FIRST CASUALTY

Gabriel Wolfe Book 4

Andy Maslen

TYTON PRESS

Published by
Tyton Press, an imprint of
Sunfish Ltd
PO Box 2107
Salisbury SP2 2BW

T: 0844 502 2061
www.andymaslen.com

Cover illustration copyright © Darren Bennett
Cover design by DKB Creative
Author photograph for the print edition © Kin Ho
Edited by Tom Bromley
Formatted by Polgarus Studio

ALSO BY ANDY MASLEN

The Gabriel Wolfe series
Trigger Point
Reversal of Fortune (short story)
Blind Impact
Condor

I dedicate this book to my parents.

Acknowledgments

I owe a huge debt of gratitude to the people who supported me and helped me while I wrote this book. As well as the members of my Readers' Group and Inner Circle, who are too numerous to thank individually, I would like to single out the following kind/talented/patient souls:

Clare Allen

Jason Anderson

Marina Anderson

Alison Barclay

Giles Bassett

Darren Bennett

Tom Bromley

Valerie Bush

Mark Dawson

Mike Dempsey

Gina Gough

Kin Ho

Jo Kelly

Michelle Lowery

Tom Pinnock

Rob Richardson

Nick Warren

Thank you all.

Andy Maslen
Salisbury, October 2016

"In war, truth is the first casualty."
Aeschylus

1

Firefight

GABRIEL Wolfe looked down at the bloody bullet wound in his right thigh.

"Britta! I'm hit!" he shouted.

Britta Falskog whirled round, still firing her SA80 assault rifle in five-round bursts over the top of the fallen tree she was using for cover.

"I'm coming. Can you move?"

"Not sure. Hurts like fuck."

"Hold on."

Britta ducked down, rested the SA80 against the rough bark of the tree, and unclipped her two remaining grenades from her belt: a white phosphor and a high explosive. Holding one olive-green steel sphere in each hand, she pulled the pins out with her teeth, let the springs fly, then counted to two and lobbed them into the path of the incoming fighters.

Three seconds elapsed, during which she grabbed her rifle and crawled over to Gabriel, who had cut away his trouser leg and was staunching the bleeding with a QuikClot sponge he'd pulled from his medical kit.

With loud bangs a half-second apart, the two grenades exploded. There were screams from the enemy fighters as the shrapnel hit them. The white phosphor was worse, exploding outward in a cloud of burning chemicals that stuck to the skin and kept burning all the way down to the bone.

Britta pulled her pistol and popped up again, firing into the small clearing where the enemy fighters had fallen. None returned fire. Their AK-47s lay on the ground near their owners, who were maimed, burning, bleeding or all three. She vaulted the log and rushed towards them, killing each man in turn with a double-tap to the head.

Now she ran back to Gabriel. His face was white and his lips were drawn back from his teeth.

"Help me with the field dressing," he said, grunting rather than speaking.

Britta unravelled the bandage and wound it tight round his thigh, holding the QuikClot sponge in place against the wound. He drew in a sharp breath through his clenched teeth. She checked the other side of his leg.

"No exit wound. Round's still in there. Fuck!"

"We need to go," he said. "Get me up."

Britta shouldered her SA80, bending to grab his arms and pull him to his feet. He pulled upwards and transferred his weight to his good leg. Gingerly, he put some weight on the right and almost collapsed, biting back a scream as the pain intensified. Blood squelched out round the edges of the clotting sponge and through the dressing, running over the pale skin of his leg and into his boot.

In the distance, they could hear shouts and gunfire. More fighters. More Kalashnikovs. More machetes. More trouble.

With Britta supporting him, Gabriel was able to limp along. Their progress was agonisingly slow. The undergrowth was thick and Britta had to slash at it with her parang every few steps to clear a path he could negotiate. Even with the razor-sharp blade, it was sluggish going, and the enemy fighters were getting closer.

"Wait," Gabriel said, pulling Britta to a stop. "We won't outrun them. Not with me like this. I'll hold them down and you go. Whatever happens, Don can pull you out."

Her blue eyes flashed. "Fuck you, Wolfe! I'm not leaving you. We'll fight these fuckers off, then I'm getting you out of here or we'll go down together. OK?"

Gabriel nodded, his mouth set in a grim line of determination and pain. "Over there," he said, and pointed to a clump of tree ferns with fat brown trunks covered in scales of tough, hairy bark.

Britta half-dragged, half-carried him to the ferns and they flopped behind them, backs to the trunks.

With a grunt of effort, he unshouldered his own SA80 and pulled back the cocking lever.

"How are you for ammunition?"

She patted the bandolier that ran diagonally across her chest. "Got three clips. Thirty rounds. How about you?"

"Five. Plus whatever's in the mag."

"We've got maybe ninety rounds between us then. SIG?"

"Two full mags and a handful loaded."

"I've got one spare, one just loaded. MP5?"

"Out. Dumped it."

"Me too."

"It's going to be tight."

Britta swiped the back of her hand across her high forehead then pulled the plait of copper-red hair straight out from the back of her head. "When was it ever not?"

A burst of automatic fire shredded the foliage of the ferns as somebody opened up with an AK-47.

Britta and Gabriel rolled away from each other onto their bellies and shimmied sideways along the ground like crabs, taking up firing positions on each side of the clump of ferns.

"Come out, British cowards. Die like men," a voice called from about thirty yards away. Its owner sounded like he was laughing. "Or we can come and get you. You can eat your own balls while we watch, if you like."

Another burst of fire. The Kalashnikov's 7.62 mm rounds slammed into the trunks, showering Britta and Gabriel with sharp chips of bark.

"British?" Britta mouthed at Gabriel.

"Balls?" he mouthed back, grinning despite his wound as adrenaline neutralised the worst of the pain.

Gabriel looked into Britta's eyes and she nodded. An old, familiar signal.

The man who'd issued the threat went down with half his head missing as a three-round burst from Gabriel's SA80 hit him in the face. Three other militiamen rushed forward, AKs held at their hips, set to full auto and spraying bullets at Gabriel and Britta.

Britta hit the leftmost man in the groin, doubling him over and leaving him screaming in the mud. The centre and right-hand men swerved, only to be caught by a long burst from Gabriel. The burst took them both in the torso, tearing great holes through their bodies, smashing and liquefying internal organs before exiting from their backs in showers of blood, bone and tissue.

Gabriel was starting to believe they might, just, get out of the unholy shitstorm they'd got themselves into. But then a sound he hated almost more than any other shattered the calm that had descended: a booming, thudding, and very, very loud, automatic weapon had opened up from way back beyond their last position.

A "Dushka".

The DShK heavy machine gun, Soviet-manufactured, didn't kill you so much as obliterate you. Its makers had designed it to take out materiel rather than people, and its 12.7 mm calibre rounds would put a football-sized hole through anything softer than armour plating.

Whoever was behind the Dushka had them pinned down and was methodically chopping away at the tree ferns. Huge umbrellas of leaves tumbled from the tops of the ferns and fell to cover Britta and Gabriel. As the Dushka's rounds crashed into the trunks, they tore out lumps of wood that fragmented into lethal shards sharper than the best tactical knives.

"Switch to single-shot!" Gabriel shouted.

Britta nodded again and Gabriel knew she understood: if they were to stand any chance against the remaining fighters advancing on them, they had to take out the Dushka.

Gabriel knew Britta was the better shot of the two of them, and had completed a sniper course in her Swedish Special Forces training. He could see her listening hard, trying to pin down the position of the heavy machine gun. Gabriel peered through the broken fern fronds, trying to identify the firing path of the rounds still smashing into the trees in front of him.

They both reached the same conclusion. The shooter was off to their right, two o'clock. Probably standing in the bed of a pickup, Gabriel thought. A Toyota Hilux, or a Land Cruiser if they had a bit more cash. That would put his head about ten feet off the ground, and his torso and the Dushka maybe two feet below that.

Gabriel closed one eye and sighted down the SA80's barrel, aligning the iron sights on an imaginary machine gunner. He tightened his finger on the trigger and squeezed, slowly and steadily as his gunnery instructors in the SAS had taught him, until the rifle almost seemed to fire itself. The 5.56 mm round tore into the trees. The Dushka kept firing, pouring red-hot, copper-jacketed lead into the rapidly diminishing cover hiding Gabriel and Britta.

Now Britta began firing, too. She was systematic. One round high, one low, one to the left, one to the right. The Dushka kept firing.

Then it stopped. Gabriel's heart leapt. She'd done it! The super-Swede had actually taken out a Dushka that was completely invisible.

The roar of the heavy machine gun was replaced with taunts.

"Come out, pussies!" one voice called, a high-pitched giggle following the words.

"We're going to fuck you up bad, man. Yes we are," called another, deeper voice.

"Take your heads into Maputo and go bowling," yelled a third.

Then the Dushka started up again, only now its deep, bass roar was joined by the excitable chatter of three AK-47s being fired in unison and in full expectation of a quick victory. The shooters burned through their magazines in a matter of seconds and had to stop to reload.

In the gap, Britta squeezed off another six rounds in quick succession. There was a scream. One more down.

But the enemy were still firing, even though they'd lost a man.

There was a slashing rustle ahead of the tree ferns. Someone had cut their way through the undergrowth into the small clearing. Gabriel risked a look.

A tall, grinning man stood there, machete in his left hand, Kalashnikov held by the pistol grip in his right. Gold teeth glinted across the front of his mouth. A single round from Gabriel's Glock put him out of action, his heart smashed by the 9 mm Parabellum round that left a gaping exit wound big enough to put a fist into.

"How're you doing?" he whispered to Britta. She didn't reply.

He looked over.

Britta Falskog was lying on her back. Her eyes were closed. Blood was running down her forehead, obscuring the freckles that spattered her face like caramel-coloured snowflakes.

Gabriel crawled over to her and pulled up her right eyelid. The eye was rolled back in its socket. He bent to her chest and listened for a heartbeat. Couldn't hear one. Put his ear to her nose. No breath either.

"Britta!" he whispered hoarsely. "Come on!"

He knelt astride her and began thumping her chest. Not the interlaced fingers of TV medical dramas. These were full-power punches that would crack ribs. He leaned forward, pinched her nose and covered her mouth with his own before blowing fiercely into her, trying to put breath back into her lungs.

"Too late, my friend," a voice said from above him.

He looked up into a brown face, cut with dozens of V-shaped scars on both cheeks. The man grinned, revealing a double row of gold incisors. Then he drew a pistol.

2
Packing List

"THIS is straight from the horse's teeth?" Britta Falskog asked.

The line was crackling with static and her voice kept wobbling as if she were underwater, but Gabriel heard her well enough.

"It's 'mouth' not 'teeth' and yes it is. I just came home straight from Downing Street. Barbara Sutherland as good as said I can go back to Mozambique to retrieve Smudge's remains, assuming I can find him."

"Couldn't you just go on your own, as a private citizen?"

"Of course I could. But then I'd have no logistical support, no back-up if things got hairy, and most important of all, no access to military records. How would I find out where we'd been extracted from? No, this is much better. I'm going to find him, Britta."

"Oh, Gabriel, that is such a result."

"I know. It's just an in-principle 'yes' at the moment. I need to talk to Don, see what the deal is with equipment and support."

He took a sip from the glass of chilled Meursault on the kitchen counter, savouring the taste – flint and peach – as it rolled down his throat.

"So you're in Salisbury now, yes?"

"For the foreseeable future. I haven't got any projects coming up and I

7

really need a break. I was thinking of seeing that guy Fariyah Crace recommended, Richard Austin."

"Fariyah. She's your shrink, right?"

"That's right. She said he's done a ton of work with PTSD sufferers."

"Wow! You're happy to say it. That's a big change."

Another sip, larger this time.

"It is. But I can feel it. You know? I can feel there's a chance to put things right. For Smudge. For me, too."

"I wish I could be there."

"Can you get down for a couple of days?"

"Not a chance. I'm surveilling some *kuksugare* who's trafficking young girls from Eastern Europe into London."

"*Kuksugare?*"

She laughed. A thrilling, raspy sound that made his stomach flip. "Look it up, Wolfe. Google Translate, *Ja?*"

"*Ja, okej!*"

"Got to go. Keep me posted on this new job, yes?"

"Definitely. Now go and catch your *kuksugare.*"

The line went dead but Gabriel held the phone to his ear for a few moments longer, listening to his pulse, rushing in and out like surf.

Would it help? The therapy offered by Richard Austin? What had Fariyah called it? Eye movement desensitisation and reprocessing. His hijab-wearing psychiatrist seemed to think it was worth trying, and that was enough. But when should he call? *No time like the present, Wolfe.*

He pulled Fariyah's NHS business card from his wallet. On the back, in small, precise handwriting, was a name and a number. He dialled, holding his breath, then realised what he was doing and let it out in a controlled sigh. The call was picked up on the third ring.

"Richard Austin."

"Richard, it's Gabriel Wolfe. I hope Fariyah Crace said I might be calling you."

"Yes! Hi. I mean, it's been a while, so I thought you'd decided against it but, hello. I'm really pleased you've called."

"Fariyah thinks very highly of you, otherwise I wouldn't have."

"She and I go back a long way. In fact, we served together. You're ex-Army, right?"

"SAS. You were in the armed forces, then?"

"Royal Artillery, ten years. I met Fariyah in Afghanistan."

Gabriel poured another glass of wine as Austin talked.

"I wondered whether that was the connection. She knows my old CO. In fact, he recommended her to me."

"Yes, she was a military psychiatrist. Embedded with the Royal Marines to be strictly accurate. I don't think she ever gave up her private practice. When I got my discharge papers, I called her. I had an idea about retraining as a psychotherapist to help ex-service personnel with PTSD and other mental health disorders." Austin stopped himself. "Sorry. I'm sure you didn't call me for a rundown of my CV."

"It's all interesting background. But I really wanted to fix up an appointment to see you. I have some time on my hands."

"Let me see, hold on a moment . . ." Gabriel could hear a diary being flicked through at the other end of the line. ". . . can you come in next week? Monday morning? Or Tuesday afternoon?"

"I should be able to. I mean, yes, of course. As I said, diary's a blank page at the moment. And the weekend will give me time to get myself ready."

Austin laughed. "There's really no need to prepare. But shall we say Monday at ten, then?"

Austin gave Gabriel an address in Islington and they ended with an agreement to call again only if one or other had to move the appointment.

Gabriel went to the French doors that led from his small kitchen onto the back garden. He leaned forward until his forehead was resting against the cool glass, his breath misting it. A movement in the darkness caught his eye. The moon was almost full and in its silky, white light he saw a fox padding across his lawn. He remained motionless, watching the animal nosing in the flower bed, looking for worms or beetles, he supposed. Some sixth sense made the fox turn and stare right at Gabriel. Its eyes were ghostly, greenish-white marbles in a white-muzzled face. Its ears twitched twice, then it returned to its foraging. The human clearly posed no threat. Not to the fox, at any rate.

Gabriel spent Saturday morning researching Mozambique. It had gained independence from the Portuguese in 1975, then spent the ensuing seventeen years being torn apart by civil war as left- and right-wing armies shot their way to an uneasy peace. He assumed that one way or another Barbara Sutherland would smooth things over diplomatically so he could make his way into the forest and track down Smudge's remains. Presumably, she'd arrange some sort of back-up or military support. Otherwise, it was going to take years to find whatever was left of the SAS trooper for whose death Gabriel still blamed himself.

He made a list of supplies.

Medical Kit
Analgesic
Intestinal sedative
Antibiotic
Antihistamine
Anti-malaria tablets
Surgical blades
Butterfly sutures
QuikClot sponges
Plasters
Water purification tablets

Survival Kit
Fish hooks and line
Needles and thread
Waterproof matches
Candle (shave square so packs tighter)
Flint and striker
Magnifying glass

Kindling
Compass
Snare wire
Flexible saw
Torch, spare batteries
Knife plus whetstone
24-hour field rations

Other
Change of clothes
Plastic carrier bags for keeping spare clothes dry
Survival bag
Personal weapon, pref. SIG Sauer P226, ammunition
Night-vision goggles
Mosquito net
Human remains recovery kit (brushes, forceps, tweezers, bags)

As he wrote this last item, Gabriel realised he had been avoiding thinking about what, precisely, he would be bringing home for burial. Somewhere in his mind he had been visualising a complete skeleton. But now that he contemplated the reality of the situation, he knew he would be lucky to find anything at all. Predators and scavengers would have disturbed the body of his old comrade, maybe carried off parts of it to their dens or tunnels, or even into nests if raptors had arrived on the scene.

He put his pen down and leaned back until his head hung down over the back of his office chair.

"Smudge, mate, I'm sorry," he said to the ceiling. "But I'm coming for you now. I promise."

The two other remaining members of his patrol, Ben "Dusty" Rhodes and Damon "Daisy" Cheaney, had remained in the Regiment. But Gabriel had resigned his commission almost as soon as he got back to Hereford. He'd been unable to cope with the guilt he felt over leaving a man behind – a man he had ordered back into the teeth of enemy fire to retrieve a briefcase full of a warlord's plans.

How long had it been? He counted back to 2012. In a handful of years, he'd been hired – and fired – by an advertising agency, set up as an independent corporate negotiator, then moved into private security consulting.

As part of the last role, he'd landed a semi-permanent contract to work for The Department, an off-balance-sheet team of government-backed troubleshooters run by Don Webster, his old Commanding Officer in 22 SAS. This group of professional intelligence-gatherers and killers was deniable, funded through discreet channels neither the media nor run-of-the-mill MPs would ever discover, and charged with eliminating enemies of the State too troublesome, elusive or lawyered-up to go down through conventional legal channels.

And now, for "services rendered", Prime Minister Barbara Sutherland had granted permission for Gabriel to retrace his steps to Mozambique and recover whatever was left of Smudge's remains for a military funeral in the UK.

Gabriel lunged forward in the chair. There was someone he needed to see. Someone so important he couldn't understand how he'd forgotten about her.

3

A Long-Delayed Meeting

DENMAN Road was a narrow street of Victorian terraced houses in Peckham, in southeast London. Gabriel parked his indigo Maserati in a space about halfway along. He walked down towards the main road for ten yards or so and stopped outside a house with window boxes crammed with miniature conifers and ornamental cabbages in shades of mint-green and rose pink. The gate opened smoothly without a screech from its iron hinges. He walked the short distance up the black-and-white-chequered tiles of the path to the front door. The wood was painted a deep shade of red that contrasted with the bright brass of the letterbox, knocker and knob. It echoed the red in two panels of geometric-patterned stained glass. There was a brass-collared spyhole between them, and three locks – mortises top and bottom, and a high-end Banham smack in the middle. House-proud *and* security conscious.

Gabriel pushed the button for the doorbell and as it rang in the hall beyond the door, he felt his heart rate spike. He'd been calm all the way up to London from Salisbury, but now he was finally here, his pulse was racing. *Let it. No need to control it this time.*

Through the glass, which was lit from within, he saw a shadow moving closer to the door and then close enough to look through the spyhole. He took a deep breath and let it out slowly, wiping his right palm on his trousers.

He heard the sound of a chain being unhooked and a bolt being withdrawn. Then the door opened.

The woman standing before him was smiling, yet her eyes looked sad. The irises were the bright blue of cloudless summer skies, yet dark shadows lay beneath them on her pale, pink-tinged cheeks. She was wearing faded jeans and a white sweater over what looked like a man's shirt, pale blue with dark grey stripes. Her ash-blonde hair was tied into two tight plaits no thicker than a finger, arranged symmetrically on each side of her collar.

"Hi, Melody," Gabriel said, feeling a blush creeping onto his cheeks.

"Gabriel," Melody said softly. "I thought we'd never see you again. Come in." She stepped towards him and hugged him tightly. "I'm so glad you're here. Mike looked up to you like an older brother. I swear he loved you more than me." Melody held him at arm's length, staring into his eyes and looking him up and down. "Civvy Street obviously suits you."

"I'm sorry I haven't come to see you since . . ."

"Since Mike was killed. It's OK, Gabriel. You can say it."

Gabriel ran his fingers through his hair, ruffling it into spikes. "I know it was wrong of me. I don't really have any excuse."

"And I don't want any. Can I get you something to drink? Tea? Coffee?"

"Coffee, please."

"Come on, we can talk in the kitchen. Nat's there – Sunday's homework day."

Gabriel followed her along the hall. One wall was a mosaic of photos. A wedding picture caught his eye: Smudge and Melody emerging from the church, Melody grinning with her veil thrown back, carrying a bouquet of pure white roses. Smudge was resplendent in his ceremonial No. 1 dress uniform, a row of campaign medals above the left breast pocket of his jacket, and smiling at someone to the left of the frame.

In another photo, Smudge was holding Nathalie as a baby. A third, taken by Gabriel himself, in Afghanistan, showed the other three members of his patrol, part of the F Squadron's Mobility Troop in 22 SAS: Daisy, Smudge and Dusty, arms round each other's shoulders, smiling out of dust-skimmed faces.

Gabriel stepped into the kitchen. At a scrubbed pine table, bent over a metallic royal-blue laptop, was a girl of thirteen or maybe fourteen. She looked up as her mother and Gabriel entered the room.

"Gabriel!" she squealed. She scraped her chair back on the slate tiles and ran into Gabriel's arms, throwing her arms around him and squeezing hard enough to make breathing difficult.

"She's been impossible since you phoned," Melody said. "I managed to get her to bed before midnight last night, but even that was a struggle."

Her tone was indulgent, and her smile told Gabriel things were going to be OK.

"How are you, Nathalie?" he asked, once the girl had released him from her hug.

"I'm in Year Nine now, as you probably don't know. I'm on the school senate and I'm captain of the soccer team. I'm going to be a lawyer like Mum when I grow up. Other than that, you know, normal teen stuff." Nathalie fixed him with an inquisitor's gaze, leaning forwards as she looked up into his face. "Mum said you've got some news. Is it about Dad?"

Gabriel nodded. "Yes. Yes, it is. Can I sit down?"

Nathalie hurried back to the table and pulled out a chair for him.

While Melody made two cups of instant coffee and poured apple juice for her daughter, Gabriel asked Nathalie inconsequential questions, about what subjects she enjoyed, how her team were doing, what her teachers were like. Topics he assumed early teens wouldn't find embarrassing to talk about. When the drinks were made and sitting on the tabletop, Melody asked the question to which he'd been trying to find the best answer since the previous day.

"Why are you here, Gabriel?"

He paused before answering, and looked out of the window, at a tiny patch of lawn bordered with cut-back roses waiting for the spring. Then he took a deep breath and let it out in a sigh.

"I'm going back to Mozambique to find Sm – , to find Mike. If I can. To bring him home."

Melody reached across the foot of pine between them and gently took his hands in her own. She looked at him with eyes that glistened in the pale winter sun lighting the kitchen.

"Can you really do that? After all this time?"

He looked over at Nathalie, who was dry-eyed but frowning, as if trying to solve a particularly hard homework problem.

"You're going to get Dad?" she asked.

"I'm going to try," Gabriel said. "I have permission from the Prime Minister to go, so I think I'll have really good support from the people I was there with."

"You mean the Regiment?" Melody said. "Can they do that? Now you're a civilian, I mean."

"I'm not sure. But our old CO, Don Webster, do you remember him?"

Melody nodded.

"He's not in the Army any more but he's helping too. I think it'll be fine."

Nathalie tapped Gabriel on the arm.

"Why didn't you come to see us? Before, I mean. We thought you would."

"Nathalie, it's fine," Melody said. "Gabriel's here now and that's what matters."

"No, it's OK, Melody. She has a right to know," Gabriel said. He turned to face Nathalie and found himself looking into Smudge's eyes. "Your Dad was a brave man. One of the bravest I ever met. I asked . . . I told him to get something we'd lost and he did it without thinking because he was a very well-trained soldier. And that's when he was killed. I blamed myself for causing his death. And for having to leave him behind. I still do. I was ashamed to come and see you." He stopped talking, trying to dislodge the lump in his throat by swallowing but it seemed to have become fixed there. He swiped a hand across his eyes.

"Gabriel," Nathalie said. "Nobody blames you except yourself."

He cleared his throat, amazed at the girl's maturity. "Thank you." He looked across the table at Melody. "I'm seeing someone about it. Trying to sort it out."

She nodded. "You're a good man. You shouldn't be suffering. But there's one thing that puzzles me."

"What's that?"

"Hold on. Nat, darling, do you want to go and finish that in your room?"

The girl let out a theatrical groan. "God, Mum. I'm not a kid any more. You can talk in front of me, you know."

Gabriel smiled at this exchange.

"Yes, I know you are and I know I can. But just this once indulge me, OK?"

"Fine! Come and see me before you go, Gabriel. That's an order." She gathered up her laptop, notepad and pens and stomped off.

"So what's up?" Gabriel asked, once the sound of Nathalie's door slamming had confirmed she was out of earshot.

"Barbara Sutherland is what's up."

"What do you mean? Up . . . how?"

Melody took a swig of her coffee.

"Did you know I was studying for a law degree while Mike was serving?"

"Open University wasn't it?"

"Yes. Cost a bloody fortune. I had to borrow off my parents and get a loan. But anyway, I got my degree and then went on and did my Legal Practice Course at Westminster University. Now I work in the legal department of a non-profit organisation called Scrutiny International. We monitor governments for breaches of UN resolutions, international treaties and conventions, that kind of thing."

"And what, Barbara's corrupt, is that what you're saying?"

"Barbara? You *are* cosy with the elite, aren't you?"

"I've met her a couple of times, that's all."

Melody smiled but there was a watchfulness in her expression now. "Nobody's saying she's bent. But there are a few little blanks in her CV. A few places where an uncharitable person might decide she was hiding things from the public. When she was Secretary of State for Defence, for example, we know she was meeting some really dodgy characters in Africa. Now, we submitted a request under the Freedom of Information Act for the minutes of those meetings and they're not there. In fact, the Ministry of Defence denied they ever took place."

"Maybe they didn't."

"We checked locally. We've got sources in Zambia and Tanzania,

Zimbabwe . . ." She paused and looked at Gabriel. ". . . Mozambique. All over. She was there at the times we claimed she was. We have photos. Video, even."

Gabriel looked out of the window again. Then back at Melody.

"I'm not saying she's perfect. She's a politician, for a start. But she's a straight arrow, you have to believe me." *A straight arrow who oversees a covert assassination squad run by your husband's and my old commanding officer.*

"Just be careful," Melody said. "And bring Mike home, if you can. It would mean a lot."

"I will. Both of those things. I really will try."

Gabriel checked his watch.

"I should go. I'm leaving as soon as I can and I've got a ton of preparation to do back at home."

"I'll show you out," Melody said, getting to her feet. At the foot of the stairs she stopped and shouted out to Nathalie. "Gabriel's going, love. Come and say goodbye."

The bedroom door opened and Nathalie ran down the stairs so fast she almost slipped on the final step. For the second time, she threw her arms around Gabriel and squeezed tight before releasing him and staring into his eyes.

"Don't die," she said. "Come back safe with Dad."

"I'll try," he said, feeling the inadequacy of his words.

At the door, Melody stopped him with a hand on his arm.

"If you need help in Africa that Barbara Sutherland can't provide, call me. I said I had contacts there. I can put you in touch with them."

4

PTSD

THE following day, Gabriel turned left into a quiet residential street in Islington, in north London. He found Richard Austin's house halfway down on the right – a terraced Victorian not dissimilar to Melody's. Only, he guessed, probably worth at least twice as much in this *chi-chi* neighbourhood occupied by bankers, media types and advertising agency creatives, to judge from the number of Porsches he'd spotted on the drive in.

As Austin had said on the phone, there was off-street parking. Gabriel pulled onto the graveled rectangle that had replaced the front garden. He switched off the engine and sat for a few minutes, listening to the cooling fans whirring.

He checked his watch, a vintage Breitling Chronomaster with a black face. His father had given it to him when he'd joined the Parachute Regiment. It was something of a peace offering, as well as a present, as his old man had wanted Gabriel to follow in his footsteps, first to Cambridge and then to the Diplomatic Service. It was 9.45, early, as planned. Gabriel didn't want to sit in the car and sweat nervously for fifteen minutes, so he got out and walked back the way he'd driven to the main shopping street running east-west through Islington itself.

A cold wind had sprung up and Gabriel was glad of his overcoat. He pulled it tight across his body and tied the belt for good measure. Ahead, two young women were pushing buggies and talking to each other in an eastern European language that sounded like Polish. It wasn't a language he spoke fluently, though he could make out the odd phrase. It seemed they were nannies and he caught the words "useless man" and "she's having an affair".

After a ten-minute circuit, turning repeatedly right, he ended up back on Richard Austin's road with a couple of minutes to spare. He squeezed between his Maserati and Richard Austin's battered, avocado-green Volvo estate and pressed the doorbell. From inside the house, a melodious peal of church bells sounded and a few seconds later, the door opened.

The man standing in front of him was in his late thirties or early forties. Tall, maybe six-one or six-two, and with the beginnings of a paunch. His eyes, pale grey, were magnified by the lenses of his glasses – thick, tortoiseshell frames that sat on a long, straight nose.

"Gabriel," he said, holding out his right hand. "I'm Richard."

Austin's handshake felt odd and Gabriel looked down. The man's right hand, and the wrist protruding from the cuff of his sweater, were horribly burnt, the skin rebuilt in swirls of shiny pink that looked like melted plastic.

Austin followed his gaze down.

"Our Bradley took a direct hit from an RPG. Got a bit hot inside."

"Sorry. I didn't mean to stare."

"It's fine, but come in, come in, don't stand out there in the cold, you'll let all the heat out." Richard led Gabriel though into the kitchen. "Coffee?" he said.

"Yes, please."

The coffee made, they went through into a small, square room. On one wall there was a painting of a field full of poppies. On another, a simple line drawing of a woman seated in a chair, reading a book. In the centre of the room, placed opposite each other on a deep-red Persian rug, were a pair of matching armchairs – low-slung affairs upholstered in soft, creased leather the colour of plain chocolate and rimmed with bright brass nailheads. Between them stood a low table, its top a frosted glass slab. On the table was a box of tissues, the uppermost sheet tugged partway out of the oval slot. One wall consisted of floor-to-ceiling bookshelves in white-painted timber. Gabriel ran his eye along one of the shelves and read out some of the authors: "Alfred Adler, Sigmund Freud, Anna Freud, Carl Jung, Francine Shapiro. All the greats – but I haven't heard of the last one."

Austin gestured with the hand not carrying his mug of coffee that Gabriel should take the chair nearest the door.

"No?" he said. "Most people I see arrive having Googled her. Half of them seem to know more about her work than I do."

Gabriel sat, hitching the knees of his trousers up an inch or two. He pressed his lips together for a second before he spoke.

"Not me. I didn't want to prejudge or even really know what was going to happen. I've only been seeing Fariyah for a few sessions, so I thought I'd just do what she told me and come to see you."

"Well, I'm really glad you did. I should tell you that, although I'm not a doctor, I work to the same ethical standards. Everything and anything you tell me is confidential and my only goal is to help you get well."

"Thank you. So where should I start?"

Austin put his coffee down on the table and stayed leaning forward, his hands loosely clasped between his knees. In his sage green corduroy jeans and mustard-coloured cable-knit jumper, he could have been a university professor seeing a nervous first-year student about an essay.

"Did Fariyah tell you anything about EMDR?"

"Only that it stands for Eye Movement Desensitisation and . . ."

"Reprocessing," Richard prompted. "Go on."

"And that you worked a lot with veterans with PTSD, and it was pretty powerful juju."

Austin laughed, a soft sound that Gabriel found reassuring.

"It is," he said, taking off his glasses and polishing them on a tissue pulled from the box, before screwing it into a ball and tossing it with precision into the wastepaper basket in the corner of the room. "I'm going to be honest with you – we don't know why EMDR works. Just that it does. Shapiro came across it by accident while out walking. I'm also a qualified and registered psychotherapist and hypnotherapist, so we can explore your issues from any angle that feels right, OK?"

"OK."

"Why don't you tell me your story? Not your life story, but we can come to that if we need to. But from the time you feel your symptoms started."

Gabriel drew in a deep breath and let it out in a sigh.

"My Squadron was in Mozambique. We were there on a search-and-destroy mission to take out a warlord called Abel N'Tolo. Get his plans, put him down, exfil and extract. But we got ambushed on the way out of the village. We took heavy fire and one of my patrol, a trooper called Mickey Smith – we called him Smudge – was killed retrieving the case full of plans. I ordered him back into enemy fire to get the briefcase and he went down. We were carrying him out when another of my men lost an arm to a round from a Dushka. You know what that is, right?" Richard nodded. "We couldn't go on with Smudge. I ordered them to leave him and we beat our way back to the chopper and got out by the skin of our teeth. My last sight of Smudge was from the door of the chopper. They'd crucified him on a tree with machetes."

Gabriel stooped, eyes pricking, and snatched a tissue out of the box, wiped his eyes and blew his nose then screwed it into his fist.

"Do you want to stop for a minute, Gabriel?"

Gabriel sniffed and cleared his throat, then shook his head.

"No, I'm fine. Well, obviously I'm not fine," he laughed. "But yes, I want to talk this out with you."

"So you left Smudge behind. That must have weighed on your conscience."

"It did. The nightmares started as soon as I got back to Hereford. I resigned my commission a few weeks later and I was out of the Regiment within six months."

"And then?"

"And then I started getting flashbacks. More nightmares. And Smudge started appearing. Always with his face blown away, or hanging off. Talking to me."

"That can't have been easy. How did you cope?"

"Oh, alcohol is a great help. And I drive faster than I ought to a lot of the time. There are a lot of empty country roads near me. And I had some training in meditation when I was growing up. So, you know, I manage."

Richard pursed his lips and scratched the side of his chin.

"You probably don't need me to tell you that alcohol is probably the most common remedy PTSD sufferers resort to. We call it *self-medicating* in the trade. And your driving. Risk-taking behaviour is another classic symptom. It's been likened to a death-wish produced by what we call survivor guilt. You feel bad about having survived, so you put yourself in harm's way and almost dare nature, or fate, or chance, or God to even the score."

"Well, it hasn't worked so far, as you can see," Gabriel said, spreading his hands wide.

Richard smiled. "No. It hasn't, has it? Are you working?"

"Advertising when I left the Regiment. That didn't end too well, then I set up on my own as a freelance negotiator. Now I . . ." *Yes. What do I do now? Freelance assassin for a deniable Government black ops department?* "I do private security work. Corporate stuff, mostly, some training, a bit of protection, that type of thing." *And rescuing the families of pharmaceutical company bosses from Chechen terrorists. And going undercover in fucked-up religious cults.*

"And how are you managing with that? It sounds like very stressful work."

"It is. But it's what I'm good at. And to be honest, I don't see myself sitting behind a desk for the next forty years, tapping away on a computer or attending endless meetings."

"I can't say that would get me going either. But it sounds like you're almost doing two jobs simultaneously. Your security work, and keeping the lid on your psyche. Is there anything else going on in your life that you're trying to deal with?"

After he asked this question, Richard leaned back in his chair and folded one ankle across the opposite knee. He sat very still, watching Gabriel and waiting, not attempting to fill in the silence.

Gabriel looked out of the window as a murmuration of starlings filled the iron-grey sky over Islington, an animated dust cloud that swirled and pulsed, changing shape as if guided by some inner intelligence. He watched as holes broke through in the centre and then closed, bulges of a few hundred birds threatening to break free before being reabsorbed back into the flock. Then they seemed, collectively, to tire of this game, and disappeared from the square of sky demarcated by the white painted window frame. Gabriel turned back to Richard, who hadn't moved.

"There is something else. Fariyah thinks it may be the root cause of my PTSD. I . . ." he scragged his fingers through his short, black hair until it was standing up in spikes, "I caused my younger brother's death."

In faltering sentences, he repeated to Richard the story of Michael Wolfe's fall into Victoria Harbour in Hong Kong, and his own fugue state that followed. When he had finished, he realised his cheeks were running with tears and grabbed a couple more tissues to dry them off.

"That is quite a story," Richard said. "And it makes more sense to me than the story of your last mission in the SAS as a reason for your PTSD. I'm guessing that's what Fariyah told you?"

"More or less, yes. She's a very wise woman."

Richard smiled. "Listen, the good news is that unless there's something else you've got squirreled away in your subconscious, I think you have already started to face your demons. EMDR is helping thousands of people just like you all over the world as we speak. Not just veterans, by the way. Rape victims, rescued hostages, car crash survivors – all sorts. And we can start right now."

Gabriel sat up straight in his chair. "Really? I thought maybe we had to do lots of talking first."

"When she's referred one of her clients to me, I leave all that to Fariyah. No, we can give it a go right now."

A passer-by looking in through the window would have seen a puzzling sight. Two men sitting facing each other in armchairs. One holding a pencil up in front of the other's face and moving it left to right while the other man followed it with his eyes, his lips moving as if reciting. Inside the room, Gabriel was doing just that, talking about the moments leading up to Smudge's death while tracking the movements of Richard's pencil, his head still, just his eyes moving.

". . . that's our time up, I'm afraid," Richard said after a few more minutes. "How do you feel?"

Gabriel looked up at the ceiling and then back at Richard. "Honestly? I'm not sure. Fine, I think. Sort of light."

"It affects people in different ways. You'll probably sleep very deeply tonight. It takes a while for your brain to process the memories, but come and see me again as soon as you can and we'll do some more work."

Richard showed Gabriel to the door and they shook hands again. Gabriel looked down at the disfigured hand.

"Were you all right?" he said.

Richard looked him directly in the eye. No smile but a depth of feeling came through his gaze.

"I wasn't. And then I was. You will be, too. Call me soon, OK?"

It was eleven o'clock. Gabriel had two hours before his next appointment. An appointment with the two people who were going to help him atone for Smudge Smith's death. His former CO. And the Prime Minister.

Gabriel had just reached his car when a woman screamed and all thoughts of meetings left his mind.

5

Shining Armour

GABRIEL ran to the end of the street, straight past his car, in the direction of the screams. Rounding the corner, he cannoned into a pair of figures sprawled on the pavement, struggling over a rust-orange handbag. First to his feet was a scrawny white youth in a grey hoodie, with angry red spots all over the lower half of his face. He snatched the bag from the woman's hand. She was late fifties, well-dressed in a cream coat and matching broad-brimmed hat. Turning to run, he stopped long enough to kick Gabriel in the face. The kick was a poor one and his scruffy trainers did little damage. Then he was off, sprinting up the road towards an estate of high-rise blocks painted in optimistic shades of bright blue and yellow.

"Is Birkin!" the woman screamed in Russian-accented English. "Save it. Please. I reward."

Gabriel didn't know what a Birkin was, but he guessed it was worth more than everything the young mugger owned. He jumped to his feet and ran after the youth. His brogues were hardly made for running, but he was fit and minded to rescue what he saw as a damsel in distress. Even if this one was probably an oligarch's wife and more than capable of replacing her stolen bag.

Ahead, the youth veered right into the grassy area in front of the blocks of flats. He was heading for the warren of walkways and alleys that he clearly hoped would baffle and defeat his pursuer. Gabriel was gaining, but by the time he arrived at the entrance to the estate, the youth was crashing through a door into the ground level of the nearest block.

As Gabriel hit the door, swinging it back on its hinges with a bang, he caught a couple of curious faces staring at him from the shadows, sitting on low-slung BMX bikes that looked about five sizes too small for their riders. He could hear feet pounding up stairs just ahead and put on a burst of speed, desperate to catch his quarry before he reached his own flat.

He turned a corner just in time to see the scruffy trainers disappearing onto the half-landing on the flight of stairs. He took the stairs three at a time, and as he reached the first-floor walkway, the gap between himself and the mugger had closed to tackling distance. He didn't want to risk a dive, so lunged with his leading foot and tripped the man with a well-aimed tap to the trailing heel. Down he went, rolling expertly into a ball, bag still clutched in his left fist, and was up again and facing Gabriel.

Panting, Gabriel stood still and thrust his hand out.

"Give me the bag. Now!" he shouted.

The man bared his teeth like a cornered animal. "Fuck you!" Then a knife appeared in his right hand, its long, narrow blade sliding out from the grip with a metallic *snick*. His chest was heaving and his marred face was bloodless.

He lunged at Gabriel.

Which was a mistake.

Gabriel half-turned, grabbed the incoming wrist with both hands, then completed his turn and threw the man over his shoulder and down, hard, onto the concrete walkway.

The knife skittered away and bounced off a bright-blue front door, coming to a spinning halt in the centre of the walkway. It was in Gabriel's hand a moment later.

His opponent wasn't finished yet. He was back on his feet and leaning over the guardrail of the walkway.

"Oi! Fed. Tox. Up 'ere. Fucking cunt's robbing me!" he yelled in a cracking voice that sounded like it hadn't broken much earlier. Then he turned to face Gabriel, who'd stowed the knife in a trouser pocket. "You're fucked now, mate," he said, revealing small teeth that gleamed in the shadows of the walkway.

Gabriel could hear two sets of feet pounding up the stairs behind him. He jumped forwards, straight-arming the man in the face so that he staggered backwards, finally releasing the bag that had caused so much trouble. Gabriel tripped him again, only this time he reached down, grabbed his waist and hauled him up to and over the guardrail.

Transferring his grip to the man's ankles he pushed him right over the rail until he was head-down over the glass-strewn concrete.

Fed and Tox arrived just in time to see their friend swinging over the drop. It wasn't a huge distance, perhaps fifteen feet or a little more. But being dropped onto your skull from even half that distance would earn you a hospital trip. The full fifteen would take you straight to the mortuary. The confederates stumbled to a stop, palms raised in front of them.

"Whoa! Mate! Chill, man. Don't drop him. Easy, yeah?" the taller one said, his eyes wide.

"Get me up!" their friend screamed from six feet closer to the ground.

"Yeah, man. Let him up, OK? He ain't done nothing to you." This was lieutenant number two. Stocky, greasy hair lank across his face, crude tattoos on his neck. Neither one of them could have been more than seventeen.

"I tell you what, boys," Gabriel said. "Why don't *you* get him up. Here, you can have one leg each."

When neither man moved, he barked at them in his best parade-ground tone. A tone that had brought hard-faced veterans of desert warfare and hand-to-hand jungle fighting into line.

"I said, one leg each! Now!"

They moved cautiously towards him, eyes watchful, lips closed tight. Then Gabriel jerked the man downwards as if to let go.

They rushed forward and grabbed for their friend's ankles. Now, Gabriel did release his grip. He stepped past the two rescuers, who now looked as though they were the ones performing the gangland threat on their friend, picked up the bag on his way to the stairs then ran for the door to the stairwell, pushed through and was outside a few seconds later.

Above him he could see the struggling trio, a failed circus act, screaming at each other. The two on the deck hadn't managed to retrieve their friend and in fact, appeared quite likely to drop him. He looked up to the next storey and saw a young black woman with a baby on her hip peering down over her own balcony to watch the scene unfolding beneath her flat.

"Call the police!" Gabriel shouted up at her. "They're trying to kill him."

Then he walked away at the double, not looking back. He doubted they'd follow him, but putting distance between yourself and the enemy once your objective is achieved is never a bad idea.

Gabriel found the Russian woman exactly where he'd left her on the corner of Richard Austin's road. She was sitting on a low wall bordering a front garden, being comforted by two police community support officers: one male, a Sikh in a navy blue turban; one female and white, short where her partner was tall, thin where he was chunky. The male officer was speaking into his Airwave police radio when the woman saw Gabriel walking towards them, the rust-orange bag held against his chest.

"He is there!" she shouted, jumping up from her perch and waving frantically at Gabriel.

Gabriel arrived to be greeted by an all-enveloping hug that threatened to suffocate him, either through manual pressure or by means of her expensive-smelling, heavy perfume.

When she released him, he held the bag out to her. "Yours, I think," was all he could manage, as the adrenaline from the chase and rescue of the bag kicked in.

"You are brave man." She turned to the PCSOs. "Not like you. I tell you, go help man, but you are cowards with your radios and your 'back-up'." She put air quotes around this last word.

"Did you want to register a formal complaint, Madam?" the male officer asked, holding his hands out a little from his sides.

"Complaint, or no complaint, is no difference. You go now. I have bag and hero also," she said, looking adoringly at Gabriel, who was sitting on the wall, enjoying the exchange.

The two PCSOs about-turned and walked off in lockstep, presumably agreeing that given a choice between scrawny muggers and blinged-up

Russians, they knew who they'd rather deal with.

"Here," the woman said to Gabriel, holding out a stiff, rose-pink, fifty-pound note. "For your trouble. Is reward."

He shook his head. "There's no need. I was just lending a hand."

"You don't need my money?" A smile on her scarlet lips, crinkles at the corners of her eyes. "Is fine. Maybe you are rich man already."

"No, not really. But please, your gratitude is more than enough."

"Then take card instead. One day you need favour, maybe. You call me."

He took the card, a thick rectangle of ridged stock with gold-blocked type declaring its bearer to be:

Tatyana Garin
CEO
Garin Group

The logo was two interlinked capital letter G's. In addition to the usual contact details, the card bore a Russian phrase, transliterated into the English alphabet:

"V zolote my doveryayem"

Gabriel read it out, first in flawless Russian, which he'd learned to speak while training for the SAS, then again in English. "'In gold we trust.' That's very good."

She looked at him, eyes wide. "You speak Russian? Man of talent indeed."

"Is that your business?" he asked. "Gold?"

"Is part, yes. Mining, refining. But also diamonds, emeralds, platinum. Also saffron. You know this word? Saffron?"

"More expensive than gold, pound for pound."

"Exactly! Garin Group is world number three in precious metals and gemstones but number one producer of saffron."

Gabriel checked his watch. "I don't suppose you'd like to have a coffee with me, would you? I have to meet someone in Whitehall at one, but between then and now I'm at a loose end. My name is Gabriel, by the way. Gabriel Wolfe."

"Why not?" she said. "Perhaps you tell me your story, Gabriel? How you become brave man."

She linked her arm through his and, recovered Birkin swinging from her other hand, let Gabriel lead her to a small cafe on Upper Street. Once they were seated in a corner by the window overlooking the street, Tatyana swirled a spoonful of brown sugar into her latte and spoke.

"Many English men would not do what you did. Many Russian men, too. Was little strange, no? You were not scared?"

Gabriel took a sip of the flat white in front of him. It was excellent, deep and nutty, and not overwhelmed by hot milk.

"Most muggers are cowards as well as thieves. I just ran him down. It wasn't hard."

"You know what is Birkin? Why I screamed?"

He shook his head.

"Made by Hermès. Very rare. I wait three years for that one. Is saltwater crocodile. One hundred thousand sterling."

Now it was Gabriel's turn to widen his eyes.

"I think *I* would have screamed if I'd had a hundred-grand handbag taken away from me."

"So, why no screaming?" Tatyana said, narrowing her eyes. She leaned across the table and squeezed Gabriel's left bicep through his jacket. "Hmm. Hard muscles. Scar on face," she said, looking at his left cheekbone.

"I was a soldier. For thirteen years. So muggers don't bother me very much."

"Thirteen. In England is unlucky, yes?"

"Supposedly. I'm not really superstitious."

"In Russia, we think is very funny. No thirteenth floor in Western hotels."

He laughed. "I know. But lots of people wouldn't stay in a room with a thirteen in it, so the hotel would lose a lot of money."

"I like you, Gabriel Wolfe," she said. "You are funny as well as courageous. And you remind me of my son."

Gabriel had to perform a rapid mental calculation. Yes, it would work. Easily in fact.

"Does he live in England, too?"

"He lives with God," she said, eyes focusing on the tabletop. "Grigori is dead. He was soldier like you. Very brave boy. Fighting all over world. Came back from Afghanistan without scratch."

"What happened? If you don't mind my asking?"

Tatyana scooped the froth from the bottom of her cup and sucked it off the spoon. "He was killed in car crash. Mayfair. An Arab boy in Lamborghini also was killed. Grigori was driving Ferrari. You know these names?"

Gabriel nodded again.

"It was birthday present. Five days old. It burnt down to black shell. Grief nearly killed his father."

"I'm sorry. To lose a son is terrible." *Or a brother.*

"You have children?"

"No."

"Then you do not know. Parent's grief is worst pain on planet. Pain of birth is joy in comparison."

"You're right. I'm sorry. Again, I mean."

Tatyana reached out to place her hand, bedecked in gold and diamond rings, over his.

"Do not worry. You are kind man. But now you must leave, I think. For your meeting?"

Gabriel glanced at the clock above the bar.

"I'm afraid I must."

He stood and offered her his hand to shake. Instead, she rose from her own chair and came round the small table to hug him once more, with less pressure this time, and more tenderness, and kissed him three times on alternating cheeks.

"*Do svidaniya*, Gabriel," she said. "Remember. I owe you favour."

"*Do svidaniya*, Tatyana. Until we meet again."

6

Number Ten

AT the beginning of Downing Street, where Gabriel had pulled over, a group of schoolchildren were milling about in front of the outer set of gates, taking selfies under the watchful gaze of a couple of young female teachers. The boys seemed more interested in the weapons slung across the chests of the firearms officers grouped to the left of the gate. From his vantage point behind the wheel, Gabriel could make out the distinctive shape of the buttstocks that declared these to be SIG Sauer SG 516 semi-automatic rifles. The SCO19 officers also had Glock 17 semi-automatic pistols strapped to their thighs. Their bulky anti-stab vests and auxiliary equipment belts held Tasers and extendible batons, as well as handcuffs and black rubber torches.

One of the men marched over to the Maserati, right hand held loosely around his rifle's pistol grip, index finger covering the trigger guard.

"You'll have to turn round, sir," he said. "Right away, please."

He didn't sound unfriendly, but there was no mistaking the edge in his voice. His three colleagues were staring over and Gabriel noticed approvingly the way they'd asked the two teachers to move their class along.

Gabriel smiled back at the officer. "I have an appointment. With the Prime Minister."

"Really?" the officer said. "Turn off your engine, please." He beckoned one of his colleagues over. "Gentleman says he has an appointment with the PM."

The second officer, a sergeant, leaned down, his left hand on the roof, right resting on the butt of his Glock. "And you would be?"

"Gabriel Wolfe. I'm sure it's in your system. Perhaps you could have a look?"

"Could you step out of the car, please, sir?" The sergeant had a short-cropped grey beard and the red cheeks of a department store Santa. *He wants to know if I'm naughty or nice.* Gabriel turned off the ignition, undid his seatbelt and slid out of the seat's cushioning embrace. He was aware that the group of schoolchildren had stopped just a few yards up from the gates and were now filming and photographing his encounter. His overcoat was in the boot and a cold wind was blowing off the river just a few hundred yards to the south. A stray fast food wrapper blew along the pavement and swirled around his legs for a moment before sailing up in an eddy of cold air and whirling away over the rooftops.

"Is there a problem, officer? I really do have an appointment."

"Could you remove your jacket, please, sir?"

Gabriel shrugged the jacket off and handed it over. The sergeant squeezed it over the pockets and ran the sleeves through his hands. He seemed to be enjoying keeping Gabriel standing in front of him, in the cold. Just as he was about to ask for it back, the first police officer emerged from a small hut to the right of the inner gates and called over.

"It's there, Sarge. Look."

The sergeant handed the jacket back to Gabriel. "Do you have some photo ID, sir?"

"Of course." Gabriel dug his driving licence out of his wallet and held it out.

The sergeant examined the plastic card, squinting at the photo and comparing it to Gabriel's face.

"Very good, sir," he said. "Drive through the gates and then park in the marked bays at the far end of the street. You'll have to undergo a search by one of our officers as well, but we can do that inside. Don't want you catching cold, now, do we?"

"Sure. But I wasn't searched last time I was here. Have you uprated your security or something?"

"I can't say, sir. Now, in you go, please."

Gabriel climbed back into the still-warm interior of the Maserati, started the engine and, once both sets of wrought iron gates had opened, eased the car into Downing Street, past the famous black front door, to the visitor parking. Climbing out a second time, he made sure to collect his overcoat from the boot in case the sergeant was thinking of conducting the search outside. In fact, he was met by a member of the Prime Minister's staff, a bespectacled young man of maybe twenty-five or twenty-six, wearing a slim-cut navy suit and a tie in an acidic shade of yellow-green.

"Gabriel? Follow me, please. The Prime Minister is expecting you."

Gabriel bit back the remark forming in his head, that she had a funny way of showing it. He followed the aide, or assistant, or private secretary, or whatever he called himself, into a security building set back from the road between two of the grand townhouses invisible to the public confined outside the gates. There, he was frisked, extremely professionally, by another uniformed police officer. The man was neither rough nor hurried. He treated Gabriel's figure more as a technical exercise in where a potential assailant might conceal a weapon.

Having been deemed no threat to the Prime Minister's person, Gabriel was shown into an office where Barbara Sutherland was waiting for him, along with Don Webster. The room was lined with bookshelves. Gabriel scanned the spines. Political biographies and memoirs. Reference books. Some history. A lot of military titles. The walls were painted a forest green below a dado rail about waist-height, and white above it.

Once the aide had closed the whisper-quiet door behind him on the way out, Barbara Sutherland turned to Gabriel.

"Hello again, Gabriel. Good to see you. How's my favourite action man keeping?"

She held out her hand. No embrace like the last time they'd met. No lipstick print on the right cheek. Just a professional politician's grip, through her eye contact was lasting and warm.

"Hello, Prime Minister. Very well, thank you."

"Oh, come on, Gabriel. No need for titles. You can call me Barbara. You did before."

But you hugged me like a friend before.

"Sorry. Barbara. Hi, Don."

"Hello, Old Sport," Don said, extending a dry-palmed hand. His grey eyes looked tired and there was a tension round them that Gabriel had never seen before.

Once the three of them were seated at a circular table, Barbara spoke.

"I said last time we met that you had my permission to go into Mozambique to recover the remains of your former colleague, Michael Smith."

"Smudge, yes."

"And you still do." Barbara looked down at her hands and twisted her plain gold wedding band around her finger before speaking again. "We will lay on any logistical support you need and I think I can safely say you'll get some decent support from the Governments in Mozambique and in Zambia next door. We're one of their biggest aid donors, so we're owed."

She paused again and Gabriel could sense that she was keeping something back.

"Is something wrong?" he asked. "With my wanting to go?"

"No. Not at all. However, I need you to complete a separate assignment for me. It will be under the auspices of The Department again, like your last little jaunt to Brazil."

She was referring to an undercover mission Gabriel had undertaken that involved his infiltrating a quasi-religious cult run by a French national. Christophe Jardin had brainwashed Gabriel and had almost succeeded in having him assassinate two prominent South American politicians with a suicide bomb.

"What kind of mission?" *You should have known it would come with strings attached. She's a politician, after all.*

"The Zimbabwean Finance Minister, one Philip Agambe, is out of control. He's funnelling United Nations aid to an Islamic terrorist group controlled by one of his cousins. They killed nineteen British nurses working in a children's hospital in Kenya a couple of months ago, and three of your former comrades the month before that. It was hushed up – bad for morale –

but now we believe he's planning to overthrow the Government there."

"Believe?" Gabriel shot a glance at Don. But the older man's face was impassive.

Barbara Sutherland gave Gabriel a look cooler than the weather outside.

"You're not questioning my intelligence sources are you, love?" she asked, her Yorkshire accent sharpening like a blade. "Because as a private citizen you don't have quite the insight I do."

Gabriel ran a hand through his short, black hair, raising an uneven row of spiky tufts from forehead to crown.

"Of course not. I just remember you telling me before that The Department works under the highest burden of proof."

"And so it does, Gabriel. So it does. If it makes you more comfortable, we *know* that Philip Agambe is plotting a coup. Even though he's a Shona like the man he wants to overthrow. And although it's fair to say there's no love lost between the current President of Zimbabwe and the United Kingdom, he looks like a *Sun*-reading British patriot compared to Agambe and his poisonous friends in the Freedom Party of Zimbabwe. He has to go. And I want you to do it."

Gabriel turned to look at Don properly. He did look tired. His posture was far from the straight-backed military bearing that no amount of desk work could soften. His shoulders were rounded and there was a slackness in his face that drew his mouth down at the corners.

"What's your view, Don?" Gabriel asked.

"Don's view is that Philip Agambe is a dangerous enemy and needs removing from the picture," Barbara interrupted before the older man could even open his mouth.

"The PM's right, Old Sport. He turned a convoy of nurses into a funeral cortège. The PM showed me a dossier. Man's a bad 'un."

While Gabriel was pondering the disconnect between his former and sometime-current boss's demeanour and his words, there was a soft knock at the door and a young man dressed as a waiter appeared carrying a tray of tea and coffee things.

"Ah, thank you, Will, my love," Barbara said, all trace of the edge in her voice erased, replaced by that warm tone that she'd made her trademark in media appearances. Even journalists weren't immune, soft-pedalling on questions as Barbara Sutherland treated them with respect and folksy good humour. "Now, boys, shall I be Mother?"

7

Mission Parameters

"DON, tell Gabriel what we want him to do, would you? I'm gasping for this," Barbara said, before blowing on the surface of her tea and eyeing both men in turn over the rim of her cup.

Don cleared his throat.

"Agambe's background is as a leader of the Fifth Brigade. Know who they were?" Gabriel shook his head.

"Basically, a Special Forces unit trained by the North Koreans. Involved in a systematic programme of civilian massacres, torture and internment during the civil war in the eighties. Now he positions himself as a moderate within the party. But it's a front. You know what politicians are." He glanced at Barbara, his eyes creasing, brow grooved with worry-lines. "No offence, Barbara."

"None taken," she said, her eyes as dark as pooling blood. "Go on."

"Because he was part of the gang who helped the current president, he can do no wrong. Keeps his seat at every general election, massively popular in the countryside, where his power base is."

Don stopped for a moment and took a sip of his tea. His eyes flicked up to the ceiling, to the window, then back to Gabriel.

"I don't understand, Don," Gabriel said. "Do we really go after elected politicians? Especially ones with a popular mandate? I hear what you're saying," he glanced at Barbara, "about the nurses and the SAS boys, and that's beyond bad, obviously, but it doesn't seem like business for The Department."

Barbara spoke again, clinking her teacup down into the saucer in front of her.

"Behind his bluster, the current President actually depends on the UK to keep him in power. Without the aid and international political support we give him, he'd be out on his ear the day after tomorrow. He's also a rabid anti-communist and that's strategically very helpful in keeping the Russians out. I . . . we . . . don't want a bloody missile base or a client state in that part of Africa. Now, can we continue?"

"Yes, of course. Sorry, Don."

Don smiled. Rubbed his palms on his trousers. Then across his face.

"Agambe's funnelling aid money to equip his Islamist friends with all manner of tasty military hardware. Meanwhile, people starve. Children go unvaccinated and die of malaria. Schools rot away for lack of maintenance. Stopping him will give us the breathing space we need to pursue the next level down in his little organisation through more conventional means."

"This is all solid intel?" Gabriel asked, ignoring the glare from Barbara Sutherland.

Don gave a small nod. "MI6 and CIA joint taskforce on southern African terrorism confirmed it all, Old Sport. I've seen the report myself."

"And you want me to stop him?"

"Yes we do. You could make it look like a professional hit. Plenty of Afrikaners to the south would look good for it. Or a street attack. Then you can be on your way across the border to find Smudge."

"What about that? We've not even talked about how I'm going to find him."

"After this, we're going across the river to MI6. I've got a full briefing assembled for you. We retrieved your last-known coordinates from the extract point, detailed maps, profiles of local warlords and the disposition of their forces. Plus a quartermaster. You two can have a nice little chat about what toys you want. You'll be flying military so you can take it all with you – none of that diplomatic bag nonsense this time."

"What about local support?"

"For Zim, you're on your own, I'm afraid. For Mozambique, we can be a bit more helpful. Army, park rangers, intelligence – whatever you need, it's all going to be laid on for you. All you need to do is focus on bringing Smudge back."

Throughout this exchange, Barbara had sat silently, watching, and listening. Every now and then, Gabriel glanced over, expecting her to speak, but she just smiled, her trademark red lipstick a splash of colour as the sky turned darker and hailstones began clicking against the window.

"You know, there probably won't be much left," she said. Not unkindly, but there was no mistaking the calculation in her voice. "Not after, how long is it?"

Gabriel pinched the bridge of his nose, screwing his eyes up tight.

"Four years."

"I don't want to be too graphic, but it's hot, and humid sometimes. Scavengers will have found the poor man. Maybe even treasure-hunters."

"I know all of that. I know that even if I can find the exact tree where they . . ." Gabriel cleared his throat. ". . . where they left him, there might be nothing left, but at least then I'll know. I promised his daughter I'd bring her Dad back and I need to be able to look her in the eye and say I tried."

"Yes you do. Promises mean a lot when you're thirteen."

Gabriel looked up sharply. How did Barbara know Nathalie's age?

"Prime Minister, if there's nothing else?" Don checked his watch.

"No. You go on, Don. And take my blessings with you, Gabriel. All the way to Mozambique. And back, hopefully."

8

Tooling Up

ONCE outside, Gabriel turned to Don.

"Is everything OK? You seemed a little sub-par in there. And what's happened to Barbara? She's definitely not playing the kissy Yorkshire lass these days is she?"

"Did you bring your car?"

"Yes, it's over there."

"Let's get going and I'll fill you in on some domestic political issues you should know about."

Once inside the Maserati, and being waved through the double iron gates by the police, Gabriel asked again.

"So, tell me. What's going on?"

Don let out a sigh. It sounded as though he were trying to empty his lungs completely.

"There's going to be a general election soon. Barbara wants another term. But she's convinced there are people – 'forces' she calls them – who are out to get her. She's on edge and it's leaking into her relationships with people she ought to have a bit more time for. People like you, Old Sport."

"And you?"

"Me?" He laughed. "I'm just an old war horse. Not even properly in harness any more. I know The Department sounds like fun, and from your point of view and that of your fellow operatives, it is. Wearing black and bursting in and shooting the bad guys, that has to be better than selling insurance or whatever Civvy Street dishes up to ex-service personnel. But for me? I'm basically an administrator. I have budget meetings, protocol meetings, inter-agency meetings, staff meetings, meetings with my oppo in Langley . . ."

"The CIA know about what you do?"

"Know about it? They helped us set it up. I know I told you it was Wilson, but once our remit went beyond providing a paranoid, lefty prime minister with intel on his cabinet colleagues, the Americans were really useful in developing our methods."

Gabriel drove across the south side of Parliament Square, passing the House of Commons on his left. A blast on the horn shooed a couple of tourists from the middle of the road where they were attempting to frame a selfie with Big Ben in the background.

"Bloody tourists. Sorry, go on. The Americans?"

"Yes, I have a weekly catchup with a very senior executive in Langley. Usually on a scrambled video link, but occasionally we take turns to fly over and have what he calls 'face time'."

"But Christine must prefer you having a safer job? It's like your driver was saying to me a while back. 'Home in time for tea.'"

At the mention of his wife, Don's face clouded over like the darkening sky above them.

"She does. Especially since her stroke."

"How is she?"

"Doing OK, really. The doctors say she's made amazing progress for a woman of her age. Still a bit droopy on the left side and using her wheelchair, but she can talk again, and feed herself, so God willing she'll outlive me yet."

"Send her my love, won't you?"

"Of course. She thinks of you as a son, you know."

Now it was Gabriel's turn to sigh.

"She's the only woman who does, now."

"I know it's been tough since your parents died. Christine and I, we really felt for you. Now look lively, we need to take a left for Vauxhall Bridge."

Gabriel indicated left and pulled round a bus to make the left turn across Vauxhall Bridge from Millbank. Ahead of them, on the left side of the bridge, stood the sand and bottle-green building that housed Britain's Secret Intelligence Service: MI6. Despite looking like a cross between a 1930s Hollywood mogul's idea of 'the factory of the future' and an Aztec temple, it had withstood an attack from dissident Irish republicans in 2000.

"Where do we get in? I'm guessing there isn't a big gate with a 'way in' sign on it."

Don chuckled, the first sign that his mood was anything other than black since Gabriel and he had shaken hands inside Number Ten.

"Actually, there is, Old Sport. Just turn left at the lights onto Albert Embankment. It's on the left just before the end of the building."

Gabriel did as he was told and, yes, there it was. A forbidding steel gate in a matt green paint that matched the showier frontage facing the Thames. A blue and white 'IN' sign sat beside a 'No cycling' sign.

Gabriel pointed. "What's that for? To deter bicycle bombers?"

"Hadn't you heard? We're under attack by militant cyclists."

As the two men bantered, Don pulled out his phone and sent a short text. A second or two later, the railing-topped gates slid sideways from the centre. They were in.

"Now what?" Gabriel said.

"Security like you wouldn't believe, then we'll go and see Sam about your toys."

Twenty minutes later, having been photographed, fingerprinted, retina-scanned and subject to a body cavity search that made him long for the gentle hands of the police officers at Downing Street, Gabriel found himself walking along a bland, white-painted corridor. It was devoid of all visual interruptions, barring regular swipe-card locks, fire alarms, and notices reminding personnel to carry SIS ID at all times and never to let IT software or hardware out of their sight.

"Here we are," Don said, stopping front of a pair of stainless steel lift doors. Above them was a sign that read, simply, "QM only".

"Quartermaster?" Gabriel asked.

"In one."

There was no floor indicator above the doors, but they opened a few moments later with a whisper of changing air pressure.

Inside, the lift was as devoid of decoration as the corridor it opened onto. Observing the behaviour code of lift occupants everywhere, neither man spoke until the doors opened again onto an identical white-painted corridor.

"Come on then," Don said. "Let's introduce you to Sam."

They stopped outside a white-painted door marked with a square of aluminium etched with the letters QM. To the right was a button, which Don pressed for a second.

The door was opened by a person Gabriel took to be an assistant of some kind. She was slightly built, with straight black hair tied back in a ponytail, wearing a brown button-through cotton overall of the kind worn by school woodwork teachers. It reached to just above her knees, revealing slender calves that disappeared into a pair of lilac and white Converse baseball boots, their laces replaced with dark purple ribbons. Her face was an almost-perfect heart shape with a sharp chin and a broad, high forehead that was utterly free of wrinkles. And yet, behind her wet-slate-coloured eyes was a wisdom that belied her apparent youth. She smiled at Don, revealing small, even teeth, the canines crossing slightly in front of the incisors.

"Hello Don, brought your boy to see me, have you?" she said, stretching up to plant a light kiss on Don's cheek.

Don smiled back. "Hello, Sam. This is Gabriel Wolfe. Best soldier I ever had under my command."

She turned to Gabriel, appraising him with a single look that swept up from his feet to the top of his head, lingering for a moment on the scar on his left cheek.

"Doctor Samantha Flack. But you can call me Sam."

"Pleased to meet you," he said, shooting Don a look. *"Sam"*.

Her eyes twinkled. "Don been playing games again, has he?"

"He always did like to test me. See what assumptions I'd leap to. Got me again, I'm afraid."

"You're not the first, and I dare say you won't be the last. Now, come in to my domain and let's see about kitting you out, shall we?"

Sam led the two men over to a steel-topped bench. Dominating the scratched surface was a selection of handguns: Berettas, Glocks and SIGs. Then there were the edged weapons: everything from tactical blades to flick-knives. There were coils of wire; steel cylinders six inches long and half an inch in diameter; and dull, charcoal-grey plastic boxes the size of cigarette packets. At one end was a weapon Gabriel had last used on active service in Northern Ireland: a Heckler & Koch MP5K sub-machine gun, little more than a foot long, its stock removed and its barrel shortened to make it a practical option for concealing inside a jacket.

"Nice," was all Gabriel said.

"Indeed," Sam replied. "I know how much you boys – and increasingly, girls – like your toys. If you want anything extra – assault rifle, maybe – do say, won't you?"

Gabriel looked at the woman again, embarrassed at his initial assumption that somebody else, probably a grizzled ex-Army weapons instructor, or bearded scientist-type would be the boss. Her hair, which he had at first taken to be as solidly black as his own, carried threads of silver. And there were fans of fine lines radiating out from the corners of her eyes. Yet she didn't look older than thirty or thirty-five, despite the remote possibility anybody that young could have risen to such a key position within the Service.

"Tune out for a moment, did you, Old Sport?" Don said, with a grin. "Checking out the good Doctor, were we?"

"It's OK, Gabriel," Sam said. "It's a little game we play. To reassure you, I'm well past my fortieth birthday and I know my API-blowback from my roller-delayed weapons."

Gabriel swept a hand over his scalp. "Sorry, Sam. Residual sexism, I'm afraid. What's your doctorate in?"

"Effects of meditation and other eastern mindfulness techniques on resistance to torture," she whispered, leaning closer. "The practicals were huge fun."

She stared into his eyes.

He blinked first.

Sam broke the spell with a burst of laughter. "Oh, dear, not really in our comfort zone are we? Come on, let's have some fun with your new toys before we ship them out to your departure point. Grab a couple of the pistols, would you, Gabriel? You too, Don."

With each of them carrying two pistols apiece, like desperadoes ready to rob a train, Gabriel, Sam and Don walked to the far end of the room where a door led to a shooting range.

A bench ran along the complete width of the narrow range, except for a gap at the far end. Unlike the police and army ranges Gabriel had practised in, this bench had no partitions to separate shooters from one another.

At the far end of the room, perhaps forty feet away and mounted on thin metal frames, was a series of paper targets printed with imaginary assailants. These were not simple black silhouettes, or even cartoonish bad guys with sunglasses, brandishing improbably large handguns. Instead, they depicted a human frame from head to mid-thigh rendered in a bright yellow, with the skeleton superimposed in blue as if X-rayed. Picked out in orange were areas over the heart, the brain and the two wings of the pelvis.

"We call him Pablo," Sam said. "After Pablo Escobar. The Medellin cartel boss? Much more efficient as a training aid than the older-style targets. Depending on the mission parameters, body armour, concealment, bodyguards and so on, you can opt for different shots from kill to disablement. I'm partial to a pelvic put-down myself. Hit the ball-and-socket joint at the top of the femur and flop, down goes your man like a rag doll."

They lined up at the bench. Two pistols in front of each them. Sam left briefly, reappeared with several boxes of ammunition, and started scooping rounds out and piling them in front of Don and Gabriel.

"Standard ball, hollow-point, and my little babies on the right," she said.

Gabriel felt sure he should ask about Sam's *little babies*. "And they would be?"

"Depleted uranium; DU in the trade. You need to aim high because the weight pulls the trajectory down. But they'll go through steel plate half an inch thick. We've modified the propellant and the cartridge cases to deliver the extra *oomph* they need, so the recoil's a little cheeky, but if you're holding it properly, you should be fine. Only had one broken wrist since we developed them."

Gabriel frowned. He wasn't sure if she was joking and was beginning to realise that people underestimated Sam at their peril. Particularly if they were one of the bad guys.

"Standard ball first, gentlemen. In your Glocks, I'd suggest. Load and fire at will. Ear defenders on the wall behind you."

They each loaded the pistols, pulled the red plastic ear defenders down over their heads and levelled their weapons.

9

DU Rounds

GABRIEL stilled his breathing, and let his pulse drop to around fifty. Focused on the highlighted brain on his target.

Waited for a gap between heartbeats and squeezed off two rounds.

To his left and right, Sam and Don had begun shooting too, and even through the foam-insulated cans, the noise of three semi-automatic, 9 mm pistols firing in such a confined space was deafening.

Next, Gabriel aimed for the heart and sent three more rounds down the range, adjusting his aim as the Glock 17 bucked in his hands.

The hips next, three rounds apiece.

They carried on firing until each magazine was emptied. The air reeked of burnt cordite and the hot brass of the ejected cartridge cases that plinked and rattled as they hit the steel bench and the concrete floor. Then Sam pressed a button on the wall behind her to bring the targets, or what was left of them, swinging up towards them on ceiling-mounted wires.

Gabriel's target was almost completely unmarked by bullet holes, except for four tight groups: three to the head, and four each to the heart and the left and right pelvic joints. Don's was peppered with bullet holes in the right places but each round had hit in a different spot and clearly several had gone wide of the target. He pulled a face.

"Bloody desk jockey, that's what they've turned me into."

Sam had punched out the face of her attacker with a neat oval of fifteen shots.

"Let's switch to the hollow-points," she said.

Gabriel hand-loaded the hollow-point rounds into the Glock's magazine. While he was reloading, Sam walked down to the end of the range and set up two humanoid targets: one male, one female, both dressed in jeans and T-shirts, and equipped with dummy Kalashnikovs.

"I'll let you two compete for the marksmanship badge," Don said, when Sam returned to the shooting side of the bench. "That last performance confirmed what I've long suspected. My shooting-war days are behind me."

Gabriel looked up and cocked an eyebrow. "Nice targets."

"You don't have a problem shooting at women, I hope," Sam said. "Look, she's carrying an AK-47. She's about to blow your brains out."

"Or mine, Boss."

Gabriel startled as Smudge's voice echoed inside the insulation of his ear defenders. He whirled around but mercifully Smudge's presence was confined to the auditory realm this time. No mangled face grinning at him from the far end of the range.

Sweat broke out on his face and he wiped it away with his forearm. His pulse jerked upwards and a burst of adrenaline raced around his bloodstream, setting up a mad desire to run from the room. Breathing evenly, Gabriel fought the panic attack down, focusing on a mantra for calm he'd learned at the feet of Zhao Xi, the friend of his parents who'd virtually raised him when his behaviour at school had caused one too many expulsions.

"I'm ready," he managed to choke out.

"Off you go, then. I think I'll sit this one out, too."

Gabriel brought the Glock up to a double-handed shooter's stance, holding the barrel level with his right eye. Then, in a continuous flexing movement of his trigger finger, he discharged all seventeen 9 mm Parabellum rounds in a matter of a few seconds.

Once the smoke had cleared, Sam pointed to the target. "I think she's dead."

The dummy's head was obliterated, only the lower jaw remained. The area around the heart was shredded – there was a hole big enough to reach through without scratching yourself on the sharp edges of plastic around the exit wounds. And both thighs had sustained catastrophic damage. Had she been real, and had the head and heart shots missed their targets, the wounds to the legs would have killed her, either from shock or blood loss, or both.

"You, Gabriel, are a stone killer," Sam said, with a grin that turned the corners of her lips up. "Let's see what you make of my little babies. Load the DU rounds into the SIG, would you?"

The depleted uranium rounds were the same dimensions as the rest of the ammunition they'd been handling. But whereas the regular ammunition had round-nosed, copper-jacketed tips, the 9 mm-diameter DU projectiles were pointed, and clipped into three interlocking wedges of yellow plastic: sabots. Their job was to guide the bullet along the barrel without it yawing. The rounds were heavy, too, freakishly so, given their tiny size. Gabriel carefully slid ten into the SIG's box magazine before pushing it home into the butt with a reassuringly solid click.

Sam disappeared off down to the end of the range and left through a side door. She emerged a few moments later dragging a rectangle of dull, khaki-painted steel on a trolley. It was three feet tall by a foot wide. A single white cross had been painted about two thirds of the way up. Gabriel waited for her to regain the safety of the shooters' bench.

"I'm not planning on taking on anything bigger than a hyena, you know."

"Try it. Indulge a girl for heaven's sake."

"What am I shooting at?"

"That's half-inch thick, military-spec, steel armour."

Remembering what Sam had said at the start of the session, Gabriel aimed at the top edge of the steel panel. He gripped the SIG firmly in his right hand, cradling his curled fingers in his left.

He took a breath.

Let it out.

Squeezed the trigger.

And swore.

"Fuck. Me!"

The recoil from the pistol almost knocked him off his feet. The bang as the high-capacity cartridge discharged its uprated load of propellant was deafening, even with the defenders on. And the intense smell of the burnt smokeless powder made his nose sting.

The three of them looked down the range at the steel plate.

Halfway down exactly, eight inches below the centre of the white cross, was a perfectly circular hole, 9 mm in diameter. The backboard, comprising six inches of solid timber sandwiching ballistic foam, was burning merrily. With a rush of compressed air, automatic fire extinguishers jetted snowstorms of CO_2 over the flames. A roar of fans added to the noise as massive extractor fans sucked the radioactive by-products of the impact out of the range and into the bowels of the building.

"Fuck me!" Gabriel said. "Again."

"Good, aren't they?" Sam replied.

Don was chuckling quietly, *mm-hmm*ing through his nose.

"How the hell do they do so much damage?" Gabriel asked, his ears ringing from the noise. "Are they HE or something?"

Sam shook her head. "Not high explosive, no. It's actually pretty basic physics. Kinetic energy. Your ordinary pistol round works on the same principle. The energy it carries to the target is transferred into the target when it arrives. If the energy carried by a standard nine-mil ball round is an AA battery, a DU round is like a nuclear power station."

"And they're legal?"

She grinned. "At the moment they are, just, within the rules of war. But you must know that the rules are aimed, forgive the pun, at regular forces. We have certain . . . dispensations. In any case, all the permanent members of the UN Security Council have their own variants. Or wish they did."

"Can I take some of those with me?"

"That is rather the point. I'd suggest you take the SIG – we've modified it to cope with the increased barrel pressure and ballistic load – for the DU rounds and the Glock for regular work. Should you need them at all, I mean. You might be one of those up-close-and-personal types. Whites of their eyes and so on and so forth."

"I think we can safely say Gabriel is a 'do whatever it takes' type of a chap," Don said.

"I never say no to extra firepower," Gabriel said. "Especially in tank-buster format."

After that, they looked over the non-firearms. Gabriel selected a butterfly knife, illegal virtually everywhere, but excellent for wet work where concealment was necessary. He'd be bringing his own ceramic tactical knife.

"We've got you an encrypted satellite phone as well," Sam said. "Good anywhere on God's green Earth. Speak freely and anyone attempting to listen in will just get an earful of static."

"What about those?" Gabriel asked, pointing at the steel cylinders.

"EPGs. Electromagnetic pulse generators. Each ready-fused and operable either by delayed timer or a signal from your phone."

"What do they do, exactly?"

Sam picked up one of the devices. "Not much to look at, I know, but press here," Sam indicated a faint depression in the surface with the pad of her thumb, "and five seconds later it emits an intense thirty-millisecond burst of electromagnetic radiation in the microwave part of the spectrum that will scrub the code from every piece of silicon within a fifty-foot radius. Completely silent, odourless and harmless to human beings." She paused. "And animals." Sam indicated a couple of smaller devices, equally devoid of decoration on their dull grey plastic casings. "Couple of GPS trackers. Military-grade, none of that gap-year rubbish anxious middle-class mummies stick in their teenaged sons' rucksacks."

Gabriel prodded the EPG then turned back to face Sam.

"I made a list of stuff I thought I'd need. Can I leave it with you?"

"Of course. Hand it over."

Gabriel took out his wallet and extracted the folded paper. He handed it to Sam who unfolded it and skimmed down the list.

"Nothing too outrageous there," she said. "We'll fit out a day-sack that should give you survival capability for up to a month."

"Thanks. Oh, and one last thing."

"What's that?"

He looked left and right, then murmured, "When do I get the real toys?"

Sam's face became still, expressionless. "Go on."

Gabriel glanced at Don, then stared deep into Sam's eyes.

"You know, the magnetic watch for undoing dress zips. The flamethrower fountain pen. The amphibious Aston Martin."

Sam folded her arms across her chest. She narrowed her eyes. But Gabriel could see a twinkle there, too.

"Would you like to estimate how many agents and assorted hangers-on I've had through that door who've cracked basically the same tired James Bond joke in the last ten years?"

"Is it more than three?"

Sam poked Gabriel in the chest. "Yes. It is. 'Have you done something with your hair, Q?' 'Will it fire round corners?' 'Where's the ejector seat?'"

"Sorry. Couldn't resist it. I can see how it might get a little lame after a decade in charge of this place. But just so we're clear," he paused for a beat, "I'm not getting a jet pack, then?"

"Out!" Sam shouted, pointing at the door, before cracking a wide smile. "Don, I order you to bring me a sensible one next time."

"I do the best with the material available, Sam, you know that," Don said. "Come on, Old Sport, before she skewers us both with a rocket-propelled harpoon."

Sam's mouth opened wide. "Out, now! Both of you. Bloody overgrown schoolboys!"

10
Additional Support

SITTING side by side with his old, and now current, boss, in the Maserati, the start button unthumbed, Gabriel asked the question he'd been saving up for the right moment.

"Can I take someone with me? To Mozambique."

"Wouldn't be a redhead with a penchant for high-powered rifles and pickled herrings, would it?"

Gabriel smiled at Don's ability to divine what he was thinking without having to come out and say it.

"You knew I was going to ask, didn't you?"

"Not exactly. But I like to know my people. Especially their relationships." He paused and pinched the skin between his eyebrows, squeezing his eyes shut. "Makes a chap vulnerable, you know."

"Makes them human, as well, though, doesn't it?"

"That it does, Old Sport, that it does."

Something about his voice made Gabriel twist in his seat to look at Don. The older man was staring out through the windscreen towards the exit barrier of the car park and the forbidding green-painted steel gate beyond. His face was pulled down as if the effort of speaking in those flat tones had exhausted him.

"Is everything all right, Don?"

Don rubbed his hand across his face. "Tip top, Gabriel." He turned and offered a smile but it lacked energy, more like an expression put there by will than genuine good humour. "Just that the PM's got a bee in her bonnet about this bloody Agambe chap and she's leaning on me to take him out sooner rather than later."

Even without the skills Master Zhao had taught him back in his teenaged years in Hong Kong, Gabriel would have been able to read Don's face. *No. Nothing is right.* He frowned. No sense in pursuing it now. The more immediate concern was getting approval for Britta's accompanying him to Africa.

"If you know about me and Britta, you'll know we make an excellent team. Always did. I need someone I can trust out there."

"Why not somebody else from The Department? I have Africa specialists, Portuguese speakers, jungle-warfare veterans. This isn't some boyfriend-girlfriend thing, is it?"

"What? No! Do you really think . . ."

Don sighed. "No, of course not. Sorry, Old Sport. Just got a lot on my mind at the moment. Bloody backbenchers asking awkward questions, journalists sniffing around. Look, I apologise for that remark. It wasn't fair. Or right. But there are operational problems. For one, Britta is attached to MI5. And from what I hear on the bush telegraph, that attachment might be about to become permanent."

Gabriel's pulse ticked up a notch. "Really? They're inviting her to join?"

"If she wants it. No doubt the good lady will fill you in next time you see her. But we can't have operatives of an official British security agency – even Swedish ones – charging about foreign democracies killing elected politicians. Doesn't go down well on the world stage. Then there's the ostensible reason for your trip. Strictly speaking, recovering the remains of war dead is army business, only they don't have the budget for this type of work at the moment. But it's certainly not MI5's. Hard to see how they could assign her to a mission on foreign soil – where's the counter-terrorism angle?"

"Abel N'Tolo was a terrorist. Of sorts."

"Yes, but he was a Mozambican terrorist." Don paused. "I'm sure you want to take some time with Britta, Lord knows I would in your position. Why not make it a holiday? Go away together. I can't sanction her involvement in this bit of business and I'm sure her bosses down the road feel the same way."

"A holiday?"

"Why not? Maybe take milady Falskog somewhere hot. Just a thought. Now, shall we get going? You can drop me back at Whitehall. I have meetings, then a dinner. Bunch of extremely senior civil servants who think I run a military training programme. All Barbara's idea to maintain cover. I tell you, there'll be more knights round that table than King Arthur ever mustered round his."

Gabriel started the car. He drove out of the underground car park, waited for the barrier to be raised, then eased towards the armoured steel gates. These opened as he arrived, controlled, presumably, by some hawk-eyed security guard at the other end of the wire from the cameras mounted left and right. As Gabriel drove through, a handful of feral pigeons launched into the air where they whirled in the gathering wind like the thoughts in his head

"One more thing," Gabriel said. "Equipment reliability under African conditions. I'm thinking it might be good to build in redundancy. Maybe you could ask Sam to supply two of everything. And per her suggestion, better stick a couple of assault rifles in the suitcase too."

Don nodded. "Excellent idea. Can't have you out in the field with malfunctioning kit, can we?"

The sky had darkened to the colour of lead, and Gabriel drove in silence back over Vauxhall bridge towards Whitehall, letting the rhythm of the windscreen wipers calm his thoughts.

11

Quid Pro Quo

IT was raining properly now, fat drops that didn't so much fall from the sky as hurl themselves downwards as if in a hurry to make landfall. Gabriel didn't feel like driving back to Salisbury, and drove to a hotel he liked instead. The Raven was a small place, discreetly set back from the pedestrian and vehicular traffic on a narrow lane just north of Smithfield meat market. About as far from a corporate place as it was possible to imagine, the hotel liked to keep its rooms full by catering to its regulars and those tourists and visitors clued-up enough to avoid the chains in favour of somewhere a little less plasticky.

Checked in and lying on his bed, Gabriel picked up the house phone and hit zero.

"Yes, Mr Wolfe?"

"I'm going to need a few things for the morning, Daniel. Do you think you could have someone organise it for me?"

"Of course, sir. A change of clothes, perhaps? Toiletries? From your usual places?"

"Yes, please."

"Very good, sir. And shall we charge to your account as usual?"

"Please."

Gabriel pulled a leather wing chair round to face the darkening sky through the panelled window and, taking a good slug of the gin and tonic he'd brought up from the honour bar, settled in to take stock. He closed his eyes.

Mission: retrieve Smudge's remains from Mozambican forest. Military support, logistics, local transport, guides. Will I need scientific support? Forensic anthropologist? Price of admission: eliminate Zimbabwean defence minister who's chanelling funds to Islamist terror group and planning destabilising coup. Support from The Department including materiel. Presumably intelligence as well. Check with Don. Need to skirt round MI5 and Department regs to get Britta onboard. But how?

He opened his eyes and raised the glass to his lips, enjoying the aromatic smell of the herbs and plant extracts in the gin as it coursed down his throat. How indeed? Maybe Britta could help him come up with a plan. Maybe she was free for dinner. He got out his phone and tapped her picture.

"*Hej!* How are you?"

"Good. Are you free tonight?"

"Yes. Are you going to buy me dinner?"

"I am. There's something I want to talk to you about."

"Ooh, secret stuff!"

Gabriel smiled. "What do you fancy?"

"Chinese first, Wolfe second."

"I think that can be arranged. Chinatown?"

"Cool."

"There's a basement cocktail bar at the junction of Newport Place and Lisle Street. The door's black, no name, just a brass bell push. There's a steel plate set into the pavement with a nine cut into it. When can you get there?"

"I've got a surveillance report to write up and a debrief with my boss. Say, eight-thirty?"

Gabriel checked his watch. Three hours to kill before he had to leave. "Perfect. See you there."

"If you're there before me, champagne cocktail, please."

The call finished, Gabriel finished the dregs of his drink and headed for the bathroom.

He'd just climbed out of the shower when there was a quiet tap at the door. Gabriel tied the towelling robe around his middle and checked the spyhole. A young woman in the hotel's uniform of charcoal-grey suit and white shirt was there, holding a couple of shiny paper carrier bags with twisted cord handles. He opened the door, took the bags, and pressed a folded twenty pound note into her palm as the bags changed hands.

"Thank you, Anita. What would I do without you?"

"Wear yesterday's socks," she said, her face a mask of seriousness. Then she turned on her heel and was gone.

*

The walls of the bar flickered with shadows thrown by the candles in red glasses that lit the room. Gabriel ordered two champagne cocktails and took them to a corner table. He took a sip of his drink: buttery, toasty champagne, a deep hit from the cognac and a whisper of orange from the Grand Marnier. A few minutes later, he heard feet on the stairs and looked over to the door.

Gabriel's eyes, and those of the other patrons, travelled from Britta's flaming red hair to her black Dr. Martens boots. She was dressed all in black: jeans, hoodie under a leather biker jacket, woollen fingerless gloves. She looked around, letting her eyes adjust to the dim light, taking her time to search out Gabriel. He enjoyed the way the other drinkers seemed unable to tear their gaze away from her. Then she saw him.

"*Hej!* Cool spot." She came over to the table. He rose to his feet and they hugged. Then she pulled back and planted a kiss on his lips. "What's the news?" she said.

Gabriel outlined the brief. He had logistics and equipment in place but, as he said to her now, "What I really want is you."

"I'd love to be your number two on this one. But my bosses have me working virtually round the clock to put this people trafficker out of business."

"How come it's not a police case?"

"It would be if he was spending the money on cars, or stashing it in a Swiss bank, but he's not. He's using it to buy weapons. Serious stuff, too. He's bringing the women onto British soil, so that makes it MI5's case."

"Don gave me a strong hint that we could team up if you were to take some holiday. Otherwise, he pretty much vetoed it. Funnily enough for virtually the same grounds you just gave for following your cocksucker."

Britta threw back her head and laughed. "You looked it up, then?"

"Of course. As a professional linguist I felt it was my duty. So what are we going to do?"

Britta took a sip of her cocktail. "Here's a thought, Mr Off-The-Books. Why don't you help me deal with my trafficker, then I'm free to take some time off? A nice little holiday in southern Africa, for example."

"What do you need?"

"He's bringing another group of women in a couple of days from now. I need some audio of him to find out where and when exactly. But his house is so well guarded, we're having trouble getting the deep surveillance we need to nail the bastard."

"What if you had someone who could get inside undetected, or at least unremembered, plant a bug and get out again?"

"You mean, a person with all kinds of ancient Eastern voodoo they could use to get in under the wire?"

Gabriel smiled. She smiled back. They clinked glasses and drained their drinks.

*

It was after midnight when they returned to Gabriel's room at the Raven.

"Come and see this," Gabriel said, holding Britta's hand and pulling her through a white-painted door leading off the bedroom.

"Cool, a wet room," she said.

"Yes. I thought maybe we could get wet together. Unless you're tired, of course?"

"I'm a nightbird. What is it, a lark, not an owl?"

"Other way round. But good. Now, stand still."

Britta stood to a slightly off-centre attention while Gabriel undressed her. When she was naked, he removed his own clothes and led her into the huge shower area. Under the hot water, they embraced and kissed, wrapping their arms around each other tightly, as if they knew this might be the last comfort they'd be enjoying for some while.

Britta looked into his eyes and wrapped her arms around the back of his neck.

"Catch!" she said, then lifted her feet off the ground and jumped a little so she could wrap her legs around him.

Gabriel placed his hands under her buttocks and brought her to him. She crossed her ankles at the base of his spine and began to tilt her hips back and forth, increasing the pressure between them, then releasing it. They came seconds apart, heads thrown back and laughing, while the water streamed down their faces, pooling in the space where Britta's breasts were squashed against Gabriel's chest.

The following morning, Gabriel appeared at Britta's side of the bed carrying a deep-sided tray woven from seagrass. In its separate compartments nestled warm croissants, Danish pastries, yoghurt with fruit compote in a screw-topped jar, and tea.

"Wake up, sleepyhead," he said, nudging her thigh with his knee before putting the tray down on the end of the bed.

"What time is it?"

"Nine. I brought you breakfast. No herrings, I'm afraid."

She flapped a hand in an attempt to slap him. She missed.

"You're such a racist, Wolfe, you know that? Us Swedes have some very exciting chefs nowadays. Only the old folks eat herrings."

"Come on. We have a *kuksugare* to catch."

*

An hour later, Britta and Gabriel were standing beside an old London plane tree on a wide avenue in Kensington. They leaned against the trunk, arms around each other's waists, looking for all the world as if they were two lovers taking a moment to cuddle up against the cold November wind that plucked the few remaining leaves from the tree and whipped them high into the air. Forty feet down the road, a grand Georgian house sat back from the pavement behind wrought iron gates topped with security cameras. Over Britta's left shoulder, Gabriel watched the gates as a dark brown delivery van pulled up, the words, "Patisserie Jeannot" lettered on the side in pink script. He heard the engine quit with a phlegmy rattle.

The driver got out of the truck, went to the squawk box mounted on the right-hand gatepost, pressed a button, and spoke into the grille. After a couple of minutes, the gates swung back on themselves and two burly Arab men dressed in black nylon windcheaters and jeans came out. They spoke briefly to the driver. He turned and went round the back of the truck, opened the double doors and pulled them wide. Then he climbed inside and clambered back down, rear-end first, carrying an enormous cake box, bright pink with dark brown swirls all over it. He held it out in front of him, while one of the guards lifted the top off the box.

Clearly the box did indeed contain just cake. The guard signalled to his partner, who stood aside. With his cargo safely stored away again, the driver climbed back into the cab and drove in through the gates. The lead guard looked up and down the street, pausing on Gabriel and Britta for a second, before turning and going back inside his master's fortress.

"You see?" Britta said, her cheek just brushing Gabriel's.

"I do see. Serious muscle, serious security. I'd say a frontal assault's out of the question. What's round the back?"

"I'll show you. It's promising."

The houses on the street backed onto a similar row on the next road along. Gabriel identified the four-storey house roughly in line with the trafficker's.

"We could go in that way, down the back garden, over the fence and in through a window or side door. Or maybe even just stick a bug through the exterior wall?"

"We need a cover story to get into this house first. Any ideas?"

"I don't know. In the Regiment, we used to make sure the houses we entered were empty in the first place."

"Maybe we're tourists and our car broke down? We need to borrow their phone?"

"Seriously? Who doesn't have a mobile these days?"

"I'm Swedish. My service provider just cut my roaming. My boyfriend was mugged last night and they lifted his iPhone."

"I guess it could work. If they'll let us in, I can put them under while we go over the fence."

"Right. That's the plan. Let's go."

"What, now?"

"I have everything in my rucksack. Bug, lock-picks and check this out."

She unsnapped the flap of her khaki rucksack and pulled the top open so Gabriel could peer inside.

"Shit! Are you allowed to carry those around in London?"

He was looking down on a pair of semi-automatic Beretta M9 pistols, fitted with fat, black, cylindrical silencers. Britta flashed him a smile and batted her eyelashes at him.

"What, me, officer? Oh, well I suppose they are handguns. Will this help?" Then she pulled out an MI5 ID from inside her hoodie. It had a QR code in the bottom-right-hand corner. "They've all got scanners now. It takes them to a secure MI5 site, so we're covered, basically."

"Good to know." He looked up at the black front door, which was accessible from a flight of six black-and-white-chequered tiled steps, similar to the pattern on Melody Smith's front path. "Let's go. Darling."

They climbed the steps together, exchanged a glance, then nodded and put on worried faces, foreheads crinkled, eyes a little wider than normal. They held hands as Gabriel rang the doorbell.

Ten seconds passed and Gabriel was just wondering whether they could get away with a swift breaking and entering when the door opened. A young woman stood there: pale skin, long, straggly blonde hair, dark roots showing, a red-cheeked baby on her hip. It appeared to have recently puked onto her T-shirt, leaving dark blue patches on the otherwise pale fabric. She stood there, mute, regarding Gabriel and Britta with narrowed, suspicious eyes.

"I'm so sorry to trouble you," Gabriel began, "but our car has broken down and I'm afraid neither my girlfriend nor I has a mobile. Do you think it would be possible to use your telephone?"

The woman shifted the baby's weight on her hip then answered.

"You must speak slower. I am from Latvia and my English is not good yet."

Gabriel smiled and tried again.

"Our car is broken down. We have no mobile. Please may we come in to use the telephone?"

She nodded. "I ask lady of house. You wait here."

She turned and disappeared down a long tiled hallway and through a door at the far end.

"Still happy with the plan?" Britta asked.

"Sure, why not? Look, she's coming back."

The nanny, or au pair, or whatever the rich of Kensington called their domestics, returned, now minus the baby.

"Mrs Evans say one quick call, please. Come this way."

She led them down the hall and into what looked like a sitting room that had metamorphosed into a playroom. The floor between matching brown leather sofas was covered with brightly-coloured toys. Pointing at a phone mounted on the wall, she said, "Is there."

"One more thing," Gabriel said. As the woman turned back to him, he started speaking in an oddly disjointed rhythm, keeping his sentences simple, throwing in the odd Russian phrase, and matching his off-key delivery with a series of eye and hand movements. The young woman's bruised-looking eyelids flickered once, then twice. Maintaining his eye contact, he swayed sideways, then back the other way, like a snake mesmerising its prey. Judging his moment to coincide with her long out-breath, he reached out and tapped her sharply on the forehead. "Sleep!" he said in a low murmur. The woman gave a slight gasp, and Gabriel caught her as her knees buckled. He laid her on her front on the floor, among the squashy play mats and assorted fluffy zoo animals.

"Come on," he said. "She must have put the baby in its cot. Let's find the lady of the house."

Britta led the way down the hall to the door they'd seen the au pair go into. She knocked twice and then poked her head round the door before going fully into the room. Gabriel followed.

Sitting at the table swiping and tapping on a tablet screen was the lady of the house. Her streaky blonde hair was tied back into a ponytail with a black velvet ribbon; her smooth, unblemished skin had just enough colour to say 'winter sun' and not so much you'd conclude, 'tanning salon'. Her clothes looked very expensive. Fuchsia-pink cashmere jumper over tan leather trousers. She looked up at Britta and frowned, compressing her lips into a thin red line.

"I thought Villi showed you the phone in the front room," she said.

"I am so sorry," Britta said, laying on her Swedish accent thicker than snow in Stockholm. "She did and we are very grateful but my boyfriend wanted to ask you something. Could you listen carefully please?"

The woman looked up at Gabriel. "Well?" she said. "I'm listening."

12
Breaking and Entering

HAVING draped the lady of the house on a small sofa along one wall of the immense, extended kitchen, Gabriel and Britta left through the double doors into the garden. It was a good fifty feet from the back of the house to the fence. They ran down the path and were up and over the high wooden fence in a few seconds. Dropping down onto the far side they found themselves in thick cover provided by a thick clump of evergreen shrubs.

"Here," Britta said, reaching into the rucksack. "Take this."

She handed Gabriel one of the silenced pistols. He nodded, then racked the slide to load a round into the chamber. Britta did the same.

Peering through the branches, Gabriel could see the back wall of the trafficker's house. Unlike the front, it was scarcely protected at all. No security lights that he could see, no bars over the window or French doors, no dogs – they'd have come running by now, he thought, sheathing the tactical knife he'd taken from Britta's rucksack. Best of all, no guards. All the lights were off and although that didn't necessarily mean the house was empty – they'd seen the guards at the front after all – it suggested that things might be quiet. At least, the possibility of an international people-smuggling gang holding a meeting in the kitchen had receded.

"What do you think?" he said.

"We could plant a bug on the glass," Britta said. "But it looks nice and quiet. I'm thinking we go in, plant it under a table or shelf then leave this way. How long till sleeping beauty and her servant girl wake up?"

"Ten minutes, maybe a few more. Let's go in."

Keeping low and tracking along the hedge on the eastern side of the garden, they made their way up to the back wall of the house. Britta crawled along the wall and reached up to try the handle of the French doors.

"Locked," she mouthed. Then she retrieved a set of lock-picks from a pocket and went to work. Gabriel steadied his breathing and kept watch while Britta wiggled and twisted the two slim, hooked pieces of metal in the lock. Fifteen seconds later, she twisted the handle. This time it opened.

Inside the kitchen, they straightened and took a few moments to listen at the door on the far side. Facing each other, ears pressed against the softly shining wood, they nodded.

"Come on," Gabriel said.

Britta pulled the bug from her rucksack. It was a sliver of black plastic no bigger than the top joint of her thumb. She peeled a strip of backing paper from one side and bent to stick the bug under the tabletop.

"That's it. It activates automatically now it's been stuck down. Let's go."

As they moved towards the French doors and their escape route down the garden, the door to the kitchen opened and two men, the guards from the front of the house, strode into the kitchen, laughing loudly. Seeing two intruders, they froze for a split second, eyes widening, lips pulling back in snarls.

It was a poor time for inaction.

While they were processing the information that their boss's fortress had been breached, Gabriel and Britta were levelling their pistols.

By the time the guards realised what was happening and reached for their own concealed weapons, Gabriel and Britta were shooting.

The four muffled thuds from the muzzles didn't even make the windows rattle. At that range, the two Special Forces veterans could have dropped their men blindfolded. The double-taps to the head were fast, and thanks to the destructive power of the hollow-point Parabellum rounds, guaranteed kill-shots. They did have one major disadvantage, however.

The walls and ceiling of the kitchen were covered in runs and sprays of blood and brain matter. Bone fragments had flown out from the exit wounds and stuck to the walls or skittered under furniture.

"OK. That was unexpected," Britta said.

"Which may go down as understatement of the year. What now? The bug just became moot, don't you think? I doubt your man's going to be conducting any business here when he sees all this."

"I need to arrange a cleanup team. But now we're here, let's have a poke around."

Gabriel nodded, thinking about how he could secure Britta's services even quicker.

They left the kitchen, stepping over the corpses of the guards. At the foot of the stairs, Britta put her finger to her lips and jerked her chin upwards. Music was drifting from a room on the first-floor landing. It sounded Middle Eastern somehow – keening voices, jangling stringed instruments, and hand drums.

Drawing her pistol again, Britta climbed the stairs, keeping her feet wide and only stepping onto the edges of each tread, where the wood was less likely to creak. Gabriel followed, Beretta aimed above Britta's left shoulder into the space beyond. Once they gained the landing, Britta signalled with a finger for Gabriel to take a position to the right of the door. He stood, back to the wall, pistol in a two-handed grip level with his face, muzzle pointed to the ceiling. Britta closed her left hand on the door knob, then readjusted her grip, one finger at a time, curling them around the faceted glass ball.

They made eye contact and Gabriel nodded.

Twist, push, step through fast at a crouch, weapon out in front.

Standard room entry protocol.

Back-up man follows, levels weapon over first operative's right shoulder.

Occupants faced with two weapons, no target at expected height – operatives both have clean field of fire.

Sitting at a vast dark wood desk was a man. Gabriel took him in with a glance. Immensely fat. Swarthy. Bald but for a topknot tied with a red cord. His sausage-like fingers were flattened over stacks of fifty-pound notes.

As Britta and Gabriel entered the room, his eyes widened until the brown irises were afloat in a sea of white. In the space under the desk they could see a woman's rear end, covered, just, in a denim mini-skirt. The man pushed back from the desk and yelled out.

"Hafiz! Rafi! Help!"

The woman reversed out from under the desk. Her dull eyes were wet with tears, and when she turned and saw two armed intruders, her hand flew to her mouth, further smearing her red lipstick.

Britta pointed behind her at the open door.

"Out!" she said. "Wait for us there." Then she turned back to the fat man who was scrabbling to do up his trousers. She levelled her pistol at him. "Well, well, Omar El-Hashem. Now I have a problem."

"Yes," he said, his voice shaking. "You are fucking dead, that's your problem. When my men get up here they will kill you and then we'll put your bodies in the Thames."

Gabriel decided to let Britta do the talking. It was her case after all.

"Is that who you were calling? What did you call them? Mickey and Minnie, was it? I've got some bad news for you, *kuksugare*. They're dead. Me and my partner just sent them on their way. And I'm guessing where they're going there won't be any virgins waiting with glasses of nectar for them to drink."

The man's eyes flicked past Britta to the open door. Then back at her. Then Gabriel.

"Who are you people? You, man. Tell me, what do you want? Are you from Dmitri? We had an agreement. Girls are my business here. I control the trade and pay him a management fee. He knows this."

"Dmitri?" Gabriel asked. "I know of no Dmitri."

"Dmitri Gavas. Of course you know him. Everybody in the trade knows him. He works out of his antiques shipping firm in Chelsea."

Britta walked closer to the desk. She sat on a corner so she could look down at El-Hashem.

"Like I said, we have a problem. And the problem is, we're the good guys. Only now we're in a tricky situation. You see, there are two dead bodies downstairs. The girl's seen us. And how can I arrest you when we've slightly fucked around with due process?"

El-Hashem leaned forward, then back again as Britta's weapon came up. He pointed at bundles of banknotes in front of him. A sly smile crept over his features. He took both of them in with a look that made what he said next unnecessary, so much did it reek of corruption.

"There is much money there. If you are good guys, your government salaries are peanuts compared to what is there. To what I can pay you. Regularly."

Britta stuck her bottom lip out.

"Oh dear, now you made me even more sad. You tried to bribe us. When we are loyal servants of the Crown."

El-Hashem's hand, the one not pointing at the money, had disappeared under the desk. Gabriel had noticed but he wasn't sure Britta had. He tensed. The next few seconds seemed to stretch out for ever.

"Then fuck you!" El-Hashem shouted.

He flung two handfuls of banknotes up into Britta's face.

Britta reared back and stretched her gun arm out in front of her.

El-Hashem's hidden hand emerged from beneath the desk clutching a tiny black pistol.

He fired.

13

Briefing Britta

EL-HASHEM'S shot went wide.

Gabriel's didn't.

He put a single round into the centre of El-Hashem's forehead,

Britta fired three shots that hit the man in the head and neck. The first two blew away most of the flesh from the lower half of his face but the third tore into his carotid artery. As his head snapped backwards over the top of his chair, jets of bright scarlet arterial blood squirted over Britta before streaking long spatters of red across the ceiling and the side wall of the office.

The smoky smell of cordite and the iron tang of blood were thick in the air. The woman was screaming from just beyond the open doorway: she'd been watching.

Gabriel ran to her, shoving his pistol into the back of his waistband.

She'd sunk to her knees and he knelt in front of her and cradled her head in his palms, getting her to look at him.

"It's OK," he said. "He's dead. He can't hurt you any more. Don't be frightened. We'll get help for you."

"I am not frightened," she snapped back. "He was a pig. There are five of us here. In this house. Come. I show you."

"Gabriel," Britta said, wiping blood off her face with her sleeve. "The women. In the other house. They're going to wake up before we get back."

"Let them. You'll have to get some people round there to sort them out. 'No need for police, Madam' that sort of thing."

"I'll call it in. Though this fucking mess is going to get me suspended."

Gabriel said nothing. He turned to the girl.

"Show me," he said.

She walked in front of him, twitching at the hem of the skirt to pull it a little lower. She took him up a further set of stairs then along a narrow landing. At the end, she turned a key in the door and opened it, then stood aside.

Gabriel motioned that she should go in first.

"They don't need to see another strange man come in unannounced," he said.

She went in first and he followed. Inside the room, sitting huddled together on one of the two narrow single beds that dominated the tiny space, were four young women. They were aged, Gabriel estimated, between eighteen and twenty-five. They were all similar in looks: long blonde hair, pale-blue eyes, skinny. They looked scared, with taut facial muscles and trembling lips. They wore no make-up, and all four had dark circles under their eyes. But there was something else about their faces. A heaviness around the eyes and an unfocused gaze, maybe even a looseness to the muscles around the mouths.

The woman beside him spoke to them in an Eastern European language Gabriel didn't recognise. He spoke Russian. This sounded, to his linguist's ears, more like Bulgarian. As she spoke, he watched the other women's expressions, hoping to see them lose their wariness. Little by little, they did. The shoulders descended to a more normal position, the hands unclenched, though they still held onto each other, and their faces relaxed, which only made the slackness around the eyes and mouths more pronounced.

She looked at him. "I tell them, Omar and his guards are dead. You and woman are police, yes? We are safe now."

He nodded. "Yes, you are safe. But we're not police. Not exactly. We will call them for you now, though. Come on, we need to get you and your friends out of here."

The young woman uttered a couple of short sentences and the four women on the bed stood as one and followed her and Gabriel out of the room, down the stairs and back to where Britta was waiting for them.

"Jesus!" she said. "Is that all of them?"

"Yes," the woman who'd become their unofficial interpreter said. "There is a new batch of girls coming the day after tomorrow. Omar was talking on the phone about them just before you came in."

"Well, we'll be waiting for them when they do. Now, we need to go."

Between them, Britta and Gabriel decided that subterfuge was no longer necessary, so after Britta had cleaned the rest of the blood off her face, they left by the front door and gathered, like office workers during a fire drill, on the paved parking area behind the gates.

A few minutes later, they heard sirens. Then a screech of tyres directly outside the gate. Gabriel hit the button in the steel control panel to open the gates and, as they swung back, a marked police car nosed between them and came to a stop just in front of the small group. Behind it they could see two unmarked cars: Audi saloons in gunmetal and black with blue lights flashing a staccato rhythm from inside the radiator grilles.

A lean, fortyish man wearing a scowl and a plain grey, two-piece suit stepped out from the passenger side of the marked car and strode over to them, warrant card out in front. He was a detective chief inspector.

Britta showed him her ID card. He looked at Gabriel. Gabriel stared back. Hard. Then one of the women rushed forward and grabbed the detective's hands.

"Please," she said. "You help us now. Please. God sent them to save us from Omar."

"It's a bit of a mess in there," Britta said. "My boss is sending a clean-up team. The girls are all yours. We need to go."

"You do the glamorous bit then leave the Met to tie up the loose ends and do the paperwork, eh?"

"Well, we did break the trafficking ring without you, so yes, maybe you should do the admin on this one."

Gabriel noticed the way Britta had thickened up her Swedish accent as she spoke to the hard-faced DCI in front of her. It was a good trick. It made her seem more of an outsider, notwithstanding her MI5 status.

"Whatever," the detective said. "I assume we'll get the intel we need from you lot?"

Britta shrugged. "Above my pay grade. But one of the girls back there said they're bringing some more in a couple of days."

By this time, the DCI had been joined by three uniformed officers including a sergeant, and a female detective, who was now talking to the women in their own language.

"Come on," Gabriel said. "Time to go."

They left through the gates, not looking back.

"I told my boss about the civilians in the other house," Britta said. "He's got a team heading over there right now and they've informed the police too, so there shouldn't be any fallout for us. Or not about that part of the operation, anyway." She smiled, wrinkling her nose. "But he wants to see me straight away. Can we meet later on?"

*

"How did it go with your Boss?" Gabriel asked. He and Britta were lying side by side under a sheet in his hotel bed.

"Not so good, actually."

"Because?"

"Because, apparently, hypnotising innocent householders and then breaking in to a suspect's house without a warrant and then shooting three people dead while accompanied by a non-authorised security operative is, quote unquote, 'against departmental protocols'."

Gabriel propped himself up on an elbow and looked into her eyes. "What about probable cause? You had the intel that he was trafficking women. We heard a scream, felt we had no option but to go in to prevent violence."

"I know, I know. I said all that."

"And?"

"They're implementing damage control. Which includes putting me on administrative leave for two weeks."

Gabriel smiled down at her. "Poor you. A fortnight off and nothing to do."

She pouted. "It's not funny. What am I supposed to do? Visit fucking art galleries?"

"How about an all-expenses-paid trip somewhere hot with yours truly?"

Britta sat up and grinned, showing the little gap between her front teeth.

"That sounds like fun. Equipment?"

Gabriel looked at the gold-plated bullet between her breasts, suspended there on a thin gold chain. How it moved slightly with each beat of her heart.

"It's all covered. Two of everything. More toys than we'll need, but . . ."

"Better safe than sorry, I know. So when do we leave?"

"I was thinking first thing tomorrow. Don's lined up an RAF flight."

Her eyes widened. "Well, Mr Urgent, you don't like to keep a girl waiting do you?" She pushed Gabriel back down onto the bed so he was facing her and straddled him. "Maybe we better have one last mission briefing before we leave, then."

14
Mozambique

"WELCOME to Beira," the pilot's voice crackled over the intercom as the Lockheed Martin C-130J Super Hercules touched down on the tarmac. As they were passengers on an unofficial military flight, cleared through African Union-NATO backchannels, Gabriel and Britta simply walked off the plane, collected their gear and headed for the distant taxi rank.

The front of the terminal building was covered in huge posters advertising credit cards, obscured at one end by a vigorous palm tree. Seven-foot-tall red capital letters mounted above the roofline declared, "AEROPORTO INTERNACIONAL DA BEIRA".

Gabriel spoke reasonably good Portuguese so he was hoping language, at least, wouldn't be a problem in the days ahead. Although the sun was burning the tops of their heads, there was a cooling breeze blowing across the apron of tarmac, and the humidity was surprisingly low.

As the two figures made their way to the line of lemon and lime Toyotas and Mazdas in the taxi rank, anyone wondering about their business would have furrowed their brow. Clearly not tourists, despite the sunglasses and relaxed body language and smiles as they chatted. But not business types either: no suits, no briefcases. Engineers? From an oil company or construction firm? Possibly. The boots looked serious and those bags looked bulky. Full of tools maybe? No. They both looked lean and fit. And the woman would be an unlikely engineer out here. However many of her sex were building bridges and designing oil refineries elsewhere in the world.

If the observer were worldlier, and had travelled around the less glamorous parts of Africa, they might have wondered, mercenaries? Private security? Bodyguards? Close. But no cigar.

"Yes, boss?" the smiling taxi driver at the head of the queue said, in English. His wide smile looked genuine as Gabriel and Britta arrived at his car, a late-model Toyota Camry, sun glinting off its gleaming paintwork. "Where to?"

"We need a hotel. Not too flashy. Clean. You can do that?"

Once they had registered at the Hotel Freedom's front desk, refusing the offer of help with their bags, they made their way up to the room the clerk had allocated them – on the top floor. Gabriel's phone buzzed as they were unpacking.

"It's an email from Don," he said. "We've got a meeting with our local contact. He's a 'cultural attaché'," Gabriel air-quoted round this phrase, "which basically means CIA. We're to meet him at a bar called Sonny's, on the beach. Guy's wearing 'a revolting Hawaiian shirt', Don's words. He's sent the code phrases too. And the GPS reference for our original extract point."

Thirty minutes later, they were walking along the beach, heading for a rush-roofed cabana with a green-painted sheet metal sign on the front with 'Sonny's' hand-lettered in red gloss.

Sitting at the bar, drinking from a tall glass of pale lager, was a balding, overweight man wearing khaki shorts and scuffed beige deck shoes. His top half was covered by a baggy Hawaiian shirt patterned with flamingos flying against a turquoise and black background of palm leaves.

"What do you reckon?" Gabriel asked as they approached. "Think he's our man?"

"I hope so. There can't be two shirts that bad in Mozambique."

As they arrived and ordered a couple of beers from the barman, Gabriel turned and nodded to the man.

"Nice evening."

"Sure is," he replied in a drawl from somewhere in the southern states of the US. "Especially if you got a nice cold beer to go with it."

Gabriel took a pull on his glass of Impala. "Not bad," he said, wiping the foam from his top lip. "Brewing standards are rising in Mozambique."

The man nodded. "Especially in lagers." He held out his hand. "Darryl Burroughs."

"Gabriel Wolfe." He turned to Britta, who stepped forward, her own hand extended.

"Britta Falskog," she said, with a smile.

"Let's get a table where we can talk," Darryl said, indicating a pale blue moulded plastic table at the edge of the decking in front of the bar.

"You two working for Don Webster?" Darryl asked, once they'd sat down.

"Yes. I served under him in the SAS and now I'm freelancing for him."

"How about you, honey? You part of Don's little hit squad?"

Britta put her glass down on the table and leaned towards Darryl. "I need to tell you something, Darryl. Actually two things. First of all, no. I am with MI5. I'm here in a private capacity. Second, don't call me honey, please. This is the twenty-first century."

Darryl reared back, a wide smile on his face. "Guess we got us a genuine feminist agent, Gabriel." He held his hands out in mock surrender. "So, do you want to tell this dumb old Southern boy what he should call you?"

"You can call me Britta, or Agent Falskog. I am happy with either."

"I guess I'll call you Britta, then," Darryl said. "Agent Falskog sounds kind of formal."

"Fine. Now, maybe we can talk business."

Darryl sat forward in his chair and drained his glass.

"I've lined you up with a four-by-four. Land Rover. Extra cans of gas, roof rack, satnav, but no air con, sorry. Plus a week's rations including water. You got purification tablets?"

Gabriel nodded. "Full survival kit."

"Good, you may need them. Now, the nearest burg to your destination is a little place called Muanza. I'd suggest heading for there and establishing your forward base, then travelling into the bush on foot. We've arranged back-up with the Zambian army – strictly speaking they're supposed to keep to their side of the border, but it's the boonies where you're going: no Mozambican police or military surveillance. Your Zambian contact is a nice guy called Major Anthony Chilundika. Sounds like a typical hoity-toity Brit. Built like a linebacker."

He slid a piece of card across the table towards Britta.

"Perfect," she said.

"You guys have all you need in the way of firepower? I have some bits and pieces at the Embassy in Maputo – that's my base – but we can get anything you need through unofficial channels."

Gabriel smiled as he thought of the assault rifles, semi-automatic pistols, sub-machine guns, explosives and the DU rounds padlocked into their bags back at the hotel. "We're covered."

"Well, if you guys decide you're under-resourced in that department, just let Ol' Darryl know." He slid his card across the table to Gabriel. "I have a wide range of very interesting friends here in Mozambique."

"We will, I promise."

Darryl looked at them both in turn. "You going to recover one of your boys? That's what Don told me."

Gabriel took a swig of his beer. Wiped the foam from his top lip. "That's the plan. Just not sure what there'll be left for us to find. It was over four years ago."

Darryl leaned back in his plastic lawn chair. His belly stretched the lurid fabric of his shirt tight. "Takes a lot of character to go back for one of your own. Before I had this job, I was working with the Defense POW/MIA Accounting Agency, spending millions of dollars and probably as many hours searching for and recovering the remains of American soldiers lost in battle. Still 82,000 service members unaccounted for." He paused to swat away a fly that had landed on the rim of his beer glass. "I was mostly on Vietnam MIAs, but we were still tracking down men from World War Two and Korea, plus Iraq and Afghanistan. Sometimes we'd get lucky and find a grave. More often than not, we'd be happy with a couple of finger bones. A set of dog tags was enough to close a file, though. Stay optimistic, OK?"

The following morning, Gabriel and Britta loaded the Land Rover and were out on the main road leaving Beira at 0620. After a few miles heading northwest, Gabriel turned off the road and began driving west, towards the border with Zimbabwe. Britta turned in her seat.

"What are you doing?" Britta pointed back at the concrete motorway they'd just left. "Muanza's that way."

"We're not going to Muanza. Not straight away."

"What? Why?"

Gabriel ran his fingers through his hair.

"Because we – I – have another job to do first."

"What do you mean another job? I thought we were here to find Smudge?"

Gabriel braked and pulled to the side of the red earth road. He turned off the ignition.

"When Barbara Sutherland approved this trip, she told me I had to earn her permission, more or less."

"Earn it how, Gabriel? Why are you talking in riddles?"

"There's a corrupt politician in Zimbabwe. The man's name is Philip Agambe. He's Minister of Finance. According to Barbara, he's funneling cash to an Islamic terror group that's been hitting our troops. They killed some British nurses, too. She wants him put out of action."

Britta wiped the sweat from her forehead.

"Jesus! What happened to due process? She's got you assassinating a legitimately elected foreign politician, now?"

"It's not that simple. You're making it black and white when you know what we do is shades of grey."

"Maybe what you do is. But in Sweden, we follow rules. We're democrats. Even now, in MI5, we're acting against terrorists, not government ministers."

"Is this the Sweden where you were conducting eugenics experiments into the seventies? Sterilising people with learning difficulties, to purify the Swedish bloodline?"

Gabriel knew he'd gone too far as soon as he said it. Blood flared in Britta's cheeks and she glared at him.

"Don't use Swedish history to distract me from the facts, Wolfe. Yes, we did some bad things. Like every country. But I'm talking about right now and right here. Are you seriously telling me you're going to cross the border into Zimbabwe and kill an elected politician on orders from Barbara Sutherland?"

Gabriel saw Smudge's ruined face, smashed by a round from a Kalashnikov. Smudge's broken body, crucified on a tree with machetes through both palms. Heard the *thwock-thwock* from the helicopter's rotor blades, drowning out thought as it took Gabriel and the two surviving members of his patrol to safety.

Gabriel nodded. "That's the price for recovering Smudge and I'm paying it. I'm not asking you to help. We'll find a cheap hotel and you can stay there or do some sightseeing. I don't care."

He twisted the key in the ignition and floored the throttle. Gritty, red dust spurted from under the Land Rover's tyres as it lurched back onto the road and continued heading towards the border.

*

Nine hours later, they arrived on the outskirts of Harare. Hard-packed, red-earth side roads led away from the concrete main street. The houses were small and neat, built mainly from red brick and occasionally rendered with white or yellow plaster. The remainder of the journey to the Zimbabwean capital had passed mostly in silence, even when a shimmering pink flock of flamingos buzzed them as they drove past a lake, and a joke about Darryl's shirt might have lightened the mood.

As they drove onwards looking for a hotel, the sun dropped below the horizon, leaving deep orange fingers streaking across the sky. In the light from the street lamps the red earth of the hard-packed pavements looked a dark purple. Away to the east, an electrical storm was turning the sky pink with lightning, and distant booms of thunder rolled across the plain towards the city. They found a hotel opposite a small park, checked in and made their way up to the room. It was small, perfectly square, clean, and functional. A modernist print on the wall above the bed showed a big cat of some kind chasing down an antelope.

Britta checked out the bathroom. "It'll do," she said, with a sniff, then went to open the window. Happy-sounding guitar music, to a fast, off-beat rhythm, drifted up from a club somewhere, accompanied by a smell they'd noticed everywhere they drove in Harare: grilling meat.

Sitting on the bed, her hands dangling between her knees, Britta spoke for the first time since their argument on the road.

"Do you have a plan, then?"

Gabriel stopped unpacking the weapons, laying one of the Glocks on the desk, and went to sit next to her.

"Mugging gone wrong. I'm going to follow him home from the Parliament building and take him on the street. Make it look like a local job. The Government here isn't too keen on the British so it can't have even a whiff of foreign involvement. I'm thinking I stage the scene so the local police can make all the right deductions."

"You can't use any of this, then," she said, sweeping her arm around in a semicircle that took in the wall, where the SA80s were leaning, and the desk, where the Glock and some of the ammunition lay. "So how are you going to manage it?"

Gabriel rose from the bed and went over to his kitbag. He reached inside and withdrew a slim brass and steel rectangle about five inches long, holding it out in front of him where Britta could see it. Letting one side of it free from his grip, he flicked the butterfly knife's handle out with a deft twirling movement, then spun it in a circle before catching it in his palm and snapping it shut to clamp the blade in place.

"Shit! Where the fuck did you learn to do that? Those things are banned everywhere." Britta grinned, threw her head back and let rip, filling the dingy room with her laughter. "Oh my God. You're here to take out a Government minister and I'm worrying about the legality of your knife. Fucking hell, Falskog, you need to get a grip."

Gabriel smiled too, but there was a tautness in it that he could feel from the inside.

"I'm not proud of this, Britta. Even if he is a bad one. He's married and has a child. She's sixteen, according to his dossier. But he's financing terrorism and the murder of British civilians, let alone soldiers. I'm under orders, so it's going to happen and then we can go and find Smudge. Don't forget that's why we're here at all."

15

A Driving Job

Leaving Britta in the hotel, Gabriel walked into the centre of Harare down an arrow-straight, six-lane boulevard. It was a Monday, and in a couple of hours, Parliament would be in session. The buildings around him were mostly one- or two-storey, modern concrete and red-brick constructions. Below his feet was more hard-packed red earth. In the distance, he could see the glass and steel towers of Harare's business district, through this was still low-rise compared to the City of London.

As he waited to cross the road among a group of men dressed for business in short-sleeved white shirts and ties, and carrying briefcases, a white Metro Bus roared past. It was full and Gabriel caught a glimpse of bright headscarves in green and yellow, purple and gold, and red and white.

According to intel supplied by Don via the satellite phone, Philip Agambe would be addressing a defence spending committee at 11.00 a.m. Then he'd exit the Parliament building at noon for a meeting with the director of the Zimbabwean National Bank.

By 10.00 a.m. he'd reached the Parliament building and was conducting a close target recce – a CTR – looking for the spot where ministerial cars waited for their passengers. It took three-quarters of a circuit of the building, a two-storey, cream-coloured modernist block, before he found it on the southeast corner of Nelson Mandela Avenue and Third Street. A covered car park was designated, "Government Cars Only" on a blue-and-white metal sign.

Gabriel sat with his back to the blank wall of a copy shop, "Closed for holiday", across the street and watched for half an hour as drivers came and went with their VIP cargoes. A huge pink-flowered shrub growing in a square of earth cut out of the pavement was drenching the air with its sweet, heady perfume. He sneezed a couple of times. Some of the drivers, with nothing to do and nobody to drive were playing cards at a rickety folding table in the shade. Others polished the big black Mercedes S-Class saloons. But which one was Philip Agambe's?

Out of the corner of his eye, Gabriel noticed a pair of teenaged boys loafing against a wall a couple of hundred feet down the block. He strolled down the street towards them. As he approached, they kicked off from the wall and turned to face him. They were lean and tall – taller than him. Both had hair cropped short with intricate designs razored in by the barber. One wore gold-framed glasses, and had a squint. The other had the high cheekbones and direct gaze of a model. They watched Gabriel come closer, narrowing their eyes, hands held loosely at their sides.

"Hey, boys," he said. "I need some help. A favour. A five-dollar favour."

"What do you want?" the squinting boy asked.

"I need to know which car over there is Philip Agambe's."

"The fuck's Philip Agambe?"

"Government minister. Very powerful man."

"Fuck them, man. They all on the take."

"Like I said, I need to know which car's his."

They looked at each other. Then cheekbones spoke.

"Sounds like a ten-dollar favour."

"Seven."

"Nine."

"Eight."

"Deal."

The boy spat on his hand and grinned, offering it to Gabriel, who spat on his own and seized the teenager's hand in a grip just powerful enough to encourage him to behave himself.

"Just go over there and say you have a message for Philip Agambe's driver. Tell him he's wanted round the front. Say a security guard sent you to fetch him."

The boy nodded, then jerked his head in the direction of the car park. "Come on, Slim."

As they wandered back up the street, Gabriel following forty feet behind them, hands in his pockets, looking around him as he walked.

In they went to the covered car park and stopped at the card table. Gabriel could see them pointing out of the car park, not at him, thankfully. One of the men gestured towards the interior. Philip Agambe's driver must have been one of the polishers. The boys ambled inside until the gloom swallowed them. Out came a man in the regulation black uniform and peaked cap and walked off towards the corner of the block.

The boys followed, jogging back towards Gabriel. They stopped as they drew level.

"Job done," Slim said, smiling.

"Where's the car?"

"Right in the back. By the Coke machine."

Gabriel handed over eight dollars, which disappeared into the boy's pocket. "Thanks."

They turned and ran off, laughing and high-fiving. No doubt congratulating themselves on having bilked some journalist out of enough US currency to start a small business.

Gabriel set off in pursuit of the driver, pulling on a pair of black leather gloves and a full-face, black silk mask with gauze patches over the eye holes. He jammed a long-peaked, beige baseball cap over the mask. Keeping to the shadows in the lee of the Parliament building, he caught up with his target, as planned, at the entrance to an alley that led into the interior of the block.

He tapped the man on the shoulder and, as he turned, produced the butterfly knife with a whickering flourish. Holding the point close to the terrified driver's face, he shoved him, not roughly, but with enough force to ensure compliance, into the mouth of the alley. The man's eyes were wide, and his deep brown skin had taken on a greyish cast.

FIRST CASUALTY

"What do you want?" he stuttered. "I have no money on me."

"Give me your car keys, boy, and I might decide to let you live," Gabriel said. The mask muffled his voice, which he deepened and let slide in a lazy Afrikaans drawl.

The man nodded, thrust his hand into his right-hand trouser pocket and pulled out the chunky black plastic fob emblazoned with a silver Mercedes logo.

Gabriel curled his fist around the key.

"Turn around," he said.

"Please don't kill me!" the man said, his voice quiet and trembling.

Gabriel punched hard into the space just below the notch at the back of the driver's skull. A neurosurgeon would call the spot the basal ganglion. Gabriel's unarmed combat instructors in the SAS called it the "off-switch". As his knuckles compressed the thick bundle of nerve fibres, the man dropped to his knees. He would be unconscious for a good hour or two. Long enough.

Gabriel removed the man's jacket and collected his peaked cap from where it had rolled under a garbage bin, swapping it for his own. He dragged him out of sight behind the bin and laid him in the recovery position. Before leaving, he tucked two twenty-dollar bills into the man's shirt pocket.

The chauffeur who emerged from the mouth of the alley kept the peak of his cap pulled well down over his forehead. The jacket looked too big for him, which it was, having been cut for a man at least four inches taller than Gabriel. It wouldn't matter once he was behind the wheel but it draped baggily across his shoulders as he walked back towards the parking garage. Nor did it match the navy blue chinos he was wearing.

Reaching the entrance to the garage, Gabriel sauntered in past the card players. They looked up and one called out to him.

"Hey! Where's Future?"

"I don't know, man. I'm just the relief driver," he said, maintaining the Afrikaans accent. "That his car over there?" Gabriel pointed at the Merc sitting by a vending machine.

"That's the one," the man said already losing interest and focusing on the cards in his hand once more.

After letting his eyes adjust to the gloom inside the parking garage, Gabriel walked over to the S-Class and blipped the fob. Settling himself behind the wheel, he checked his watch. He still had an hour to wait before he needed to be out front with the motor running. He set an alarm on his phone for five to twelve, then pulled the peak down on the cap and reclined the seat. It had begun to rain. Within seconds, the water on the street was an inch deep as the torrential downpour filled the drains and overflowed across the road. To the soothing background noise of the raindrops splattering off the hard concrete surfaces beyond the exit, Gabriel Wolfe closed his eyes.

*

. . . *the noise of the rain intensified, drumming on the roof of the Mercedes, making sleep impossible. But how? The Merc was under cover. Gabriel sat up in the driver's seat to find himself in a traffic jam on the main drag through the centre of Harare. All around him, car horns were honking, angry drivers were swearing through rolled-down windows, and traffic police screamed at them, flapping their white-gloved hands in a semaphore of despair. As he watched, the gloves began changing colour as fat, red raindrops hit them, splotching the pristine white cotton with scarlet flowers. The blood poured down from bloated clouds the colour of corpses: green, sickly yellow and black. Gabriel tried to get out, but the cars on each side were jammed up hard against the sides of the Merc and the door would only open a couple of inches.*

His eyes flicked up to the rearview mirror. What he saw there made him cry out in alarm, an incoherent, choking attempt to call for help. He looked in the door mirror, at a figure making his way slowly but surely along the column of stalled vehicles.

Staggering between the stationary taxis, trucks, cars and buses, dragging himself forward on their roofs or door handles, using the machetes embedded in his palms to gain purchase on the slippery steel and plastic panels, was Smudge.

"Boss!" he called out. "You're in the wrong place. Come and get me. Now!"

He shouted the last word and Gabriel watched as Smudge's teeth flew from his ruined mouth like bullets.

Gabriel looked up.

88

There was a sunroof.

He searched frantically on the centre console for the control. There! A simple white icon on a black button. He jabbed at it with his thumb and unclipped his seatbelt. All around him, the drivers of the surrounding vehicles had turned to watch him trying to escape. Their skull-like faces split open in grins of sharp, white teeth, and they laughed as he scrambled up towards the widening rectangle of sky above him.

Half-in, half-out of the car, Gabriel turned around to watch as his former Trooper dragged himself closer and closer. Smudge was only three cars back now, and his voice had taken on a pleading tone. A smell of burnt meat drifted on the wind.

"Boss. Please. Leave now. I need you."

He held out his hands, palms uppermost and Gabriel watched, horrified, as the blades of the machetes sank and slithered through the bloodied flesh and clanged to the ground, bouncing first off the blood-streaked metalwork of the two taxis that flanked Smudge.

"I can't!" Gabriel screamed. "I've got a job to do here first. It's orders, Smudge. From Barbarian Sutherland."

"Murderer!" Smudge shouted back at him as he climbed onto the boot of the Merc, pulling himself up with clawed fingers that left bloody marks across the gleaming black paintwork.

The rain ran freely down Gabriel's face and into the collar of his shirt. Smudge's face was a red mask, his lower jaw torn away and hanging by a sinew from the left side of his neck.

The two men came face to face, Smudge on his knees, Gabriel standing on the driver's seat.

Smudge reached down inside the car and pushed the button for the sunroof.

"No!" Gabriel screamed as the wickedly sharp edge of the sunroof moved against the flesh of his stomach, pushing him back against the edge of the aperture. Then it snapped shut.

As his torso began to topple sideways, Smudge leaned closer. "Don't do it, Boss," *he whispered, before imitating a mobile phone alarm.*

*

Gabriel jerked upright, emitting an involuntary gasp and clutching his abdomen, where the phantom pain from his severed body still lingered. He wiped a hand across his forehead and checked his phone: 11.55 a.m. He thumbed the starter button and cranked the air conditioning up to full power. While he waited for the car to cool, he adjusted the seat position.

Pulling the gear selector into drive, Gabriel nosed the sleek, black car out of the garage and onto the street, which was steaming as the sun evaporated the rain from the hot tarmac.

Waiting outside the front of the Parliament building, he tried to hold onto the nightmare. *What were you trying to tell me, Smudge?* No. Not Smudge. His psychiatrist, Fariyah Crace, had explained to him that if the hallucination was telling him anything at all, it was merely acting as a mouthpiece for his own subconscious. *OK, what am I trying to tell me, then? Is that better?*

16

Death in Harare

WHATEVER Gabriel might have learnt from his subconscious would have to wait. He had no sooner parked at the side of the road outside the gateway of the Parliament building than his man, Minister of Finance Philip Agambe, appeared from the security checkpoint and walked directly towards the car.

Gabriel exited the car and walked round the back to hold the door open, keeping his head bowed and the peak of his cap dragged well down over his eyes.

"Where is Future?" Agambe asked.

Gabriel was nonplussed for a moment? Was it a code word? A secret ritual between ministers and their drivers? Then he realised. Future was the driver.

"Not well, boss," he said, maintaining his South African accent. "I'm your relief driver. Where to, please?"

"National Bank. You know where that is, I take it?"

"Yes, boss."

"Good. I don't want to keep the director waiting."

Gabriel closed the door on Agambe with a soft *thunk*.

He checked the rearview mirror. Agambe had opened his briefcase and was scrutinising papers spread out on the lid. He hadn't fastened his seatbelt. One quick check in the door mirror and he pulled out into the sparse afternoon traffic. Where the offices of the Zimbabwean National Bank were

Gabriel neither knew nor cared. He was heading for an area of the capital that politicians spoke of mainly in terms of clean-up operations, especially before international conferences.

His pulse steady at sixty, Gabriel drove through the business district. Smart, wide streets intersected at right-angles, the glass-faced buildings bedecked with global bank logos as well as local African brands. After a few minutes he emerged on the other side, heading for what his tourist guidebook had called "Harare's combat zone". Home to brothels, drug dealers and bare-knuckle boxing matches where the winner was the man left on his feet at the end of the bout, it was the last place this Cambridge-educated finance minister would ever voluntarily visit.

"Hey! Driver?" Agambe called from the back seat. "Where in blazes do you think you are taking me? Are you mad? This is The Avenues. You want to get us both killed? Turn around now and get me to the National Bank."

"Sorry, boss. We're being followed. Two white men in a dark blue BMW. I think they're armed. I need to lose them."

"Shit! Get rid of them, then. I'm calling the police."

"No! Don't do that, boss. If they're after you and they hear sirens they'll close in and do us right now. Let me lose them first."

"Fine, but get on with it. I have many enemies, you know."

Gabriel accelerated sharply, throwing Agambe back into the padded leather seat, and hurled the Merc round a couple of corners, driving deeper into the combat zone and keeping his man unbalanced, physically as well as mentally. Finally, he found the spot he'd pictured in his mind. They drove down a narrow road bordered on one side by an area of scrubland separated from the street by chain-link fencing, and on the other by a row of cheap houses and blocks of flats, the shutters of which were all closed against the sun.

Picking up speed, Gabriel aimed for the fence and burst through into the hardscrabble land beyond. Agambe screamed, an incoherent burst of his own language. The loud click in the middle told Gabriel he was a Xhosa-speaker.

The insulation inside the cabin was so effective, there was barely a sound as the fencing tore away from the metal stanchions. He brought the car to a lurching stop a few hundred yards away from the roadside, taking advantage of the cover provided by a hump of grassy red earth.

As the car's momentum transferred to the loose items inside, Agambe was hurled forwards, smashing his face against the rear of the front headrest. "Fuck! What just happened?" he shouted, after he'd bounced back into his seat.

"The end of the road just happened, Minister," Gabriel said, in his own voice.

He left the car and yanked open the door before Agambe could think of locking it from the inside. Reaching down he grabbed the man by his suit jacket and hauled him out, throwing him onto his hands and knees in the dirt.

"Who are you? You're not a driver," Agambe said, swiping at his bleeding nose with his hand.

"You're wrong, Minister," Gabriel said. "I am *a* driver. I'm just not *your* driver. I commanded a mobility troop in my Army days. It was like something out of Mad Max. We used to tear across the desert in stripped-back Humvees like fucking great dune buggies. But now I've come to tell you your shitty little game is over."

He reached into the pocket of his chinos and pulled out the butterfly knife. Agambe watched, eyes wide, as the knife executed its circular dance in the air before coming to rest in Gabriel's right hand, blade locked into place and glinting in the sun.

"What little game?" Agambe asked. "What do you mean?"

"Funding terrorism. Killing British troops. Massacring nurses. How's that for starters?"

Agambe's eyes widened. "I don't know what you mean. I'm one of the few men in the Government trying to change things for the better." Then his mouth fell open and he covered it with a hand. "Wait," he said, letting his hand fall away again. "Who sent you?"

"It doesn't matter."

"You're working for Sutherland, aren't you? She sent you to kill me."

"It doesn't matter."

"It does, it does! She's trying to silence me."

Gabriel frowned. A member of the Shona tribe who spoke Xhosa under pressure? And now, something about the man's tone made him want to hear more.

"What do you mean, silence you? Since when did terrorists' bankers want to shout about their work?"

"Don't you see? That's what this is all about. I'm going to expose her. She's going down."

With these words, Agambe lunged forward and grabbed Gabriel by the lapels. He was so close Gabriel could smell the cardamom seeds he'd chewed to sweeten his breath.

"Do not trust that woman. If you kill me she will not want you around to tell the tale. She's in bed with Gordian. She'll have you killed too, my friend."

"I've never heard of Gordian. And she won't have me killed. I saved her life."

Gabriel thought of Smudge. And of who he trusted more, his own Prime Minister, the woman who'd allowed him out here to recover Smudge's remains, or this stranger, this corrupt stranger funneling money to men who beheaded journalists and put the footage on YouTube.

"No!" Agambe screamed. "You have to believe me!"

"Sorry," Gabriel said. "The trouble is, I don't."

It's harder to stab someone to death than many people – especially amateur knife-fighters – believe. A clumsy thrust to the heart more often than not simply hits a rib, which either deflects or breaks the blade. Gabriel Wolfe was far from an amateur. He drew back the butterfly knife and stabbed upwards from underneath Agambe's lowest rib. He thrust up and kept thrusting, so that the tip of the blade found, and punctured, the heart from below, having caused almost certainly fatal damage to the man's left lung. Agambe was lifted off his feet by the force of the blow before sagging to his knees as his ruptured heart stuttered and misfired before shutting down altogether. Gabriel caught him and let him fall to one side, careful to avoid the bright red oxygenated blood now surging from Agambe's ruptured heart.

Blood cleaned off the blade, Gabriel flipped it around and back into the protective embrace of its hinged handle. Now for the cover-up. Gabriel bent by the body and pulled the jacket open before relieving the dead man of his wallet and phone. He yanked the tie downwards and pulled open the shirt collar. Gold glinted at the man's neck: an old-fashioned watch-chain, complete with a gold half-sovereign mounted with the T-bar on two shorter lengths of chain. He ripped it free, leaving a gouge in the dead man's skin. It joined the wallet and phone in the pocket of Gabriel's borrowed chauffeur's jacket. Then he crouched and hoisted the body up and dragged it back onto the back seat.

Now for the car.

After retrieving a bottle of water from a cup-holder in the centre console, Gabriel thumbed the button that opened the petrol filler cover and unscrewed the black plastic cap. He ripped a length of fabric from Agambe's shirt, twisted it into a makeshift fuse and threaded it down into the filler tube leading to the petrol tank.

He waited for a few seconds, while capillary action sucked petrol along the fibres of the shirt fabric to the ragged end . . .

. . . flicked open the lid of the lighter he'd brought for the purpose . . .

. . . and lit the end of the white cotton.

It caught at once, though the bright sunlight rendered the flames all but invisible.

Gabriel retreated fifty yards at a run then sat on the ground to wait, using the bottled water to wash Agambe's blood off his right hand.

He didn't have to wait long.

With a *whoomp*, the petrol tank of the Mercedes exploded, showering burning fuel and shards of steel around the limousine. One by one, the expensive plastics, fabrics and foam seat pads ignited, adding their own individual smells to the blend of acrid black smoke and volatile chemicals released by the combustion.

Burning in a kaleidoscopic mix of lime green, tangerine and turquoise flames, the car sagged in a series of jerks as the tyres blew out with loud pops. The previously glossy black paintwork bubbled and cracked, giving off a sharp metallic tang as the expensive minerals mixed into the paint began to burn.

Gabriel got to his feet, smacked his palms against his thighs to dispel the dust and marched back to the road to search out a taxi to take him back to the hotel.

17

A Creeping Doubt

WHEN Gabriel arrived back in the room at 12.45 p.m., Britta was lying on the bed reading, stripped to a pair of pale-grey knickers and an olive-green vest. The electric stand fan was switched to maximum power and she'd positioned it at the end of the bed in an effort to keep cool. She sat up as Gabriel came through the door. He'd dumped the chauffeur's jacket and cap in a garbage bin behind a chicken restaurant while searching for a taxi. Not knowing why, he'd kept the gold chain.

"How did it go?" she asked, eyes searching his.

"Agambe's dead."

"You OK?"

"Yes, of course. Why wouldn't I be?"

She reached out to him with an outstretched hand, and pulled him down to sit next to her.

"Like I said. You just murdered an elected politician."

"On the orders of another."

"Yes, and I'm not sure whether that makes it better or worse."

"What it makes it, is over. That part, anyway. I need to call Don, then we should get going. I want to be out of Harare before the Right Dishonourable Philip Agambe's body is discovered."

"Any risk of prints or forensic evidence?"

"Shouldn't be. He'll be beyond recognition by now and so will any prints or physical evidence I left. Anyway, I'm not on any criminal databases and Don will have ensured my Army records and prints stay secure inside The Department's files."

Britta stood and pulled on her trousers and a shirt.

"Make the call then."

Gabriel frowned. "In a second."

"What is it?" she asked.

"It's probably nothing. But he asked me if Barbara Sutherland had sent me."

"What?" Britta sat down again.

"Almost straightaway. He said he was going to take her down."

"Probably meant with his friends in the terror cell."

Gabriel nodded. "You're right. Just a final bit of boasting."

But what was that about Gordian?

He hit the speed dial number for Don on the satellite phone. After a few seconds during which Gabriel looked at Britta and gave her a small, tight smile, Don answered.

"Hello, Old Sport. What news?"

"Agambe's dealt with. Now Britta and I need to get back to Mozambique."

"Good man. Call me when you're in place and we can sort out some on-the-ground support."

"I will, but Don?"

"What is it?"

"Something Agambe said to me. He asked if Barbara Sutherland sent me. Said he was going to expose her."

There was a momentary pause during which Gabriel could hear his boss breathing steadily.

"Grasping at straws, Old Sport. Knew you were going to deliver The Queen's Message and was trying to buy time."

"I suppose so. I mean, how could a rogue Zimbabwean Government minister expose our PM?"

"Exactly. Now, listen. I have to go. Meeting some high-up in the Ministry of Defence who goes by the unlikely name of Sir Bruce Babbage. I suspect mowing the lawn would be a more interesting hour. Call me from Mozambique, like we agreed."

"Of course."

The line went dead.

"Everything all right?" Britta asked as she laced up her combat boots.

"Good question. Is it? Something's off here and I don't know what it is."

*

They reached Muanza at 10.00 p.m., having taken turns driving. It was a poor-looking place, with white-painted circular huts roofed with thatch intermingled with modern concrete buildings. The red-earth road was home to goats, chickens and sleeping men clutching bottles in outflung hands, as well as the sparse traffic.

After checking into a cheap hotel, situated another grubby rung down the ladder of comfort and respectability, Gabriel and Britta laid out their kit on the sagging double bed.

"Are you sure we need all this?" Britta asked, hands on hips as she looked down at the array of high-tech weaponry and explosives in front of them.

"Better . . ."

". . . Safe than sorry. Yes, I get it. Your favourite catchphrase, right?"

He frowned. "I don't know, Britta, I mean there's no civil war, no militias. Or not as far as we know. This should be cleared at the highest level. We should be able to just go in using the GPS, sweep the area and find him. Then leave with the remains and get back to England on a military flight."

She closed with him and slung her hands round his waist. Looked up into his dark brown eyes with her ice-blue ones.

"For an analytical man that was a lot of 'shoulds' and 'don't knows'. What's bothering you?"

Gabriel reached round to the back of his head and scratched his scalp.

"That's the trouble. I don't know. It's just, Agambe seemed so sure of what he was saying. How could anyone be so quick to identify who was behind their assassination? Even if that person was bankrolling terrorists? And why was he speaking Xhosa if he was a Shona? Sutherland said her intel was so good. Surely they'd have got his identity right?"

She pulled him closer and stretched up to kiss him.

"I don't know. Come on, stop moping. Let's go out for a beer or two and something to eat."

They repacked the assault rifles, sub-machine guns, pistols and the rest of the materiel and shoved it all into the wardrobe. Then Gabriel reached in and pulled out the two Glocks. He handed one to Britta and tucked the other into the back of his waistband.

Britta looked at him and grinned.

"Better safe than sorry, *hej*?"

He grinned back. "Fast learner, aren't you?"

Gabriel had also brought a flexible bike lock in his luggage, and now he threaded the heavy-duty, braided steel cable through the doors of the wardrobe and spun the combination wheels to lock their armoury away.

On the street, it was already dark. Warm, too, and humid. From somewhere behind them came the sound of a party. Women's voices were singing in beautiful harmony, underlaid with the clink of bottles and raucous male laughter. Gabriel's mouth watered as the ever-present southern African smell of grilling meat reached his nostrils. Britta kicked out at a pair of chickens dithering in front of them. The birds scurried away with protesting clucks. Under low-wattage street lighting, they made their way to a brightly lit bar on the corner of their block. The sign above the door announced "Bar Pele" in vivid green and yellow neon. Making sure their windcheaters covered the butts of their pistols, Gabriel and Britta pushed through the flimsy wooden door to the bar and went inside.

The patrons were all black, but seemed untroubled at the arrival of this pale-skinned pair. Britta attracted more attention than Gabriel, and a couple of wolf-whistles carried above the sound of the band playing fast township jazz in a corner. But the atmosphere was friendly and after exchanging a few smiles with the men and women between them and the bar, they found a couple of stools, ordered two lagers and some fried chicken and plantain chips.

Above the bar, a flat-screen TV was tuned to a sports channel with the sound turned down. Sipping their beer while they waited for their meals, Gabriel and Britta stared up at the TV, half-heartedly watching the floodlit soccer match. At half time, the channel switched to a newsreader pulling a professionally stern face above her navy suit jacket and white blouse.

The marquee running along the foot of the screen announced, "Zimbabwe mourns reformist minister, Philip Agambe."

Gabriel clutched Britta's bicep and nodded. Then he signalled the barman.

"Please turn up the sound," he said.

They came in part-way through the news report.

". . . was discovered in the burnt-out shell of his Government car," the newsreader said. "We go now, live, to the scene, where Mr Agambe's wife, Marsha, is talking to Prudence Kwenda."

The picture changed. In the foreground, an attractive black woman, slim and immaculately dressed in a black linen dress, her cheeks streaked with tears, was being interviewed by a female reporter from the Mozambican channel.

"My husband was murdered by somebody hired by, or under the direct orders of, Barbara Sutherland, the British Prime Minister," she said. "He was about to expose Mrs Sutherland at the Fourth Southern African Development Conference."

"Expose her for what?" the reporter asked, before aiming the bulbous foam-covered mic back at Agambe's widow.

"For her involvement in illegal land and property deals in my country in the 1990s funded by further illegal transactions involving blood diamonds smuggled out of the Democratic Republic of Congo." She turned to face the camera, so that she appeared to Gabriel to be addressing him directly from the other side of the glass screen. "Listen to me, whoever you are. You killed a decent man. An honest man. A loving father and husband. But you did not kill his dream of ridding Zimbabwe of the corrupting influence of the British State. I will continue his work. I will speak at the conference in his place".

After this threat, the segment ended and within a few more seconds the TV station had returned to the soccer match.

Britta turned away from the TV to look at Gabriel.

He felt her gaze but couldn't meet it. Something was going badly wrong. Barbara Sutherland was the decent one, the honest one. *She* was a loving mother and wife, and above all a good politician. She wasn't corrupt. Couldn't be.

18

A Phone Call

VAIL, COLORADO

NINE thousand, four hundred and seventy miles away, pale-grey woodsmoke was curling from the chimney of a timber ski lodge in Vail, Colorado. Inside, Robert Hamilton sat, sipping champagne, in a white leather and walnut Charles Eames lounge chair, his feet propped up on the matching ottoman. The chair was the genuine article, as he liked to point out to visitors – a prototype, in fact. Signed on its underside by Charles and Ray Eames themselves and insured for two hundred and fifty thousand dollars. His patrician good looks – luxuriant blond hair swept back from a clear, high forehead, sharp, blue eyes, strong nose, cruel mouth – were set off by the expensive clothes he wore, from the duck-egg-blue cashmere sweater to the hand-stitched, suede Gucci moccasins.

The open-plan living area was vast, at least thirty feet long by twenty across. Tawny cow hides and sheepskin rugs carpeted the floor. A wall of floor-to-ceiling glass gave an uninterrupted view across the snow-covered hillside, punctuated by trembling birch trees. The rest of the furnishings were a mixture of antiques and modern classics. Black leather and chrome Barcelona chairs lined one wall, facing a squashy bottle-green Chesterfield sofa, its leather cracked with age. Classical music was playing from speakers recessed into the pine ceiling. And in one corner, standing on the floor, a tall Lalique glass vase held two dozen bird of paradise flowers, which Hamilton's wife had flown in from a nursery in Arizona every week the family was in residence. Their orange crests and blue-green bracts were one of the few spots of bright colour in the otherwise sombrely decorated room.

Hamilton was CEO of Gordian Security, Inc. His company had no need to publicise its activities, or even its existence. In fact, Hamilton and his colleagues preferred to keep their collective heads well below the parapet and had taken extensive precautions to ensure their organisation was invisible to search engines. Had they bothered with an advertising agency, or a public website, they would have bragged of their expertise in "international crisis management", "global security solutions" and "traditional and non-traditional defence resourcing". To those who might wish to do business with Gordian, the meaning of these anodyne phrases would be clear: mercenaries drawn from ex-military, Special Forces and law enforcement personnel; undercover agents, similarly recruited from the ranks of the CIA, Secret Service and the FBI; and weapons. Lots of weapons. Lots of sophisticated, expensive weapons. In crates. Unused. For sale to anybody with deep enough pockets.

Hamilton's phone rang and he transferred the cut glass flute of champagne to his left hand to answer it. He checked to see who might be calling. It was a business contact. A rather important business contact. He looked up at the fair-haired youth lounging against the marble mantelpiece.

"Christopher, would you give me a moment please?" he said, his cultured drawl redolent of several generations of Manhattan privilege.

"Of course, Dad. Game of snooker later?"

He nodded. "Why not?"

With the room to himself, he answered the phone.

"David, this is an unexpected pleasure," he said.

"Hello, Robert. How are you?" A man's voice. As upper-class as Hamilton's, but formed at a public school in England, as opposed to Connecticut.

"Busy. Though we're at the lodge in Vail just now. Zoë's on the slopes as we speak. I'm here for a little skiing, a little business. You know how it is."

"Yes, I do. Which is why I'm calling. Have you seen the news from Harare?"

"Naturally. One monitors the news from all the countries where one has interests."

"We can't have Marsha Agambe presenting that dossier to the SADC. It would be ruinous. For all of us."

"Yes," he drawled. "Certainly an awkward spot you've got yourself into."

"*We've* got ourselves into? Listen, Robert. We have our papers too, you know. A little insurance policy. If the shit hits the fan, you might need to sell that delightful little ski lodge to pay for your lawyers."

"What do you propose," Hamilton paused, "*we* do about the widow Agambe?"

"Do you really need me to spell it out for you?"

"In the circumstances, I think I would rather you did just that."

"Very well. Send a team in and deal with her."

"I think that can be arranged. One thing, though?"

"What?"

"Your operative. Oughtn't you to ensure his silence?" Hamilton looked down and picked a piece of lint from the crease of his trousers. "Wouldn't do to leave him at liberty. One hears terrible stories of black ops guys getting all moralistic from time to time. Buying a whistle and then puffing out their pink little cheeks for all they're worth."

"That's very true. Though without evidence, he couldn't do anything that would hurt our operation, even if he wanted to. I had planned to deal with him back here, but it might be better for him to meet with some sort of accident in Africa. Easier to shift the blame then. Can you have your people take care of him?"

"Of course. We have plenty of ways of finding out where's been and where he's travelling to. Send me his picture, then consider it done. As will be Mrs Agambe."

19

Company

THE following morning, with Britta at the wheel of the Land Rover, they drove out of Muanza. They were following the satnav to the GPS reference supplied by Don Webster. As they powered northwest, the sky ahead boiled with tremendous rainclouds, huge charcoal and purple thunderheads that looked like mountains floating above the horizon. The acacia trees gave way to palms as the terrain on each side of the red-earth road changed from dry scrubland to denser forest. A wind had sprung up, nothing savage, but enough to move the Land Rover about on the road from time to time, causing Britta to swear in Swedish and grip the wheel more tightly.

"*Jävla Helveta!* The steering's shot on this. Maybe the suspension bushes are worn too. It's like driving a thirty-year-old Volvo."

"It's just the road surface. Don wouldn't have lined up a duff vehicle."

"Fine. I guess the wind is coming over stronger now."

Britta was right. The palms to each side of the road were thrashing from side to side as gusts of wind flew towards them ahead of the oncoming rain. The sky had massed into a solid wall of towering storm clouds, lit on their upper surfaces by the bright African sun, but coal-black on their underside. The space between the clouds and the road ahead was streaked with grey, as if an artist had run her thumb from the graphite cloud edges to the ground.

The first spots of rain pattered against the almost vertical windscreen a few minutes later. Britta switched on the wipers and almost at once snorted with laughter.

"Those are the worst windscreen wipers I have ever seen. They're shit!"

The thin blades of rubber were no match for the rain, which had intensified to a steady beat on the glass. All they did was combine the water with the patina of red road dust to create a uniform film of plum-coloured mud across the glass.

"Pull over," Gabriel said. "I'll adjust them. Push them in a bit."

The temperature had dropped. Gabriel shivered as the rain thrashed down on his shoulders and ran down the inside of his shirt. He gripped the driver's side windscreen wiper and carefully bent the thin metal structure inwards to apply greater pressure against the glass.

"Try it now!" he shouted to Britta, and wagged his index finger from side to side for good measure.

She got the message. The newly modified wiper swept the red paste from the glass, helped by the raindrops hitting the screen like bullets. Gabriel was shivering now. His shirt and trousers were soaked with freezing rain as he jogged round the front of the Land Rover to bend the other windscreen wiper into its new improved configuration.

A blinding flash of blue-white lightning erupted from the storm clouds over his head. The air crackled as ozone molecules were cooked out of the air. The lightning made landfall in a stand of palms about two hundred yards to the east of their position. Almost immediately, the accompanying thunder battered their eardrums with a roaring explosion.

Gabriel had his fingers on the door handle when a distant movement back on the road made him stop and look up. Wiping his eyes, he squinted through the rain. In the distance, far enough behind the storm to be still throwing up a cloud of red dust, was a vehicle. Something was off about its silhouette. That far back it should have been tiny. It wasn't. It was wider than a normal car, but taller too. Not a truck either.

Gabriel climbed back in.

"We've got company."

Britta looked at him quickly but didn't waste time asking questions.

Instead, she grabbed a pair of binoculars from a cubby in the space between their seats and clambered into the back.

"Humvee," she said.

"That's what I thought."

"Who drives black Humvees?" Britta asked. "Not the local warlords. They'd have a Toyota pickup or a Land Cruiser."

"Not the Army. They have Landies like this one."

They exchanged a glance. It was a look borne of long experience, both separately and during their time running joint operations together in the late 1990s. A look that said, "Trouble".

"Private contractors," they said in unison.

Britta slammed the gear lever into first and took off, spraying rooster tails of red mud from all four wheels as the Land Rover squirmed and wriggled, before finding grip and lurching forward.

Even with Gabriel's modifications to the windscreen wipers, the rain was making the screen an almost solid curtain of water.

Britta slewed to a stop. She unbuckled herself and twisted in her seat to face Gabriel, who'd done the same.

"Strategic assessment?"

"We've been set up."

20
A Fashion for Killing

FLORENCE

THE celebrities in the front row of the haute couture show in Florence were absorbed in the bizarre geometric outfits being paraded in front of them. As each model stalked the length of the catwalk on stilt-like legs, the magazine editors, fashion designers, pop stars and A-list actors applauded, took photos on their phones and shared their opinions of the outfits with their social media followers. Alone amongst them, ignoring the beaded dresses, slashed silk and feathered waistcoats, a strikingly attractive woman paid close attention to the screen of her phone.

Her cheekbones were higher than those of the beautiful models hired by the designer for his triumphant collection. Her wide-set eyes were almond-shaped and a mid-brown colour with greenish tints echoed by the emeralds in her ears. Her forehead was broad, high and unlined, though from good genes rather than injections of botulinum toxin. It was framed by long, dark hair, as straight and fine as brushstrokes from a Japanese calligrapher. The tip of her nose was tilted up, giving her the air of a woman constantly scenting the breeze, like a cat. But it was her lips that dominated her face, full and of such a deep red as to look almost bruised. She was slim, but not skinny, possessing an athletic build her floor-length gold silk dress only partially concealed. The cutaway sleeves showed off streamlined deltoids, biceps and triceps that spoke of many hours in the gym lifting free weights.

The screen bore a short message:

Sasha. Please call me.

She stood, smiling at her neighbours, a famous soccer player and his jewellery designer wife, and made her way to the lobby of the hotel. There, she called the number displayed beside the text.

"Thank you for calling, Sasha."

"No need to thank me, Robert. What can I do for you?" she said, waving away a waiter who was approaching bearing a tray of champagne glasses and a hopeful smile.

"I have a somewhat urgent job that I need you for."

"I'm taking some time off. As I think you know. That last project took rather more of my time than I really wanted it to."

"I know, I know. And I'm sorry. I had hoped the additional compensation would restore Gordian to your good graces."

She smiled. Then beckoned to the waiter she'd just dismissed, mouthing, "changed my mind". Taking a sip from the flute of five-hundred-euros-a-bottle vintage Krug, she returned her mouth to the phone.

"As indeed it did, darling. So tell me, who is causing you so much trouble that you feel the need to interrupt my holiday?"

"Her name is Marsha Agambe. She's . . ."

"The widow of Philip Agambe, until recently Minister of Finance in Zimbabwe."

"You knew?"

"Oh, Robert, your *naïveté* is touching. In my profession it pays to stay abreast of developments in the corridors of power, wherever they run to and from."

"*Touché*, Sasha. Well then, Marsha Agambe is the target. Your usual fee, I assume? I have your bank details from last time."

"Yes, my usual fee." She looked down and smoothed the gold silk over her thigh. "Doubled."

"Doubled?"

"For interrupting my holiday."

There was a pause, during which Sasha Beck drained her glass and signalled to the waiter, who had been hovering nearby, for another.

"Of course. Three million dollars. What else do you need from me?"

"Well, a deadline might be nice."

"I'll leave the precise timings up to you, but she must be dead before the Southern African Development Conference. It's in three days' time."

"And she will be. Thank you, Robert, for your continuing faith in me."

"You always repay it. In fact, I wonder whether I might ask you for a small favour?"

"A favour? Robert, you know I am a businesswoman first and foremost. Favours aren't part of my regular inventory. But tell me anyway."

"Mrs Agambe may have been contacted by British mercenaries. I think they might be the ones who killed her husband. If you come across them, perhaps you would be good enough to let me know."

21

The Second Ambush

ABANDONING the Land Rover, which now represented a target rather than protection, Gabriel and Britta ran to the trees and crawled under a low tangle of vines and broad-leaved plants. Before leaving the car, Gabriel had collected one of the weapons packs from the loadspace. Now he flipped open the catches. Britta snorted then wrinkled her nose in disgust.

"What's this? You want to take on a Humvee with a couple of SIGs? You can't just shoot the tyres out. That's military armour coming for us."

Gabriel returned her look of doubt with a grim expression of his own.

"They're not standard P226s. They're modified. Chambered for high-power DU rounds. Get it right and we can take them out in one go. Vaporise whoever's inside that Humvee and turn it into a Roman candle. Watch it, though. They've got a hell of a kick."

Britta's eyes widened so that white showed all the way round the bright blue irises. She swept her eyes clear of a few strands of hair, which had turned from copper to a deep brown as the rain soaked it.

"Depleted Uranium? In a pistol. Are you nuts? It'll blow your fucking hand off!"

"It won't. I've tried them."

She shook her head, but picked up one of the pistols anyway.

"Heavy," she said.

"Strengthened barrel. But mainly the DU. Aim high, they drop more than regular rounds."

They crept into position, about thirty yards apart, bellies squashed down into the mud, and took up spots where they could see the Land Rover.

Gabriel gripped the SIG with both hands, cradling his right hand in the palm of his left. He locked his right elbow and braced his entire arm as best he could. Over to his right, he could see that Britta was doing the same.

Thirty seconds later, the Humvee roared up the road and pulled in, twenty feet behind the Land Rover. Two men, both white, heavily-muscled and dressed in black from head to toe, climbed out. Without shouting a warning, they levelled their pistols, squat black weapons Gabriel couldn't identify through the driving rain, and emptied their magazines into the back window of the Land Rover.

OK. Bad men. Definitely bad men. Permission to engage.

Gabriel laid the SIG on its side and pulled his Glock from his waistband. No point wasting tank-buster ammunition on soft targets. Sensing that Britta would be doing the same, he aimed at the man on the left and shot him centre-mass with three closely grouped rounds.

The men collapsed simultaneously, their blood spraying out into the rain and turning a translucent pink.

Now for the main event. Without waiting for any more men to get out of the Humvee, Gabriel switched back to the SIG.

He re-braced his arm, gripped the butt tightly, looked along the iron sights and squeezed the trigger.

The heavens chose that exact moment to unleash their biggest fusillade of thunder yet. But the roar from the DU round was audible above the boom. A deafening percussive noise was accompanied by a two-foot jet of flame as the tiny projectile flashed from the muzzle and began the short journey to the target.

Free of the barrel, the dart shed its three guiding yellow sabots, which flew away like wasps.

Three milliseconds later, having flown in a virtually flat trajectory, the sharp point made contact with the Humvee's armoured flank in the centre of the driver's door.

One millisecond later, a second DU round, fired by Britta, penetrated the rear passenger compartment.

Propelled by the uprated loads of smokeless powder in their strengthened brass cartridges, the two DU darts bored through the Humvee's steel armour as if it were made of cheese. Compressed by their own force of impact, they emerged into the cabin of the Humvee from their perfectly circular cross-section entry tunnels one millimetre shorter.

Their dissipating kinetic energy caused massive compression waves and generated enough heat to increase the internal temperature of the Humvee to a thousand degrees Celsius. The waves killed the occupants instantly. The heat reduced their flesh and bones to their constituent atoms before the darts left the Humvee via perfectly circular, 9 mm diameter tunnels drilled through the hardened steel.

The grey mist that until recently had been human beings was sucked out through the exit tunnels, where it vanished in the explosion as the Humvee and the ammunition it carried blew apart.

The entire destruction of their pursuers had taken one and a half seconds, from the moment the firing pin of Gabriel's SIG hit the percussion cap to the point that the Humvee burst outwards and caught fire.

Gabriel and Britta hunkered down under the vegetation, hands over ears, eyes squeezed shut. Chunks of steel plate and fragments of Plexiglas showered down around them, thumping into the softened ground and stippling them with splotches of liquid red mud.

The smell of the flaming pile of wreckage, which until moments earlier had been a $300,000 Humvee, was an acrid stench, equal parts burning rubber and the sharp tang of steel heated to the point of ignition. Overlaying it all was the faint but unmistakable smell of charred meat.

"Keep down!" Gabriel shouted as Britta raised her head to get a better look.

Moments later, further stocks of small-arms ammunition inside the Humvee began exploding. Bullets flew out in all directions, whistling past them, shredding leaves, smashing branches and ploughing narrow furrows along the ground. Gabriel and Britta were sheltered from the volleys by a sturdy ironwood trunk that had toppled in front of them in the blast.

Once the rounds had all discharged, Gabriel signalled with his index finger. Gingerly they extracted themselves from their improvised bunker and stood. The rain was easing off and the few drops still falling sizzled and flared as puffs of steam as they hit the red-hot metal of the dead Humvee.

"Who the fuck were they?" Britta said, swiping her forearm over her face to dislodge the bigger mud clots that clung to her freckled cheeks.

"Not sure, exactly. But the kit, the clothing. The build. I'm thinking either South African or one of the US outfits that support their guys in Iraq and Afghanistan."

"Well they're fucked now, that's for sure. I never liked those guys, even when I was fighting alongside them. Always looked like they were enjoying the killing too much, you know what I mean?"

Gabriel nodded.

"So you said we'd been set up. Anybody in mind? You must have made a few enemies working for Don Webster, or on your own account. Anybody with enough cash to hire that lot?"

Gabriel paused before answering, aware that a crucial insight was locked away behind a door in his mind. He thought back to his original conversation with Barbara Sutherland and Don in her sitting room in Downing Street. The pause didn't last long. Just long enough for the tumblers in the lock to fall into place . . .

Don's oddly distracted manner as they left the MI6 building after meeting Sam Flack.

Click.

Philip Agambe's scream in Xhosa.

Click.

His dying words, about Barbara Sutherland.

Click.

The threats repeated by Marsha Agambe.

Click.

The door swung open. And Gabriel didn't like what he saw in the room behind. Disliked it so much he started to deny the thought itself.

"I have no idea," he said. "Or, rather, I have an idea, but it's such a shitty one I don't want to believe it. I don't think I even want to say it out loud."

Britta swept her arm out to the horizon.

"Look around. You could rig up a PA system and scream it into the mic – I don't suppose there's anybody for a hundred miles in any direction who'd hear you."

He frowned, wishing she'd laugh at what he was about to say, fearing she wouldn't.

"I think it might be Barbara Sutherland."

Britta spat out the water she'd just taken from a bottle.

"Fuck! What? You think the Prime Minister of Great Britain put out a contract on us with some heavy-duty paramilitary dudes in a Humvee? Jesus, Wolfe, I know you've got your problems, but that is properly crazy, even by your standards."

He'd got his wish. But it didn't make him feel better. Instead he put the case before Britta.

"I know it sounds a little crazy . . ."

"A *little* crazy? No, Gabriel, it sounds completely, one hundred percent, batshit crazy. That's what it sounds."

He waited for her to finish and tried again.

"I know all that, but," he held up a palm to encourage her silence, "look at what we know." He held up five fingers and started counting off points, a habit he'd picked up from Don Webster. "One, Barbara authorises the trip. So she knows I'm here. The only other person who knows where we are is Don, and I trust him with my life. Yours, too. Next point, Philip Agambe should have been a Shona-speaker, according to Barbara. She told me off for not having the same quality intel as her. How come she got that wrong? Plus, he asked me if she'd sent me to kill him. How would he know that? And his dying words. That he'd take her down. Third point, Marsha Agambe on the TV. Making the same threat to expose her." He finished counting and searched Britta's face for a sign that she believed him. Her face was impassive.

Not a line on her forehead, not a crinkle at the corner of her mouth.

"That's a nice, neat story to explain your theory. But how about this? One, Barbara Sutherland owes her life to you, remember. Two, in case you'd forgotten, she's a democrat. She goes to G7 meetings, NATO Security Council, European summits, all of that. Do you really think she's spending her quiet time ordering foreign agents to assassinate her own people? And three, why?" Her eyes wide now, Britta spread her hands in front of her, palms uppermost. "Why would she do it, Gabriel? What motive could she possibly have?"

He looked away, wondering the same thing. *Why does she want me dead?* He was doing her bidding. He was loyal. He was working for The Department, for God's sake. The protocols they all operated under meant that blowing the whistle on any of his work would be the equivalent of putting a pistol to his own temple and pulling the trigger.

"Honestly? I have no idea. Come on, we'd better get going. I hope the Land Rover's still good to go."

"Fine. But I think you need some sleep or some meds or a bloody big drink, because I'm not buying your theory about Barbara Sutherland, regardless of that business in Harare."

The Land Rover was driveable, though the rounds from the private security men had blown out the windscreen. Gabriel knocked out the rest of the glass from the steel frame with the barrel of his Glock. "Dust protection might be a good idea," he said.

They improvised masks from rags they found stuffed in a storage cubby in one of the rear doors. With Gabriel taking the wheel, they left the scene of their attempted murder, the stink of burnt-out Humvee making them wrinkle their noses behind the bandannas that gave them the look of Wild West cattle rustlers.

*

After six hours' driving, taking two-hour shifts behind the wheel, they were both ready for a break from the relentless buffeting delivered by the Land Rover's primitive suspension.

"Shall we find somewhere to camp?" Britta said from the passenger seat. "I'm beat."

"Me too. According to the satnav, there's a small lake coming up in a couple of miles. Let's push on till we get there."

"Sounds like a plan."

Ten minutes later, they arrived at the shoreline of the lake. Too small to have a name, it was still a pretty spot, with a flock of red-legged waders paddling in the shallows picking some sort of shellfish out of the mud beneath the water. The birds took off in a swirling cloud of white and grey as the Land Rover disrupted their peaceful feeding with its diesel clatter and fumes. Finding they weren't under threat, the birds returned in ones and twos, then larger groups, until the entire flock, numbering many thousands, were calling to each other in staccato bursts of chirruping as they resumed feeding.

"I'm hungry," Britta said. "And not for any more of those shit *stridsportions*, either."

"You don't like our field rations?"

"You ever had beef stew that tasted like that squeezy stuff they gave us?"

Gabriel wrinkled his nose and pulled his mouth down. "I've eaten worse."

"Me too. And now I want to eat something better. Look around you, Wolfe. This place is teeming with game. We're dressed in camo and we have two hunting rifles courtesy of the British Secret Service. Let's go hunt ourselves some dinner, *ja?*"

Gabriel couldn't help smiling. In all the years he'd known Britta Falskog, which were now in double figures, he'd never tired of her enthusiasm for shooting her own dinner.

There had been a time in Bosnia when, at the end of a long, cold and arduous day hunting a Serbian war criminal, she had insisted they go out with a sniper rifle to "find something tasty for the pot". To the delight of their comrades, they'd returned an hour later with a small roe deer slung between them on a tree branch. The taste and smell of the roasted venison had stayed with him ever since, as had the aura of complete and utter stillness given off by the Swedish sharpshooter next to him as she watched and waited for the doe to move clear of a stand of young birch trees.

22
Plan B

AMONG the predominantly male invitees to the reception at Downing Street, Barbara Sutherland stood out in her flame-red suit and high-heeled black shoes.

A tall man appeared silently at her left elbow. "Excuse me, Prime Minister," he said. "May I introduce you to His Excellency the Minister for Arms Procurement, Sheikh Al-Bashravi ibn al-Ahmadi?"

"Thank you, David," she said, then turned to greet the short, fat Arab man in traditional robe and headgear who had just been brought over to meet her. His brown eyes twinkled in the light from the chandeliers and his thick, black moustache gleamed with some sort of oil or wax. He bowed slightly then held out his hand.

Leaving his charge to the attentions of the Sheikh, the man the Prime Minister knew as David Brown – elegantly dressed in a handmade suit, woven navy-blue silk tie and highly polished black shoes – slipped away from the reception.

His phone's screen displayed two alerts. A missed call, and a text:

Webster on Thames path opposite Houses of Parliament.

He dialled the 'missed call' number.

"Robert. Tell me it's done," he said.

"I'm afraid not. We were following the whole thing on a satellite link. Your two operatives were rather better trained than our squad of ex-jarheads. Better equipped, as well."

Brown scratched the tip of his nose. "What do you mean, two?"

"I assumed you knew," Hamilton said. "We picked up two figures in the Land Rover Webster supplied."

"I wasn't expecting him to take reinforcements." He paused, just for a moment. "Never mind that for the moment. What are you going to do now?"

"Relax. I have an alternative plan. Do you happen to remember that nasty business in Zambia a couple of years ago? Couple of feuding warlords took to cutting each other's supporters' hands and feet off?"

"Vaguely," Brown said, thinking of some photographs he'd been given in a briefing. "Those bloody Africans are always chopping somebody into stewing steak. Why?" he asked, pausing to smile at a Scandinavian diplomat passing him on her way to the reception.

"Because we equipped and trained the winning side. 'The Rock and Roll Boys', they called themselves, with, if I might say so, a startling lack of originality."

"Just get on with it, Robert. I really don't give a flying fuck what they were called or whether they won any prizes for literary effort."

"Their head man is one Jonathan Makalele, though he calls himself General Rambo. We supplied weapons, ammunition and tactical training to Makalele and his gang of cutthroats. He owes me a favour. Rather a large one, in fact, since he now controls a sizeable goldmine and half the industrial protection rackets in his little corner of Mozambique. I was thinking, I might suggest he be on the lookout for a couple of white insurgents sent by British intelligence to infiltrate his supply chain and take him out. That should be enough to have the General locking and loading. I can't believe your guys can withstand a full-blown assault from a warlord and his crew."

"They'd better not. What do you need from me?"

"From you? Well, a GPS reference for wherever they're heading would be nice. It would make an ambush a lot simpler than our last attempt."

"Fine. I'll have it over to you as soon as I can. And just promise me Wolfe and this mysterious sidekick of his are history."

"Hyenas will be snacking on their remains within forty-eight hours. That's a promise."

"I wouldn't make promises to me, Robert, unless you are one hundred percent sure you can keep them. Now, you must excuse me, I have a Prime Minister to manage."

Ending the call, Brown returned to Barbara Sutherland's side. She excused herself from the Arab man and walked to a quiet corner of the reception with Brown.

"What is it, David?"

"I'm afraid I am needed at the office."

Outside, buttoning his navy-blue overcoat against the icy wind blowing up Whitehall towards him, and swinging a tightly-rolled black umbrella, Brown strode off towards the river.

*

About forty-five minutes later, as Don Webster was walking along a stretch of the path beside the Thames, looking across the river to the Houses of Parliament, a tall man in his sixties wearing a long, dark overcoat and carrying an umbrella veered into his path. Don tensed for a moment before relaxing. Muggers didn't wear shoes with that degree of shine on the toes.

"Mr Webster?" the man said.

"Yes. Who are you?"

"Oh, that doesn't matter. But I wonder whether I might have a word with you. About your wife."

Don frowned. "What about my wife?"

"I heard she had a stroke. I hope she's recovering well."

Don's eyes blazed and he clenched his fists. "That's none of your bloody business. Who the bloody hell are you?"

"I am somebody who works closely with the Prime Minster. In fact I just left her side. Now, I'll tell you another condition that lays people low, Mr Webster. Apart from strokes, that is. Multiple sclerosis. Such a terrible disease.

I hear it can make people suicidal. A friend of your wife's died recently, didn't she? What was her name? Georgina Paris. Was that it?"

Don set his mouth in a grim line, breathing loudly through his nose. Then he spoke.

"Yes. Georgie died two weeks ago."

"At The Paxus Institute in Lucerne."

"What of it?"

"Oh, nothing. I mean, flying off to Switzerland to be sent to the Great Beyond by some ex-Nazi with a syringe full of morphine and a bloody great bottle of sleeping pills, well, if that's how you choose to end it all, good luck to you, I say." The tall stranger looked down into Don's grey eyes, and smiled. "It's just that the law is quite clear. You must make the journey under your own steam. Mrs Paris, now, she was confined to a wheelchair, wasn't she?" Webster glared at him but said nothing. "I wonder if you can tell me where your wife was two weekends ago, Mr Webster. Actually, don't. I know exactly where she was. As, I suspect, do you. Or did you two build in some plausible deniability?" The man's voice took on a sing-song sound. "Oh, *no*, officer. I thought she'd gone to visit her *sister* on the Isle of *Wight*. I had no *idea* she'd taken a British citizen to Switzerland to be *euthanised*."

"What do you want?" Don said in a low voice, his eyes hooded.

"I want your chap on manoeuvres in Mozambique disavowed. Taken off the internal phone directory, the coffee rota and the secret Santa list. I don't want you to have any contact with him. Not so much as a text. Make me happy, and I think I can persuade my good friend the Attorney General to ignore Mrs Webster's transgression. Otherwise, who knows? The Crown Prosecution Service might find they are briefed to take an interest in Mrs Webster's actions. Horrible to be recovering from a stroke in prison, I'd imagine. It might even bring on another one."

The man watched as Don's face contorted, a snarl masquerading as a frown of concentration. Five seconds passed in complete silence.

"You can't . . ."

"Oh, but that's where you're wrong. I can. And I will, if you force me to. Now. What's it to be?"

"Fine," Don said quietly. "I'll make the arrangements."

"Jolly good. Well, I'll bid you farewell."

He held out his hand. Don took it reflexively, then almost immediately winced with pain. The man's long fingers were wrapped around the back of Don's hand and the fingernails, as sharp as knives, were digging into the thin skin there. Don pulled, but the grip was as tight as a vice.

"Naturally, this conversation never happened," the man said. He allowed Don to withdraw his hand, which was engraved with four bloody crescents.

23

Let's Play Some Rock and Roll

JONATHAN Makalele had once been a teacher. That is, until a team of South African RENAMO mercenaries had torched his school. They had also shot and killed his wife, who acted as secretary, matron and janitor all rolled into one. The white-skinned arsonists, in their khaki shorts, were laughing as they doused the building in petrol. Elvis Presley was singing in the background, his voice blaring across the clearing from their four-wheel drive.

But that was all in the past. A long time ago. After a period of mourning, he had chosen a new name for himself. And a new career. He was General Rambo, and he had personally killed twenty men. He didn't believe any of that team of mercenaries were among them, but there was always hope.

Now, the General had issued his orders. Kill the British agents infiltrating his territory.

*

The Rock and Roll Boys were sitting around in a loose group near their Toyotas. The rising sun threw spears of yellow for tens of miles across the almost flat plain behind them. One glinted evilly off the muzzle of the machine gun mounted behind the cab on a Hilux pickup.

They had eaten well the previous night. Bushmeat – monkey, deer and a porcupine – pit-barbecued and wrapped in palm leaves to keep the meat moist. Today was going to be a good day. A day for fighting. A day for heroes.

Their camp was alive to the sounds of fighting men preparing for action. Weapons being stripped, bolt actions being tested. Dirty jokes and the laughter that followed. Calls to the younger ones to fetch more beers or another joint. And, beneath it all, electric guitars, drums, saxophones and the voice of Elvis Presley.

Into their midst strode their local commander, Nuria Chissano. As always, she was immaculately turned out. Her olive-green fatigues were pressed with sharp creases, her black boots were shining. Initially, there had been grumblings from some of the men. After all, everybody knew a woman's place was in the kitchen. Or on her back. But after she'd dumped a couple of the bigger men on their arses and given them each an extra facial scar or two with the point of her knife, the grumblings had quietened.

Reaching the centre of the camp and standing with her back to the still-smoking remains of the previous night's fire, she stopped. Legs apart, hands on her hips, chrome plated revolver snug in its polished leather holster, she surveyed her men. To her, they were all men, even the young ones like Little Richard. Only twelve, and short like his namesake, he'd shot five men since being inducted into The Rock and Roll Boys. Now he had the eyes of a stone killer and they were turned on her now, watching and waiting for her orders. She flashed him a brief smile and he smiled back, chin up, thin chest out, Kalashnikov cradled in his lap like a baby.

"Listen up!" she shouted, then immediately dropped her voice to a low tone that had this crew of killers leaning forward, eager not to miss anything. "General Rambo and I spoke this morning. He has given me his orders. Two British security agents are heading our way. Orders from their government are to spy on us and destroy our operation. So guess what?"

"We going to play some Rock and Roll, Mama Chissano?" called Little Richard.

There was laughter at this, whistling, stamping and clapping of hands.

She looked down at her little killer and smiled once more. The corners of her brown-gold eyes crinkled.

"Tune up, Little Richard. You going to be a rock star today!" Then she thrust her chin out and addressed the group as a whole. "Get your shit together. We got a long drive ahead of us. We move out in fifteen minutes."

With a toss of her braided hair that set the glass beads clinking against each other, Chissano marched off, leaving her band to load their weapons and collect their gear. Sitting on an outcrop of smooth rock with an unimpeded view across the tree-studded plain to the forest beyond, she consulted her phone again. Chissano cut and pasted the GPS coordinates for the incoming spies into a geolocation app and waited for the map to zoom in.

Shading her eyes with a flattened palm, she stared across the plain to the south. A dust devil whirled by: red, powdery earth whipped into a five-foot column that danced magically in front of her for a few seconds before dissipating as quickly as it had arrived.

From behind her, Chissano heard the sound of the Land Cruisers and the Hilux starting up. She wound one of her braids around the others and tied it tight, enjoying the feel of the plait as it ran through her callused fingers. First they'd find them. And then they'd kill them. They'd film it for the General. It would make a good training aid. Like he said, "Nobody fucks with the Rock and Roll Boys."

24
Killshot

GABRIEL and Britta grabbed the SA80s and walked away from the lake. A breeze had sprung up, blowing off the water towards them. It was good news, meaning their own scent would be carried away from the game. About three hundred yards into the forest they found what they were looking for: a sturdy baobab tree with a trunk wider than the Land Rover. Its foliage was the same mixture of greens and browns as their camouflage fatigues.

Gabriel boosted Britta onto the lowest branch and then swung himself up. Together they climbed higher, aiming for a broad, cradling V between two branches as thick as a man's waist. The bark was rough and scraped at Gabriel's palms as he clambered up beside Britta.

"Perfect sniping spot," he said.

"*Ja!* Now we just need a target. A nice, fat little gazelle for instance."

"Any DLT would be good."

She turned, grinning at him as the evening sun slanted across her head from behind, bringing out the coppery colour of her hair as it blew around her face.

"DLT?"

"You know," he said, returning the smile. "Deer-Like Thing."

"Ha! Going to add that to my little book of Wolfe-isms when I get the chance. Now shut up and spot for me."

Beside him, Britta wriggled tighter against the tree bough, flattening her body until she had moulded herself to its contours. She brought her right knee up against a thick bulge of wood and used it to brace herself. He watched as she laid her cheek against the stock of the rifle and sighted through the scope. With her left hand, she flicked the fire-select switch to single-shot then returned it to the hand-guard.

Gabriel put the binoculars to his eyes, adjusted the focus until he could see each bird on the lake with pin-sharp clarity, then began, slowly, to sweep from right to left. Nothing bigger than a pelican appeared in the field of view of the binoculars so he tracked further back across the water to the far bank.

There! A lone antelope. He had no idea what species. It was the colour of cinnamon on its upper surfaces and a pale cream below. Its ears seemed absurdly large for its head, and they revolved incessantly, like miniature radar dishes. He was about to nudge Britta when something in the far distance caught his eye: a tall, narrow column of smoke – little more than a hair's width across. The optics that rendered the DLT in such detail compressed the depth of field so that the smoke appeared to be issuing from its head. In reality he had no idea how far away the plume of smoke was. The plain was so flat and the visibility so clear it could have been hundreds of miles.

"I can see dinner," he whispered, aware, even as he said it, that there was no need for silence. But seeing the beast so close through the binoculars made him feel it was necessary, as if it was just beyond his grasp and might bolt if he startled it. "Something else, too. Smoke."

"What kind of smoke," she whispered back.

"Not sure. Could be a camp fire."

"More of those mercenary types, do you think?"

"I doubt it. They'd be too smart to signal they were coming after us. It'd be cold field rations like you were complaining about."

"So should we move on? Find better cover?"

"No. I don't think we need to. It could be a tree smouldering after a lightning strike. It could be nomads cooking. I'm not sure who'd be out here, but if they're happy to have a fire then I think we can be too."

"OK. So where's dinner?"

"Beyond the lake, your ten o'clock. Maybe fifty yards behind the far bank. There's a group of three acacia trees. It's in front of them and to the left."

Britta manoeuvred the rifle's barrel in the direction he'd indicated, searching for her target.

"Found him."

"Him? You can tell at this distance?"

She grunted. "Him, her, who cares? It's dinner. Now, quiet. This isn't quite the rifle I'd pick for a shot like this. I need to concentrate."

Gabriel watched as she zeroed in on the antelope. Watched as her back rose and fell with her breathing, slowing and smoothing out as she brought herself into the calm, clear zone every sharpshooter cultivates when they need to make a kill.

Her index finger tightened on the trigger, squeezing gently but firmly until it began to move.

The report, when it came, was deafening. Flame flashed as the 5.56 mm round exploded out of the muzzle.

Gabriel watched the round drill a hole through the animal's flank and burst its heart, before leaving on the far side in a pink spray. The antelope toppled sideways, blood gushing from entry and exit wounds. He patted Britta on the shoulder.

"Nice shooting."

"Thank you. Shall we collect our dinner?"

The buck turned out to be too awkward to carry back to their camp so they butchered it where it lay, taking a hind leg back with them and leaving the rest for whatever scavengers or predators got to it first.

With the meat roasting over a fire, Britta took a swig of water they'd collected from the lake and purified with a couple of iodine tablets. She winced.

"I'm still not happy with that shit that happened back there," she said. "We're basically in the middle of nowhere and a bunch of ex-US marines or whatever show up in a Humvee, tracking us, clearly, and try to take us out. Whose orders were they really following? That's what I want to know."

"I've told you what I think."

"Yes. And I told you what I thought of what you think. Isn't it more likely to be a local warlord? Or even some powerful friends of Philip Agambe?"

"Maybe. But I left nothing they could use to identify me. And how many African warlords go in for ex-Marine-types to do their dirty work?"

"I don't know. I really don't. I can't think straight right now."

Gabriel pointed at the blackened joint of meat on their improvised spit over the flames.

"Then don't. Let's eat instead."

25
A Childhood Story

THE antelope meat was charred on the outside and pink in the middle. It tasted like venison – dark and gamy – though the texture was tough and fibrous. They ate slices carved off with Gabriel's tactical knife, pausing to wipe the grease from their chins and smiling as their bellies filled with the hot meat.

The sun kissed goodbye to the horizon and slipped away. Mozambique not being on the Equator, the sunset was not a sudden switching off of the light, but the rose-pink streaks that flared across the sky were still gone within five minutes, plunging Gabriel and Britta into a dark so total it seemed as though Earth itself had vanished, leaving them floating in space on a small patch of dusty ground.

The fire glowed, its meagre light dwarfed by the immensity of the star field over their heads. Gabriel lay back, resting his head on his arm. He stretched out his other arm and Britta joined him. He looked up into the darkness of the African sky, each star like a bullet hole shot through a black velvet curtain, revealing a brighter world beyond.

"We're going to find him, tomorrow," Gabriel said. "I can feel it. Something to take back to Melody and Nathalie."

"How will you feel then? Knowing you've done your duty to Smudge?"

"Better. I hope. It's just . . ."

"What?"

"I'm not sure my PTSD was caused by what happened to Smudge."

He felt Britta's hand pat its way up his chest until it came to rest on his cheek.

"What do you mean?" she asked. "I thought that's exactly what it was all about."

He inhaled deeply, catching the smell of the roasted meat from the leg-bone they'd tossed away from their basic camp.

"I had a brother. His . . ."

"No you didn't! You always told me you were an only child."

"His name was Michael," Gabriel said, as if Britta's interruption hadn't happened. "When I was nine and Michael was five, Mum took us to a park down by the harbour in Hong Kong to play. I had a rugby ball with me and one of my passes went over Michael's head and into the water. I sent him to get it and he just jumped in, hit his head and drowned. I killed Michael, Britta. I killed my little brother."

"Oh, my God, that's terrible," she said, wrapping her arm around his chest and squeezing. "But, I mean, how come you found this out? Did you have hypnotherapy or something?"

"No. Well, yes. I'm having therapy now. It happened on my last mission. In Brazil, you remember? The fake religious guru? I started hearing a voice in my head. Not Smudge. God bless him, I'd actually started to get used to him. This was a much younger, lighter voice. And it said, 'Gable'. That was how Michael said my name. It became a family nickname for me. So when I got back to London I called Zhao Xi and . . ."

"Sorry. Zhao Xi?"

"He more or less brought me up afterwards. I was in a lot of trouble at school anyway and the fighting and indiscipline just got worse after Michael. He was a friend of my parents, a local Hong Konger. He became my tutor, and I guess my guardian."

"Was he the one who taught you all that Eastern shit? The meditation and the hypnosis?"

"He was. And it wasn't. Shit, I mean. *Yinshen fangshi's* got me out of lots of trouble since."

"Sorry. But now you have to explain again. *Yin*-what?"

Gabriel smiled in the darkness. Her Swedish frankness, and her unwillingness or inability to notice when she was irritating him, were pulling him out of the melancholy mood into which he'd been sinking.

"*Yin* . . ." he said.

"*Yin* . . ." she repeated. "*Ja!* Got that."

"*Shen.*"

"*Shen.*"

"You're a pain, Falskog, do you know that?"

"Yes, but don't stop my Chinese lesson now, Master Wolfe. It's my first one ever."

She nudged him in the ribs.

"*Fang.*"

"*Fang.*"

"*Shi.*"

"*Shi.* Got it! *Yin-shen fang-shi.* Which means what, exactly?"

"Which means, 'the way of stealth'."

"Aha! Like the time you pulled that pistol right out of that dude's hand in Kabul? And he was all, like, 'What the fuck just happened?'"

"Yes. That."

"*Okej!* Pretty cool guy, huh?"

"Yes, very. So, when I called Zhao Xi, it was the middle of the night in Hong Kong, but he picked up on the second or third ring. Like he always knew I'd call one day. He told me the whole story. How I went into some sort of trance or fugue state for a fortnight and when I came out of it, I couldn't remember a single thing about Michael or any of what had happened. After that, my parents just cleared the house of anything to do with Michael and they let him fade away. In the house, anyway. I'm sure they kept grieving for him, but they never spoke about him from that day on."

Gabriel stared upwards, trying to identify the unfamiliar southern constellations, but it was hard because the individual pinpricks of light kept doubling and blurring. He felt a cold tickling from the corner of his eye down onto his neck.

Far in the distance there was a high *yip-yip*. Then a deeper coughing grunt. Night hunters on the move.

*

Gabriel's watch said 5.45. Sunrise. Away to the east, over a range of mountains the colour of heather, the sun was climbing steadily higher, sending rose-pink fingers across the sky. A breeze was whipping along, moving the upper branches of the acacia trees on the plain and ruffling the surface of the lake. The birds were still in residence, cackling noisily as they squabbled over fishing rights. Down by the water's edge, Gabriel watched as a herd of zebra drank, taking turns to lift their dripping muzzles from the water and watch for trouble.

While he waited for Britta to wake up, he walked over to the Land Rover and opened a pouch of the field rations, squeezing the muddy meat paste into his mouth and then washing it down with some of their precious stash of bottled water, not wanting to start the day with the taste of bleach in his mouth.

Gabriel stripped and cleaned the pistols, then the assault files, using the familiar sequences of movements to quiet his mind. Then he checked over the Land Rover using an old mnemonic his very first army instructor had taught him. POWER: petrol, oil, water, electrics, rubber.

The gas tank was half-full and when he untied and shook the jerry cans on the roof, they sloshed reassuringly. Under the bonnet, everything was as it should be. The dipstick revealed a slick of clearish yellow oil between the MIN and MAX marks, and the radiator was topped up to just below the tops of the metal strips beneath the cap. Gabriel twisted the key in the ignition. All the dials flicked to life and, not that he thought they'd be needing them, but the indicators and all the headlamps and sidelights were operational. Finally, he inspected the tyres, visually, and by feel, running the palms of his hands around the deeply grooved treads. No thorns, sharp stones or random metal spikes greeted his questing fingertips. OK, good to go.

He wandered over to Britta's hunched form inside her sleeping bag and prodded her experimentally with the toe of his right boot.

"Fuck off," she grunted.

*

Ten minutes later, they were sitting in the Land Rover, Britta behind the wheel, the engine idling. He plugged the satnav into the cigarette lighter socket and held it on his lap. As they waited for it to boot up, Britta turned to him.

"Are you ready for this?"

"What do you mean?"

"Well, you've been torturing yourself over Smudge's death ever since you left the Army and now you're so close to where it all happened. I just hope you're all right, you know?"

She reached over and squeezed his thigh. Her lips were compressed and she was frowning, the tiny muscles surrounding her eyes tight with concern.

"I am all right. Really." He ran a mental check of his emotions as he said this. Found he was surprisingly calm. No elevated heart rate. No anxiety fluttering in his stomach. No self-doubt. *We go in. We find something that proves it was Smudge. We go. I do my duty.* "Can we go now?"

"But what if there's nothing left?" Britta asked. "It's been a long time. You know, scavengers, on four legs, or two. Maybe he's gone."

"I know all about the odds. But I'm not leaving without proof we found him. There will be something, even if it's just the tip of one of those damned machetes embedded in a knuckle bone. Now, let's go. Please."

Gabriel did his best to smile but found his face had become inert. Inside he felt . . . nothing. Not hope. Not fear. Just an emptiness. Because he was beginning to suspect something awful. That this entire business had never been about Smudge at all. He was on the wrong continent, looking for the wrong body. A voice, faint as the breeze, whispered in his ear.

"Gable. Come and get me. Come and find me."

He nodded. *I will, Michael. Just let me do this first.*

Taking his nod for the signal to go, Britta, still frowning, pushed the gear lever into first and pulled away.

26

Infiltration Complete

TWO hours later, having driven cross-country the whole way through alternating tracts of open savannah and thickly forested land, the female voice from the satnav piped up.

"You have reached your destination."

They were in a clearing surrounded by acacias, maybe one hundred feet by fifty. Big enough to land a helicopter.

Britta stopped the Land Rover and yanked on the handbrake, which emitted a protesting squawk. They got out, stretching and easing off the stiffness in muscles battered by the warring between the rough terrain and the Land Rover's suspension.

"This is the place?" Britta asked, shading her eyes as she scanned a circle around their position.

"It looks the same, but there's not much to get a fix on. We were in a hurry to get out and we'd just lost Smudge."

"Can you remember which way you came?"

He paused before answering, repeating Britta's action and turning in a circle, straining to dig back into his memory for a clue as to where they should aim for.

He shook his head.

"There's nothing. But I have an idea how I can get it back. Let's have a brew first though. I'm gasping."

"A brew?"

"Tea." He smiled. "Being back here, dressed in camo, it feels just like it did then. Back in uniform. The Army jargon. Tea was always a brew."

While the water in the little aluminium billycan came to a boil, they unloaded their gear: two assault rifles, two MP5K sub-machine guns, two pistols, grenades, extra clips of ammunition.

"Do we really need all this?" Britta asked. "We're in the middle of nowhere. We haven't seen a human soul or even a sign of one since we took care of those mercenaries."

Gabriel thought back to the plume of smoke he'd seen the previous night, spotting for Britta.

"Could be a waste of energy. But there are still elephants in Mozambique, rhino, too. Where there's ivory, there's poachers. Those guys are hardcore. They're all ex-militia or gangsters. Poaching's more profitable than fighting, but they keep their shooters. So it's . . ."

"I know, I know. Better safe than sorry. Right. Let's check these, drink our tea and then go. You going to tell me how you're going to recover your memory?"

Gabriel poured boiling water into the two tin mugs they'd brought, added teabags and powdered milk. He handed one to Britta, then took a cautious sip.

"Self-hypnosis. I need ten minutes. Perfect quiet, perfect stillness. Can you keep guard?"

"Sure. I'll be over there by the stand of trees."

Britta got up and walked over to a cluster of acacias. She set her back against the trunk of one of them, put her tea by her side and laid her SA80 over her lap. Gabriel watched her go, focusing on the thick red plait of hair that descended from the nape of her neck, and the way it glinted like newly stripped copper wire as the sun hit it. He nodded at her and smiled, then sat, cross-legged, in the shade of the Land Rover.

*

Gabriel closed his eyes, allowing the orange blobs of light swirling across his eyelids to distract him.

Then he drew in a deep breath and held it for a couple of seconds, before letting it out slowly through his mouth.

Little by little, he let go of conscious thoughts, using the old technique Master Zhao had taught him as a rebellious teenager in Hong Kong. He heard his mentor's voice now, a soft whisper from long ago and far away, firm, but loving, instructing his younger self. *"Do not fight for calm, young Wolfe Cub. Let it find you. Focus on the breath. Only the breath. In for four. Hold for one. Out for four. Hold for one."*

In this way, he had learned to slow his pulse and visit parts of his mind that were inaccessible when he was ruled by his teenage instincts to grab for everything, seize it, fight for it.

Gabriel felt a settling, physical, yes, but also mental, as if he had entered a lift and found a new floor below the one he lived on. He could still hear the sounds of the exterior world – wind moving leaves in the trees and the distant keening of a bird of prey somewhere high above his position – but they seemed to belong to a different place to the one he now inhabited. Now was the time to ask: "Which direction do we go from here?"

A snatch of shouted instructions floated just beyond reach. Gabriel knew better than to strain for it. He returned to his breathing and waited. There! Stronger now. Audible. *"Northwest from here, boss!"* It was the voice of Corporal Ben "Dusty" Rhodes – a five-year-old echo from a time when Gabriel had served Queen and Country openly, as a Captain in the SAS, not clandestinely, as an operative in The Department.

A picture swam into view in his mind, as if he were watching himself on TV.

Gabriel Wolfe and Ben Rhodes move away from the scene of the firefight where they just lost Smudge. They stagger along, supporting a one-armed man between them. The casualty is Trooper Damon "Daisy" Cheaney, the troop's medic. His face is white with shock. Where his left arm ought to be, there is simply an absence. Unless you count the bloody stump trailing tatters of flesh around an ugly, fractured bone, half-covered with a field dressing and cinched tight with a tourniquet to stop the bleeding.

They reach the clearing where a helicopter waits, rotors chopping the air, its skids barely kissing the ground, impatient to get away. The aircrew in their drab, green flight suits and white helmets like eggshells pull them aboard, and up rears the helicopter, lurching over as the pilot turns sharply to head away, out of reach of the 12.7 mm rounds from the Dushka heavy machine gun mounted on the warlord's Land Cruiser.

And Gabriel looks down.

The enemy fighters have left the village.

They have left Smudge, too.

They have left him crucified on a tree, his hands pinioned to its fat, bulging trunk by machetes.

His head hangs down onto his chest.

A buzzard perches on his left shoulder, feeding steadily on reddish-grey morsels of the exposed brain.

The chopper falls away to the left and flies them to safety.

*

Gabriel let his eyelids flutter open. The afterimages dancing across his vision rendered the scene in front of him in shades of pale blue and green. Standing, he called over to Britta.

"It's southeast from here. The village, I mean. Once we get there, we can work our way out looking for the tree."

"Right," she called back, getting to her feet. "Where do we start?"

"Over there, those trees. I think we came from that direction. The village should be through there, maybe half a mile."

"Come on, then. Let's get going. And we should turn these on." She pointed at the portable GPS unit clipped to her belt. "Didn't you say we had back-up?"

"Yes. Don told me he'd lined up support from the Zambian side of the border."

They switched on the units, which immediately began pinging their position to the US-owned Global Positioning System of orbiting satellites.

The SA80s slung across their backs, and the MP5Ks under their armpits, they walked side by side, through the screening acacias towards the site of Gabriel's last, fateful mission for the SAS.

27

A Bird's-Eye View

ONE thousand feet above the forest, soaring on a thermal, a black-shouldered kite flies lazy circles. The raptor is watching the land beneath, searching for the plumes of smoke that might mean human habitation and therefore food. Or the remains of a kill from one of the ground-dwelling predators. It will hunt when it needs to, but scavenging is easier – less energy to expend and less risk of damaging its fragile flight feathers and light but brittle bones.

Directly below its right wing, it catches movement. Three vehicles are throwing up dust trails as they move southwards. The kite watches, tilting its head this way and that, as the vehicles, and the humans riding inside or on top of them, drive through the scrub.

A few seconds' flying from the position of the moving vehicles is a fourth. This one is not moving. Two humans are walking away from it.

The humans are hard to pick out against the ground. Their coverings blend in with the earth and scrub.

They are carrying the guns – black and charcoal, straight lines and sharp corners – that have destroyed so many of the birds and mammals on which the kite relies for food. Long ones strapped across their backs, small ones across their chests, and smaller ones still on their hips.

The moving vehicles stop. Humans dismount and begin spreading out in a line as they creep towards the hunting pair. One remains in the back of the open vehicle, standing behind a big gun fixed on a pole. The fourteen on the ground also carry guns.

The guns spit flame and thin wisps of smoke drift up towards the kite, acrid on the warm wind. Having observed similar skirmishes in its three-year life, it senses the possibility of a meal and flies tighter circles over the warring humans.

The humans begin falling. The kite sees the bright blood. Synapses flash in its brain. The blood in its muscles pumps faster and it allows itself to lose a few hundred feet as it watches the humans killing each other.

Two of the humans, the ones from the fourth vehicle, are retreating. This is only right. The kite itself has often retreated in the face of attacks from jackals, wild dogs and the much larger vultures that bully their way to the front whenever a kill is discovered.

They hide themselves behind a fallen tree and fire their guns from there. More of their pursuers fall. More blood splashes onto the ground, its vivid hue setting off sensory explosions in the kite's brain.

Puffs of smoke, grey and white, blossom in the clearing. Bodies fall.

Then the human that has stayed behind in the vehicle begins firing the long gun. Flame bursts from one end and the kite picks up the distant chatter of its voice, even at this height.

More firing. More deaths. More beautiful bright beads of blood.

Then, as if lions had arrived and scared off bickering jackals, all movement stops. The air falls silent, just the rustle of wind through the kite's pinions.

Far below, one human stands over another. It points a small gun down at the other's head.

28

"You're All Out of Moments"

FROM his position kneeling beside Britta's body, Gabriel looked up into a brown face, incised with dozens of V-shaped scars on both cheeks. The man grinned – all his front teeth were gold. Then he drew a pistol, a geriatric, Russian-made Makarov. He spoke.

"Time to go soldier-boy. Your bitch is dead. On your feet."

Waggling the pistol, the lean fighter stood back. Without a wound, Gabriel would have eased closer and then disarmed him. It wasn't difficult. You just had to be prepared to strike quickly and without fear. But the blood running down his thigh and into his boot was slowing him down. He stood, wincing with the pain from the gunshot.

"You should take me to your boss," Gabriel said. "You could get a nice, fat ransom."

"That's General Rambo to you!" the man spat back, cuffing Gabriel across the temple with his non-gun hand, a hard blow that unbalanced him and forced him to put his weight on his injured leg. "I fight for him on my home ground. Not like you. Another lily-white, racist mercenary come out to Mozambique to kill Africans for money."

"You have me all wrong," Gabriel said, grunting with the pain and the effort of not showing it. "I came out here to bring a friend home."

"Ha! What friend? You have no friends here. This is a land for black men."

"He *was* a black man. His name was Michael Smith. We called him Mickey. Sometimes we called him Smudge."

The militiaman relaxed a couple of degrees and some of the aggression in his manner left him: the muzzle of the Makarov dropped a fraction.

"What sort of name is that? Smudge? Because he was black? You're a racist, man. Like I said."

"No. He was a friend. We called him Smudge because of his surname. Smith – like a blacksmith. They get smudges on their faces from the forge."

"So how you going to bring him home? Sounds like he's dead to me."

Gabriel tried to stand erect, despite the pain. He needed to get on the same level as the militiaman physically as much as psychologically.

"He is. He died a long time ago. Out here. I want to find whatever's left of him and take it back to his daughter in England."

Gabriel watched as the man's grin changed into a thoughtful expression. The man pulled at his lower lip. His gun arm dropped another inch or so. Any moment now and you're mine, Gabriel thought.

The man laughed. A hard cynical sound.

"You know how big the forest is? Hyena or buzzard will have eaten your friend by now. No. He's gone and soon you'll be joining him. You can explain man to man why you left him to rot so far from home. Now move!" The Makarov's barrel had jerked up to the horizontal again and was pointing straight at Gabriel's stomach.

Gabriel moved ahead and limped along in front of his captor towards a clearing.

When they arrived in the trampled-flat circle, they were met by a ragtag band of heavily-armed fighters, aged, in Gabriel's judgement, from ten to thirty. Each man, and boy, carried a Kalashnikov assault rifle – crude assemblages of varnished plywood and pressed steel, yet reliable enough to be the battle rifle of choice for dozens of countries and hundreds of militias all over the continent, and far beyond. The Soviet-made rifles looked comically oversized in the hands of the boys. Yet he knew only too well how African warlords depersonalised their captives until they were ready not only to carry guns but to use them without compunction. It kept food in their bellies and clothes on their backs. And, more importantly, blood flowing in their veins.

The fighters were wearing an assortment of clothing, from military fatigues to sportswear, the camouflage completely at odds with the neon colours and bright logos of the T-shirts and tracksuit trousers. Several were wearing mirror-lensed, Ray-Ban Aviator sunglasses, or, at any rate, cheap knockoffs bought in Maputo. All of them wore machetes at their hips. One man, a rangy six-footer with a striking afro held in place with a strip of bright scarlet satin, was toting a light machinegun. A belt of long brass cartridges dangled from the breech and he wore two further belts crossed over his torso. He caught Gabriel looking at the weapon and grinned. Then he called over.

"Hey white man! You like it? She my baby. Not that Russian shit. Not Chinese, neither. Know what she is?" Gabriel did, having a photographic memory for infantry weapons, no matter who'd made them, but he kept his mouth shut. The man swaggered over and stuck the muzzle of the gun into Gabriel's face. "South African. How about that? SS-77. Seven-point-six-two."

"Very impressive. Strange weapon for a fighter like you to end up with."

The man laughed. A deep, throaty rumble. "Bought it. All legal. One of them Afrikaners raising money for their cause down south. Then I tried it out on him and got my money back, eh boys?"

He turned around and grinned at his comrades who obliged with a chorus of mocking laughter directed at the presumably dead Afrikaner gun dealer.

Then he turned back to Gabriel.

"Maybe I should try it out on you, too. What you say?"

"I say I'm worth more to you alive than dead. I'm British. On government business."

The tall man, who with every utterance seemed more likely to be their leader, paused. He scratched his chin with an exaggerated, theatrical flourish and looked upwards, pouting, as if pondering a philosophical point.

He looked back at Gabriel. Then down at his leg.

"What's that, one of our AKs? Must be hurting quite a bit, no?"

"I've had worse. I took a hit from a bullet ant in Brazil. Now that did sting."

The man reached down and prodded the field dressing with a long finger, making Gabriel flinch with the pain. "Well now. We can't have you saying us Mozambican boys don't know how to shoot properly, can we?"

Then without any warning he took a step back and kicked Gabriel hard, over the entry wound.

Gabriel screamed and fell over sideways clutching his thigh with both hands as fresh blood welled through the thick pad of cotton and out from under its edges.

The laughter was genuine this time, and his tormentor took a bow as they clapped and whistled and stamped their booted feet.

Gabriel could feel reality slipping away. The pain had set off flares in his head and the laughter had taken on an echoey quality as if heard from the other end of a tunnel.

Come on Wolfe. Don't go down without a fight.

The machine-gunner strutted in a tight circle, encouraging the others with outspread hands, the SS-77 hanging from his shoulder on an improvised strap made from a leather belt. A couple of them had their hands resting on the crude wooden handles of their machetes. Still clutching his bleeding thigh, Gabriel edged his right hand down into his boot and closed his fingers on the hilt of his black ceramic tactical knife. He'd had the blade in the Parachute regiment, taken it with him into the SAS and then "forgotten" to hand it in when he left the Army for good.

He was going to die, he knew that. But he was going to take a couple of the enemy down with him. He waited for the man to complete a revolution and end up back where he started, within an arm's length of Gabriel's right hand.

In a continuous movement, Gabriel pulled the knife from its sheath inside his boot and brought it around in a flat, sweeping arc to slash the back of the man's right ankle. He fell with a scream as his Achilles tendon parted with an audible snap. Gabriel's blow also severed the man's posterior tibial artery. Jets of bright scarlet blood sprayed out from the wound, covering Gabriel and several boy-soldiers with a mist of fine droplets.

Gabriel reared up, leaned over the fallen man and stabbed through his right eye and down into his brain. The eyeball burst with an audible *pop*, and a squirt of clear liquid hit Gabriel in the face. The man jerked once with a great convulsion that arched his back almost double, then flopped, lifeless, onto the grass.

Two or three of the other fighters surged forward, pulling pistols, aiming their Kalashnikovs, unsheathing their machetes. But a shout pulled them all up short. All eyes swivelled to the owner of the loud voice.

Pushing her way through the wild-eyed fighters was a woman dressed in immaculately tailored olive-green trousers tucked into high, black combat boots glossy with polish. Her shirt was an exact match for the trousers, virtually uncreased and decorated with gold bands across the epaulettes, which were buttoned down beside her collar. Her hair was braided into dozens of long, knobbly strands, decorated with yellow, green and red glass beads. She was strikingly good-looking, with a wide mouth, elliptical gold-brown eyes and a short, straight nose with flaring nostrils.

"That's enough!" she yelled as she gained the centre of the group. "You! Stand up!" she shouted at Gabriel. "Now," she added, as he struggled to his knees. She drew a revolver from a polished brown leather holster on her right hip. It was chromed, but he still recognised it: a Smith & Wesson Model 29.

"Nice piece," he said through gritted teeth.

"This? Sure is. Takes forty-four magnum loads. Just like Dirty Harry, yes?"

"You're much better looking than Clint Eastwood."

She laughed at this. "I'm General Rambo's second-in-command, you know that? And you flirting with me? In the middle of my forest? In the middle of my country?"

"Why not? I imagine you're going to kill me. I might as well enjoy my last moments."

"Yeah, well, you're all out of moments. I liked Elijah," she said, pointing at the lifeless machine-gunner at her feet. "He was a good fighter".

Then she straightened her right arm until Gabriel could look straight down the long barrel of the Model 29. He could see the blunt copper tips of the rounds in the cylinder's chambers and fancied he could see the one that would shortly burst its way into his skull.

Using her thumb to pull back the hammer, she cocked the pistol with a loud click. No need for that on a double-action gun like the Model 29, Gabriel thought. Just squeeze and keep squeezing. Guess it makes the kill more dramatic.

He waited.

His pulse was steady.

Maybe this would be fine. To die out here, in the same patch of ground where he'd left Smudge.

He closed his eyes.

29

The Third Ambush

GABRIEL opened his eyes again. He stared at the woman holding the revolver. Deep into those gold-brown eyes. Then his eyes flicked upwards. He heard something. A deep chatter made by only one helicopter in the world. An Apache Gunship.

Her eyes followed his.

"Shit!" she shouted. "Take cover!"

Leaving Gabriel tottering on his wounded leg, she turned and fled for the trees, followed by the rest of the gang, a couple of whom rashly started shooting upwards with their AK-47s as they retreated. All they were doing was giving the onboard heat-seeking targeting system something to lock onto.

The big, angular chopper materialised low over the trees, low enough for Gabriel to see the markings on the side. They looked like US designations. Was someone, somewhere, looking after him? He had no time to think. With the Apache's nose tilted forward, the co-pilot opened up with the 30 mm M230 chain gun.

Like a swarm of flaming mad hornets, thousands of red-hot rounds poured down into the trees sheltering the militia fighters. The tall palms and deciduous trees were shredded in seconds, branches crashing to the ground and burying the unfortunate platoon of Rock and Roll Boys. And Girl.

Gabriel fell to the ground and rolled and scrambled as fast as possible away from their hiding place. He knew he'd be safe: the gunner would have infra-red, computer-guided targeting software, maybe even locking the 30 mm cannon to his own helmet position; so as long as kept down and still, he'd be OK.

After what felt like minutes, but was in all probability only ten seconds, the gun fell silent. Gabriel had found a huge section of rotted log on the edge of a dried-out mud wallow and hauled himself behind it. He had a feeling the Apache crew weren't finished. He was right.

The gunner fired a missile from one of the mounts under the stubby wing pylons. With a whistling roar, one hundred thousand dollars' worth of Hellfire air-to-ground missile curved down from the Apache, trailing white smoke from its rocket motor, and detonated in the centre of the now flattened stand of trees with a devastatingly loud explosion.

The flash was so bright, Gabriel was temporarily blinded, even with his head covered by his arms. A fine rain of wood chips, mud and red specks of vaporised fighters drifted across from the blast site and coated Gabriel in a slimy mess that stuck to his sweaty skin. It smelled bad: burnt flesh, stagnant water and rot. General Rambo's fighters would be taking no further part in their conflict over land, drug supply routes or whatever lay at the heart of their fight with their rivals in this part of Mozambique.

A man's voice, an American voice, amplified and distorted by a loudspeaker, boomed down at the clearing. The voice was coming from the Apache.

"Gabriel Wolfe, identify yourself. This is US Marine Corps Lieutenant Todd Slater. Repeat. Gabriel Wolfe, identify yourself."

Gabriel struggled to his feet, grabbing at a six-foot length of broken branch at his feet and, using it as a makeshift crutch, hobbled into the centre of the clearing. He held his free arm upwards, palm out, and waved.

He had to shield his eyes from the dust and fine grit sucked into the air by the Apache's rotor blades. The broad leaves of the palm trees were thrashing around in the downdraft, adding their clatter to the chopper's racket.

The Apache hovered, not setting down. The loudspeaker was still switched on and he caught the end of an exchange between the man who'd spoken and somebody in a command centre. A second voice, heavily inflected with a Texan drawl, blared across the smoking clearing.

"Gator Three this is Blue One. Visual confirmation, that's your man. Gabriel Wolfe, British Intelligence. We're sending a medevac chopper."

"Roger that, Blue One. Subject positive ID Gabriel Wolfe, British Intelligence. Medevac chopper en route. Maintaining cover. Gator Three out."

"Roger that, Gator Three. Blue One out."

"You hear that, sir?" the first man's voice boomed down at him, the tone now more concerned than official. "You're being pulled out. Stand by."

Gabriel waved again and limped back to his log to sit and wait.

The Apache gained height but maintained its position directly over the clearing.

Ten minutes later, the sound of another set of rotor blades mingled with the Apache's, setting up a thumping, asynchronous beat that seemed to pulse inside Gabriel's head.

He looked up to see a green-painted helicopter swinging in from the west in preparation for a landing. He recognised it instantly. It was a Sikorsky HH-60 Pave Hawk. He'd sat in identical choppers in theatres of war from Latin America to the Balkans during his military career, either being dropped into hot zones or extracted from them once the fighting or intel-gathering was done.

The pilot made a perfect three-point landing dead-centre in the clearing. From the open rear door jumped a tall, dark-skinned man in an olive-green flight suit. He ran over to Gabriel. Up close he wasn't merely tall, he was a giant – over six feet six and built like a prop forward. His face was dominated by a huge, bushy moustache.

He offered his hand, which Gabriel shook.

"Mr Wolfe? Major Anthony Chilundika. I am with the Zambian Army, on, what shall we call it, a humanitarian mission?" He winked. "Would you come this way, please?" The warm, pleasant voice that emanated from the Major's deep chest spoke of Oxford and Sandhurst.

Gabriel took the arm that Major Chilundika had proffered and leaned heavily on the bigger man for support.

"Thank you, but we can't go yet. I came with a partner. She's dead, over there. The militia got her." He pointed with the broken branch at the spot beyond the clearing where Britta lay. "I want to take her body back with us. I'm not leaving her."

"This is most irregular," Major Chilundika said. "My orders were quite specific on this point. One operative to be extracted." Seeing the way Gabriel's eyes flashed and his jaw clenched, the Major batted away an imaginary paper. "No matter. Take me to her."

Beyond the log where they'd taken fire, Britta lay still, just as he'd left her. The Major let go of Gabriel's arm and knelt over Britta. He placed his ear against her chest and then took her pale wrist in his oversized hand, pressing the tips of his first and middle fingers firmly but gently against the mud-spattered skin on its inside.

He paused for a few seconds, then looked up at Gabriel.

"Forgive me, but your diagnostic skills are perhaps in need of refreshment. Your colleague is alive. I suspect she is in shock. She needs attention. We have a medic on the helicopter."

The Major unclipped a walkie-talkie from his belt and spoke briefly and clearly.

"Medic! This is Major Chilundika. I need you here now, please. Bring your crash kit. Out." Then he turned to Gabriel. "She will be fine. Now, let us get you back to the helicopter. By the look of that leg you need a little help yourself."

Suddenly, Gabriel became fully aware of the pain from his gunshot wound. Somewhere amongst the muscle and sinews of his thigh was a 7.62 mm Kalashnikov round and it hurt a lot worse than a bullet ant sting.

"Actually, you're right. I need to sit down."

With that, Gabriel let go of the improvised crutch and the major's shoulder and collapsed into the red dirt.

30

Extracted

"MR Wolfe, sir. Can you hear me?"

Gabriel opened his eyes. The noise from the chopper's rotors was deafening without a flight helmet and he had to crane his neck upwards to catch the Zambian major's words. Chilundika smelled strongly of cologne, a lemony scent sharp against the background smells of aviation fuel, grease and the musty smell all military transports seemed to give out from their metalwork and canvas webbing.

"How's Britta?" he asked.

"Your colleague is going to be fine. She must have fallen against that tree trunk. Our medic has just finished stitching her scalp. He pulled some bark from the wound. Just a mild concussion. No lead poisoning, eh?"

Major Chilundika laughed, showing a wide row of even white teeth that flashed below his moustache. Gabriel made to push himself up onto his elbows, but the burly officer placed a huge, plate-like hand onto his sternum and forced him back to the floor of the helicopter.

"I need to see her," Gabriel said.

"Then turn your head. There she is."

Gabriel did as Chilundika instructed. Britta lay with her head to one side so he could see her face. Her eyes were closed and she had a field dressing bandaged across the top of her head. He could see her chest rising and falling.

He thought back to an earlier time when he had misdiagnosed death. *Good job you're not an undertaker, Wolfe. You'd be burying them alive.*

"How about me?" he asked, craning his head to look down at his thigh.

"That is why you must lie still. No artery damage but we can't have you capering around with a Kalashnikov round still inside you, now can we?"

"How did you find us? And why were the Americans involved? Where are you taking us?"

"So many questions! We found you because, very sensibly, you activated your personal GPS sets. We have been waiting for a signal since Colonel Webster informed us of your mission. Our American friends have been training the Zambian Army in search and rescue techniques. They were delighted to be able to participate in a live exercise. We are taking you to Mikango Barracks. We have an excellent trauma surgery team there. They will patch you up and once you are fit, they will discharge you and we can talk about where you go next. I assume you will wish to return to England?"

"I'm not sure it's going to be that simple."

"No?"

"No. I have some unfinished business in Mozambique. The reason I came out in the first place." *And possibly in Zimbabwe, although I may need to call a friend first.*

"Oh, I think that would be most unwise. The Rock and Roll Boys are just one of a number of extremely well-armed and aggressive gangs in this part of the country. I'm afraid I cannot permit you to return. I am sure Colonel Webster would feel exactly the same."

With that, Major Chilundika stood and went forward to talk to the pilots, leaving Gabriel under the watchful eye of the medical officer.

*

At the military hospital at Mikango Barracks, Britta and Gabriel were separated: she for brain scans, he for emergency surgery on the bullet wound in his thigh.

Coming round from the anaesthetic, Gabriel sat up in bed, groaned at the pain in his head from the drugs and lay back down.

"Hey!" he called in an urgent whisper. "Britta. You OK?"

She stirred, brushing at some imaginary creature crawling over her cheek, and mumbled:

"What? That you, Wolfe?"

"Yes, it's me. Jesus, I thought I'd lost you."

"Me, too. You, I mean." She opened one blue eye and focused across the yard of space that separated their beds. "I thought they'd hit you and I stood up. I tripped and fell. Must have banged my head." She reached up and touched the bandage across the top of her head, wincing as her fingertips instinctively found the tenderest spot under the dressing.

"They think it's just concussion," Gabriel said.

"How about you?"

He reached under the covers to where the bandage covered his stitched-up leg, then turned his head to the bedside cabinet, where a Kalashnikov round, dark with his own, dried, blood, stood like a miniature copper obelisk in a glass petri dish. "I'm fine. Bullet's out. Just a bit sore, that's all."

Actually it feels like a rhino just stuck its horn through my leg but I guess you probably already know that.

"Don't bullshit me, I can always tell when you're lying. So you want to tell me what went down back there?"

"I wish I knew. I think someone has decided we're surplus to requirements," he lowered his voice to a hoarse whisper, "now that Agambe's out of the way."

"So are we safe here?"

"I hope so. Even if she finds out where we are, I don't think there's much she can do. The Zambians aren't going to let a crew of US privateers swan in here and start shooting, still less some gang-bangers with AKs and machetes."

"I hope to God you're right. Because I have the mother and father of all headaches right now and I really need to sleep."

"Sleep, then. I've got a plan, but it can wait till you're ready to hear it."

Britta's voice, when she spoke, sounded far away and very, very tired.

"Good. You always have a plan. Tell me later."

Moments later she was snoring quietly. Gabriel lay back on his pillow, staring at the ceiling fan as it rotated slowly above his head. He did have a plan and it was going to take him to the one person on Earth who wanted to see him dead more than the British Prime Minister.

*

Three days later, Major Chilundika was putting Gabriel and Britta into a Zambian military transport plane to fly them back to Harare.

"Sorry about your weapons," he said, as the Jeep rolled to a stop on the runway. "But as much as I owe a debt to Colonel Webster, I can't allow you to leave Zambian soil packing that heat, as our American friends would no doubt put it. I suggest you find a commercial flight from Harare back to England as soon as you can. Put this whole bloody business behind you."

"We can't thank you enough, Major," Gabriel said, offering his hand.

"Please. Think nothing of it. As I said, it made a nice little training exercise for my men. Perhaps you can send my regards to Colonel Webster when next you see him."

"I shall. It's a promise."

"Good," the Major said with a smile. "I have made the necessary arrangements with my counterpart in Harare. You will be provided with temporary papers. May I suggest you do not outstay your welcome."

Gabriel nodded. Then he and Britta turned and boarded the plane, a Dornier Do 228.

As the plane lumbered along the runway, they looked out of the window at the tall, ramrod-straight officer, who stood, waving, on the tarmac as the backdraft from the two turboprop engines threatened to whisk his beret off his head. Britta turned her head to Gabriel.

"You are nuts, you do know that, right?"

"She'll see me. She has to. I've got a contact back in London who can make the introduction."

"This isn't some networking trip, Gabriel. You killed the woman's husband. She'll be waiting for you with police. Probably with a gun. I would be."

Gabriel looked down at his hands, which were clenched together between his knees.

"I have to try. When we get to Harare, I'm going to call Melody Smith. She said her organisation has people on the ground in Africa. Mozambique, Tanzania, Zimbabwe. All over."

"I admire your faith. Especially since we left all our weapons behind with the lovely Major Chilundika."

"He was right. He had no choice. Frankly, I'm amazed we're getting the VIP treatment out of here. I half expected to find ourselves being shipped straight back to England."

Three hours later, the Dornier touched down at Harare International Airport with a tearing shriek from the tyres and a jolt that would have thrown them out of their seats had they not been strapped in.

"Sorry about the bump," the pilot's voice crackled over the intercom. "These babies handle differently when they don't have a full cargo."

Gabriel and Britta collected their kitbags, salvaged by Major Chilundika from their Land Rover after their rescue, and walked down the steps from the single passenger door. The temperature was in the low seventies. A breeze was blowing east to west across the runway, bringing an earthy smell from the distant savannah and bending the flimsy trees at the edge of the airfield into graceful curves that sprang back as each gust abated.

The roar from the engines made speech impossible, so, hand across his nose and mouth to prevent the swirls of dust choking him, Gabriel pointed to the terminal building before shouldering his bag and heading away from the plane.

As they reached the building, the Dornier's engine note rose in pitch and volume and they turned to see the plane rise into the air, climb at a shallow angle and then bank to the right before heading back towards the Zambian border. Two Zimbabwean soldiers came out to greet them. They were handed slim packets that contained all the necessary papers to permit them to travel into and then out of Zimbabwe. They still had their British passports and the dollars Gabriel had brought with him. Plus one very important rectangle of white card, printed with the contact numbers and email address of Melody Smith.

Sitting inside the terminal building, sipping from a cold can of mango juice, Gabriel used his satellite phone to call Melody.

"Hello?" she said, from five thousand miles away, on a line so clean she could have been sitting with her back to Gabriel.

"Melody, it's me, Gabriel."

"Oh, my God. Where are you?"

"I'm in Harare. Listen, we got close but we were ambushed. I didn't get to where we left Mike. I haven't given up, but there's something I need to do while I'm here. Something really important."

There was a long pause, during which, Gabriel could hear clicks and electronic bleeps on the line as the various satellites and continent-bridging fibre-optic cables kept the fragile connection alive.

"What am I going to tell Nat? You promised her you'd bring her Dad home."

"And that promise still holds. It's just, I'm going to have to figure out a new plan."

Melody sighed. "You said you had something important to do in Harare. What does that have to do with me?"

Gabriel took a deep breath, then let it out slowly, looking at Britta, who reached out and took his hand. Squeezed it, and gave him an encouraging smile.

You said that your organisation had people on the ground in Africa. Here in Zimbabwe."

"Yes, we do."

"Can you put me in touch with them? I need to fix something. Something I did on the orders of that person you warned me about."

There was a pause.

"Oh, no, Gabriel. Tell me it wasn't you. Tell me you didn't kill Philip Agambe."

Now it was Gabriel's turn to say nothing, though he knew he was broadcasting his guilt through his silence just as eloquently as if he'd stood up and confessed in a court of law. "How did you hear about it?" he finally asked.

"Not on the news," she said, her voice sharp and tight. "The mainstream media here don't care about a minor black politician getting killed in Africa.

But when you know which websites to check, you can find out what you need to know. It's part of my job. Oh, Jesus, Gabriel, why? Philip Agambe was a good man. He was honest, which is a bloody rare thing in politics anywhere."

Gabriel rubbed his hand over his face. "Like I said. I had my orders. Only now I'm beginning to wonder whether the story I was fed about Agambe was fake. So I need to check. And that means I have to meet his widow."

"Let me make a call or two. Can I give our contact your number?"

"Of course. Just make it quick, can you?"

"I will. What have you got yourself into, Gabriel?"

"I don't know. But I'm going to find out. Then I'm going to put it right."

31

Repentance

A knock at the hotel room door: loud, confident. Gabriel rose from the bed to answer it, checking the spyhole first. Outside, his face distorted into a bulging sphere with a protuberant, flat nose stood a tall, brown-skinned man, sporting a lime-green trilby with a black-and-white-chequered band. He opened the door and let the hat's owner in.

"You're Marcus Rudzungu?" he asked.

"You think there are two hats like this in Zim?" the man said, with a smile, pointing to his unusual headgear.

"It is as described, certainly," Gabriel said.

"Better than all that code word nonsense." Marcus looked over Gabriel's shoulder and doffed his hat to Britta. "Good day to you, Madam. A friend of Gabriel's, I assume?"

Britta stood and came over to shake hands with the tall Zimbabwean.

"Pleased to meet you."

"Likewise, dear lady, likewise. So, I receive a call from Melody Smith in London. Says a friend of hers – no, wait, better make that two friends," he grinned at Britta, "is in Harare and wants to meet with Marsha Agambe."

"Did she tell you why?" Gabriel pointed to the hard chair under the desk, which Marcus pulled out and sat astride, like a detective from a seventies cop show.

"Just you urgently had to speak to her."

Gabriel pressed his lips together, realised he'd not be able to speak and relaxed them again.

"I killed her husband."

Marcus's eyes widened and he reared back in the chair so far Gabriel thought for a moment he'd topple backwards, forgetting there was no backrest to save him. Then he burst out laughing.

"Oh, my God, you had me going there for a second. Philip Agambe was killed by a mugger out in The Avenues. A very bad neighbourhood," he said, turning to Britta. "Stabbed for his wallet and phone and then put back in his ministerial car, which the mugger set on fire."

Britta glanced at Gabriel, who remained still, looking at Marcus Rudzungu with mouth downturned. Gabriel reached into his pocket and pulled out his fist. He held it out to Marcus and uncurled his fingers.

Coiled in the centre of his palm was a gold watch-chain, mounted with a gold half-sovereign. It bore Queen Victoria's portrait on one side, St George, mounted on horseback, thrusting a long spear into a dragon, on the other.

"This belonged to Philip Agambe. I took it from him after I killed him. His widow will confirm it's his. I need to meet Marsha Agambe. She said she's going to continue her husband's work. That she intends to expose the Prime Minister – the British Prime Minister – at the Southern African Development Conference. She may be in danger. Some very bad people – I don't know who – are after Britta and me. They've already had two goes at killing us. I don't want Marsha Agambe to meet the same fate as her husband."

Marcus held out his hand and Gabriel dropped the chain into it. The strong brown fingers closed tight around the gold. He looked up at Gabriel. His mouth was set into a grim line.

"You know, Gabriel, when I tell Marsha Agambe that her husband's assassin wants to meet her, I do not think the prospect will fill her with joy."

"I know. But please try. Her life is in very real danger."

An hour later, Gabriel's phone rang. It was Marcus.

"Marsha Agambe says she wants to meet you. But I tell you my friend, you'd better be straight with her. One hundred percent. Marsha has some powerful friends of her own, and her brother is a policeman. I hope you know what you are doing."

The phone clamped between cheek and shoulder, Gabriel looked over at Britta, then down at his hands, which were clamped together, fingers interlaced, knuckles white.

"So do I," he said.

*

Marsha Agambe had chosen a very public place for their meeting. Africa Unity Square, directly opposite the Parliament Building on Nelson Mandela Avenue. Gabriel left Britta in the hotel and walked the two miles to the square on his own. He was still limping from the bullet wound, but the medics had given him some powerful painkillers. He wondered whether she would have asked her brother to arrest him, or simply hired someone to kill him, as Barbara Sutherland had hired Gabriel to do the same thing to Philip Agambe.

Today, Harare was blanketed by high, white clouds. A cool breeze was blowing through the city, whipping up small whirlwinds of rubbish and dust that eddied at street corners. Ahead, sitting on a low wall that bordered an ornamental pond with a fountain at its centre, sat a slim black woman dressed in a black trouser suit and a small, black, pillbox hat with a veil pulled down over her face.

Gabriel looked around, searching for bodyguards, but the widow Agambe appeared to be alone. She raised her head and turned to face him. He walked on, drawing closer, straining to detect even the slightest glimmer of an expression beyond the veil that might indicate the woman's mood. There was none. She sat perfectly still, waiting for him to arrive.

When he did, he stood in front of her. She looked up into his eyes and finally he could see her face. The eyes were dry and the mouth, outlined in deep red lipstick, was pulled into a tight line. Not knowing what else to do, he knelt in front of her and sat back on his heels, so that he was looking up into her face.

"Mrs Agambe," he said. "My name is Gabriel Wolfe. I killed your husband on the orders of Barbara Sutherland."

He stayed in that position, ignoring the pain from his cramping muscles, waiting for a sign from her that he might get up. Finally, after several minutes during which she maintained her poised silence, she spoke.

"When Marcus told me you wanted to see me, I began planning your death. I have friends who could make it happen and then make it so nobody would ever know you had been here in my country. Until I saw you coming, I was still convinced it is what Philip would have wanted. He hated the British and their malign influence on Zimbabwe and on Africa as a whole. Even this square is based on the Union Jack. Their aid-for-trade deals, their defence contracts, their pious hand-wringing over starving Africans when it is their own greed and corruption that has caused so much suffering. Look over there, Mr Wolfe." She nodded in the direction of a busy crossroads. He followed her gaze. "Do you see the fellow with the shopping bag?" Gabriel nodded. "He has a gun in there. A pistol with a silencer. All I have to do is remove my veil and he will walk over here and shoot you. And over there?" She turned and raised her chin in the direction of a wheeled fruit stand under a tree with spreading branches, casting a deep pool of shade on the northern side of the square. "Together they could load your body under the top of the fruit barrow and wheel you away from here to a place far away from prying eyes. A place occupied by a pack of wild dogs who are always hungry and never fussy about what they eat."

Gabriel returned his gaze to hers. "I wouldn't blame you if you raised your veil. I came to Africa in search of redemption. To search for the remains of a friend of mine whom we lost in battle. I willingly paid the price Barbara Sutherland demanded of me. But now I have started to wonder whether everything she told me was truth or a convenient fiction."

There was another long pause after this speech. Gabriel looked left, at the man leaning against a railing, the lethal shopping bag still at his feet. Then he looked right, at the fruit seller and his makeshift gurney, ready to spirit Gabriel's corpse away to be turned into dogfood. Marsha Agambe looked down at Gabriel and bestowed on him a small, sad smile.

Then she reached up to pinch the lower edge of her veil between her thumb and forefinger.

32
Truth and Reconciliation

GABRIEL tensed. Despite his desire to pay for his crime, he knew he would not wait to be shot, down on his knees. Marsha Agambe tugged down on the edge of the veil, settling it under her chin.

"Get up, please, Gabriel," she said. "I do not know why I am doing this, but I feel I should trust you. I cannot forgive you for killing my husband. Not yet, anyway. But you must help me now."

Sighing as much from the pain in his muscles as from relief, Gabriel got off his knees and sat beside Marsha on the low wall. When he looked around, the man with the shopping bag had disappeared into the crowds ambling through the square, and Marsha Agambe's other friend was busily selling his brightly coloured local fruits to a small queue of customers.

"Tell me," she said. "Did my husband suffer?"

Gabriel found her nobility almost unbearable. No screaming, no slapping or punching, no beating her fists against his chest, just a quiet dignity reflected in her tone of voice that was more sad than angry. He thought back to the moment he had taken Philip Agambe's life. The sudden weight of the man's body against his own, the fading shine on his eyeballs, the gasping exhalation carrying his final breath away into the warm midday air. Had he suffered? Of course he had suffered! Violent death is never pain-free, and to be murdered in your home city by a foreign assassin – that would fill your last moments on earth with suffering of the most intense kind.

"It was quick. He did not suffer. I am so very sorry."

He felt tears starting from his eyes and dashed them angrily away. If anyone had a right to shed tears it was the woman in front of him, yet she sat beside him, holding his hand in her own and staring at him with a look he couldn't read.

"I will grieve for my husband when the time is right," she said. "But for now, I must remain strong. I must continue Philip's plan through to its conclusion. Perhaps you can help me after all. Can you come to my apartment tonight?"

"Of course. What do you need me to do?"

"I want you to see his files for yourself. Then I will know I can trust you to protect me."

*

On the roof of the Metropolitan Insurance Building on the southwestern corner of the square, Sasha Beck lay on her belly, protected from the grime by a six by four-foot dust sheet made from charcoal-grey, rip-stop nylon.

Anyone at a gun fair or in an arms dealer's stockroom looking for a rifle to match the long-barreled weapon in front of her would be disappointed. It was made to her own specifications by a middle-aged gentleman living in Oberndorf am Neckar, a pretty town in Baden-Württemberg, Germany. Herr Brandt was a former employee of Heckler & Koch, and he supported his large and happy family entirely on the proceeds of the bespoke weapons he fabricated in his basement workshop. The rifle's accuracy at ranges of up to seven hundred and fifty yards was as good as, if not better than, any commercially produced rifle. But that wasn't the primary reason Sasha Beck bought her equipment from him.

Brandt's forte was producing weapons systems that could be dismantled quickly and stowed in the sorts of unobtrusive rucksacks, musical instrument cases or even shopping bags that wouldn't attract a second glance as their owners made their way, casually and openly, away from the scene of their latest assignment.

Being entirely handmade and using no mass-produced components, they offered other advantages. They were untraceable, unregistered and would never show up on any police or criminal intelligence database. Only the ammunition and the telescopic sight were bought-in. The rifle was chambered for .338 Lapua Magnum rounds. The telescopic sight was a Schmidt & Bender PMII. The latter had cost her four thousand dollars, and the salesman in the gun shop had congratulated her – genuinely, she thought – on her choice.

Now, she lay her cheek against the cool aluminium stock and sighted through the scope on Marsha Agambe's breastbone. This was merely a reconnaissance, however, and her trigger finger was curled around the outside of the guard.

"Who are you, handsome?" she breathed, as she moved the cross hairs a foot to the right. "Making a move on the black widow so soon after her husband's unfortunate demise, are we?" She tutted. Then smiled. "You'd better be quick, my brown-eyed friend. She won't be around for much longer."

*

Back at the hotel, Gabriel and Britta ate club sandwiches they'd ordered from room service, washing the spicy chicken and bacon down with cold lagers.

"How's the head?" Gabriel asked.

She touched the dressing. "Not too bad. Still got a headache, but considering the firepower we were up against, I'll take that. How's the leg?"

He looked down. Gingerly, he touched his fingertips to the spot beneath his trouser leg where the dressing was. "Same. It hurts but I can deal with it. The pills help. Do you want to talk about who's after us?"

Britta finished her mouthful and took a long pull on her bottle of lager. She wiped her mouth with the back of her hand.

"You do, obviously."

"Yes, I do. I told you what I think. If you can't accept that Barbara Sutherland is out to silence Philip, and now Marsha Agambe, can you think of a plausible alternative? Who'd have the money and the contacts and the motivation to send a bunch of black-clad heavies into the Mozambican forest to take us out, and then when that didn't work, a bunch of bloody gang-bangers?"

She didn't answer immediately. That was something Gabriel had always valued whenever they'd been on operations together. When other voices were calling for a full-frontal assault, all guns blazing, Britta Falskog would be working the intel, looking for an angle. Frequently, that meant they achieved their objective quietly and efficiently, without filling the air with hot lead and grenade smoke.

"First of all, are we even sure the two events are connected? You kill Philip Agambe, a known terrorist financier. Then we encounter the Humvee boys and we deal with them. Then the warlord gang or whoever they were. Apart from timing there's no link that I can see. Maybe we were straying on someone's territory. Maybe the Humvee guys were at war with the other lot and thought we were going to join them."

Gabriel finished his own sandwich and drained his beer.

"What about, Barbara Sutherland tricks me into taking out a political enemy then sends a posse of freelance Special Forces types to wipe us out? Then, when that fails, she recruits a local militia gang to finish the job?"

"Come on, Gabriel," Britta said, pulling on her plait. "Can you really see a British Prime Minister just picking up the phone to a warlord in the middle of fucking nowhere and saying, 'Oh, hi, General Whackjob. Listen, could you just send some of your crew to kill a couple of British Government agents?' How would she know somebody like that even existed? It's not like they'd have met at a party."

Gabriel stood and walked to the window. They had a room on the tenth floor and the whole of downtown Harare was spread out before him. He looked across to a neighbouring tower block, wondering who was working there, whether they were routing calls between foreign Prime Ministers and local warlords in return for a slice of the fee. He turned back to her.

"A middleman."

"What?"

"A middleman. A go-between. A broker."

Britta laughed, breaking the tension, revealing her gappy teeth.

"All right, Mr Dictionary, I know what a middleman is. Let's say you're right. Barbara Sutherland *has* taken out a contract on you. She knows some dodgy 'intermediary'," she made air-quotes around this word, "and arranges two ambushes. Well, they both failed, so what now? Is she going to send tanks after us next? A couple of Apaches? A bunch of your former colleagues? Or my current ones?"

Gabriel shook his head. "I don't know. I'm hoping we're under the radar for now. Even if Major Chilundika reported back to her somehow, he doesn't know precisely where we are now, so neither does she. Or, if not her then whoever is behind all the shit that's been following us around."

"What next, then? We got so close to finding Smudge. Are you going to try again?"

Gabriel sighed. "Jesus, Britta, I want to. More than anything. But we're rather under-equipped now. No vehicle. No weapons, which I really do feel we need. And no support. Just some cash, our passports and a couple of GPS units. I think we need to get ourselves away from here and then regroup. There's something else, too."

"What?"

"I don't want you involved any more. I want you to get home and then report for duty. Keep quiet about the whole thing. You weren't on the passenger manifest of the flight out, Don made sure of that. And I told Major Chilundika you were a South African guide I picked up in Maputo. I snagged your documents in the helicopter so there's no intel anywhere on this continent to show you were even here."

Britta stood, hands on hips, eyes blazing. "You want me gone? What about you? What are you going to do? Don't play the knight in shiny armour with me. I could kick your ass from here to Stockholm. With or without a weapon."

Gabriel couldn't help the smile, but held back on the correction. "Believe me, I am in no doubt you could put me down any time you chose. But things are getting complicated, surely you can see that. I can't risk your life as well as mine. I'm seeing Marsha Agambe tonight and I'm going to work to keep her safe until the conference. Then I'm flying out. If – when – the shit hits the fan, I have no idea what's going to happen. I could be charged with treason or given a knighthood. I just don't know, and there's no reason for you to get tangled up in it."

Britta sat back down on the bed, fingering the fine gold chain where it crossed the notch of her collar bones. He saw that a red blotch had crept up onto her throat. For a while, she just stared at him and he stared back, noticing the way the sun caught the coppery notes in her eyelashes, the freckles that spattered the bridge of her nose, the look of equal parts fury and determination mingled in her expression. Then something changed. The tension went out of her jaw. She blinked.

"If I go, promise me no heroics. Just keep an eye on Marsha Agambe then get the fuck out of this bloody place."

He went to sit next to her on the edge of the bed and put his arm around her shoulders.

"No heroics. It's a promise."

33
Pillow Talk

THE elegant, well-spoken, sixtyish man lying in bed in his Barbican apartment was known to his MI6 colleagues, and the Prime Minister he purported to serve, as David Brown. His real colleagues knew him only as Strickland. The organisation for which he worked was straightforwardly commercial, yet its financial value exceeded the GDP of all but the 21 biggest economies in the world. In its distant past, the organisation had built railways, communications networks, nuclear power stations and transport infrastructure. As it grew, it acquired the banks, law firms and insurance companies that had hitherto supported its expansion. By the time Strickland joined, it had abandoned tangible goods altogether, finding greater return on investment in manipulating global markets, international trade regulations and, eventually governments themselves. Strickland was its area manager for the UK. His role was equal parts political liaison, enforcer and corrupter of public officials.

Now, he looked down at his phone as it buzzed and swiveled on his bedside table. The screen bore a familiar name.

He picked up the phone. "I do hope you bring me good news, Robert. I'm not in the mood for excuses."

"Sadly, the news is not good."

"Why? What happened?"

"The Rock and Roll Boys have played their final concert, or at least this particular group have. They were about to deliver the coup de grace when they themselves were ambushed. It would appear the Zambian Army came to the rescue of the dynamic duo. I have no idea how, but they have disappeared."

"If the militia, or whatever they were, were killed then how do you know all this?"

"Jonathan Makalele, their boss, told me himself. He took a second team in to find out what had happened. He found one man still alive, or alive enough to tell him it was a Zambian helicopter and possibly an American, too."

"Shit! And what about Marsha Agambe?"

"Mrs Agambe is alive, for the moment. But I have contracted with a highly skilled person in what you might call the outplacement business. She will see to it that our little problem ceases to be a problem. But I can't push her. She does things with great care, and her due diligence would make many a corporate lawyer blush for shame."

"Do you ever listen to yourself?" Strickland hissed. "You sound like a fucking civil servant. Why don't you call a spade a spade?"

"Very well. I have hired a professional killer to murder Marsha Agambe. She takes her time because fucking up isn't in her playbook. How's that? Better?"

"Much."

"Indeed. So perhaps we might keep our plain English for face to face meetings from now on."

"Just call me when your HR manager has outplaced the candidate."

"Of course. But tell me, what are you going to do about the two operatives? They're in the wind, now. Comfortable for them, perhaps, but not for you."

"You mean, what am I going to do now that you fucked up royally? Oh no, wait a minute. Fucked up royally, twice. And it's not comfortable for *us* by the way. You're still not out of the woods. I'll have to put my thinking cap on, won't I? As I said before, without proof there's not much he can do.

Maybe I can buy his silence if he ever shows up again."

"And the mystery partner?"

Finally, Strickland's patience snapped.

"Look!" he hissed. "Given that I can't use any of the official state security apparatus, I'm doing the best I can. You, on the other hand, have been about as much help as a rubber spanner. So forgive me, but why the fuck don't you come up with some suggestions of your own instead of asking these stupid fucking questions?"

Now it was Hamilton's turn to pause. Good, Strickland thought, I've finally put you on the back foot.

"It's a fair point. I apologise for my failure, my repeated failure to nip this little issue in the bud. Let me ask around. If he shows up and we identify him, we'll take care of things."

34

Paying His Respects

RESTAURANTS jostled for space at the start of Marsha Agambe's road. They were selling every kind of food, but with a heavy emphasis on barbecue. The smell of spices and grilling meat lingered in the air, overlaying the traffic fumes as city workers made their way home.

It was seven that evening, as they'd agreed. Few cars passed Gabriel as he walked down the tree-lined street looking for her apartment block. The apartment buildings each had a name, mounted on a signpost at the pavement end of a long paved walkway. Marsha Agambe's was called Kenyatta. Her number was 1005.

As he approached, a low growling snapped him out of the reverie he'd descended into. A scruffy, yellow-and-brown dog stalked towards him from the cover of a group of trees in the grass lawn to the front of the apartment block. Teeth bared, hackles spiked up like a Mohican down the nape of its neck, the dog stood, stiff-legged, on the pavement in front of him. It had no collar and no obvious owner.

Gabriel stood quite still. He'd fought dogs before. And won. But he had no desire for a rematch with the species this evening. He lowered his gaze, avoiding any eye contact the beast might perceive as a threat. The dog's lips were retracted, revealing an impressive set of yellow incisors and inch-long canine teeth. The growling continued, a low rumble that triggered primitive neurochemical responses in Gabriel's brain. Responses he ignored, since they were saying, "run or fight", and he wanted to do neither. Despite the shiver of fear bouncing from his knees to the pit of his stomach, and the sweat on his palms, he knelt down in front of the hip-high animal.

Gabriel succeeded in his aim, which was to confuse the dog. It stopped growling and whined instead. Then it cocked its head to one side. He looked up from under lowered eyelids. The teeth were covered again. He stretched out his right hand, knuckles uppermost, intending to offer it for the dog to sniff. But then it backed up, and barked, twice, very loudly. He could see it was making ready to spring at him.

Out of the shadows, a slim-built figure dressed in the navy and khaki uniform of the Harare police emerged and shouted at the dog.

"Bazu! Down!"

The dog whipped its head round at the noise, and though its hackles were still erect, it complied with a whine, sliding to the ground on outstretched forepaws until its belly was in contact with the concrete pavement.

Gabriel stood, careful not to make any sudden movements, and faced the stranger, who carried a pistol in a brown leather holster on his right hip.

"Thank you. Is he yours?"

The man placed his right hand on the butt of the pistol. "He is a she, and yes, she is. Who are you and what are you doing here?"

"My name is Gabriel Wolfe. I am here for a meeting with Marsha Agambe. You know her?"

"I am her brother, Foreman. I was named after the great American boxer, you know? Gorgeous George?" Gabriel nodded. "Do you have some ID?"

Gabriel pulled his passport from an inside pocket of his windcheater and held it out to the man. After scrutinising the passport, Foreman handed it back.

"Since Philip was murdered, we have become wary of strangers, as I am sure you can appreciate. You have done our family a great evil. But I respect your decision to try to atone by helping Marsha. Come with me, please."

"What about Bazu?"

The man laughed. "She stays on patrol." He looked down at the dog, who was sitting at attention, her head high between her front paws, ears pricked, muscle-tone high. "Stay, Bazu!"

The dog whimpered but remained immobile as Foreman led Gabriel inside the apartment block. He pressed the call button for the lift then turned to Gabriel.

"Are you armed, Gabriel?"

Unusually for him, Gabriel was able to answer, truthfully, in the negative. "No," he said. "Would you like to search me?" He held the sides of the windcheater open.

"I think it would be remiss of me not to, don't you?" Foreman said. Bending, he ran his flat palms up Gabriel's legs in four efficient sweeps, side to side then front to back, left leg then right. Standing, he ran his hand around Gabriel's waist, then up his ribcage, over his chest and then around his back. Finally, he patted the windcheater all over, squashing the pockets in his fists.

"Very professional," Gabriel said with a smile as Foreman completed his frisking.

"Thank you, white man. We are not amateurs in the Harare Police department, you know."

The lift bell pinged, saving Gabriel from further embarrassment. Two minutes later, they were at Marsha Agambe's front door on the tenth floor. Foreman knocked. Gabriel felt the tension that had ebbed away from the confrontation with Bazu boiling back up in his stomach. The door opened and Marsha Agambe beckoned them inside. She wore the same black trousers from their earlier meeting. No jacket, now, just a simple, white, cotton shirt.

The kitchen was spotless, furnished with white wooden units, a stainless steel sink and a plain pine table with four chairs. Gabriel sat at the table, opposite Marsha Agambe. Foreman remained standing. Gabriel asked the question that had been on his mind since their first meeting.

"Mrs Agambe, I have to ask this. Why have you not gone to the police?" He looked round at Foreman as he said this.

She looked at him with soft brown eyes, unveiled this time, except by the grief that kept them hooded.

"I could have done that very easily. But what good would it do? Would it bring Philip back? Would it help me expose your Prime Minister? Would it leave me open to further attacks? This way, I have you to help keep me safe until the conference. Do that, and we will see. I am not a saint, Gabriel Wolfe. But I try to be true to my faith. To forgive. I expect you are the sort of man skilled in evading capture. Maybe you will get out of Zimbabwe before the police find you."

Gabriel inclined his head.

"Thank you," he said in a quiet voice. Then, "You said you would show me the evidence you have against Barbara Sutherland."

"And I will. But first, I want you to tell me something."

"What?"

"The story she told you, to make you believe it was right to murder my husband."

35

A Test of Character

GABRIEL took a deep breath, aware that he was facing another test of his character. He turned his head as his chair moved a little. Behind him, Foreman had placed his hands on the backrest.

"She told me that your husband was channeling UN aid to an Islamist terrorist group run by a cousin of his. It was responsible for the deaths of nineteen British nurses and three members of the SAS. She told me he was planning a coup here in Zimbabwe."

As he relayed the narrative Barbara Sutherland had outlined for him as justification for Agambe's murder, Gabriel realised two things at the same time.

First, that was how he saw his actions now. Not as a "targeting", a "mission goal", or even a "kill", but as a cold-blooded, brutal, and premeditated murder.

Second, that he wasn't sure he believed the story any more. It was too clean, too perfect. Enough moral outrage to overcome his queasiness about going after an elected politician, an anti-terror message, and the endorsement of MI6 and the CIA to round the whole thing off. But then, Don said he'd seen evidence, a dossier from Barbara. Was there room for doubt, even at this stage? It would have to wait. Marsha Agambe was smiling at him, but her forehead was creased with lines.

"You know, I could give you chapter and verse about Philip's character. About his fanatical belief in democracy. About the scrupulousness with which he runs – he ran – his department, and even his personal affairs, so that no whiff of corruption should ever swirl about him. But I do not need to do any of that. I can give you a single fact that will puncture that woman's lies." She glared at him. "Philip's parents were both only children. No siblings, either of them. And therefore no cousins. It is a matter of public record. You can look it up if you don't believe me."

It was a lazy error. But somehow, Gabriel knew it was precisely the sort of lazy error an overconfident politician, backed by powerful friends in two separate intelligence agencies, would make. She'd probably added it in herself as a bit of back-story.

"I don't need to check. I believe you. All I can say is that I was set up. In fact, there were two attempts to kill me and . . ." he had been about to say "my partner", but something held him back. Why drag Britta any deeper into this unholy shitstorm than she was already? "Clearly they failed. But only just."

Marsha Agambe leaned back in her chair. She raised her hands to her face and rubbed her eyes with long slender fingers.

"Foreman," she said. "Could you get the dossier, please? And perhaps some beers. I am sure Gabriel is thirsty."

Foreman moved from behind Gabriel and left the room. He returned a few moments later carrying a thick black cardboard folder, held closed with a red rubber band. The folder was at least an inch thick and stuffed with a variety of document types to judge from the different colours, sizes and thicknesses of paper that peeped out from between its dog-eared covers. He set it on the table and turned to the fridge.

While Foreman popped the crown caps from three bottles of lager, Marsha pulled the thick rubber band from the folder. Turning it round to face Gabriel, she opened it and placed her finger on the top document. It was a photocopy of a bill of lading for military hardware of some sort. Gabriel recognised the style of the text, but not the individual reference numbers.

"When Barbara Sutherland was Secretary of State for Defence, she paid many visits to Africa, helping weapons manufacturers ply their dirty trade. That is when we believe she began taking kickbacks. Everything is in there, Gabriel. Ten years' work by my husband and his associates. Not just here in Zimbabwe, but internationally. He had links with a great many people who were all united in their desire to root out corruption, wherever it was to be found."

Gabriel interrupted her. "I'm sorry, but would any of those associates have worked for Scrutiny International?"

"Yes. How do you know of them? They are not exactly high-profile."

"It doesn't matter. I . . . read about them somewhere. You were saying?"

"I was saying that the missing link in the chain came into his possession just a month or so ago. Testimony from a London gemstone dealer confirming that conflict diamonds had found their way into the hands of your Prime Minister and then been traded illegally. There is a solid chain of evidence linking her to illegal trade in arms, blood diamonds, sanctions-busting, you name it."

"You've got a copy, right?"

"At my lawyer's office: Alice Rukuni. She is a partner at Penduka, Ballantyne and Farai. They are the third-biggest firm in Harare. I left explicit instructions that they should make it public if anything happens to me before the conference."

Gabriel reached for the folder, to bring it closer. As he did so, Marsha Agambe looked down at her chest and flicked her fingers over the fabric of her shirt. She tutted.

"What is that?" she said.

He looked at her. A small red dot, perhaps an eighth of an inch across, hovered over her heart. As she brushed at it, the dot rippled across the backs of her fingers.

His lips formed themselves into the shape of a warning shout. But it was too late.

The kitchen window blew inwards and Marsha Agambe's white shirt puffed out, a red blossom flowering in place of the neat dot. The door of the low, glass-fronted cupboard behind her exploded, masking the sound of the shot, which had caught up with the supersonic bullet. Needle-pointed shards of glass flew out in all directions to join those from the shattered window. Blood spewed from her back, spattering the wall in a circle of droplets and sprays.

As her body slumped on the chair, head flung backwards, arms thrown out and down to the sides, Gabriel pushed back from his own chair and jumped to his feet, heart pounding, palms slick with sweat, head jerking from side to side, searching for cover. Then he looked down.

The red dot was back, spider-still over his own heart. He willed himself not to move, even though every fibre of his being, every instinct, was screaming at him to drop to the floor before the assassin could get another shot in.

Something curious happened.

The dot wagged from left to right, as if shaking its head.

Then it centred on his heart again.

"Foreman!" he shouted. "Are you OK? Where are you?"

Out of the corner of his eye, he saw Foreman stroll back into the kitchen. He hadn't seen him leave, he now realised. Had thought he was still pouring the beers.

"Oh, I am fine, believe me. And soon I will be more than fine. Soon, I am going to be a very rich man." Then he pulled his pistol, an old Browning .45 calibre, its steel barrel scratched and pitted. He pointed it at Gabriel.

"What are you doing? Someone just killed your sister. We have to get out."

But instead of moving towards the door, Foreman just looked down at the dead body of his sister, prodded her hip with his toe then turned back to face Gabriel, grinning.

"Technically? She was just my half-sister. Always one for bossing me about with her high-toned morals. But now I've got a payday coming. Plenty of people in this country are doing very well, thank you, without her blowing the whistle. They promised me enough money to leave this stinking country and move to America. But first we're going to get rid of you, my English friend." He extended his right arm, aiming the pistol at the centre of Gabriel's face. "When I'm done here, it will look like you killed yourself in remorse after murdering my sister."

Gabriel remained still. Remained calm. It wasn't particularly difficult, since the red dot had slid off his chest, jumped back six feet to the wall beyond, then jumped forward again as it found Foreman Agambe's neck and crept upward until it was resting on his right temple. Gabriel squeezed his eyes tight shut and turned his head away.

Foreman laughed. "Don't worry. It will all be over soon."

Foreman's head exploded with a dull smack, covering Gabriel in blood and brain matter and bits of bone and hair. The report from the sniper's rifle was a dull thump from somewhere outside the broken window. Gabriel moved to grab the folder from the table, but another round from the unseen assassin's rifle burst it into a cloud of paper fragments. He turned and ran for the front door, pausing only to grab a thin navy windcheater he assumed belonged to Foreman. He took the stairs rather than the lift, hurtling down them three at a time.

From above, he heard two more rounds burst into the flat. This time, the impacts were followed by a dull roar as furnishings, books and papers caught fire. Whoever the shooter was, they'd switched to incendiary rounds. The place would be an inferno in seconds. As he passed another landing, he jammed his elbow through the glass of a fire alarm, bringing residents out from their apartments, faces anxious, shouting to each other above the clanging fire bell.

Now wearing the windcheater, which hid the worst of the bloodstains on his clothing, Gabriel reached the ground floor and ran into the street, heart racing, wondering whether the shooter would decide to kill him after all. Bazu was still prowling, but, having met Gabriel once, seemed disinclined to put up any sort of challenge. She looked in his direction, sniffed loudly, then trotted off across the road, presumably to find somewhere a little less likely to set her coat on fire.

There was a tap set into the wall on the side of the apartment block, and Gabriel stopped long enough to wash his face and hands. Walking quickly but avoiding breaking into a run, Gabriel retraced his steps along the street, back towards the commercialised end, with its bars and restaurants. Half an hour later, having stopped at a crossroads as a convoy of fire engines sped past, he'd reached his hotel and was pulling a business card from his wallet.

36

Appointment with Counsel

"THIS is Tatyana."

Gabriel sat back on the bed as relief flooded his system.

"Tatyana, it's Gabriel Wolfe. I rescued –"

"Yes! My knight in shining armour. How can I help you, dear Gabriel?"

"I'm in a spot of trouble. In Zimbabwe. Harare, as a matter of fact. I need to get home but I have a feeling my passport won't be enough to get a scheduled flight. I think I'm under surveillance. I wondered . . ."

"If I could help? Of course, silly boy. Do you know what? I am in Sierra Leone right now. We have a diamond field here. There was trouble with local gang. They thought we would pay them protection money. All sorted now, I am happy to say. So can you stay, how do you put it, under radar, maybe for one day longer?"

Gabriel glanced instinctively at the window, even though the curtains were drawn tight, admitting not so much as a glimmer of moonlight.

"Yes. That shouldn't be a problem."

"Good, good. Listen, then. I will tell my pilot we have new flight plan. London, yes, but by way of Harare. When we are landing, tomorrow evening, I call you. You must get to airport and meet me in zone for corporate jets. How, I do not know. But you are man of action, so will find way. My plane is easy to find. Purple and gold Boeing Business Jet

Three. Very pretty. Garin Group logo on side."

"Thank you, Tatyana. Until tomorrow evening."

"Yes, Gabriel. Until then."

Gabriel suddenly realised he was hungry. The club sandwich he'd eaten with Britta seemed like a very long time ago. He ordered a steak and a beer from room service and settled down on the bed to wait.

"Fuck me, you're in a hell of a mess," he muttered, as he flicked through the channels on the TV. He found a local news channel and watched idly as a reporter stood outside the apartment block that, until very recently, had been the home of Marsha Agambe. It was now a partly smoking ruin, with firefighters running behind the reporter, uncoiling hoses and directing the thick jets of water up to the tenth floor.

He leaned over and grabbed a notebook and pencil, both imprinted with the name of the hotel, and started scribbling notes.

Philip Agambe: compiled dossier on Barbara Sutherland showing alleged corruption. Murdered by GW.

Marsha Agambe: stopped from presenting dossier at SADC by unknown assassin.

Foreman Agambe – meant to kill GW, having betrayed (?) sister for payout from local opposition. Killed by UA as above.

Barbara Sutherland: set up GW to murder GA to get rid of possibility of exposure? Or honest politician being attacked by Islamist terror financier and wife?

Don Webster: evasive, uncomfortable at last meeting. Why? Under pressure from PM? Still trust him 100%.

GW: under surveillance. But not shot by UA. Why? Unrelated murder?

Dossier destroyed. Copy with MA's lawyers in Harare. <u>Track down and see with own eyes for definitive proof.</u>

Gabriel underlined the final sentence of his notes. It seemed to offer the best chance of getting conclusive proof of the rightness or wrongness of Philip Agambe's claims. How this squared with staying under the radar, he wasn't sure. But he had to know.

The steak, when it came, was leathery, despite his having asked for it medium-rare. He chewed as much of the brown meat as he could manage, ate the mashed sweet potato – surprisingly good, rich with butter and black pepper – sank the beer, then walked to the window. Standing to one side, he lifted the thick curtain away from the frame just enough to peer out at the moonlit city beyond.

The streetlamps cast a sickly yellow glow over everything but they were dim and there were plenty of shadows. A body could stay in the lee of the buildings, or keep to back streets, and move about unseen and undisturbed, with a bit of luck. But would Lady Luck be smiling on Gabriel tonight? He only knew of one way to find out.

Ten minutes later, he left the hotel, the collar turned up on his windcheater, which was now reversed so that its navy blue lining was outermost. It was half-past nine, and the streets were largely free of traffic.

Gabriel had checked out the location of Penduka, Ballantyne and Farai on a PC in the hotel's lobby. As soon as he could, he took a left down a narrow side street. He walked to the far end then turned right, intending to track north, parallel to the main road, following the long side of a rectangular route that would bring him out at a crossroads. The law firm's offices were two hundred yards farther down Simon Muzenda Street.

The street was dark except for occasional patches of light spilling from bars and the waxy sheen cast over the road by the moon. Through habit, drilled into him by SAS and military intelligence instructors, Gabriel kept to the outer edge of the pavement. Alleyways opened onto the street every half a block or so and these pitch-black canyons seemed tailor-made for muggers, drug dealers, pimps and prostitutes. Basically, people Gabriel neither wanted to meet, nor had time for.

Lady Luck had gone for a tea-break.

As Gabriel approached one of these black slits between two buildings, a tall, dark-skinned figure stepped out, followed, a second later, by two more.

Not one of the men was under six feet tall, and two of them were correspondingly broad through the chest.

The third man was fat rather than muscular, though his sheer girth meant he was packing a certain amount of beef under all the blubber.

Their grins, as he slowed and then stopped, glinted in the moonlight.

Like him, they wore baseball caps pulled down over their eyes.

Unlike him, they had knives in their hands.

Not dainty little flick-knives, either. These were more like the sorts of tools a butcher would use for jointing a carcass: deep-bellied, steel blades that caught the light and winked at him from their edges. Edges, he had no doubt, sharp enough to remove a man's hand without stopping for muscle, bone or sinew.

Gabriel pulled up short, leaving a seven-foot gap between him and his adversaries. Now he stood, feet shoulder-width apart, hands hanging loosely at his sides, turning his head slowly in a short arc, fixing each man with eye contact for a split second, before moving on to the next. A steel dustbin stood to one side of the entrance of the bar behind him. He'd noted it as soon as the men had emerged from the alley.

"Hey, white boy. You are a long way from home, yes?" This was the first man talking. One of the fitter pair of the three.

"Yes, I am. I have no money, look." Gabriel slowly pushed his hands into the pockets of his windcheater and pulled them inside out.

"Fuck you! Of course you have money."

They made no move to close with him. Gabriel squared his shoulders, trying to maximise his size, though as he was several inches shorter than they were, and slim where they were heavily muscled, or just lardy in the case of number three, that achieved little.

The man doing the talking was right, as a matter of fact. Gabriel had a roll of twenty-dollar bills in his left-hand trouser pocket and more strapped round his waist with tape.

"No, I don't," he said. "But I'll show you what I do have." His right hand opened to reveal the butterfly knife. He flipped it up with a steely rasp, and around on itself, until the handles closed on the blade, which he held up nice and high, in the man's eyeline.

He waved it from left to right. "See how the light catches it? Nice and sharp. You want my money? You have to get past my friend here first."

The three men stood still, though they had spread out into a line. The leader spoke.

"Julius. Take him."

The fat man looked at his boss, then back at Gabriel, then at the knife in Gabriel's hands. Then he lunged forward, butcher knife held high over his head.

As he came within stabbing distance, his knife descending towards Gabriel's chest, Gabriel stepped to one side. The big man's movements were so clumsy and slow, Gabriel had the eerie sensation he had somehow entered a slow-motion version of the scene, where he moved as an insect might among humans.

He needed to stop these three and continue with the mission he had set himself, but he didn't want to leave any more corpses behind when he left Zimbabwe.

As the big man sailed past him, Gabriel kicked him on the ankle, tangling his legs under him.

Falling, the man threw his arms out.

Gabriel caught his right wrist and twisted hard.

The man yelped as nerves and ligaments were mashed against each other inside his wrist, and dropped the knife.

Leaving his man to crash heavily to the ground, with a sound that suggested he'd fractured his cheekbone on the pavement, Gabriel bent and retrieved the butcher knife. He jumped back, delivered a short but brutally effective kick to the fallen man's throat, eliciting a choking cry and ran back to the bar, where he snatched up the lid of the bin by its rim.

"Come on, Thomas, we can take him, and his money," the gang's leader said.

They started towards Gabriel, but he had another trick waiting for them. He swung his arm back then flung the steel lid over their heads. The lure of the flying disc was too strong, and both men looked straight up at it. In the time it took them to straighten their necks, Gabriel moved closer and chopped first one, then the other, across the throat.

They staggered back, looking at him, eyes wide with surprise and, *good*, fear for the first time. They clutched their throats and were focused entirely on trying to drag air into their lungs past their rapidly swelling windpipes.

Gabriel had never been keen on the more balletic karate moves Master Zhao had occasionally demonstrated to him during his apprenticeship in Hong Kong: the jumping kicks and spinning manoeuvres designed to throw opponents off balance mentally as much as physically. Now, however, he felt it would be appropriate.

As his body rotated in midair between them, the men must have sensed they were on the losing side of this particular conflict. What happened next confirmed it. Gabriel's boot heels connected with a temple here and the point of a jaw there. They went down like creatures stunned by a slaughterman, their butcher knives clattering to the pavement between them as they fell.

Looking around, breathing heavily, Gabriel realised he was still not alone. A small group of children were watching him. They wore scruffy T-shirts and hoodies, zip-up cardigans and jeans, trainers and wide-eyed expressions of admiration. He collected the other two butcher knives from the ground and dropped all three down a drain in the gutter a few feet further up the street. They landed with a shallow splash.

He unpeeled a twenty from the roll in his pocket and held it out. The children hung back.

"It's all right," he said offering them a smile. "They were bad men. I was defending myself. Take the money and don't tell anyone you saw me. Okay?"

An older girl, maybe the same age as Nathalie Smith, came forward, taking tiny steps. She wore her hair in braids, coiled tightly on the top of her head. She stretched her arm out in front of her and gently plucked the banknote from between his fingers.

"Are they dead?" she whispered.

He shook his head.

"No. Just sleeping."

"Good." She looked over at the man who'd done all the talking. He lay still, eyes closed, leant half-upright against the wall of the building. She walked over to him and kicked him in the stomach. "They make us give them half what we make from our jobs."

The she turned to her entourage.

"Come on!" she shouted. "Who wants fried chicken?"

They all shouted at once then turned and ran off back down the street.

Marvelling, once again, at the strange ways of children, Gabriel moved away himself, taking a right into a brighter street, then a left and another right figuring he should put as much distance between himself and his attackers before they regained consciousness. He estimated the lawyer's building was ten minutes away.

37

Antisocial Climber

SASHA Beck was an expert in all the ways one might separate a person from the life force that pulsed in their blood vessels, nerves, muscles, brain, and that mysterious entity called a soul. She had also acquired specialist knowledge in a range of complementary skills. These included explosives, commercial and improvised. Breaking and entering. Computer hacking. Free climbing. Forgery. And physical transformation.

She sought out her instructors on the Internet. They were always in need of extra money and were invariably glad to make some on the side in return for sharing their expertise. Actors, computer programmers, demolition experts, career criminals, athletes. She knew where to find them and exactly what to offer them. It was another of her talents.

On this particular evening, she was drawing on the techniques taught to her by a Frenchwoman named Marielle Zadou.

Marielle was a free climber – a lunatic in Sasha's opinion – who set off for the tops of vertical cliffs wearing only two pieces of Lycra and a pair of thin-soled, rubberised canvas shoes, and carrying nothing for the ascent but a pouch of powdered resin.

However, their relationship as master and pupil did mean that she had just been able to scale the exterior of the office block in which Penduka, Ballantyne and Farai conducted their business. She had ascended the rear of the building, despite there being neither fire escape nor any sort of drainpipe. Now she rested on a window ledge no more than five inches wide, careful to keep the small black rucksack she carried away from the wall so it didn't lever her off the ledge.

Pulling a dull, red, rubber sucker the size of a side plate from her belt, Sasha placed it against the window and twisted the plastic covered handle through ninety degrees. She felt the vacuum build under her fingers and gave the sucker an experimental tug. It was glued to the glass as tightly as a limpet to a rock.

Sasha withdrew a glass cutter and inscribed a circle around the edge of the sucker. With a jerk, she pulled the glass disc out from the window. Reaching in, she bent her wrist so that she could unlatch the handle. Then it was a simple matter of leaning out seven storeys above the traffic and pedestrians while she half-pulled-half-pushed the window out so that she could shimmy round the frame and slide her body into the office.

Hamilton's intelligence was gold-plated. The back wall of the open-plan office was decorated with the firm's name in foot-high, brushed aluminium letters. As a partner, Alice Farai enjoyed the luxury of a private office. There they all were, arrayed down the longer side of the main space, glass from waist-level upwards, dark wooden panels from there to the thickly carpeted floor. Sasha walked between the spotless desks in the centre of the room. She held a slim, black, rubber torch, and swept its narrow blue-white beam along the offices. *And look, darling! They've even painted her name on the door to make our job easier.*

The door was locked. Had Sasha been planning merely to steal the dossier, she would have picked the cheap lock in seconds, tutting at its slipshod construction and rudimentary engineering. As, on this occasion, she had no such plans, she reared back and kicked the door open with a crash and splintering as the frame gave way. Once inside, she stopped for a moment.

"Now, Miss Farai," she said aloud. "Desk drawer or filing cabinet?" It didn't really matter, since she intended to break into every locked space in the office till she found what she was looking for. But Sasha prided herself on her ability to intuit where normal people might hide their treasures. "It's a client folder, like any other. But I bet Marsha Agambe told you to guard it with your life. Eeeny, meeny, miney, mo," she said in a sing-song voice, before crossing to the desk. "Into the desk drawer you must go."

The drawers were locked on a common rail located behind their fronts. With nothing on hand to force them, Sasha fished her lock picks out of her belt. She inserted the two slim steel tools and gave them a few twists to separate the tumblers inside the barrel. Then, using a gentle bumping movement with the heel of her hand while holding the picks in place, she had the lock open.

Reasoning that the top would hold a few items of stationery, maybe some paper handkerchiefs and a packet of painkillers, she started with the deep drawer at the bottom. It housed a set of suspension files, each topped with a plastic label holder enclosed the letters of the alphabet.

"Oh, darling. This is too easy," she whispered.

Pushing her fingers down into the first, fat, hanging V of card, Sasha extracted all the documents within and laid them on the desk in front of her. They were enclosed in individual manila card wallets, hand-lettered in neat blue capitals with the client's name at the top-right. The second file bore the name, AGAMBE. She opened it. Then hissed out an oath. "Shit! I didn't climb up here for your fucking last will and testament, darling, now did I?"

Standing up and knocking the fatly padded leather chair over behind her, she hurled the thin wallet of papers at the wall. It opened in mid-flight, spinning the sheets of paper into the air, which was still cool from the day's air-conditioning.

"The filing cabinet it is, then."

After another few seconds' work with her lock picks, the steel cabinet was broached. Starting at the top, Sasha worked methodically, running her fingertips along the tops of the suspension files, searching for the dossier on Barbara Sutherland.

The top drawer yielded nothing. She moved down to the second. Again, after a careful study of each file inside, she puffed her cheeks out and slammed the drawer shut with a clang. She hit her target inside the third drawer. Unlike the first two, it did not contain any suspension files. Instead, it held a stack of shallow cardboard boxes, each secured with a red ribbon, tied with a bow over a knot.

"Well, now," she breathed. "What have we here?"

Sasha lifted the stack of boxes out and squatted down beside the filing cabinet to start her search. Using a short-bladed knife, she slit all the ribbons and opened the boxes one by one. As each box failed to reveal the dossier, she tossed it away, scattering its contents on the carpet. With one to go, she frowned as she lifted the lid. Then she smiled, all the tension draining way from her facial muscles. Inside the box was a pale blue folder, secured with a thick brown rubber band. Written across the top were two words:

SUTHERLAND / GORDIAN

Her brief from Hamilton had been clear: destroy any and all files relating to his company. But Sasha believed in the power of information. She decided to make the files vanish, though not in the way her client wanted. Smiling, she pinched the black plastic clips holding her rucksack closed, loosened the drawstring and slid the folder inside.

Her hand, when it emerged, was closed around a lump of Semtex the size of a grapefruit. It smelled of putty and hot plastic. Her colleagues in the business laughed at her for using "that old Soviet rubbish", but as she liked to point out, it was just as destructive as more modern plastic explosives, such as C-4, and far easier to get hold of.

Sasha pushed a blasting cap into the Semtex and wired the whole lot to a battery and a cheap watch she'd bought from a street vendor the previous day. With the watch's timer set for ten minutes, she squashed the grey lump down onto the desk, wiped the greasy residue off on her trousers and headed back for the window.

Two minutes later, her plimsolled feet hit the ground and she turned and walked off towards downtown Harare. She found a bar that didn't look too fussy about dress codes, went in, bought herself a large gin and tonic, and settled down in a corner booth to wait.

38

The Absence of Evidence

EMERGING back onto Simon Muzenda Street, Gabriel stopped and looked around to get his bearings, then continued on towards the crossroads and the office building housing Penduka, Ballantyne and Farai. Ideally, there would be a back entrance, perhaps protected by a flimsy lock or a door secured with a push bar, neither of which would present much of an obstacle.

When he had identified the building, a handsome edifice of red brick and sandstone rendered a soft grey by the moonlight, he turned down a side street, looking for the rear entrance. As he found the even narrower road that led to the back of the office block, something made him look up. What he saw made him dart into the shadows and watch more closely.

A slender, black-clad figure was climbing down the outside wall of the building, apparently without ropes or gear of any kind. The figure, as it neared the ground, resolved itself into a female form, with long, straight black hair tied up somehow. She reached the ground and strolled off away from Gabriel, before disappearing round the far corner of the block.

There had been times, during his military service, first in the Parachute Regiment, and then in the SAS, when Gabriel had heard an inner voice telling him in no uncertain terms that he and his men were in terrible and immediate danger. Not in the way he still occasionally heard from Smudge, though. And even those moments were becoming less frequent since Fariyah Crace had explained how his hallucinations were really his own subconscious attempting to communicate with his conscious mind. No, these early-warning messages were more like intuition, enhanced by some of the world's toughest training, and then given voice.

Gabriel had learned to trust this inner voice, and it had had saved lives each time he had listened. He listened now. It was telling him that to attempt to enter the building now would be an extremely unwise course of action. Yes, the figure might have been a mere cat burglar after property deeds, jewels or stacks of high-denomination dollar bills. But the explosions and burning-plastic smells of the apartment block fire were still fresh in his mind. As was the sight of the bullet-riddled corpses of Marsha Agambe and her brother. So he tended to believe that she was connected to – or the same person as – their killer.

What would I do, if I'd been hired to assassinate Philip Agambe's widow and erase all traces of a potentially incriminating dossier against Barbara Sutherland? Torch the apartment, obviously. Yes, but what else? Search out the copy. There's always a copy. And destroy it.

He looked up at the building. And waited.

He counted his heartbeats.

. . . One . . .

. . . Two . . .

A pigeon alighted on the pavement in front of him and began pecking around a scrap of discarded fried chicken.

. . . Four . . .

A good-looking black couple passed him, laughing, holding hands.

A taxi sped by, electric guitars blaring from its stereo.

. . . Seven . . .

. . . Eight . . .

. . . Nine . . .

The explosion was almost beautiful.

Above the loud *crump* as the Semtex detonated, the hypersonic blast wave pushed the floor-to-ceiling ball of fire outwards in a compressed sheet that shattered every window. The flying splinters of glass were lit by the moon and for a moment appeared to be a floating layer of diamonds, suspended above the street on a sheet of orange fire.

The smashing began seconds later as the glass hit the pavement and road.

A few pedestrians who were too close screamed as they suffered cuts from the tumbling shards and fell to their knees or sat heavily against cars or on the kerb.

Car alarms were set off by falling lumps of masonry smacking into their thin steel roofs. And overlaid on the whole scene of destruction was the smell: burnt paper, the sharp ozone tang of electrical fires as PCs and office equipment caught fire, and the acrid, throat-catching aroma of plastic and upholstery foam turning into gas.

From his vantage point, Gabriel watched as the remains of the law firm's documents flamed and fluttered in the breeze, swirling in eddies and miniature whirlwinds, glowing fragments of blackened paper, their edges crawling with strings of orange sparks.

Somewhere among them were the remains of the dossier allegedly incriminating the British Prime Minister in corruption on a breathtaking scale. And now? There was nothing. The Agambes were dead and their "evidence" had been reduced to carbon atoms swirling and separating in the air above Harare.

Sirens interrupted his train of thought, and soon the streets around the building were blocked by fire engines, police cars and ambulances. *Time to move on, Wolfe. You're done here.*

*

A faint ringing from the cocktail glasses hanging from their bases in racks above the barman's head sounded a tinkling counterpoint to the *basso profundo* rumble from the Semtex detonating.

As a fan of Mozart, Puccini and Verdi, Sasha often imagined her work in terms of the voices of each member of an opera cast. Knives were the sopranos:

virtuosi but temperamental, requiring great delicacy in how they were handled. Pistols were the tenors: flashy showoffs that demanded centre stage. Rifles were the baritones: less glamorous than their slighter colleagues in the armourer's locker but equally devastating. And explosives were the basses: deep-chested shouters who could make the walls of your chest vibrate. Or, if you were the target, burst like a balloon.

Now she smiled, raising her glass to her reflection in a mirror on the far wall and signalling to the barman for another gin and tonic. The other customers had run from their tables and disappeared onto the street where they were busy filming the conflagration on their phones or texting friends about this latest outrage on Harare's streets.

As the barman placed the new drink on her table, releasing its perfume of juniper and quinine substitute, the door opened and in walked – *of all people, darling!* – the man from the Agambes' apartment. Sasha watched him intently, taking in his muscular but not overdeveloped build, his dark eyes and his short, straight, black hair. Something about the way he carried himself lit up a sign in her brain. "Soldier", the sign said, in bright, white letters. It wasn't a problem. She'd dealt with soldiers plenty of times in her career, and besides, he was cute. It was why she'd shot the idiot brother as well. The question that flickered on and off behind the sign was this: is he one of Hamilton's missing mercenaries?

As he turned from the bar with a gin and tonic, she smiled at him and raised her voice so that he would hear her, adopting, on a whim, an accent from the Deep South.

"A dangerous place, Harare. One never knows what sort of devilry might occur."

He looked over at her, and came over.

"It certainly is. May I join you?"

She nodded and pushed a chair out towards him with her right toe.

*

Gabriel took in the woman's appearance in a glance. She was strikingly good looking. Straight, dark hair pinned up at the back of her head with a couple of coils escaping to lie against her long, pale neck. Lips a deep, blackish red, almost as if she'd stained them eating cherries, the lower fuller than the upper. Her black eyebrows were finely curved and perfectly graduated from a square edge at the bridge of her nose to tapering points just above the outer edges of her eye sockets. Below them, her eyelids were shaded in a smudgy combination of purple and gold. Asked to estimate her age, he would have said, mid-thirties. Too old to be scaling office blocks and blowing them up? He wasn't sure. Maybe he could find out.

"Name's Cordelia," she said. "Lipscomb."

She held out her hand, which he shook as he sat down.

"Rhodes," he said. "Rhodes Cheaney."

"My, my, how very *exotic* we both sound. Were our parents afraid of conformity, do you suppose?"

Gabriel thought back to his English father, a career diplomat, and his half-Chinese mother, a private tutor. They had lived and breathed conformity, except for the single rash act of their marriage itself.

"I suppose they must have been. Thanks for inviting me over. It's a bit lonely out here." He raised his glass and watched her eyes as she clinked hers against it, raising a loud ping from the rim.

"In Harare? Or Africa? You sound like you're a long way from home."

"I am."

"British?"

"Mm hmm," he said. He sipped his drink and relaxed as the cold gin hit his stomach.

"I, myself, am an American. Though perhaps you figured that out for yourself?"

Gabriel smiled. He was beginning to like this glamorous woman with her antebellum manners.

"Well, your accent is something of a giveaway."

"So is yours, dear boy. Tell me, what brings you to this, if I may say so, *Godforsaken* country?"

Her eyes narrowed slightly as she asked her question. A casual observer wouldn't have noticed, but Gabriel was not a casual observer. He had been trained to notice things.

He noticed this.

"I'm a doctor. I come out from time to time to do *pro bono* work – eye operations at the children's hospital. How about you?"

"A physician," she breathed. "Giving sight back to those poor little black children. And for nothing. You truly are a saint. For myself, I'm afraid I am somewhat below you in the pecking order of virtue."

"What do you do?"

"I am an attorney. What you British would call a barrister."

"Defence or prosecution?"

"Oh, prosecution. I like to put the bad guys away." Then she winked.

The bar refilled as the patrons finished their texts and uploaded their videos, and the noise level increased. Sasha leaned closer to Gabriel.

"If I may ask, is there a Mrs Cheaney? I don't see a wedding band, but I know men are less concerned about such things."

He shook his head. "No. Footloose and fancy free."

"Oh, I am sure you won't remain single for too much longer, looking the way you do and with such . . . obvious qualities. But tell me, do you travel out here alone every time? Surely you have someone to chaperone you?"

"No, just me."

Gabriel knew she was probing for clues about his true identity. Maybe he could return the favour.

"And you, Cordelia. Are you over here for a case? I didn't realise American lawyers could practise overseas."

"No, I left my law books in Georgia. I've been visiting with family. My sister and brother live here. They're missionaries. Can you believe it? In this day and age, it sounds so old fashioned. But I found out tonight they're moving on to new pastures."

"And apart from your family, do you have any other friends here? Other lawyers?"

"Sadly, no. Although from what I hear, it can be a tough place to practise."

Gabriel could almost hear the rapiers clanging as they fenced this way and that, looking for an opening without appearing to. He decided, whoever she was, she was far too skillful to give anything away. He drained his glass.

"Well, I must go, I'm afraid. I have a delicate operation tomorrow that I need to prepare for. It's been a pleasure."

He stood, hand extended, and she matched his movements. They shook hands and then he turned to go.

"I hope we meet again, Rhodes," she said. "I would love to find out what makes a man like you tick."

He walked through the drinkers without looking over his shoulder. He could feel her gaze drilling him right between the shoulder blades.

39

Not Alone, After All

THE next morning, at 0815, Gabriel sat in his hotel room, eating smoked ham rolls and drinking the passable coffee he'd ordered for breakfast from room service.

A "Do Not Disturb" sign hung on the outer door knob. He had no intention of leaving the room until Tatyana texted him to say his ride had arrived. And if she didn't text? Then he would exfiltrate under his own steam. He still had the card Darryl Burroughs had given him on their first night in Zimbabwe. He still had a pocket full of US dollars. And he still had his wits. They had got him out of worse scrapes than this.

After showering and dressing, he sat at the desk, picked up the satellite phone and called Don. He'd briefly considered buying a burner phone in one of the many shops that seemed to sell them, but just as quickly dismissed the idea. The satphone was encrypted, at least, and he had no idea whether Sutherland would be able to discover who was calling Don from a foreign burner.

Aha! So we're sure she's behind it then, are we?

The phone at the other end began to ring with a furry sound, then the recorded message clicked in and Gabriel's heart jumped a little as Don's familiar, soft voice began to speak:

"This is Don Webster. Leave a message, Old Sport."

At the final two words, it did more than jump a little. It leapt right into his throat. "Old Sport." Don's name for him. It was a message. Had to be. That Don wanted him to make contact. But what to say? He hung up. He needed to think. He cast his mind back to their previous conversation. He wanted to let Don know that the attempts to silence him, permanently, had failed, and that he was still alive and in the game. And a code word that would let Don know his identity, but nobody else. Five minutes later, he dialled again. After Don's outbound message finished, Gabriel left his own, in an Australian accent.

"Mr Webster? I'm calling from Babbage's? Give us a call, mate, and we can fix up a time to deliver your lawnmower. Bye for now."

Would it fool any spooks who were monitoring Don's calls, trying to get a fix on Gabriel's location? Gabriel had no way of knowing. But he had to try to reach his old CO somehow. As he ended the call, his personal phone vibrated – two short buzzes – on the nightstand. He jumped up and crossed the floor to the bed in two long strides and snatched up the phone. It was a text alert. The faint characters hidden by the unlock screen said, "Britta." He swiped his unlock pattern, a simplified Chinese character that meant truth, and tapped the icon.

Back safely. Wasn't missed. At flat. Take care. I love you. B x

"I love you, too, Britta," he whispered. Then stopped, and frowned. "I do?" he asked, in a louder voice this time. He sat down on the bed and cradled the phone in his hands, looking at the text. When had that happened? He'd thought they just enjoyed each other's company, whether between the sheets, in a restaurant or exchanging automatic fire with African militia, or hired muscle driving Humvees.

His thumbs hovered over the screen until it faded to black and he had to reswipe his unlock pattern. The process repeated itself a dozen times before he answered.

Good. I will. You take care. I love you too. G x

He pressed SEND.

"Fuck me, Falskog, that's a complication I really could have done without."

But he was smiling as he said it. His insides felt jittery, but not the anxious worms of doubt squirming in his stomach before closing with the enemy. More like the feeling he used to get before taking to the pitch for a rugby sevens game back in Hong Kong, where, as a teenager, he'd excelled at the fast-moving sport.

Gabriel found he was running through all kinds of possibilities in his head for a life back in England with the red-haired Swede he was apparently in love with. Married with children, pushing buggies through a park in Chiswick near her flat? No. Too conventional. Living in a city-centre apartment in Stockholm, teaching the kids to sail? Better. Running a discreet private security firm offering protection to A-listers, living like gypsies in expensive boutique hotels in Manhattan, London, Paris and Beijing. Better still. He shook his head, like a dog trying to rid itself of fleas.

"How about disavowed, disappeared or dead? Every trace of your former existence wiped from the record like pen off a whiteboard?" he muttered.

The image didn't appeal. He went to the window, opened a slit in the curtain on the left side and peered out. The sky was a uniform whitish-grey. People crowded the pavement, cars and trucks jammed the road, and small motorcycles wove amongst them. Through the rudimentary double-glazing he could hear the constant bleating and blaring of the vehicles' horns.

A plan existed in his mind, but it was vague. Pressed to explain, Gabriel would have said, "Get to London, confront Prime Minister, expose her to British media, keep head down till smoke clears." Was it realistic? Almost certainly not.

Early on in his Army career, Gabriel had realised that captain, the rank he'd attained in the SAS, was the highest he would ever rise. He was a tactician, not a strategist, gifted with the ability to achieve short-term goals efficiently and effectively, but not able, or, if truth were told, interested, in developing long-term solutions to big problems.

How to clear that block of flats of enemy combatants? *Leave it to me, Sir.* How to get from this *wadi* to that town in stripped-down dune buggies? *I'm on it, Sir.* How to achieve peace between warring religious groups intent on exterminating each other in the name of God? *Got to go and clean my weapon, Sir.*

But what other options did he have? It seemed clear to Gabriel now that, barring a development he was incapable of imagining, Barbara Sutherland had instructed him to kill an innocent man. And she was behind two separate attempts to take him, and Britta, out. If he went back to England and just resumed his normal existence, there'd be black-clad men in balaclavas and leather gloves hauling him from his bed at three in the morning. Or a tragic car accident. No. He had to pursue the new mission. Take down Barbara Sutherland before she did the same to him.

He spent the next couple of hours doing a condensed version of his regular fitness routine: press-ups, squats, bicep curls using his bag, and yoga poses, which he held for five minutes each. The poses weren't relaxing. A couple of them were so uncomfortable they bordered on excruciating. But they taught self-discipline and also stretched out the fascia around his muscles, which had often taken enough punishment that he wanted to leave them alone. He'd been taught this style of yoga by a woman he'd met at a cocktail party.

Clara Lane didn't look like a yoga teacher. Her appearance was more like that of the account managers at the advertising agency he'd joined after leaving The Regiment: high-heeled, sparkly shoes; lots of makeup; and a thousand-watt smile that made him feel lightheaded when she directed it at him.

As he discovered at his first class with her, she didn't sound like a yoga teacher either. "Come on, you babies!" she'd called out in an accent that was pure South London, "You're not on Daddy's fucking yacht now! High plank!" The memory made Gabriel smile. She reminded him of a Regimental Sergeant Major he'd known in the Paras.

As he leant forward, breathing deeply and swearing continuously under his breath after squatting with his toes bent back for what felt like an eternity, his phone rang.

"This is Gabriel," he said.

"And this is Tatyana. You are in pain, dear Gabriel. Are you all right?"

"Hi Tatyana. No, I'm fine. Just finished a workout, that's all."

"I am not sure such workout can be good for you. Listen, we are here. In Harare. At airport. You remember my instructions?"

Gabriel steadied his breathing before answering.

"Yes. I'll come to the corporate jet zone. Your plane is a purple and gold Boeing. A Business Jet Three. Garin Group logo of two interlocking gold 'G's."

"Good boy! You remembered everything. We will wait until you arrive. And one last thing."

"What's that?"

"I hope you like vodka!"

*

Forty minutes later, he was standing on an access road looking through the chain-link fence at the area of Harare International Airport reserved for corporate jets. And there was Tatyana's plane. It stood out in its imperial livery among the Learjets and other small aircraft – a purple and gold Rolls Royce in a crowd of white hatchbacks.

He took a quick look around. The access road, cracked and dusty, with scrubby weeds growing up through the centre, was deserted. He looked up at the top edge of the fence. No cameras and, thankfully, no razor wire. Finally he scanned the ground between his position and the Garin Group Boeing. No airport personnel, no passengers either. Just a clear expanse of yellowish tarmac between him and his ride home.

Taking a few steps back, he dropped his bag from his shoulder to the ground and then hefted it by its webbing strap. He executed a couple of turns, whirling the bag out at the end of his right arm, then released it like a discus thrower and hurled it up and over the fence. It landed with a thump and a puff of dust on the far side, about two or three yards from the bottom of the fence. Climbing chain-link hardly counted as surmounting an obstacle in Gabriel's book, and he was up and over in a few seconds. He stooped to collect his bag then walked at a quick march towards the plane. There were a couple of soldiers on the other side of the runway, but they had their backs to Gabriel, looking towards the terminal building. Curls of smoke drifted upwards from their cigarettes.

When he reached the plane's gleaming side, he realised he had no idea what the protocol was for gaining admittance to a corporate jet. The doors were all closed and there didn't appear to be a bell push anywhere in sight. Just as he was beginning to wonder whether Tatyana was even inside, a crop-headed man in a tight-fitting black suit, white shirt and dark blue tie materialised at his right shoulder.

"You are Gabriel?" he asked, though he made it sound like a statement of fact.

"Yes. Tatyana is expecting me."

The man held out his palm. "ID?"

Gabriel fished his passport out and held it up with the photo page outwards.

The man stood, his slabby face a mask of inscrutability as he studied the passport, then flicked his black eyes to Gabriel's own features.

"Fine. You wait."

He pulled out a walkie-talkie and spoke a few words of Russian into the mic.

"Vash posetitel' zdes'"

Yes, I am here, Gabriel thought. And I'm quite keen to be aboard, if you don't mind.

The man nodded then turned to Gabriel. "They lower steps. Stand back, please."

With a muted groan of hydraulics, the passenger steps descended from the side of the plane and moments later, Gabriel was being kissed voluptuously, several times on both cheeks, by Tatyana Garin.

"Here you are, my dear Gabriel Wolfe," she cried, finally releasing him from her embrace and the cloud of expensive-smelling perfume he remembered from their previous meeting. "Now it is I who rescues you from dragons, yes?"

Gabriel smiled at this effusive Russian billionaire and her extravagant way with the English language.

"Yes, and I am truly grateful."

"Come, come," she said. "You must be thirsty."

40

A Girl's Best Friend

TATYANA poured out two huge glasses of vodka from a cut-glass decanter. The spirit making the ice cubes chink smelled of raspberries. She held her tumbler out to Gabriel.

"Chin chin!"

"Cheers!"

He sipped the pale-pink spirit – it was smoother than he had been expecting and the heat it delivered to the pit of his stomach warmed rather than burnt.

"We should strap ourselves in," she said. "I ordered pilot to take off as soon as you are on board."

"We don't have to wait for clearance?"

"When you are as rich as I am, clearance comes as part of package."

He buckled his seatbelt. The cabin was luxurious in a way that suggested an oceangoing yacht rather than a first-class cabin on an airliner. It was panelled in what looked like walnut, with paler inlays marking off the panels from each other. Each square panel had an inlaid Garin Group logo at its centre in a gold-coloured wood. The seats were vast, more like armchairs, with extendible foot rests and wide, padded arms. They were upholstered in white leather decorated with purple piping along the seams. Gabriel sat opposite Tatyana, facing forward. Between them, a low table, in a matching inlaid style to the walls, was bolted to the floor. Purple and gold silk curtains were tied back beside each of the windows and the colours were picked up in the thick pile carpet that covered the floor and the first foot of the walls.

As the engines roared and the Boeing gathered speed along the runway, Gabriel looked out of the small Plexiglas window. He was leaving Africa without the one thing he had promised to find – a sign that Smudge had breathed his last oxygen on this continent. He sighed. So much had happened that he wasn't proud of. Worst of all, he felt betrayed by one of the few people he had felt he could believe in.

The pilot altered the trim on the ailerons and tail flaps, and the plane parted company with the tarmac, gaining hundreds of feet in altitude in a few seconds. As the airport beneath him dwindled, he turned back to face Tatyana, who was watching him with a worried frown on her immaculately made-up face.

"Why so sad?" she asked.

"I went to Mozambique to recover the remains of a friend of mine and instead I was deceived into committing a dreadful crime. Then I witnessed a couple more and I was powerless to do anything about it. Now I'm going home empty-handed and I have to visit my friend's widow and say I failed."

"That is sad. But is not shameful. If you were deceived and then powerless, then was not your fault. Tell me, dear Gabriel," she said, leaning over the table from her seat and patting his left knee, "who deceived you?"

Gabriel swallowed, trying to equalise the pressure in his ears, which were throbbing uncomfortably.

"You wouldn't believe me."

"Try me. I am woman of world. I have met many liars in my life."

"Barbara Sutherland."

Tatyana's eyes narrowed.

"Barbara Sutherland, British Prime Minister?"

He nodded. "The very same."

"Yes. She is good liar. I met her at embassy party in Washington last year. She said she could never do business with our President. But I have seen her with him in Moscow. In restaurant I own. Definitely not talking about

207

politics, I can tell you. What is story with you and Barbara Sutherland?"

As the plane continued climbing, Gabriel took another sip of the vodka, then pinched his lower lip between thumb and forefinger.

"A while back, there was an attempt to seize power by force in the UK. I stopped it, with some help, and saved her life in the process. Since then, I've been working for her, more or less directly. As a pat on the back for a successful mission I completed, she said I could ask her a favour."

"What did you ask for?"

"I asked if I could go back to Mozambique to find the remains of a former comrade of mine from the Army."

"That is honourable thing to do. Like before, with bag. You are good man, Gabriel."

"That's the problem. I'm not sure I am any more. The price for being equipped for the trip was . . . to commit a deeply immoral act, on her instructions."

"Sutherland?"

"Yes. She lied to me to save her own skin."

"Listen, Gabriel. I am not police. So whatever you did is between you and your conscience. But tell me and maybe I can help you put things right."

He paused. Should he admit his guilt for murdering a foreign politician to a woman he had only met once before today? The decision took an instant.

"I killed a man who Barbara Sutherland said was channeling money to a terror group. Now it looks like he had information that would show she was corrupt. She'd been involved in some sort of deals involving defence contracts, land and diamonds."

Tatyana finished her vodka and placed the glass on the table. The she unsnapped the catch on her seatbelt and came to sit next to Gabriel.

"In defence, I am not expert. In diamonds, I am expert. Probably these were blood diamonds. You know this phrase?"

"I've heard of it, but I don't really know what it means."

"Is when warlord, or government even, sells diamonds in exchange for weapons to fight civil war or insurgency. Reputable traders like Garin Group have piece of paper for every diamond shipment called a KPC."

"KPC?"

"Kimberley Process Certificate. It says 'this diamond is from accredited source, not war zone'."

"But why would she be involved with blood diamonds? Why not ones with a KPC?"

Tatyana smiled and patted his arm. "You pick up diamond lingo very quickly. KPC diamonds are traceable. Blood diamonds are not. Like unmarked bills. Very useful currency if you want to do secret deals. Except for one thing."

Gabriel twisted round in his seat so he faced Tatyana directly.

"What one thing?"

"Without KPC is very difficult to turn blood diamonds into cash."

"So you'd have to get someone to forge one for you."

"Da. Or steal blanks. But that is very difficult. Forging much better."

"If you had blood diamonds and the paperwork to show they were legal, where would you trade them?"

"Oh, many, many places. Amsterdam, Cape Town, Manhattan, Tel Aviv, London. Plenty of gem merchants will buy certified diamonds."

"Is there a central register of traders? Somewhere you can look up who's been active in the market?"

She shook her head. "Is very secretive trade. For understandable reasons. But is not *completely* secret. If you know who to ask."

"And you know who to ask?"

"I am Tatyana Garin. I know everybody in global diamond trade. You leave this with me. Maybe I can sniff out something – is right phrase? – that might help you."

"You know it might bring down the Prime Minister of the UK?"

She snorted and flapped her hands, making her many rings click against each other. "Is not my problem. Prime ministers come and go. Kings and queens. Tsars and tsarinas. Even presidents. You know words of famous song, Gabriel. Only diamonds last forever."

*

Sixteen hours later, the jet's tyres met the tarmac at London Luton Airport. As the plane taxied to a stop at the private terminal building, Tatyana got to her feet. She had been asleep for much of the flight and her eye makeup was a little smudged from the mask.

"I have second driver in terminal, dear Gabriel. Tell her where you want her to take you. I have your number. I will call you when I have something useful to tell you."

"Thank you, Tatyana. For getting me out of Zimbabwe. For your help with this business. I feel I owe you, not the other way around."

She smiled, pulling him into an embrace, and whispered in his ear. "In my business, always is favours. One way, then other. But we can be friends, yes? Nobody owes anybody. Is OK?"

"Yes. Is OK."

"Do svidaniya."

"Do svidaniya."

*

Beyond the discreet brushed-steel barrier of passport control, which he moved through without incident, Gabriel could see a small group of chauffeurs, standing around, talking into phones or holding up name boards. Only one was a woman. She wore a dark purple trouser suit with a small purple and gold enamelled double-G pinned to her lapel, and she wore a peaked cap low over her eyes. She held a rectangular whiteboard with his name printed across it in neat block capitals.

He walked over and smiled at her.

"Mr Wolfe?" she asked. Though it was more confirmation than question. He nodded. "Come with me please."

*

Two hours and ten minutes later, the silver Mercedes S-Class drew up on the gravel outside Gabriel's cottage. Gabriel climbed out, stretched and retrieved his bag from the boot. The chauffeur refused his offer a cup of tea and, as he stood in his drive, reversed back onto the main road and took off, back, he assumed, to Tatyana's London office.

Inside, the fatigue he'd been keeping at bay overwhelmed him like a tidal wave. He dropped his bag, climbed the stairs as though they were a mountain, stripped off his clothes and fell into bed. He slept for twelve hours. Twelve dreamless hours.

When he woke, it was to the sound of rain hammering on the windows. He looked out over his garden to the woods beyond. Through the bare trees he could just make out the spire of Salisbury Cathedral in the distance, a narrow, pale-grey spike rising out of the land beyond the wood.

He showered and dressed, then went downstairs to make a pot of tea, mixing Kenyan Fannings, Russian Caravan and Earl Grey leaves in the pot. While the fragrant tea was brewing, he pulled out a sheet of paper from a drawer and grabbed a pencil from a mug on the kitchen counter.

Across the top, he wrote a single two-word question.

What now?

41
Shift Work

SOMETHING Philip Agambe had said in his final seconds came to Gabriel. It was bouncing off the edges of his consciousness like a moth at a window lit from inside, but he couldn't get it to settle. He closed his eyes and breathed deeply, letting his mind quieten, waiting for the familiar state of heightened awareness to descend on him.

Philip Agambe's terrified face loomed out of the dark at him, eyes wide and staring, lips pulled back from his teeth in a grimace of fear and despair.

Gabriel could feel the cold metal handle of the butterfly knife in his hand and smell the bitter sweat rising from the man he was about to murder in cold blood. Bile rose in his throat and he swallowed it back as he willed himself to hear the words coming from Agambe's lips:

"She's in bed with Gordian."

His eyelids snapped open and he jotted the word down on the sheet of paper in front of him. What did it mean? Had he even heard the word correctly? Maybe it was Gordon. A man's Christian name, or anybody's surname.

He opened the lid of his MacBook Air and launched a browser. He Googled, "Zimbabwean politician Gordon". Precisely zero useful hits, just a bunch of irrelevant pages about a former British prime minister. He widened the search to the whole of southern Africa. Apart from a long-dead colonial administrator, nothing again. After twenty minutes trying an increasingly absurd set of search terms, Gabriel gave up on the idea of the word as a person's name.

"Well then," he muttered. "If not a person, then a company. And maybe it is Gordian."

He typed, "Gordian Zimbabwe" and immediately groaned in frustration as a series of pages were displayed, all using the metaphor of the Gordian Knot in relation to southern African politics. It seemed Alexander the Great had once solved the puzzle of an intricately tied knot nobody could undo by slicing through its middle with his sword. Ever since, the phrase had come to mean an intractable problem.

Turning away from the screen, he doodled a knot on the paper, adding coils, turns and twists until the image took up almost half the space on the page.

"Are you a company?" he asked the doodle. "Gordian Group? Gordian Limited? Gordian Incorporated?"

Returning to the search engine, he tried every variant he could think of, from the obvious forms of incorporation – Ltd, Inc, LLP and PLC – to more esoteric designations including the Finish OY, the Polish SA and finally, the Albanian Shpk, all fruitlessly. If there was a corporate entity in the world calling itself Gordian, it had managed the seemingly impossible feat of hiding itself from Google.

He wrote *Gordian – company?* on the sheet beside the huge knot. Then he added a note: *would Melody know?* If her organisation was monitoring global corruption, maybe they'd have sources on the ground who could point him in the right direction.

There was someone he wanted to speak to a lot more urgently than Melody Smith, however. Someone either with hands blackened by dirty money, or who had been set up even more cleverly than he believed he had been. The only problem was, getting to see Barbara Sutherland wasn't simply a matter of knocking on her front door.

Then he remembered. It was an election year. That meant Sutherland would be all over the place. Travelling on trains. Appearing in the constituencies of loyal MPs whose campaigns could do with a boost from the party leader and sitting Prime Minister. Making stump speeches at dockyards and factories. Reading stories to groups of bored-looking eight-year-olds. Yes, she'd have a security detail, but he was used to defeating people much better-trained and motivated than they would be.

Within fifteen minutes, he'd assembled a schedule of the Prime Minister's appearances for the next two days. It was laughably easy. He just scanned social media, searching for "Prime Minister coming" and a few other variants, and the posts revealing her itinerary piled up. But Gabriel wasn't cracking a smile. His mouth was set in a line and the muscles in his jaw were clenching and unclenching as he planned an intercept.

The place he chose was a car factory in Oxfordshire. It was a straightforward drive to get there, and by its nature, it would be physically easy to infiltrate. At most, he was expecting some chain-link fencing. At best, a stroll through wide-open gates. He could pose as a journalist; he'd done it once before. But on the whole, he favoured a covert approach. He had a day to prepare. More than enough time.

Next, he called Britta.

"*Hej*. How are you? And where are you?"

"I'm back home. I swung a favour. Flew back in style on a corporate jet, too. How the other half lives, eh?"

"Well, I don't know about that. I flew economy and it was a fucking nightmare. Screaming babies and drunk tourists for fourteen hours is not my idea of fun." She paused, and he listened to the sound of her breathing. "I got your text," she said, finally.

"I got yours, too."

"So?"

"So, what?"

"What do you mean, 'so, what?', you numbskull? I said I loved you and you said It back. Doesn't that mean anything to you? Or were we just being polite?"

"No! I mean yes. Yes, it does mean something and no, I wasn't just being polite. It's just, I don't know, I've never been in this situation before. And I'm caught up in a little bit of business, in case you'd forgotten."

"But you did mean it? You do love me?"

"Yes, Britta Falskog, you crazy Swede, I do love you. And I want to see you. Badly. But I just can't. It's too dangerous. I don't know what she's going to do and you're not visible to her, so I think we should keep it that way."

"Fine. I'm back at work anyway. My boss relented and put me back on active duty. But if there's anything I can do for you, you let me know, OK?"

"I will. I promise. I have to go. I need to get in touch with Don."

Gabriel ended the call and sat there, staring at his phone's screen for a minute longer, wondering whether it was possible to lead a life where you loved someone and got married and did all those normal things other people did, and still run around the world burgling office buildings, planting bugs and shooting bad guys. He knew a man who'd know. But he had a feeling he needed to use a little subterfuge to make contact.

After a half-hour round trip, he was back at home with a cheap mobile phone and twenty pounds of credit. He called Don Webster's number. Just when he was resigning himself to leaving another message, Don picked up. His voice sounded guarded.

"Who is this? How did you get this number?"

"Don, it's me."

The older man sighed, then spoke. "Quiet! Just listen. I'm going to give you a number. Wait ten minutes then call it."

He read out a set of digits. Then he hung up.

It was a landline. *Why the home phone, Don? And why the wait?*

The ten minutes passed for Gabriel with glacial slowness. Even with a career's worth of 'standing by to stand by' he found the wait unbearable. Nine minutes later, he stood, finger hovering over the phone's buttons. As the second hand on his watch passed ten he started punching in the number Don had given him.

The phone answered on the first ring.

"Hello, Old Sport. I wondered whether you'd find a way to reach me."

"Where are you?"

"Village phone box. There's a committee been formed to apply to turn it into a library – bloody silly idea – but for now, one can still use it for the purpose God intended."

"Are they monitoring your phone?"

There was no need for Gabriel to explain who 'they' were. Both men understood the term's meaning in all its infinite variety.

"Not sure, Old Sport. And remember, to a certain extent, I *am* 'they'. But one can't be too careful. Here's the situation. Barbara has expressly forbidden me to talk to you, offer you help or even acknowledge your existence. Some sort of spook accosted me the other day. They're putting personal pressure on me. There's not a lot I can do for you. But not a lot doesn't mean nothing. Need a shooter?"

"I don't think so. I'm not planning on taking her out like I did that poor sod in Zimbabwe."

"No, but if they get desperate enough they might arrange to set some of our friendly neighbourhood firearms officers on your scent. 'Rogue SAS veteran on the loose', that sort of thing."

"I'm still not sure."

"Look, I tell you what. That hotel you favour in London, what's it called? The Crow?"

"The Raven."

"I'll have one of my lads leave a package for you there. If you feel the need, you can collect it. If you don't, we'll retrieve it later. How about that?"

Gabriel smiled at the thought of his boss leaving a loaded pistol behind the reception desk of a hotel for him, like an umbrella.

"Sounds good. Thank you. Are you all right, Don? You sounded strained when you took me to meet Sam that time."

"Me? I'm fine. I've faced worse than this in my time."

"It's just, you looked, I don't know, off, every time we discussed this mission back in London."

"Let's just say Barbara's documentary evidence against Philip Agambe failed to meet The Department's normal standards. I queried it. She insisted it was kosher and ordered me to proceed. And that was that. Look, I can't help you further. And we can't speak again for a while. If you're doing what I think you are, we may be able to in the future. Do what you think is right, Gabriel. And good luck."

The line went dead. Gabriel held the phone to his ear for a few more seconds, listening to the unbroken tone, picturing Don Webster striding away from a red phone box in the heart of a picturesque village, past a duck pond to a half-timbered Elizabethan house and a wood-burning fire. He shook his head to dispel the image.

*

By seven the following morning, Gabriel was halfway to the car plant. He kept the Maserati to a steady seventy. Being stopped by the police for speeding would hardly help his plan to accost the British Prime Minister and – he realised he had no exact idea of how – interrogate her about whether she was up to her elbows in blood diamonds-for-arms-for-land deals in Africa.

At eight, he rolled to a stop in a layby a mile from the plant. Dressed in jeans, work boots, a dark grey hoodie and a leather jacket, he hoped he'd pass for a factory worker. He pulled a baseball cap down over his forehead and set off along the road towards the factory. The morning shift were arriving, mostly by car, though some were on motorbikes and a few cycled or walked towards the factory gates. Gabriel merged into the foot traffic and, keeping his head down and his hands jammed in his jacket pockets, wandered through the gates and into what he thought of as enemy territory.

Already, the media were assembling in front of the main building. Vans with satellite dishes on thick telescopic mounts were clustered to one side, and in front of the shallow flight of steps, a dozen or more smartly dressed news presenters were checking levels with their crews or rehearsing short pieces to camera.

Photographers and reporters were massing in a wedge of notebooks and long lenses several people deep. The workers were being marshalled into a well-organised crowd and the air was alive with good-natured banter about the imminent visit of the Prime Minister.

Gabriel hung back, finding a spot on the edge and off to one side of the crowd. Behind him, he noticed a stack of plastic crates that presumably had once held components of some kind. They had labels written in German on the side.

A cold wind had sprung up, raising clouds of fine grit and dust from the concrete in front of the offices. There were complaints and jeering as the workers pulled their coats and jackets tighter around them.

"Come on, Babs," a loud male voice called. "We've targets to hit, you know."

There was a ripple of laughter at this and a medley of other voices joined in.

"Yeah, come on, Babs. It's too cold to stand around here. You'll be losing votes if you don't hurry up."

As if heeding their summons, a British Racing Green Jaguar swept up the access road and in through the gates, followed by a black Range Rover with all the windows except the front windscreen blacked out. The latter vehicle disgorged its passengers first: a squad of four six-footers. They were lean but blocky men with regulation short haircuts, watchful eyes and curly wires leading from their right ears inside their jacket collars.

Moments later, the driver of the Jaguar got out and opened the rear door for his passenger. And there she was. One of the most powerful democratic politicians in the world. And possibly one of the most corrupt.

Barbara Sutherland.

42
Big Game Hunting

AT once, there was an electronic clattering as every one of the photographers pressed their shutter buttons. Above the whirring of the cameras and the calls for Barbara Sutherland to, "look this way, please, Prime Minister," one of her media minders called for silence and patted the air with her hands. The crowd fell silent and Barbara Sutherland smiled out at them, her lipstick a bright slash of scarlet in the dismal, grey, winter light. She waited a few seconds and then began her speech.

From the back of the crowd, Gabriel turned away and stacked a couple of the plastic crates on top of each other. He climbed up and turned back to face Sutherland. He stood erect, removed his cap and folded his arms. Then he simply waited.

While Sutherland continued with her crowd-pleasing messages about support for British industry, ensuring competitiveness abroad and job security at home, he let his eyes rove left and right, monitoring the security detail. Like him, they were watchful, scanning the crowd, looking for trouble. But they were alert to sudden movements, figures rushing towards the Prime Minister, arms drawn back, hands clutching solid objects. Gabriel kept completely still.

Then came the moment he'd been waiting for. Sutherland was talking about the need to remain vigilant against destabilising forces. She meant militants within the trade union movement, but it was an apt phrase for the role Gabriel had adopted. As she swept the crowd with her gaze, she spotted him.

She stumbled over her words, mispronouncing the name of the firm's managing director. Gabriel held her gaze then broke eye contact. He stepped off the boxes and moved back, away from the crowd. Reaching a gap between two long steel-clad sheds, he turned back. She had resumed her speech, but even at this distance he could see a flush had crept up her neck. He waited for her eyes to lock back onto his own. They did. He walked away to his left and found a quiet spot to sit out the rest of the speech.

After another five minutes or so, the crowd clapped and whistled dutifully. Gabriel knew from his research that a quick tour of the plant was scheduled before the Prime Minister would be whisked on to her next appointment. He circled around the perimeter of the factory and made his way to the front of the building, where the cars were parked.

From behind a container left by a delivery truck, he watched as the Prime Ministerial party emerged from the doors of the factory. She shook hands with the managing director, a slim, short, bespectacled man with thinning sandy hair. Then, batting away a volley of questions from the journalists, she strode towards her Jaguar.

Her staff may not have realised the significance of her rapid glances to left and right, but Gabriel did. He stepped out from the cover of the container, directly into her eyeline. Once again, she caught his eye and this time she made a move. Pulling one of her minders to one side, she pointed to the container. Gabriel tensed, ready to run. But there was no need. She was coming on her own, marching towards him on her high heels, not stumbling despite the gravelly surface.

"Gabriel Wolfe," she said, smiling for the first time. "What the bloody hell are you doing here, my love? Are you stalking me or something? You could always deliver your report in the normal way. I might even pour you a glass of that Burgundy you like so much."

"Two questions, Barbara," he said. "Have you ever owned diamonds? Who or what is Gordian?"

Her eyes gave nothing away. "Only the one on my finger," she said, brandishing her left hand at him, "and I haven't the faintest idea. What happened in Zimbabwe? Did you do what I asked?"

"I'm sure you know that I did. But I didn't manage to complete my own mission. W –" he checked himself, "I was intercepted. Twice. I thought you might know something about that."

"Look, Gabriel, love. I have no idea what you're on about and I really can't stop to chat. It looks pretty bloody odd my coming over here, anyway. I had to tell my lads I'd come over faint and needed a moment on my own. Come and see me at Number Ten. Tomorrow. Early, say seven a.m. I'll have someone rustle us up a couple of bacon sandwiches."

Then she turned and picked her way across the weedy expanse of hard standing back to her puzzled-looking crew of minders. Moments later, the Jaguar and its Range Rover escort sped away through the gates leaving a cloud of petrol fumes hanging in the damp air behind them.

*

Gabriel was parked in a little square on the east side of London's Smithfield market by noon. He walked the few hundred yards to The Raven and pushed the front door open. Inside, he was greeted by the familiar smell of apples. Very little daylight penetrated the reception area of the hotel, and for that reason the staff always kept electric lights burning, which gave the place the air of being perpetually evening.

"Good afternoon, Mr Wolfe," the female receptionist said with a wide smile. "I'm afraid we're full tonight. But . . ."

"I don't need a room, thanks, Martina. Has somebody left a parcel for me?"

She bent to look beneath the counter and straightened again, holding a cardboard carton the size of a large shoebox. The top was marked F.A.O. G.WOLFE in black marker pen.

"Here you are," she said. "Be careful. It's heavy."

"Thanks," he said, taking the box from her with both hands. "I'll see you soon."

Back at the car, he resisted the urge to open the carton and instead laid it on the floor of the boot, then spread a picnic blanket over it. He needed a base where he could examine its contents and formulate a more detailed plan.

He called Britta. The phone went straight to voicemail. He adopted a servile tone.

"Oh, yes, hello, Miss Falskog? This is the West London Game Meats Company. Your leg of antelope is being delivered by one of our drivers later this afternoon. You'll need to be in to sign for it. Thanking you."

Then he started the car and pulled away from the square, heading for the Thames and then west towards Chiswick.

For the middle of the day, the traffic through London was moving fast. Using steering wheel, accelerator and brakes with equal vigour, he made it through the centre and onto the A4 dual carriageway running west to the M4 motorway in thirty minutes.

Ten minutes after that, he was pulling up outside the converted Victorian house where Britta lived. He got out and tried the doorbell. There was no light on the other side of the stained glass, no blurry figure coming to let him in. So he turned and went to wait in the car.

After four hours, he was beginning to wonder whether he should quit and find a cheap hotel when an Air Force-blue Saab convertible raced up the road and slid in behind his car with a protesting squeal from the tyres. He slid down in his seat.

There was a loud rapping on the passenger window. He looked over and let out a sigh of breath he'd been unconsciously holding in: Britta. He climbed out, and she ran round the back of the car and threw her arms around him.

"Oh, Jesus, you're a sight for painful eyes! I got your message. Come on. Let's go inside."

He laughed at the way her English idiom buckled under stress, kissed her hard on the lips then let her lead him inside, stopping briefly to retrieve the package from the boot.

Over coffee with a shot of brandy poured into it, he explained where he'd been and what he'd been up to.

"And she didn't call the cops or set her attack dogs on you?" Britta asked.

"Nope. In fact, if you took what she said at face value she gave nothing away. She acted surprised, but then why wouldn't she? Last thing she knew I was in Mozambique looking for Smudge, then I turn up at her photo opportunity like Banquo's ghost."

"What did you ask her again?"

He took a sip of the strong, alcoholic coffee. "I asked her if she owned any diamonds, just to see if she'd give anything away, not because I thought she'd own up to having a bucketful of blood-diamonds under the bed. And I asked her if she knew what or who Gordian was."

"What did she say?"

"She said no diamonds. Apart from her engagement ring. And she claimed not to know about Gordian. Who aren't on the web, by the way."

"That doesn't mean anything. Half the people I investigate aren't on the web. Or not the surface web anyway."

"The which, now?"

"The surface web. Where the companies and bloggers and social media sites are. All the cat videos and inspirational quotes are indexed so search engines can find them. But there's a whole other web, called the deep web. All the stuff search engines can't see. Most of it's harmless: corporate intranets, stuff you find using search boxes, broken links. But there's one part of the deep web where all the really bad shit happens."

Gabriel frowned. "There's pretty bad shit on the surface web, isn't there?"

"Yes. But we're talking arms dealers, drugs, protection, assassins, some truly evil people who do stuff with women and children you do not ever want to have to see, believe me. And that's called the dark web. Stuff they *intentionally* hide. You need a special browser called Tor to find it. And even then, you have to know a ton of entry codes and passwords. I can do some digging there for you. See if Gordian comes up."

"That would be good. Because without concrete evidence and my gut feeling, what have I got, really? The last words of a man trying to save his own skin? His embittered widow and an alleged dossier I never saw?"

"Yes. And two separate attempts to kill us, don't forget."

"I haven't, believe me. I thought you'd bought it back there."

"I know. My chest is still bruised, you know. I might have to get you to take a look later." She grinned. "If you can bear it."

He frowned, then nodded. "I should think I could manage that."

She grinned, then pointed to the cardboard box.

"What have you got there? Cake?"

"Something Don left for me at The Raven."

"Come on then," she said. "Open it."

Gabriel placed the box on a coffee table and ran his thumbnail down the tape holding the flaps closed. He pulled them open and bent them back. Under a folded sheet of bubble wrap was what he had hoped to see. A SIG Sauer P226 semi-automatic pistol. Next to it, a spare box magazine. And next to that, denting the layer of bubble wrap beneath the pistol, a white cardboard box about five inches square. He eased the top off to reveal the blunt copper noses of fifty 9 x 19 mm Parabellum rounds.

43

Rooftop Safari

BRITTA picked up the pistol and dropped the magazine out from the butt. It was full. She slotted it back into place.

"Nice," she said, weighing it in her hand and then aiming it at an Andy Warhol soup can print on the wall. "What're you going to do with that? Kill Sutherland?"

"No. But it might help focus her mind on answering my questions."

"I thought she already did that. You said she denied it all."

"She did," he said, pushing twenty rounds home against the spring of the spare magazine. "But I didn't believe her. Besides, what else is she going to say in a public space? 'Oh, yes, I'm up to my elbows in African blood thanks to my illegal dealings in conflict diamonds and arms contracts.'"

Britta clanked the pistol down on the coffee table.

"What makes you think she'll answer any differently just because you're pointing a nine-mil in her face?"

He shrugged. "Honestly? I don't know. But I'm running out of inspiration, so unless you have any better suggestions, I'm going with that."

"How about come to bed?"

He smiled. "That's definitely a better suggestion. For now, at least."

Upstairs, Britta led Gabriel along the hallway to her bedroom. More Scandinavian style: white bed linens, a bedstead made from what looked like wrought iron and driftwood, pale abstract prints on the wall. She undressed him then pushed him back onto the bed.

"This is the first time I've had sex with a man I was in love with," she said.

"You never loved Per, then?"

"Mr Super-cop? No, I never loved him. Not really. Even when we were together, he was a borderline asshole."

Under her indigo jeans and white T-shirt, Britta was wearing plain white cotton underwear. She unsnapped her bra and shimmied out of her knickers, then joined Gabriel on the bed.

Their lovemaking was tender, rather than passionate. Almost as if they wanted to try out this new way of being together carefully, without spoiling it.

When she reached her climax, she cried out his name. He finished a few moments later, arching his back as he reared above her, before lowering himself to one side and burying his face in the curve of her neck.

After her breathing had stilled, she spoke.

"Seriously, Gabriel, are you sure this plan of yours is a good idea? It's pretty much a losing bet, whichever way you look at it. If she's innocent, then you're never going to work for Don again. In fact you'll be lucky to escape prison. And if she's guilty as charged, you're giving her even more of a reason to get rid of you."

Gabriel folded his arms behind his head and stared at the ceiling.

"But that's the trouble, don't you see? If I do nothing, and it *was* her behind those attacks on us in Mozambique, she's just going to try again. At least if I confront her, I have a chance of finding out the truth. Yes, if I've screwed up then I'm finished as an operator for The Department. I'll probably have to leave the country. But if I'm right, then she just becomes the enemy. I have to believe that somewhere in this country there are people who'll help me."

"Well, here's one for a start. Now, all that," she reached down and gave him a squeeze, "has made me hungry. I fancy pizza. Something with lots of chilli."

*

Once the delivery boy had taken his tip in exchange for the flat cardboard box containing their dinner, Britta closed the door and brought the pizza over to the kitchen table. With a couple of glasses of Chianti poured, they ate.

"You need anything else for your little adventure?" she said, through a mouthful of pizza. "Knife? Disguise? Lock picks?"

"I brought a knife." He showed her his treasured ceramic tactical knife that he'd 'liberated' from the SAS when he resigned his commission and managed to bring out of Zimbabwe. "As for a disguise, I doubt anything that would work for you would work for me. Unless . . ."

"What?"

"Have you got any wigs?"

She laughed. "Oh, I have some very lovely wigs. Would you like to see?"

"After this, yes please. And if you can spare a set of lock picks, I wouldn't say no."

The pizza consumed, the wine drunk, they returned to Britta's bedroom. She pulled open the second drawer in her dressing table and pulled out three wigs.

"OK," she said, pulling the first wig on, a long blonde one, straight as cornstalks. "You have your basic glamorous nightclub look. Probably not for you, hey?"

He smiled, and shook his head. "Not this time."

"No. Didn't think so. Then there's this one." She bent her head over the still-open drawer and swapped wigs before turning round to face him again in a curly, shoulder-length black number. "Ta da! Rock chicks rule." She growled out this last sentence.

He wrinkled his nose and shook his head again. "Too much hair to get in my eyes."

"Huh! Beggars can't be choosers, you know. Fine, this is the last one." She swivelled round, swapped wigs once more, then posed in front of him, hands on hips. "I call this one 'the Swedish pixie'. You like it?"

He took his time appraising the final option. It was short and straight, pale blonde, framing her face like the cap on an acorn. Then he smiled.

"I'll take it!"

*

At three the following morning, Gabriel slid out of bed, dressed quietly, picked up the blonde wig, the SIG Sauer and the spare magazine and was out of the flat and behind the wheel of the Maserati in ten minutes. Britta didn't stir, even when he caught one of the narrow iron legs of her bed between his toes and muffled a stream of Anglo Saxon.

Half an hour later, he parked on a meter on Tothill Street then made his way, hands deep in jacket pockets and hood up over his new pale yellow hair, to the corner where Whitehall met Birdcage Walk. He looked all around – nobody about. The building on the corner of Parliament Square was easy to scale thanks to the deep grooves cut between the blocks of stone, and in less than three minutes he was standing on the roof, the SIG Sauer a reassuringly uncomfortable presence in the back of his waistband.

The view was stunning. He looked south where the London Eye stared, unblinking, over the river Thames. North to the old Post Office Tower, a cylindrical sixties office building that looked like a science fiction author's idea of 'the skyscraper of tomorrow'. East towards the random assortment of flamboyant contemporary skyscrapers erected by developers and architects clearly compensating for something. And west, across parks and green spaces and the gradual lowering of the building heights, as hubris gave way to a more everyday vision of a city as somewhere to live and work. Maybe to get married and raise a family.

He was glad of the extra layers he'd put on. The wind was piercingly cold and driving rivulets of tears out of his eyes and across his numbing cheeks. Turning towards Trafalgar Square, he began to navigate the unfamiliar roofscape. His progress towards his destination was unhindered by any canyons created by side streets, and he was able to pick his way across one rooftop after another, skirting constructions housing lift gear, air conditioning units and other utilities necessary to keep a modern office building functioning for the safety and comfort of its inhabitants.

Nearing his objective, he was startled by a sudden explosion of noise and feathers, as a pair of peregrine falcons erupted from their nest. The birds wheeled over his head, keening their distress and annoyance. He avoided the nest altogether, not wanting to draw the parents' wrath down upon his head. But he could still hear a demanding cheeping coming from the tidy bowl of twigs, scraps of plastic bags and fast food containers the raptors had fashioned into a home for their brood.

Then he saw it. The divide between one building and the next where Downing Street cut through the solid mass of architecture. Far too wide at the Whitehall end of the street to cross without descending to the heavily defended ground, it narrowed at its northern end to an eight-foot gap.

Gabriel got to his hands and knees and crawled right to the edge of the parapet to look over. The distance to the ground was fifty or sixty feet. Enough to ensure that a fall would be not just fatal but messy as well. As he moved away from the edge and stood again, he had a flashback. He was standing on a clifftop in the Outer Hebrides in January of 2005. A training exercise for a group of applicants to join the SAS, himself among them. The others were Morgan, Beaumont and Smith.

That last man was Smudge, whose bones still lay in that damned patch of land in Mozambique, unless hyenas, wild dogs and vultures had carried them away.

On that day, their task had been to jump across a five-foot gap between the island itself and Old Tom, a three-hundred-foot basalt column rising out of the North Atlantic. The exercise was a test of nerve rather than athletic ability. Even an averagely fit human being would have been able to clear the gap had it been, say, marked out with tape on the floor of a gym. But with a bitter wind swirling around their heads, and a platoon of armed soldiers at their backs, there was nothing simple about it.

Morgan, Beaumont and Gabriel himself had made the leap easily. But Smudge had messed up. He would have tumbled to his death had Gabriel not anticipated his shortfall and been ready to grab his flailing arm and pull him to safety.

Shaking his head to clear away the cloudy image of that make-or-break moment, Gabriel shoved the pistol an extra inch down the back of his waistband, then backed up twenty feet . . .

. . . crouched for a second . . .

. . . drew in a breath . . .

. . . and sprinted.

Arms outstretched as they had been all those years ago, Gabriel sailed out over the abyss and landed a foot inside the low retaining wall, his boots landing virtually silently on the roof of Number Ten Downing Street.

He looked at his watch. Four o'clock. Perfect. She'd either be deep underwater or in the early stages of sleep if she'd been up late working on papers. Either way, she'd be less than alert. Which would make what he had to do that much easier.

44
Within Striking Distance

AT ground level, Downing Street had the unobtrusive but effective security of a military base. Armed police. Narrow gates. Plus some hidden countermeasures the public would never find out about but which were more than capable of disabling all but the most determined of terrorists.

On the roof, it was a different story. It was almost as if the architect had decided to offer would-be intruders as wide a choice of entry points as possible. There were heating and air conditioning ducts, glass skylights and unprotected sash windows just a foot below the parapet. Gabriel ignored all of these. Instead, he simply stuck the blade of his knife into the space between the latch and frame of a maintenance door and cleared the tongue from the striker plate. With his other hand he pulled the steel-clad door towards him.

A set of narrow unpainted wooden stairs led down into the interior of the building.

Keeping his feet to the edges of the treads, where there would be less chance of ill-fitting joints betraying his presence, he descended to the top floor of the house.

At the bottom of the flight – just ten stairs in all – was another door. White-painted timber this time and with a simple spherical brass doorknob above a brass escutcheon screwed over the keyhole. The wig was making his scalp itch, but he kept it on. Anything that might disorientate Barbara

Sutherland, even for a second, would be an advantage. And it would certainly help if he was observed leaving, whichever route he chose.

The lock took under thirty seconds to pick. Gabriel was breathing steadily, keeping his heart rate under control, but the flutter of excitement and anxiety in his gut was making it hard to do that and concentrate on his mission. He decided to let his heart do whatever it wanted, and his adrenal glands too. His focus was on reaching the target.

Gabriel pulled the door towards him, then twisted the knob. He thanked the handyman or woman who had kept the door and its hinges oiled – it opened without so much as a squeak. Once inside, he closed the door behind him, without letting it latch shut. Any sound his feet might have made was deadened by the thick, blood-red hallway carpet. He made his way to the flight of stairs.

At Britta's flat, they'd sat, hip to hip, Googling 'floor plan Ten Downing Street'. The master bedroom, labelled 'Bedroom 1' on the plan was on the northeast corner of the first floor. Now, he made his way down the stairs, pulse bumping in his throat, heading for a showdown with the woman who was either out to kill him, or who would want to shortly thereafter, but would probably settle for arrest and prosecution.

From a previous visit, confined to daylight hours and a ground floor sitting room, Gabriel had met the Prime Minister's son, Tom. He'd been five or six then. *So a bit older now. Please, God, don't let the kid be a sleepwalker.*

Reaching the first floor, which was as well-carpeted as the second, Gabriel paused for a couple of seconds to get his bearings. He looked over the bannisters to locate the front door. *That's west. So over there is northeast.* On the balls of his feet, palms sweating, head itching furiously under the scratchy wig, he stepped as if on eggshells round the balconied hallway. Finally, he reached the door behind which, if he had calculated correctly, lay Barbara Sutherland.

Her husband was a serving RAF officer. Whether he was serving a tour or at home on leave, Gabriel had no idea. It was the one part of the puzzle he'd been unable to pin down in advance. Even the web had its limits.

He stood for an eternity with his hand on the doorknob, breathing quietly but deeply. *It all happens now, Old Sport*, a voice said in the space inside his skull where all his disembodied advisers spoke from, whether alive or dead: Smudge; his long-dead brother, Michael; Britta; and, on this occasion, Don Webster.

Looking down, he watched his hand turn the knob. It was just as silent as the other door had been and he released it against the spring and opened the door by a few inches. He could hear snoring. Which had to be a good sign. If there were two people in there, then one was asleep. If it was just the Prime Minister, he had a sitting-duck target.

Brushing a stray blonde hair away from his mouth, he risked peering around the edge of the door.

45

Confrontation

SHE was sitting up in bed, in a low-cut, black silk nightgown. In front of her, spread out on her lap, were some sort of Government papers. The red box in which they had been sent lay near to the end of the bed. A pair of rectangular, black-framed reading glasses perched on the end of her nose. Beside her, a hump in the bed clothes revealed that the snorer was her husband. In the act of reseating the glasses on the bridge of her nose, she looked up and over at Gabriel. He was pointing the SIG at her.

She could have screamed. Woken her husband. Had Gabriel arrested and thrown in the Tower. She did none of these things. Instead, she stared at him for a time, then pointed at him and made a shooing gesture with the backs of her fingers. He withdrew, and waited just outside the door.

Moments later, pulling a white dressing gown around herself and tying the belt at her waist, Barbara Sutherland appeared. She closed the door behind her, taking exaggerated care to engage the latch without making a sound, then glared at him and hissed:

"You've got a bloody nerve. Follow me. And put that bloody gun away."

She swept past him, down the hall and turned left into a room at the far end. Keeping within a single pace of her back, Gabriel tracked her along the softly carpeted hallway and into the room, which turned out to be another bedroom, furnished with a double bed and a couple of arm chairs.

Once inside with the door shut behind them, Sutherland spoke.

"Suppose you tell me what this is all about. It's not the most usual way members of The Department present their reports to me."

Gabriel decided to go along with the fiction that he was still a loyal, trusting and, above all, unsuspecting, member of the unofficial task force of spies and killers maintained by the Government to eliminate those on its 'most wanted' list.

"I went to Mozambique, crossed into Zimbabwe, killed Philip Agambe, returned, tried to reach the site where I suspected Smudge' remains to be and was ambushed by a crew of ex-US Marine types. They failed. I pressed on and was then ambushed a second time by a gang of local, I don't know, militia or something. They hit me in the leg and were about to execute me when I was pulled out by the Zambian air force with some help from the Americans."

He paused to see whether Sutherland was reacting at all to any of this but her face was still. No expression to give her away. Inscrutable.

"Very impressive, I must say,"

"What was impressive?"

"Well," she said, "fighting your way out of not one, but two, ambushes . . . all alone. Nobody to help you?"

Realising he'd been perilously close to giving away Britta's presence, he tried to regroup.

"Like I said, the Zambians crossed into Mozambican airspace to pull me out of the second one and I just got lucky in the first. Some of the toys Don provided were brutally effective."

"Then what?" she asked. "Did you go back for Trooper Smith's remains?"

"I couldn't. The Zambians took all my weapons and I didn't judge it safe to try again, given how many people seemed to be out to get me."

Now she did smile, ever so slightly. It was a fleeting expression but Gabriel picked up on it all the same.

"So then what?"

"So then I went back to see Philip Agambe's widow."

"That was an unusual decision. What did you say, 'Hello, I just assassinated your terrorist-financing husband and now I want to pay my respects?'"

Gabriel took a breath. Reacting to her provocation now would undo all his work in getting here.

"I told her I was the man who'd killed her husband, yes. But I begged for her forgiveness and said I'd been set up. She had a dossier that she claimed proved that you, Prime Minister, were up to your elbows in blood diamonds, corrupt arms deals and land purchases in southern Africa."

Sutherland's lips compressed into a thin line. She appeared to be deciding on something.

"Claimed," she said, finally.

"Pardon?"

"You said Marsha Agambe had a dossier that she 'claimed' showed I'd been involved in some sort of dodgy dealings. So you didn't see it, then?"

"No. I was about to look at it when a sniper shot her. Her brother was working against her and he pulled a gun on me but the sniper got him, too."

"So it's entirely possible that the two of them were in cahoots with Philip Agambe, laying a false paper trail to incriminate me and camouflage their own actions?"

"It is. That's why I'm here. I want to believe in you. I saved your life, remember? And now I'm working for you, even if it's indirectly, against Britain's enemies."

Now, she smiled at him. Leaned towards him and laid a hand on his knee.

"Look, love. Don told me about your medical condition. The PTSD. I know the last few months have been tough on you. I understand, really I do. You've been under enormous strain. But you have to understand, breaking into Number Ten in the small hours of the bloody morning to interrogate me about supposed wrongdoings in Africa. Well, you can see how it looks from my side, can't you?"

The earnestness of her tone disorientated Gabriel. What if she were telling the truth? What if she really was being set up by the Agambes? He had a foolproof way of finding out. Hypnosis. He altered his breathing pattern, and began a sequence of eye movements, locking onto hers and then leading her gaze in a pattern of left-right movements taught to him decades earlier by Zhao Xi.

"Of course I . . . can see . . . how it looks to . . . you . . . Barbara, but that's why . . . I . . . had to some to . . . see –"

She interrupted him, shaking her head and blinking rapidly.

"What the bloody hell do you think you're playing at? Are you trying to hypnotise me?"

She stood up, and placed her hands on the arms of his chair, effectively trapping him there unless he wanted to physically force his way past her. Glaring down at him, she spoke at a normal volume.

"You're not right in the head, my love. You need help. Professional help. I know you've been under enormous strain, but really, don't you think it's time to sort yourself out?"

"You may well be right. But now isn't the time. I'm going to make an educated guess that you don't want to wake up the household – or get the police involved – any more than I do. So I'm going to leave now."

She stood over him for a couple of seconds, breathing heavily, then stood back and to one side. As he pushed up from the chair she laid a hand on his arm, stopping him for a moment.

"I'm going to put this whole episode down to your mental health condition, my love. And you're right, I don't want to wake John or Tom and I certainly don't want to call the police. For one thing, John sleeps with a gun in his bedside table – he's not supposed to have it here, but what can I say, he's overprotective. For another, I don't think you're in your right mind, so turning you over to the police wouldn't be in your best interests. But I do want you gone from my house, right now. And I suggest you take some leave. Maybe a lot of leave. See a shrink or someone who can sort out your problems for you. Now get out. I need some sleep before I face that mob in the House tomorrow."

She stood to one side and let Gabriel stand.

"Thank you," was all he said. He looked at her. Her face wore an expression of sadness, eyes creased at their corners, forehead wrinkled, mouth pulled down. Without another look, he left the room, crept along the hallway, made his way upstairs to the second floor, and was out on the rooftop a few minutes later.

It was still dark when he climbed down onto the street fifteen minutes later.

It was still dark when he sat behind the wheel of the Maserati five minutes after that, put the car in gear and cruised away from Tothill Street.

It was still dark when he climbed into bed beside Britta at the end of a nerve-wracking thirty-minute drive to Chiswick, during which he must have checked his rearview mirror a couple of hundred times.

In truth, Gabriel Wolfe had never felt so much in the dark as he did at that precise moment.

Then he thought of somebody who might be able to shed a little light.

After a couple of hours' fitful sleep, more dozing than anything else, he was up and dressed again, showered, shaved and on his way out of the door. Britta was still asleep, though she'd turned over when he'd got out of bed and mumbled something he couldn't make out before rolling herself up in the duvet, leaving just a few strands of her long, copper-coloured hair showing.

At seven-fifteen, Gabriel pulled into a parking spot on Denman Road.

46

The Third Copy

GABRIEL walked up the path to Melody's front door and stretched his fingertip towards the doorbell. Then hesitated. *What am I going to say?* Then he stopped hesitating. *For God's sake, the way things are going this can't possibly make things worse.* He pressed the bell push firmly, holding it down for a count of three before releasing the shiny porcelain dome. The ring was surprisingly loud, and made him jump.

"I'll get it, Mum!" came Nathalie's voice from the other side of the door. He watched as the shadowy outline of the thirteen-year-old girl grew larger in the panes of stained glass set into the upper half of the door.

He heard the scrape as Nathalie put the chain on – *sensible girl* – then the door opened and her brown eye scrutinised him through the crack.

"Oh, hi, Gabriel. You're up early." The eye disappeared. "Mum! It's Gabriel."

The door closed a little and the chain scraped again. Then Nathalie opened the door. She was dressed in school uniform. A dark blue blazer with sky-blue trim, black and white tie, white blouse under a black jumper and black trousers.

"Hi, Gabriel," she said. "Do you want to see Mum? She's just getting dressed. Are you hungry?"

"Hi, Nathalie. Yes I do and yes I am. Got any toast?" He was starting to

239

understand how to talk to teenagers, or this self-possessed teenager, at least.

"Come in, then. I'll make you some."

He followed her along the hall to the kitchen and sat at the table while she dropped two slices of bread into the toaster.

"I can make you tea if you want?"

"That would be lovely. You look very smart, by the way."

"Thank you. I go to an academy." Adopting a stagey "posh" voice, she intoned, "We require all our students to maintain high standards of behaviour and to wear the correct uniform at all times." Then she giggled. "That's from our website. You get sent home if your tie's crooked."

"A bit like the Army."

At this, her face clouded, just for a moment, but Gabriel realised he'd said the wrong thing.

"Have you come about Dad? Here's your tea, by the way."

He took the proffered mug and sipped the tea.

"Yes. Did your mum tell you?"

The girl nodded. "She said you tried and you got really close to your objective but then you got into some trouble and had to abandon the mission."

He smiled, impressed with her self-control and easy way with military language.

"That's right. But I'm not giving up. I have a plan and I'm going back to Mozambique. But that has to wait, just for a while."

Melody appeared in the kitchen doorway and, grateful for the interruption, Gabriel rose to meet her.

"Wow!" he said. "Are all the women in this part of London as smart as you two?"

She was dressed for work in a tailored, dove-grey suit over a white shirt. She stepped forward and hugged him.

"Flatterer! How are you? Pour me a tea would you, Nat?"

Munching the toast and drinking tea, the three of them sat round the kitchen table, for all the world like a little nuclear family on a workday. Daughter ready for school. Mum off to work as a lawyer for an international corruption-monitoring charity. Dad trying to escape his past and avoid being slung in prison for breaking into Number Ten and brandishing a loaded pistol at the Prime Minister. While the adults talked, Nathalie was texting her friends.

"I saw what happened to Marsha," Melody said. "Please tell me that wasn't anything to do with you."

He shook his head. "I promise. But I was there. She was . . ." he looked across the table at Nathalie.

"Oh, fine," she said, rolling her eyes. "I'm going round to Georgia's house to pick her up. Tell me everything later, Mum, OK?"

Her mother smiled. "The good bits, darling."

"Fine. Bye Gabriel. Hope you liked your breakfast."

Then she did a surprising thing. She leaned over him and kissed him softly on the cheek. Before he could even react, she'd turned and was out the front door.

"She can tell when people are troubled," Melody said. "She's always been drawn to hurting souls, ever since she was a baby. Are you hurting?"

Gabriel realised that he was so troubled he didn't know what was preventing him from collapsing physically, weeping, running into the street screaming, or all three. Yes, he did. Training. Self-discipline. The mission. He took a deep breath and let it out in a sigh, willing his shoulders to drop from the position adjacent to his ears where he'd jacked them.

He nodded.

"Marsha Agambe was killed by a sniper. And her brother, too. It sounded like he was taking kickbacks from someone who wanted her out of the way. I tried to get a copy of her dossier from her lawyer's office, but someone got there before me and blew the place sky-high."

"So I heard. Do you think it was the same person? The killer and the bomber?"

He nodded. "Had to be. Those sorts of skills tend to walk around together in the same body. So we're buggered, basically. I even tried to confront Barbara Sutherland last night but she's just denying everything. I mean, what if she's clean? That's still a possibility isn't it?"

"Wait. What? How did you . . . I mean where did you confront Sutherland? Surely you didn't . . . ?"

Somehow his actions of the last twelve hours suddenly struck him as funny. He grinned.

"Surely I did. Went over the rooftops and down through a maintenance stairwell."

Melody's eyes popped wide open.

"Gabriel! You broke in to Number Ten? What are you, insane?"

He was laughing now and she joined him.

"I think I may be."

"What, I mean, did you climb into bed with her and have a little chat with her under the duvet?"

"Couldn't. Her husband was there. Didn't think a threesome was appropriate."

She shrieked at this. Gabriel felt his laughter threatening to turn into an unstoppable fit and he suddenly slapped himself on the right cheek. Melody stopped instantly at the violence of the action.

"Sorry," he said. "I could feel myself losing it there. The point is, without evidence, either she's going to get away with it, or . . ."

"Or what?"

"Or isn't there just the smallest chance she's telling the truth? Couldn't your contacts have got it wrong?"

Dabbing at her eyes with a paper tissue, careful not to smudge her eye makeup, Melody sighed and shook her head.

"Come with me," she said and stood up from the table, pushing her chair back.

She led him out of the kitchen, along the narrow hall and up the stairs. At the end of the upstairs hall was a door. She opened it. Beyond was a home office, PC humming on a desk facing out over the road, the wall to the left of the desk lined with filing cabinets, the one to the right occupied with a small leather armchair and a swan-necked reading lamp on a side-table.

"Do you always dress like that just to work from home?" Gabriel asked.

"I'm going into the office today. Normally, I'm a little less formal. But

242

with Nat in her uniform, I like to make the effort. Can't have her looking down her nose at slummy mummy, can I?"

"I suppose not."

"Now, sit there," she said, pointing to the armchair. He did as he was told and watched as she jiggled the mouse to wake the PC. "There!" she said, double-clicking on an icon on the desktop and then keying in an unlock code.

Gabriel leaned forward and watched as the zip-file unpacked itself and several dozen files of different types popped up in a new window.

"She sent you a copy?"

Melody nodded as she double-clicked a PDF file. "I met Marsha two years ago at a conference. We hit it off. When you killed . . ." she turned in her chair, her face a confused mask of emotions, including anger and embarrassment. "When Philip was killed, she sent the dossier to me through a secure file-sharing site we all use. Look."

She pointed a finger at the screen.

There, in crisp detail, almost as if someone had taken it and simply stuck it behind the glass of the screen, was a document. It was a list on a World Diamond Exchange Ltd letterhead. The type was an old-fashioned font like Times or Garamond, the logo a remarkably crude drawing of a multi-faceted diamond resting in the pan of a weighing scale. It was some sort of account statement.

Against the pre-printed heading, "Account holder", someone had written, in blue biro by the looks of it, "Gemma Northfield". But there was also a '1' by the final 'd', set as a superscript character, balancing above the tip of the ascender. At the foot of the page, the meticulous book-keeper had added, in small but completely legible cursive script, a matching superscript digit, and two words.

Barbara Sutherland.

The rest of the details were hard to decipher, but one phrase gave Gabriel no trouble:

Seven (7) diamonds, 19.25 carats total, mix., F colourless – VVS/VS, Cognac, Intense Pink, Fancy Blue.

Beside the description of the gemstones were three letters: *KPC.*

Gabriel pointed. "Kimberley Process Certificate. That guarantees they're not conflict diamonds. She's innocent. They're legal. This isn't evidence of anything."

"Isn't it? Look closer." Melody pointed at the acronym. There was a superscript '2' half a millimetre northeast of the 'C'.

Gabriel registered the tiny digit then searched for its twin at the foot of the page. And there it was. Was this final, irrevocable proof that Barbara Sutherland was been playing him all along?

47

A Trip East

2 UNVERIFIED serial number. Prob. forgery. Apply discounted value to trade.

"It's still just a document," Gabriel said. "These days anyone with Photoshop on their PC could knock up something like that."

"You really want her to be innocent, don't you?"

"Don't you?"

"I haven't decided. It's complicated."

"Because exposing the British Prime Minister for something she might never have done would destabilise the country?"

"Oh, believe me, it would definitely do that. But there are all sorts of other considerations. Aid payments could be affected, relations with the developing world. All kinds of delicate negotiations. In truth, I'm really not sure what to do. If she really is dirty then, yes, I do want to take her down. But I'm not sure if that's just my heart ruling my head. I was going to take it in to work today and ask to speak to our Director."

Gabriel's mind was working overtime on very little sleep. But it had come up with an idea.

"Listen, I'm going to leave the country for a bit. There's something I need to do. But can you send me a copy of the dossier, then sit on it until I get back? Please? I can get to her in a way you can't, and I think I can find out the truth – whatever it is – without the shit hitting the fan. Plus, she's dangerous. You could be targeted if you go public."

"I don't know, Gabriel. People have died because of this. And she's behind it all."

"I know you think that. And if you're right then I hate it as much as you do. More, actually. Look, strategy was never my strong point, but you have to see the long-term impact. You could just send that to the media and drop a bomb on her head that would take her out completely. But it might take a lot of other people, too. Or you could box clever, use it against her, but only her. Call it a surgical strike, if you want."

Melody turned her swivel chair around so she was facing Gabriel.

"Why are you so keen to protect Barbara Sutherland?"

"I'm not. But," he pressed his lips together then released them, "I love this country. My father said something to me once that I've never forgotten. He said, 'Politicians come and go. And so do diplomats. But the institutions we serve, they endure.' I believe that. It's what I've always fought for. And if you go public, I'm just afraid of what the fallout would be. We'd look like some banana republic where the president's using the economy like their own personal piggy bank. I don't want that. Do you?"

She shook her head. Then she spoke.

"I'll do you a deal. Bring me concrete proof – of her guilt *or* her innocence. And bring me something of Mike we can bury." She reached across the foot of space between them and took his hands in hers. "I loved him, Gabriel. With all my heart. I never blamed you for his death. Not even for a second. But you're the only person on Earth I trust to find him for me."

She was dry-eyed as she said this, but Gabriel wasn't. He felt a tear force its way out of his eye. He dashed it away with a knuckle.

"It's a deal. I won't come back until I have."

*

Gabriel called Britta while he sat in the car outside Melody's house.

"Hey, you," she said. "Where did you disappear to?"

"I needed to see someone. About Sutherland. She could be dirty. I've seen some documents. If they're genuine then she's as dirty as fuck. I mean up to her elbows in the shittiest, most corrupt . . ."

The realisation hit him like a round from an M16. There was a real possibility that his own Prime Minister, the woman who'd been giving the orders as Defence Secretary when he'd been in uniform, was bent. Britta spoke, interrupting his thoughts.

"Back up a little. What do you mean 'if they're genuine'?"

He swiped a hand over his mouth and jaw. "All I saw were some digital files. Not actual paper."

"Huh! My sister's kids could whip you up a Swedish driving licence on their laptops in less time than it would take you to apply for a real one. I told you before, she's a democrat. A British democrat. You do know the rest of Europe looks at your politicians and wishes they were ours."

"What, even the Swedes?"

She laughed. "No, we're far too perfect. But everyone else does. I mean, the Italians?"

"Isn't that a bit racist?"

"*Ja! Det är korrect!* True, also. Listen, what are you going to do now? You're not a documents expert. Or an IT guy. How are you going to check those things you saw are genuine? I'm about to go into the office, by the way, so we'd better keep this short."

"Honestly, I hadn't really thought. I mean look at the facts. I broke into Number Ten Downing Street last night and confronted her. She denied everything and she had no reason to doubt that I believed her. She thinks my PTSD is making me behave irrationally."

"Yeah, but if I was her, I'd be starting to watch you like a hawk. Maybe put a couple of people on your tail from Special Branch."

"Maybe. I think I need to get out of the country for a while. I need to find somewhere to go where I can put a plan together. I'm going to find out the truth. But I also made a promise to Melody to go back to Mozambique and find Smudge for her."

"No pressure there, then. Where will you go?"

Gabriel had a vision of a harbour ringed by high-rise developments, a city of neon, with forested hills beyond, but he didn't want Britta to be in possession of any information that might put her in danger.

"I don't know. I've got a couple of ideas."

"But you don't want me to know because it would put me at risk."

He smiled. "Something like that. Although I'm sure you could take care of yourself."

"You better believe it. I have to go. Sounds like you do, too. Send me a message if you can. Just to let me know you're all right."

"I will." He paused. "I love you."

"I love you too, Wolfe. Now, go."

*

The traffic out of London heading east was heavy. Gabriel's route home lay in the other direction, but he'd decided on a whim to call on Don at his base at MOD Rothford in Essex. He wanted to see his boss face to face and try to winkle out of him what was making him so cagey.

Arriving at the gates of the base, he found himself hoping they'd be guarded by one of the men he'd met on a previous visit. They'd joked about his "flash motor" and urged him to "give it some" before he'd driven sedately round the perimeter road to find Don's quarters.

No such luck.

He pulled up by the guard house and a tall, black soldier carrying an SA80 assault rifle across his chest strolled over to meet him as he got out of the car.

"Good morning, sir. Can I help you?" the soldier said, his deep voice equal parts politeness and suspicion.

"I hope you can. I've come to see Colonel Webster." Gabriel remembered that although Don had left the Army, the soldiers and civilian staff on the base had all referred to him by his old rank.

"Colonel who, sir? Webster? I'm sorry, sir. Our CO is Colonel Mayhew."

"Sorry, I know that. Colonel is just an honorary rank. He's just plain Mr Don Webster. He's in charge of Special Operations. He's based in the Admin Offices."

"Sorry, sir, nothing like that here. This is a training base." The soldier's face betrayed no emotion, or understanding.

"Look, it's fine. I served under Col –" he corrected himself, "Mr Webster in the SAS. I came to see him here not too long ago."

The soldier squared his shoulders and stared down at Gabriel, resting his right hand over the trigger guard of his weapon.

"I don't care if you served under him in the Galactic Space Rangers. Sir. I told you there's nobody of that name working here. Now, turn your car around please and move on."

Gabriel stood, rooted to the spot, for another couple of seconds. Then he shook his head, muttered an apology and climbed back into his car. He reversed out onto the road and roared away from the gates, tyres screeching as they struggled for grip. *What's happened, Don? Where are you?*

*

Gabriel reached home in three hours, having exceeded the speed limit for all but a ten-mile stretch of road-works. Leaving the Maserati plinking and ticking on his drive as its engine and exhausts cooled, he went inside and packed for a trip. Suits, shirts, ties, cufflinks, polished black Oxfords, underwear, but also jeans, T-shirts, hoodie, black combat trousers, boots, and running gear.

Twenty-four hours later, Gabriel was descending the steps from a Cathay Pacific Boeing 777 onto the tarmac at Hong Kong International Airport. The air was muggy and warm, and Gabriel's clothes stuck to his back and chest.

He took the Airport Express train to Hong Kong Island, squashed among Hong Kongers and international tourists who stared across the greenish waters of the Zhujiang river estuary to the city beyond.

Free of the crush of the train, Gabriel made his way to a taxi rank. The noise all around him was disorientating after the long, relatively peaceful flight. The slap of shoes on concrete formed a pattering background to the honking of car horns and the ding-ding of the double-decker trolley cars as they approached their stops. Local voices speaking Mandarin, Cantonese and English swirled in and out of the Babel of tourist languages.

Gabriel hailed a white-roofed, red taxi and slid onto the rear bench seat.

There was no air conditioning so he wound the window down, letting in the smell of traffic fumes, street cooking and incense. The driver sped away, using the horn as Gabriel would the indicators. They passed between dizzyingly tall skyscrapers, jolted down back streets packed with low-rise buildings housing restaurants, fast food joints and mobile phone shops and then emerged onto a highway taking them into the hills overlooking the glistening towers of the financial district.

He arrived at the house mid-morning, and, as the taxi pulled away from the kerb, he leaned against, rather than pressed, the doorbell.

His heart was racing. Butterflies in their thousands were swarming inside his stomach. His palms were damp with sweat. And yet what he felt deep inside – at his core – was hope.

A figure materialised beyond the pale-green frosted glass in the door, and a key scraped in the lock.

The door swung inwards.

And there he was.

48
Reunion

ZHAO Xi rocked back on his heels. His dark eyes opened wide and his mouth spread wide in a toothy smile.

"Wolfe Cub?" he asked, in Mandarin. "Is that you? It is!"

The old man stepped forward and pulled Gabriel into an embrace that had a strength behind it that belied his slight frame. Gabriel hugged him back, and as he did, felt a lightness inside he hadn't felt for a long time.

When, finally, Xi released him, it was to hold him by his shoulders, at arm's length.

"You look tired Wolfe Cub. Come, come inside. I will make tea."

The house was sparsely furnished, although every wall was lined with books, and it smelt wonderfully of cooking. The aromas of garlic, ginger and chilli permeated the ground floor, and the salivary glands at the angle of Gabriel's jaw began prickling as the smells reached his brain.

Gabriel dropped his bags by the bed in the room Xi showed him to and followed him back out to the kitchen.

"I'm sorry I didn't call ahead, Master Zhao," he said. "But I needed to get out of the UK in a hurry and I thought it best not to leave any sort of trail."

Xi spoke while he busied himself boiling water and spooning tea into a dull green ceramic teapot with a bamboo handle.

"Are you in trouble, then?"

"I am. But I think maybe I can sort it out."

"I am sure you can. I will do all in my power to help you, of course. Now, here is tea. And are you hungry?"

Gabriel nodded. "Very."

"Then we will eat first and talk of old times, then you can explain more about this trouble in which you find yourself."

Gabriel sat on a high stool at a scrubbed wooden worktop. He watched Xi wield a razor-sharp cleaver, slicing peppers, carrots, a giant white radish and some pak choi into slivers so fast the edge of the cleaver was blurred. A piece of translucent-fleshed fish was cubed and the whole lot went into a wok half-full of the garlic, ginger and chilli broth Gabriel had smelled on his arrival.

"There is another reason I am here, Master Zhao," Gabriel said.

"Of course there is."

"I want to know about Michael. About what happened that day."

"And you will. I can take you to see the place where it happened. The old house. And his grave."

At the mention of the grave, Gabriel's pulse spiked and he gasped involuntarily. In all the time he'd been thinking about Michael, since recovering the memory of his younger brother, he'd never once stopped to ask himself whether there would be a place where he could visit him.

"I never thought about a grave."

Xi smiled, deepening the lines around his eyes and the deep grooves running from the wings of his nose to the corners of his mouth.

"I will take you there. But now we eat."

The food was excellent, and the flavours of the fish braised in the aromatic and spicy broth took Gabriel flying backwards through time to a younger version of himself: sitting at this same table, eating with this same man, wrestling with his urges to defy authority at every turn, to talk back, to run away.

Once the meal was cleared away and the plates and chopsticks washed in the stone basin, Xi filled two glasses with a pale honey-coloured spirit and motioned for Gabriel to follow him into the sitting area. He handed him one of the glasses and they clinked the rims together.

"Your health, Wolfe Cub."

"And yours, Master." The liquid was sweet and packed a hefty alcoholic punch that burned the back of Gabriel's throat. As its heat mellowed and spread outwards from his stomach, he at last felt ready to talk. "Please tell me about Michael."

Xi sipped from his glass then turned his gaze on Gabriel.

"He was very different from you. Obedient where you were unruly. Thoughtful where you were impulsive. Gentle where you were aggressive. And he adored you, Wolfe Cub. Remember that. You were his older brother and could do no wrong as far as he was concerned. He would defend your behaviour to your parents and to me."

Gabriel swallowed down a lump that had solidified in his throat.

"What about the day itself? Tell me again what happened. Don't leave anything out."

"Lin – that is, your mother – had taken the two of you to play down at the little park by the harbour. We can go there tomorrow. You brought a rugby ball with you. You were obsessed with the game. It was the only school activity you really enjoyed. Michael pestered you to play a simple game of catch with him. This game went on for a few minutes and then, according to your mother, you told Michael to move back so you could practice kicking."

The rest of the story confirmed what Gabriel already knew, ending with Michael's drowning and his own descent into darkness.

"And then what?" he asked, when Zhao Xi finished speaking. "You said before, when I called, that I went into a coma or something."

"We didn't know what it was. The doctor did not either, though he used clever language to obscure the fact. You lay in bed for two weeks. Either you were sleeping or you were awake, with your eyes open, but seeing nothing, saying nothing, doing nothing. You ate nothing. Just the odd spoonful of soup. And you drank water if the cup was pressed to your lips."

Gabriel watched his old teacher carefully as he retold the story, hoping that some new detail would present itself that would help him make sense of the tragedy for which he had been at least partially responsible.

"How did it stop?"

Xi rubbed a liver-spotted hand over his eyes.

"One morning, you appeared in the doorway to the kitchen and asked for breakfast. A boiled egg. Your parents were eating their own breakfast and were astonished to see you. Your mother prepared your meal and then they both watched as you ate it. They telephoned me and I came as fast as I could. You were talking, walking, smiling. I asked you this one question. I said, 'Gabriel. Do you remember what happened with Michael?' And do you know what you said?"

Gabriel had a clutching feeling in his gut and thought he knew the answer all too well. "Tell me," he said, finally.

"You asked, 'Who is Michael?', and you had a look of such open curiosity on your face, I will never forget it. Your mother burst into tears and left the room, but your father told you that Michael was your younger brother. He did not mention the accident."

"What happened then? What did I say?"

"Just that he was playing a trick or joking. Because he knew fine well you didn't have a brother. I took you for a walk then. Your father had to go to work and your mother had gone to lie down. I asked you in several different ways about Michael, but it was clear to me that you really had no recollection of him at all. It was as if your mind had wiped itself clean, like a cook cleaning out his wok. Nothing of Michael remained inside."

"But there was something, Master Zhao. In the end. Wasn't there? Because last year I heard his voice inside my head. Calling me 'Gable'."

Xi nodded. "Somewhere, deep down in your soul, you had saved one part of your memories of Michael. 'Gable' was his name for you because he couldn't say Gabriel. Until the accident, it had been the whole family's pet name for you. Afterwards, we went back to calling you Gabriel."

"You said they put all the photos of him away."

"Yes. You became angry and that is when your real troubles at school began. It became too upsetting for your mother, and for your father, too, though he was better at hiding his feelings than she was. When you came to live with me, things became easier for them, but we agreed never to mention Michael to you until the day when you should come and ask freely about him yourself."

Gabriel finished his drink and set the glass down on a small red lacquered table beside his armchair. He scrubbed his eyes with his sleeve. The bare facts of the story weren't new to him, but hearing the story retold in his master's soft cadences, sitting with him above the city where it had all happened . . . this was too much to bear.

"Master Zhao, I am so tired. Would you forgive me if I just went to bed now?"

The old man simply inclined his head.

Gabriel stood, and left the room, head hanging. He was asleep less than a minute later.

The following morning, Gabriel awoke at dawn. Outside his bedroom window, starlings were singing so loudly it sounded as though they might be in the room with him. Despite the troubles he had left behind in England, and the detailed retelling of the story of his brother's death, he felt ready to face everything. Barbara Sutherland. Whoever or whatever Gordian was. The mystery southern belle in the bar in Harare. All of them.

After thirty minutes of push-ups, sit-ups and yoga poses in his room, he pulled on his running shoes and left the house by the back door. The day was overcast, but mild. Gabriel alternated between short sprints and longer periods of steady running, working his body harder with each sprint, until he could feel his heart operating at peak capacity. High above the harbour, he could see ships steaming into Hong Kong, boats skippered by sailors eager to get out on the water, and the many super-yachts owned, he assumed, by China's new super-rich, still berthed at the Hong Kong Royal Yacht Club.

He closed his eyes and listened to the birds and the distant blaring of ships' klaxons.

Something made him frown, but he couldn't pinpoint what it was. He felt at peace. Nothing was bothering him, despite the forces ranged against him.

Then he realised. No voices. Smudge was leaving him alone. And even though he was so close, the young boy's voice that called him 'Gable' was silent, too. Was it the effect of being close to his childhood guardian, he wondered? Master Zhao had always seemed to have infinite reserves of patience. He had never once rushed Gabriel into saying or doing anything, but had let him come to the decision by himself. He shrugged. Whatever it was, he didn't mind.

He ran back down the path to Xi's house, showered and changed into jeans and a T-shirt and went to find some breakfast. Xi was in the kitchen sipping tea from a small, white cup, the porcelain so thin as to be translucent.

"Good morning, Wolfe Cub. Would you like some tea?"

"Yes, please, Master Zhao."

"Have you eaten?" Gabriel shook his head. "Then we will eat. I usually start the day with homemade *baozi*. You remember? Pork dumplings. You used to love them."

"That sounds perfect."

Sipping the smoky-flavoured tea, Gabriel watched Xi preparing the food. He looked for a sign that he should begin his story. But Xi seemed entirely taken up with preparing and steaming the dumplings.

"Do you want to know why I'm here, Master?"

"Do you want to tell me?"

Gabriel laughed. "You haven't changed at all. Yes, I do want to tell you. I really, really need some advice."

"Then begin. But when the food is ready, we eat, yes?"

"Yes. Of course."

Gabriel began with his and Britta's abortive trip to find Smudge's remains. And how Barbara Sutherland had given him permission to go, once he agreed to kill Philip Agambe. With a short break while they ate the pork buns, fragrant with coriander, the story took half an hour. Xi nodded occasionally, furrowed his brow at others, but mostly sat perfectly still, listening intently.

When Gabriel reached the end – "Then I took the boat Dad left berthed for me in Southampton, crossed the Channel and flew out here to see you" – Xi nodded more emphatically and then clapped his hands together with a pop.

"The British Prime Minister is in league with a person or company called Gordian. She has been trading blood diamonds for political influence. You killed one of the people who could have exposed her. A mystery assassin killed the other. You confronted the Prime Minister at Number Ten Downing Street and she denied everything, naturally. But she has already tried to have you killed twice and you believe she will again."

"That about sums it up, yes."

Xi steepled his fingertips together under his chin and looked up at the ceiling, where a bamboo-bladed fan creaked arthritically.

"You must discover who or what Gordian is. Even if the Prime Minister does want you dead, they are helping her. She must be stopped. But so must they. There is someone I know here in Hong Kong who might be able to help you. A very powerful man. Not a completely legal man, but then, you are not completely legal yourself, are you?"

Gabriel shook his head. "Not exactly, no."

"First, the harbour, though. You wish to see the place where Michael died. And where he is buried?"

"Yes, please."

"I will call my friend. Then I will take you. Meet me at the front of the house in ten minutes."

49
Family plot

THE streets were packed with people, all dodging the scaffolding poles, backhoes and road-works, arranged as if by a malevolent hand intent on booby-trapping the pavements. One street was devoted exclusively to restaurants and a cluster had specialised in selling "stinky tofu" as their English-language signs proudly boasted. Gabriel wrinkled his nose as the smell – a combination of burnt blue cheese and overcooked duck liver – rolled out of the doorways and air-conditioning extraction vents.

The park, when they reached it, was a simple square of mown grass dotted with benches and picnic tables, perhaps fifty yards to a side. It was separated from the harbour on its eastern side by a wide pavement and a low retaining wall. Under the pale grey sky, a group of elderly ladies in loose-fitting cotton smocks and trousers extended their arms and legs in graceful, slow movements. Xi led Gabriel to the pavement and pointed to a ladder leading down to the water.

"That is the spot where Michael jumped in. He could have used the ladder but I think he wanted to impress you. We do not know exactly how he injured his head, perhaps there was something from one of the ships floating on the water. Your mother said you just shouted his name as you watched, then dived in after him. Do you remember anything now you are back here?"

Gabriel stared down at the greenish water, willing himself to recall even a fragment of the scene. The sound of a splash, or the smell of the water, the feeling of the cold on his skin. Nothing came. He could only recall Michael because he had been told the story by Xi and combined it with a couple of fleeting auditory hallucinations. His brother remained a void in his mind.

"There's nothing there. It's just a blank."

Xi touched him on the arm. "Do not worry. Perhaps now is not the time for you to remember. You were brave. That is what matters. You went in after Michael and you pulled him out. It is sad that you were unable to save him. But . . ."

"But I killed him, Master. Didn't I? I kicked the ball too high for him and I told him to fetch it out."

"You were young, Wolfe Cub. And you were an older brother. You did what older brothers do the world over. But taunting and bossing are not killing. It was an accident. That is all. An accident."

Gabriel sighed and scratched his scalp. "I know. The trouble is, the accidents I get involved in tend to get people killed."

*

As they approached the cemetery, Gabriel felt oddly calm. He had expected to feel afraid or anxious, but there was nothing. No fluttering butterflies in his stomach. No sweating palms. No breathlessness. They walked side by side along the gravelled path between the headstones until Xi laid his hand on Gabriel's shoulder to slow him down. He pointed to a small, polished slab of black granite, perhaps two feet high by one across and four or five inches thick. In front of it, a few sprigs of pink magnolia sat in a glass vase.

Gabriel looked over at the grave. "The flowers?"

"I put them there. I tend the grave. It was a promise I made to your parents."

"Thank you."

Gabriel inhaled deeply. He squared his shoulders. Then he walked, alone, away from the path, towards his brother's grave.

He knelt in front of the stone and read the carved and gold-filled inscription aloud.

"Michael Francis Wolfe. Nineteen eighty-five to nineteen ninety. Beloved son and brother. Taken from us too soon." He closed his eyes, strained to recall the face that belonged with the name. With the voice that had spoken to him and called him 'Gable'. There was nothing. He opened them again. "I'm sorry, Michael," was all he said. Then he stood, turned, and walked back to Xi, who was waiting for him on the path.

"How are you feeling?" Xi asked, his head cocked to one side, a soft breeze ruffling his fine grey hair.

"I don't know. I don't feel anything. I thought maybe there would be this rush of grief or shame or something. But no, there's nothing there. I'm sorry, Master."

"Do not be sorry. We wish to impose order on the internal world as much as on the external world. But neither is ours to control. We must simply act, and let our feelings take care of themselves."

Gabriel shrugged. "That's just it, Master Zhao. I have no feelings."

"Come. You need to focus your mind on something else for a while. Did you pack training clothes?"

"Yes."

"Good. Then I will give you some instruction in *Yinshen fangshi*. We can see whether you have been keeping up your practice."

50
The Golden Dragon

THAT evening, at ten-thirty, Xi and Gabriel stood outside an ornate golden door flanked by carved wooden dragons. The seven-foot-tall reptiles held illuminated glass globes in their fanged mouths. The dragons themselves were flanked by two more monsters: men wide of chest, thick of bicep and seemingly carved from the same hardwood, though wearing black suits rather than a skin of gold paint. Despite the expert tailoring of their jackets, Gabriel detected telltale bulges under the left armpits of their jackets. Above the door, in red neon Mandarin characters, was the club's name. Golden Dragon. What else?, Gabriel thought.

Xi had told him to dress well for the visit to Fang Jian. He had therefore donned a plain grey, lightweight suit with a navy windowpane check; a white shirt with a herringbone weave to the cotton, and French cuffs secured with gold-plated nine-millimetre pistol rounds; a knitted navy silk tie with a square end; and his polished black Oxfords. Xi himself wore a traditional Chinese suit with a high collar, in black silk, and matching slippers.

In Mandarin, Xi told the doormen, "We have a personal invitation from Fang Jian."

"Name," one said, his features scarcely more mobile than those of the reptiles to his left and right.

"I am Zhao Xi and this," he extended his right hand, palm outwards, "is

261

my friend from England, Gabriel Wolfe."

The doorman unhooked the thick, twisted scarlet rope from its brass pole and motioned for them to enter the club.

Beyond the cloakroom area was a red-and-gold silk curtain. They pushed through it. Gabriel had been expecting loud music, the blare of conversations held at shouting level to make the participants heard, shrieks of drunken laughter. Instead, the Golden Dragon was subdued. Such music as there was came from the clatter and skip of ivory balls bouncing around roulette wheels, the flicker of cards being dealt and checked, the rattle of dice and the clack of dominos on hard wooden tables.

The air was thick with cigarette smoke. It hung in a bluish haze above the heads of the gamblers. Gabriel's nose twitched and he sneezed, twice. He realised how rare it was in England now to inhale that pungent, bitter smell in a public space.

The Golden Dragon's patrons were dressed in Western-style lounge suits or dinner jackets for the men, and cocktail dresses for the women. There was a lot of gold in evidence, shimmering over the curves of the women's bodies, dangling from their earlobes or draped over their collarbones, and worn on the fingers of the men like eighteen-karat knuckledusters.

Between the gamblers and the occasional knot of spectators, waitresses weaved, carrying aloft circular trays of drinks. They wore red cheongsams, slit up the right thigh and embroidered with more golden dragons. These beasts clawed their way up from the women's knees, over the hips, around the back to the chest, where their open mouths snarled at any punter who got too close.

Gabriel scanned the room, looking for the man they had come to see. Knowing nothing of the man's appearance, he was at a disadvantage to Xi, who smiled and waved, before descending the flight of stairs carpeted in more scarlet and gold, and walking into the centre of the room.

Coming towards them through the crowd was a wide-shouldered man with the build of a heavyweight boxer. He wore a gold dinner jacket over black dress trousers. Even at this distance, Gabriel could see that the backs of both hands were inked in colourful designs.

Arriving in front of them, the giant smiled at Xi, revealing large, yellowish teeth, and enveloped him in a bear hug. They clapped each other on the back, then released their arms.

In Mandarin, he asked Xi, "Is this the Wolfe Cub?"

"Yes. Do you remember him?"

"He has grown into a man, but yes, I see something of the spark he had as a boy."

Xi turned to Gabriel. "Wolfe Cub, this is Mr Fang."

Gabriel extended his hand, which Fang ignored with a roar of laughter. "Why so formal? Don't you recognise me?" before grabbing Gabriel and enveloping him in another crushing embrace.

When he could draw breath again, Gabriel scrutinised the man's face. The nose had been broken at some point and the flat planes of the cheeks bore a couple of old knife scars.

"I'm sorry," he said, sticking, like the other two men, to Mandarin. "I can't place you. Have we met before?"

"Come to my office and I will tell you."

They followed him across the floor of the club and Gabriel noticed the way the waitresses flowed around Mr Fang like river water round a boulder, while the punters eyed him nervously and bent closer to their cards, dice or brightly coloured chips.

Inside Fang's office, the noise of the excited gamblers dropped to a murmur. On a sleek silver monitor fixed to one wall, eight full-colour views of the gambling floor were tiled on the screen. The room was lit with a soft, yellow light from four more of the golden dragons with glass globes in their jaws. Everything in the room came in the club's signature colour scheme of scarlet and gold, from the buttoned leather armchairs and matching sofa, to the low lacquer table between them, and on to the wallpaper. Sitting dead centre on the table was a golden ice bucket and three tall flutes, decorated with yet more dragons. Protruding from the surface of the ice was the foil-wrapped neck of a champagne bottle. Gabriel recognised the design. It was Pol Roger – his favourite brand, and also, he'd found out at a Regimental ball, Winston Churchill's too.

Pulling the bottle free of the ice with a metallic rattle, Fang gestured with his other hand for Gabriel and Xi to seat themselves on the sofa. With a loud pop, he opened the champagne and filled the glasses.

"A toast," he said, switching to fluent, if ungrammatical, English. "To Wolfe Cub who grew up into Wolfe."

They clinked glasses. Gabriel let the champagne slide down his throat, enjoying the prickling of the bubbles on his tongue and, as they tricked his stomach into letting them through into the gut, the almost immediate hit from the alcohol.

"You said we had met before, Mr Fang," Gabriel said.

"Yes, we have. Tell me," he said, extending his left hand, showing Gabriel the back, "you know what fish this is?"

Gabriel examined the tattoo. The fish was plump, with large silvery-blue scales, and barbules drooping from the corners of its wide mouth. It was clear that the background of water lilies and abstract green and turquoise swirls extended back inside the man's cuff and up his forearm.

"It's a carp."

"It *koi* carp. Very special fish. And scales should really be white, but that hard effect to achieve with tattoo needle. Now do you know me?"

Gabriel stared at Fang. The clang when the penny dropped was almost audible. "Wait. The White Koi? Are you . . . ?"

Fang threw his back and roared with laughter. Dabbing his eyes with a display handkerchief he whisked from the pocket of his dinner jacket, he returned his gaze to Gabriel.

"Yes! I am Ricky Fang. I don't know why we take English names in those days. Maybe we think it make us sound cool. You came asking me for job. You were just small boy. You arrive on little bicycle, offering to deliver drugs for me. Do you remember?"

Gabriel smiled at the memory. It was the story he'd told Fariyah at one of their sessions together. He'd seriously fancied himself as a drugs courier, whizzing around Hong Kong on a BMX bike with five-dollar bags of weed or coke stuffed into his jeans pockets.

"Yes, I remember. Only I got into a fight with one of your boys and you threatened to cut my throat if I ever showed my face again."

"Ha! Don't worry, I won't carry out my threat. Now, tell me. Why does my good friend Xi bring you here? You know what I do, who I am?"

Gabriel nodded and took another sip of the champagne. "I know what the White Koi is. And I know you are the man in charge. Can I say it? You run a triad."

All business now, his face grim after the humour of a few seconds ago, Fang leant across the table towards Gabriel, his shoulders bulging under his jacket yet not straining the seams. Excellent tailoring, Gabriel thought. Better than your goons on the door.

"That is right. I am very bad man. Breathing same air as me put you on list at police headquarters. Right. At. The top!"

He slammed his hand down on the table, making Gabriel jump. Then he burst out laughing again. "But don't worry, Wolfe Cub. If they come for us, we go down fighting, eh?" Gabriel smiled, shaking his head and trying to recalibrate his emotional responses to this bear-like man and his sense of humour. "Xi tells me you are in trouble of your own. Is that right?"

Gabriel turned to look at Xi.

"Go on Wolfe Cub," he said. "Mr Fang can help you. I am sure of it."

51

How to Kill a Snake

GABRIEL explained the situation once more, hoping Xi wouldn't mind hearing the details all over again.

"And what do you think I can do for you?" Fang asked, when Gabriel had finished.

"I'm not sure. I have a vague plan of getting her to admit what's she's been doing and recording it. And I need to retrieve my friend's remains from Mozambique. And there's this mysterious Gordian, which could be a person, but I feel it's more likely to be a company. An American company. One with access to mercenaries and military-grade hardware."

Fang drained his champagne, belched loudly, then refilled all three glasses. He sat back, legs spread, and slapped his meaty palms down on his thighs, looking first at Xi, then at Gabriel.

"There is a snake in a hole. You want snake dead, because it threaten your family and attack your livestock. But it only comes out when you are not there to kill it. You could put your hand into the hole, but then it bite you and you die. What do you do?"

Gabriel thought for a moment. A test. He was used to tests. But they were usually physical or logistical, not exercises in lateral thinking.

"I stick a gun barrel in there and start shooting."

"Terrible idea! Snake just retreat further into tunnel. You will never hit it."

"Grenade, then."

Fang smiled, clearly enjoying himself. "But snake's burrow is beneath your house. Blow up burrow and you destroy own home."

Gabriel smiled back and opened his arms wide. "Then I must give up and learn from a master snake-killer."

Fang nodded. "There another triad here some years back. They call themselves the Coral Snakes. In beginning, White Koi and Coral Snakes live side by side happily. But their leader very ambitious man. He tried to muscle in on our businesses and territories. It become necessary to deal with him and his organisation. But he always very cautious about going out in public. Many bodyguards. But I know of something he want so badly, he abandon his own rules."

"What was it?" Gabriel asked, leaning forward, ignoring his drink.

"Painting. By young mainland artist. Very collectable. Very valuable. China has many billionaires now, just like Russia. They want art as well as fast cars and gold. He think he can join them if he has this painting. It bought at auction few years before by unknown buyer. I put out word on street I have it. Then, guess what?"

""I don't know. What?"

"The man contact *me*. The rival he trying to put out of business. Say he want the painting and can we sit down together and hammer out deal."

"You didn't have the painting though, did you?"

"Your boy see the truth of things quickly, Master Zhao. He has a wise teacher."

Gabriel turned to look at his old teacher. The old man smiled and inclined his head.

"I did not have painting," Fang continued. "I get someone in Guangzhou create copy instead. Librarian, can you believe it? The man was genius. I send photo to Coral Snake leader and say we meet at workshop of old carpenter we both know."

"How did you persuade him to come without protection?"

"I say to him I have people watching building and streets leading to it. We see muscle and deal off."

"Did it work?" Gabriel asked.

"Like charm. He comes on time to the workshop. Alone. I set up fake on easel by carpenter's workbench. Bench has clamps screwed along one edge and vices bolted to the wood. Woodworking tools hang on wall behind bench. Where practised hand can find them without looking away from work."

Gabriel could feel what was coming next, even if the hapless Coral Snake leader could not. "And then?"

"And then, while he lost in admiration of my fake, I hit him on back of the head with wooden mallet. When he comes round he clamped to top of workbench. Then I hammer out deal. After that, Coral Snakes slide away and find another house to nest under."

Xi spoke, startling Gabriel, who had been absorbed in Fang's story.

"What do you learn from Mr Fang's tale, Wolfe Cub?"

Gabriel paused before answering. His mind was processing the story and using it as an overlay on the map of his own challenges.

"You draw the snake out of its hole far enough then cut off its head with one swift, sharp strike."

"Exactly!"

"I need to find a way to draw Sutherland out into the open, away from her minders and then deal with her so she stops being a threat. I need something she is desperate for."

"And does such a thing exist? No, let me rephrase that, because everyone has something they are desperate to possess. Do you know what she wants so badly that she would meet you, alone, to acquire it?"

Gabriel thought of the dossier on Melody's computer.

"Yes. I do."

"Then you can follow Mr Fang's example and you can triumph."

What about Smudge? And Gordian? There are too many loose ends. I can't just go back to England. I need some help.

Gabriel took another swallow of the champagne and looked straight at Fang.

"Mr Fang. Thank you for telling me your story. And for welcoming me after my behaviour the last time we met." Fang inclined his head. "I need to ask you for some help with other, related problems."

The big man leaned forward.

"Zhao Xi bring you to me. So ask for whatever you need," he said.

"I need a fake passport. And I need someone with computer skills. Really, really good computer skills."

The crinkles in the big man's forehead disappeared and his narrowed eyes widened again. "I thought you ask for something difficult. Send me your passport and new photos. It take forty-eight hours. Second thing also easy. In my organisation is boy called Wūshī. You know word?"

"Wizard."

"He *is* wizard. But with code, hacking, whatever. I introduce you to him." Fang checked his watch. "Believe it or don't, even clubs like Golden Dragon must close from time to time. I have business across town. But you stay in bar as long as you like. Order more champagne, on the house. When you ready to leave, my security men on the front door lock up after you. And take this."

Fang gave Gabriel a business card, which he pocketed. Then Xi and Gabriel stood, following Fang's lead. The three men walked back to the gaming floor, which was now deserted apart from the croupiers and dealers tidying up their stations, stacking chips and plaques and disposing of used decks of cards.

"I am tired, Wolfe Cub," Xi said after they had shaken hands with Fang and he had disappeared. "You stay. I will see you in the morning."

Gabriel took a seat at the bar. As the last of the staff left, leaving eddies in the pungent smoke curling lazily in their air on the stairway leading to the exit, Gabriel smiled. At last, he could see an end game that he might just win.

52

Hello Again, Darling

BEFORE leaving, Fang had been quite clear in his instructions to the barman.

"My friend stays here as long as he wants. You serve him. You don't charge him."

Then the big man had left, accompanied by two slightly built women dressed in white leather, whom Gabriel suspected could inflict unimaginable pain and suffering on anyone unwise enough to attempt an unscheduled meeting with their boss.

It had been a long day, but Gabriel was wide awake. He signalled to the barman.

"Bring me a bottle of the Pol Roger, please."

The bottle brought, and a tall, rose-pink flute set beside it, the barman vanished through a door. Gabriel unwrapped the white foil himself this time, enjoying the way the heavy yet pliable metal twisted between his fingers. He removed the wire cage around the top of the bottle and dropped it onto the bar. Then he held the cork still with his right hand and twisted the bottle to let the pressurised carbon dioxide inside escape with a hiss. "Pops are for *arrivistes*," a diplomat friend of his father had once confided to him at the beginning of an Embassy reception.

He was just tilting the rim of the glass to his lips when a couple of muffled thuds from beyond the door made him look up. The red and gold silk curtain over the entrance bellied out towards him. Then it was swept aside and a woman stepped into the space between the tables. It was the woman he'd drunk gin and tonics with in Harare.

She had taken the club's dress code and perverted it, just a little. Instead of a cocktail dress, she wore black dress trousers, a fitted dinner jacket over a white silk blouse and bootlace tie secured with a silver clasp of some kind, and high-heeled, cream and black snakeskin boots. Where she had been sitting for their previous meeting, now she was standing and Gabriel could take in her physique. She was about five feet six, with an athletic build that spoke of long hours training in a gym somewhere. She moved gracefully, sinuously, always on balance, weight distributed carefully, feet light on the ground. She was carrying a zipped, black leather document case in her left hand. And a pistol in her right, aimed at his chest.

Keeping very still on his bar stool, Gabriel identified the pistol: a Smith & Wesson M&P Shield. Chambered for .40 calibre rounds, it would take his head off at this range, even with the matt-black cylindrical suppressor screwed into the end of the barrel. Clearly, the woman had a strong sense of personal style – the gun was chrome plated, with ivory panels just visible each side of the grip.

He glanced behind him at the door through which the barman had left.

"Don't bother, darling," she said, strutting over to him. "Who do you think let me know you were here? People like Fang Jian think they are the only ones who can command loyalty." She winked at him. "They're not."

"You seem to have lost your accent," Gabriel said, noticing that the silver clasp holding her string tie closed was a cast of a hollow-point round, *post-impact*: an ugly flower with sharp, jagged petals.

"Why, I do declare, so I have," she said, returning to her southern belle persona, just for a second. Then she was all business again, using her own voice, an accent Gabriel classified as southern England with an upper-class filter. Cut glass, but playful, like his champagne flute with the addition of a tiny plastic mermaid. "I've got some bad news for you, Gabriel Wolfe."

"How do you know my name? And who the fuck *are* you?" Gabriel said. "Really?"

The woman looked at him, smiling enough to expose the tips of her teeth between those amazing, bruised-looking lips.

"Me, darling? I'm Sasha Beck."

"And you normally show up in bars after hours and shoot the door staff?"

"Not at all. But they were in the way. Normally I only shoot people when I'm paid to. Which is why I know your name, to answer your first question. It's part of my business to know the names of everyone I've been hired to kill."

Gabriel had faced people holding guns on him before. The fact she'd been hired rather than recruited, sub-contracted or kidnapped didn't really matter to him. He just knew he had to keep her talking long enough to figure out a way past her. "You blew up the law office in Harare didn't you?"

She nodded. "A little bit of housekeeping."

"And, what, you're a hitwoman?"

"A what?" She threw her head back, exposing a slender white throat, and laughed. "We're not in some kind of Raymond Chandler novel, you know. I prefer the term 'assassin'. It has greater historical resonance."

"OK, so you're an assassin. What are you doing in Hong Kong?"

"I could ask you the same question. It's a free country, more or less."

"I'm researching my family history."

She arched her thin, black eyebrows.

"Really?" she drawled. "You don't look the type. Genealogists are more the beige cardigan and horn-rimmed spectacles type."

"Now who's inhabiting a novel?"

She licked the tip of her index finger and painted a mark in the air.

Tell me, Gabriel," she said, closing one eye and tracing a triangle over his face with the muzzle of her pistol, "as you're so interested in research, would you like to have a look at some documents I acquired in Harare? It was just before our first meeting."

The dossier! At last.

He steadied his breathing before answering. "Yes, please."

"I thought you might. Here."

She held out the document case. For a second, Gabriel considered trying to disarm her, then changed his mind. Something told him she'd be expecting a move and would drill a bullet into his skull if he so much as looked at the gun. He reached towards her and took the case.

"Smart boy," she said with a smile. "Have a read. But don't spend too long. It took me bloody hours to get through it all."

Gabriel pulled the rubber band off the folder and opened it. Inside was an inch-thick sheaf of documents. The papers were of differing sizes, colours and weights, some with letter headings, some without, some even with Zimbabwean Government stamps across the top, or adorned with shiny, red, wax seals plastered down over pink ribbons.

The top sheet of paper was a list of contents. The title read:

Evidence of Barbara Sutherland's involvement in corrupt arms/diamond/ land deals.

Underneath were a series of numbered items:

1. *Trips to Democratic Republic of Congo by B Sutherland.*
2. *Copies of forged Kimberley Process Certificates from Rambeka Diamond Field.*
3. *Financial statements from Sutherland's a/c at Hoffner & Albrecht, Zurich.*
4. *Invoices for munitions, targeting software, weapons systems, Gordian Security, Inc.*
5. *Emails between B Sutherland and Robert Hamilton, Gordian CEO.*
6. *Video of B Sutherland at Hotel Panafrica, Kinshasa, meeting R Hamilton and Emmanuel Chinandia, Minister of Defence.*
7. *Minutes of cabinet defence and security committee meetings.*
8. *Testimony of Jonathan Makalele AKA 'General Rambo', leader of gang known as The Rock and Roll Boys (regard as dubious).*
9. *Statements from B Sutherland's account at World Diamond Exchange Ltd under alias "Gemma Northfield".*
10. *Contracts for land purchases in Zambia, Kenya, Mozambique: co-signatories, B Sutherland, R Hamilton, W Chinandia.*

Gabriel turned the page. The list continued, eventually reaching 29 on the third sheet of paper. He turned over and began reading the first document.

While he read, flipping backwards and forwards through the pile, noting documents he'd seen on Melody's computer and rubbing the back of his neck occasionally, Sasha poured herself a glass of the champagne and wandered round the bar, never letting her aim deviate from the centre of his head.

*

Thirty minutes later, sitting back on the stool facing Gabriel, she spoke again.

"Well?"

He jerked his head up.

"These aren't forgeries. Not all of them. They can't be. She's dirty."

"I'm afraid so, darling. Your Prime Minister has been a very naughty girl. She's wasted in politics, though. I could introduce her to some people who would make this sort of thing look like pin money." Sasha reached across the table and slapped the folder shut with the flat of her hand. "I can't let you keep it, I'm afraid. Much though I imagine you would like to."

She put her fingers to her lips and whistled, a shrill, pure note, rising and falling, that could have brought a taxi to her side from the other side of the city. Instead, a squat, heavily tattooed Chinese man entered the bar on silent feet. She handed the folder of documents to him and whispered something Gabriel couldn't catch. The man nodded and then ran from the bar.

"Do you like stories, Gabriel?" she asked.

He nodded, still stunned from the realisation that his suspicions about Barbara Sutherland were correct. "I love them."

"Then pour yourself another drink, and one for me, and I'll tell you how I became an assassin. It's the last story you'll hear. In this world, at least. But it's a good one. I promise. Oh, and please don't try anything clever with the bottle. I have extremely fast reactions."

53
Gabriel Wolfe is Dead

GABRIEL turned round slowly and reached for the bottle. Then with his back still turned, even though he could almost feel the pressure of her finger on the trigger, he poured two generous glasses of the champagne. He handed one to Sasha and leaned back against the bar.

"I'm all yours," he said.

As Sasha began her story, Gabriel closed his eyes. It would make him seem less of a threat. He started a breathing exercise that would lower his heart rate and prepare him for action.

While she talked, he listened. Not to the details, just to the sound of her voice. Its rhythms, cadences, tone and speed. All perfectly normal. As her story came to an end, with her training at the hands of a Serbian killer, he opened his eyes again.

". . . and I've been an assassin ever since," she finished.

"If you don't mind my asking, how many contracts have you worked since then?"

She looked straight at Gabriel, her lips curving into a smile. "You sure you want to know?"

"I'm just curious."

"Sixty. But numbers one through thirty were all in the first three years. I've slowed down a bit. I get to be more . . ." she paused, looking upwards, ". . . selective."

"So that's a little more than five kills a year. On average, I mean. What do you do the rest of the time?"

"I read. Classics, mostly. And I like art. I travel around. There are some amazing galleries. The Uffizi, the Prado, Chicago Art Institute, the Guggenheim. Don't worry, darling. I fill my time."

"And now you've come to kill me."

"And now I've come to kill you."

"You know I have killed people myself."

She nodded. "I did my research. It doesn't change things. Doesn't make you special. Not even unique. One guy? He was a mass-murderer, a bona fide serial killer. Ukrainian. Slaughtered and ate fifty-four people, from Kiev to Murmansk. A Russian Mafia boss hired me after the guy made *steak tartare* out of his sister-in-law."

As they talked and drank the champagne, Sasha's left hand didn't waver by so much as a millimetre. The suppressor was now pointing directly at Gabriel's chest. She'd already chambered a round. All it needed was a seven-pound pressure on the trigger and the .40 calibre round in the chamber would explode out of the muzzle and punch a fist-sized cavity through his torso.

"But who hired you to kill me, Sasha?" he asked now, looking intently into her eyes.

"I'd love to tell you, Gabriel, you'd find it so hard to deal with, but I'm afraid my perfession . . ." she shook her head, ". . . my professional ethics forbid such a . . . disclosion. No. That's not right."

A frown crossed her face, smooth, high forehead crinkling as various possibilities raced through her rapidly failing mind.

Gabriel had known better than to try hypnosis. Sasha Beck wasn't the sort of woman who'd blithely fall into a trance so he could kill her. At the first sniff of a change to his speech pattern or breathing she'd plug him where he stood. However, he'd had an alternative.

Just as he was leaving the club, Fang had pulled a small zip-lock bag from his jacket pocket and shown Gabriel the contents.

What are they?" Gabriel asked, looking at a dozen or so pale-blue, circular pills, just a few millimetres across, each one imprinted with a 'P'.

"It's a new drug in Hong Kong. For date rape. Like Rohypnol only much stronger. Ketamine-based. They call it Panda. We confiscated them from a customer."

"You care about date rape?"

"I care about my image. Date rape bad for business." He smiled. "It much harder to launder money through my club when police always sniffing around."

"I don't need date rape drugs, Mr Fang."

Fang laughed.

"No. You handsome fellow. I bet you have all girls you want. But you also get into trouble from time to time, you already told me that. Maybe these will get you out one time."

Using *Yinshen fangshi*, Gabriel had dropped one of the pale-blue pills into Sasha's glass of champagne while she'd sauntered around the casino. Now, he had to be ready to move. As she felt her grip on reality slide she'd almost certainly shoot.

He watched her closely.

"Are you OK?" he asked, tensing his muscles, ready to move.

"Oh, you naughty man," she said. Her eyes looked black – her pupils had blown up all the way to the edges of her irises.

No doubt she meant to pull the trigger but her synapses were gluey with the drug. Gabriel reached her before she could react.

He darted out his right hand and clamped it around the slide of the pistol. The pressure stopped it moving forward and releasing the hammer as she squeezed the trigger. For good measure he jammed his thumb down in front of the hammer, preventing the firing pin striking the rear of the cartridge in the chamber.

With his left hand he punched her hard on the tip of her long, straight nose. The blow snapped her head back, and as she fell backwards he twisted the gun out of her grip and sideswiped her across the left temple. The combination of the punch, the pistol-whipping and the industrial-strength anaesthetic coursing through her bloodstream put her down. Gabriel caught her as she slumped and, with his hands under her armpits, lowered her to the ground.

First he checked her for other weapons. Inside the jacket he found a shoulder holster, empty. The Shield's home. He patted her down, checking the back of her waistband. On tour in Northern Ireland, he'd never gone anywhere socially without a Walther PPK tucked into the back of his jeans – "nightclub guns" they used to call them. Sasha obviously didn't feel the need. From her waist, he moved to her ankles, pulling up the hems of her tailored dress trousers over the snakeskin ankle boots. *Aha! A pro would never leave themselves without a spare.*

Strapped to her right ankle in a slimline leather holster was a small semi-automatic pistol. Gabriel unsnapped the catch securing the pistol and withdrew it. The stampings on the slide confirmed what he had already concluded from the striking grey and black design and the compact size: it was another Smith & Wesson, a 2213, chambered for .22 rim-fire cartridges. More of a gun for plinking at piles of beer cans out on a farm than serious professional work, but what it lacked in stopping power it made up for in concealability. And in the hands of a killer like Sasha Beck, more than capable of taking her man – or woman – down.

A trickle of saliva had emerged from the corner of her mouth and was tracking across her cheek. Gabriel fished the display handkerchief from the pocket of his suit jacket and dabbed the spit away. Then he undid his tie, rolled her onto her front and lashed her right wrist to her left ankle. He used his tactical knife to cut the flex from a table lamp and used it to cross-lash her left wrist to her right ankle. Only amateurs lash wrists together. Anyone with any training, whether Special Forces, counterintelligence or a more unorthodox source such as Sasha's, would be free in seconds.

Once his would-be assassin was secure, he turned back to the bar and poured himself another glass of the Pol Roger. Then he settled himself into a chair and waited.

She was out for ninety minutes. A small mewing sound escaped her lips, as if she were a child having the beginnings of a bad dream. Gabriel stood. He walked over to where he'd hog-tied her and knelt by her head, watching her eyelids intently. Now, they flickered, rising and falling in spasmodic contractions, as if they weighed too much for the small muscles behind them to lift them clear of her eyeballs. This was the moment Gabriel had been waiting for.

Groggy from the Panda and the blows to her head, she would be susceptible to the ancient hypnotic techniques taught to Gabriel by Master Zhao. He began speaking, a metronomic monologue that conveyed virtually no meaning beyond a simple instruction to relax and think of nothing. Behind the syntax and the semantics, riding on his words like a hidden code, he instructed her brain to allow him unrestricted access while remaining conscious itself.

He stroked his fingers across her brow then tapped her, twice, sharply, an inch above the point where the upper edges of her eyebrows would intersect if they continued their arched progress towards the bridge of her nose.

"Sasha. Can you hear me? I want you to say my name."

Her voice was a breathy whisper. "Gabriel Wolfe."

"Good. Do you remember why you came here?"

"To kill you."

"So tell me, Sasha. Who hired you to kill me?"

"Can't tell you."

"Yes you can tell me. I want you to tell me who hired you. Who is your client?"

Sasha's forehead contracted, and her eyebrows drew together. Her bruised red lips compressed and her eyelids wrinkled. Then her face relaxed and she spoke.

"Robert Hamilton."

"Who is Robert Hamilton?"

"He's CEO of Gordian Security."

"Where did you meet when he gave you the contract?"

"Didn't meet. Phone."

"How are you normally paid?"

"Wire transfer."

"OK, good. Thank you. Now, listen to me and repeat what I say. The contract on Gabriel Wolfe is completed."

Her drowsy lips moved. "The contract on Gabriel Wolfe is completed."

"Gabriel Wolfe is dead."

"Gabriel Wolfe is dead."

"Good. You can stop repeating now." Gabriel was seized with inspiration. "Tell me the unlock code for your phone."

"Six, seven, one, nine, one."

"I am leaving. You will sleep. Count down in threes from seven hundred and ninety seven."

Drawing a shivery breath, Sasha began counting backwards. She reached seven hundred and eighty two before her voice tailed off and her breathing settled into a still, quiet rhythm as she slept. Gabriel bent to her chest and extracted her phone from her inside jacket pocket.

"You dropped your phone in Victoria Harbour," he whispered.

On the walk back to Xi's house, Gabriel called Fang.

"Mr Fang, it's Gabriel Wolfe. After you left there was a visitor to the Golden Dragon. She killed your door staff and I think you should replace your barman too – he's not to be trusted."

"Who is she? Where is she?"

"Her name is Sasha Beck. She's an assassin. She was sent to kill me. I left her at the Golden Dragon. She's not going anywhere. Could you keep her out of circulation for a couple of weeks for me?"

"As I say, Wolfe Cub. Whatever you need. I will go back to the club now. Thank you."

Gabriel noticed a photo booth outside a pharmacy. Five minutes later, a still-sticky strip of miniature Gabriels was drying in the night air between his fingertips. Suddenly hungry, he ducked into the first restaurant he passed. It was lit with bright fluorescent strip-lights that gave the place a cold, bluish cast and turned the diners' faces an unhealthy whitish-grey. The restaurant, it turned out, only served a soft, creamy milk pudding in various flavours. Too tired to change venues, he ordered a banana-flavoured dish from the waitress and spooned the warm and surprisingly tasty concoction into his mouth. The canteen-style seating arrangements meant he was joined moments later by a couple of young Hong Kongers who barely spoke to each other, so engrossed were they in their smartphones.

Before he went to bed, he placed the strip on top of his passport on the kitchen table with a note asking Xi to send it all to Mr Fang. The last thing he did before sleep overtook him was to send a text from Sasha Beck's phone. He scrolled through the list of contacts until he found Robert Hamilton.

```
Contact completed. Gabriel Wolfe dead. No wire
transfer this time. Sending someone to collect
in person. US bearer bonds. Text when you have
them.
```

That puts you on notice, you bastard. I'm coming for you.

54

The Wizard Works His Magic

Gabriel woke to the sound of Xi talking. He checked his phone. It was eleven o'clock. There was a text waiting from Hamilton.

```
US Bearer Bonds not issued since 1982. May take
some time to locate. No problem. Thank you.
```

Forty minutes later, Gabriel was standing outside an apartment building on Ko Shing Street. He pressed a button and after a few seconds a tinny voice crackled from the intercom speaker.

"Who is it?"

"Gabriel Wolfe. Mr Fang – "

"Yeah, yeah. I was expecting you. Come on up. Sixth floor, number six-one-four."

The door latch buzzed and Gabriel pushed through into the lobby.

The lift smelled of incense, a heady jasmine perfume, so strong as to be almost sickly. Gabriel was grateful when the doors opened and he could step out into the hallway on the sixth floor. He turned left, realised he'd picked the wrong direction and turned back on himself, finding Wūshī's door twenty feet beyond the lift. He knocked three times and stood where anyone peering through the spyhole would get a good look at his face.

The door swung inwards and there stood the wizard: a slightly built man in his late teens or early twenties, bleached blond hair gelled up into a pompadour, high cheekbones and a nose ring.

"Come in, Man," he said. "I got my machine purring away waiting for you."

Gabriel smiled as the geeky Hong Konger with a fake American accent led him down a narrow hallway and into a room that could only be described as a control centre.

Dominating the small room was a desk on which sat three flat-screen monitors behind a wireless keyboard and mouse. On a shelf to the left of the desk sat a dull golden cylinder about nine inches in diameter and maybe a foot tall. It emitted a quiet hum. Cables in yellow, black and a startling cobalt blue snaked away from it to the monitors, a printer and a couple of other peripheral devices whose purposes Gabriel couldn't even guess at.

"Nice," Gabriel said, nodding at the cylinder, which he assumed was the guy's computer.

"Nice? She's better than nice, man. She's ripped. I built her myself. Faster than a speeding bullet, more memory than a herd of elephants, know what I'm saying?"

The shelves were crowded with toy robots, replicas of spaceships from science fiction films and scale models of superheroes, the men with absurdly overdeveloped muscles, the women with huge breasts and impossibly narrow waists. A toffee-apple red electric guitar stood in a corner, a dozen or so bright green plectrums stuck to the headstock.

The room smelled of fried chicken, and a small pile of fast food cartons teetered on one end of a bookshelf. There were two chairs pulled up in front of the desk: a big leather recliner and a smaller, mesh-backed number with a matching seat that appeared to float a couple of inches above the gas strut supporting it.

Wūshī took the leather chair and Gabriel sat beside him, surprised at the comfort offered by the space-age contraption in which he was sitting.

"Mr Fang said you needed some help tracking down a company?"

"Yes. It's called Gordian Security. Its CEO is a man called Robert

Hamilton. They're not on the surface web, I've searched."

"Oh, the surface web? Sounds like somebody's been doing his homework. Your teacher tell you about the deep web?"

"Actually, she did. Until then I'd never heard of it."

"Yeah, well, it's kind of like the bottom part of the iceberg. Look, I'll show you."

Wūshī clicked on an icon on his desktop – a white skull and crossbones on a red square – and the screen displayed a basic-looking browser, just a solid black background with a white search box and a menu bar at the top. The logo in the top-right corner of the screen was a snake eating its own tail. Beneath it was the word, "Tor".

"This is where all the truly weird, illegal and evil shit goes down. None of it's indexed, so your regular, vanilla search engines can't see it. Most of the sites are encrypted, too. You need to know in advance where you're going and what the passkeys are. So, let's just type Gordian Security in here and see what we get."

Gabriel leaned forward as Wūshī hit the Return key. A split second later a handful of results popped up: the first looked like it pointed at a corporate web site.

```
Gordian   Security   Inc.   Defense   contracting,
security strategy, specialized military equipment.
```

"Try that," he said, feeling his pulse notching up by a few beats per minute at the thought of getting closer to the man who had tried to have him and Britta killed. Twice, he reminded himself.

The mouse clicked. Up popped a graphic of a knot. A very beautifully drawn and extremely complicated knot. There were no other icons, navigation buttons or text of any kind on the screen.

"Now what?" Wūshī asked, leaning back and picking at an angry-looking red spot on his neck. He moved the cursor over the knot and immediately a free end of the rope flicked free and waved seductively to one side. Wūshī clicked on it and held the mouse button down and the arrow icon changed to a grabbing hand. He moved the cursor to the right and slowly the rope began to unravel. It seemed to vibrate as if tautening, and then it snapped back into the body of the knot. "Shit! We have to undo this fucker. It's going to take all night."

Something he'd written in a notebook back in his cottage was knocking at the door of Gabriel's consciousness, waiting to be granted admission.

"Wait," he said. He closed his eyes and tried to picture the page in front of him after he'd Googled 'Gordian Zimbabwe'. There! A search result talking about the Gordian knot. "You don't need to unpick it. You just need to cut it."

"What do you mean, 'cut it'?"

"Like you would with a sword. You know, slice it through the middle."

Wūshī shrugged. "You're the boss." He held the mouse button down and swiped the cursor from right to left through the centre of the knot. It stayed in position. "Maybe we need to go the other way," he said, repeating the action, but this time swiping from left to right. Still the knot hung in space before them, unmoving and definitely not unravelling.

"Try slicing downwards," Gabriel said.

Down went the cursor, through the centre of the knot, and with a smoothly animated transition, the ropes flew apart and tumbled in slow motion to the bottom of the screen, where they faded and then disappeared.

Wūshī turned to look at Gabriel. "I think we're in."

55
Proof Positive

WHEN Gabriel and Wūshī looked back at the screen, it was filled with a corporate home page illustrated with tough-looking, ex-military types in black fatigues carrying an impressive array of automatic weapons, from M16 assault rifles to shoulder-launched, FIM-92 Stinger anti-aircraft missiles. Beneath the logo in the top right-hand corner, a knot like the one Wūshī had just cut, in black and grey, was a slogan:

Fighting the good fight. Always. Everywhere.

"Go to the Contact Us page," Gabriel said.

And there, as if inviting him to join them, was the company's street address:

Gordian Security, Inc.
Tactical Campus
11785 Lincoln Street
Shiloh, PA 17899

"This is fantastic," Gabriel said. "Thank you."

"What, this? This is, like, baby stuff. What do you really want?"

Gabriel ran a hand through his hair. "What I really want is to find out whether Hamilton has been emailing Barbara Sutherland. She's—"

"The British Prime Minister. I check the news sites, you know. I'm not a total code monkey."

"Sorry," Gabriel said. "Shouldn't have jumped to conclusions."

"No problem. I fit the stereotype."

"So, is that even possible?"

"Sure it's possible. They'll be encrypted, but that's what makes my job interesting."

"And what is it exactly? Your job, I mean? Do you work for Mr Fang?"

"On and off. But if I told you what I do for him, I'd have to learn to code with my toes. That's what he said when he hired me. He showed me his knife. It looked wicked sharp, man."

Gabriel held up his hands in mock surrender, smiling. "It's fine, I was just being curious."

"I'll need some time, maybe a day, to get into their mail server and poke around to find Hamilton's account. You want me to send the stuff to you?"

"That would be great."

Wūshī held out his phone, the screen facing Gabriel. "Email me and I'll send you the stuff when I get it. You want everything, yes?"

"Everything you can get, yes."

"You know how to unpack a zip file?"

"I think I can just about manage. You know, if I can find the right key on my big-button phone."

Wūshī nodded his appreciation. "Got me back. Cool."

Gabriel watched as the young man's slender fingers scuttled over the keyboard. After a minute or two he realised he'd disappeared from Wūshī's perception, to be replaced by the dancing lines of white-on-blue code, so he got up, patted the young guy on the shoulder and let himself out of the flat.

*

At three the following afternoon, while he was sitting with a gin and tonic on a wicker chair looking out over the mountains looming above Xi's house,

Gabriel's phone buzzed. The alert told him he had an email from wushi@daimahauzi.com. He clicked the icon and read the message:

Zipped all the files. Check it out.

A few moments later, Gabriel was frowning with concentration as he read the first of a series of emails between the CEO of a private defence contracting firm based in Pennsylvania, USA and the Secretary of State for Defence of the United Kingdom. The first email was from 23 August 2012. By the time he reached the three at the end of the chain, he had a sick feeling in his stomach as if a black toad were squatting there, leaking poison into his guts.

From: Barbara Sutherland
To: Robert Hamilton
Subject: Search and destroy mission: target Abel N'Tolo

Robert,

SAS are planning to eliminate Abel N'Tolo and take his plans for the diamond field capture.

Will call with mission details.

Suggest warn/equip AN'T urgently. Have worked too long on this to start again with new local contact.

B

From: Robert Hamilton
To: Barbara Sutherland
Subject: Re: Search and destroy mission: target
Abel N'Tolo

Barbara,

Agreed. Thank you for the intel. Once our
counter-mission succeeds, are you ready to move
ahead with our arrangement?

R

From: Barbara Sutherland
To: Robert Hamilton
Subject: Re: Re: Search and destroy mission:
target Abel N'Tolo

Robert,

Yes. Ready and waiting. I have all relevant
accounts set up including for the diamonds.
Defence procurement contracts and sourcing
protocols also finalised.

B

Gabriel's jaws were clenched so tight his back teeth were aching from the pressure and he had a violent desire to hit something. Or someone. Before he could hurl his smartphone deep into the undergrowth beyond the garden wall, he placed it, hand shaking, on the glass-topped table next to his empty glass.

He stood, suddenly, knocking over the chair, and swore, loudly.

"Fuck! She fucking set us all up."

He thought, first, of Smudge, brains blown out through his face by a 7.62 mm Kalashnikov round, his lower jaw flying away into the forest. Then of Damon "Daisy" Cheaney, who'd lost his left arm to a .50 calibre copper-jacketed projectile from a Dushka heavy machine-gun. The breakdown he'd almost had before resigning his commission. The nightmares, flashbacks, hallucinations and sudden uncontrollable rushes of anxiety or suicidal feelings. All now lying at the door of Barbara Sutherland, who had betrayed her own troops, her own country, in the pursuit of wealth.

Pacing up and down in the garden, between neatly clipped box hedges and towering bamboo and banana palms, Gabriel didn't hear Xi approach. He started when the older man laid a hand on his shoulder.

"What is the matter, Wolfe Cub?"

As he looked at his old teacher, Gabriel's eyes filled with tears. He let them come, until they were running freely down his cheeks and dripping from his chin. He sank to his knees, laid his forehead on the ground and wept, pounding the soft green moss with both fists.

How long he stayed there, he had no idea. When his racking sobs finally ended, he looked up to see that Xi had not moved. Now, he did. He squatted beside Gabriel and took both of his hands.

"Come with me. You need to exercise."

*

The fighting room in Xi's basement was just as Gabriel remembered it. Bare of any furniture, laid with thin canvas pads in the centre of the wooden floor, racks of Kendo sticks, practice swords with dulled edges and throwing stars lining the walls. Because the house was built on a slope of the mountain, one long wall was composed of floor to ceiling windows, which gave onto the harbour.

Both men were wearing white outfits of loose tunics and short, wide-legged trousers. Both were barefoot. Both wore bamboo masks secured with leather straps and buckles.

Xi went to the weapon rack and selected two Kendo sticks. The thick bamboo would not maim but it could still inflict a powerfully painful bruise. He threw a stick to Gabriel who caught it one-handed. Then they faced each other, two yards apart, bowed low, and began.

Driven by his anger and overwhelming hatred for the woman he had once sipped cold Burgundy with and called by her Christian name, Gabriel lunged forward and slashed down at Xi's head. By the time his stick arrived, it whistled through empty air.

Xi had simply been in the way one moment, and gone the next. With the end of his own stick, he jabbed at Gabriel's mask, knocking his head back with a clack as bamboo met bamboo.

Breathing heavily, Gabriel danced away then returned in a sliding leap, feinting with the stick to Xi's head before reversing the direction of his blow, aiming for the right forearm.

Once more, Xi seemed, simply, to dematerialise then rematerialise out of range. His chest was still, unlike Gabriel's, which was heaving in and out as his overstressed lungs struggled to suck in enough oxygen.

This time, Xi swept his stick right to left, slapping into the side of Gabriel's head.

Gabriel retreated a second time. He shook his head and re-centred himself. In a third furious attack, he plunged forward, stick whirling, jabbing, and managed to land a blow on Xi's left shoulder. This time Xi fought back in full heat, and the two men spent the next three minutes engaged in a flurry of feints, counter-feints, lunges, parries, jabs and cuts. The rattle of the sticks sounded like small-arms fire.

Twenty more minutes passed in bouts of furious fighting. Finally, Gabriel held his right hand up, palm outwards. He went to replace his stick and pulled his mask up and over the back of his head. His face was wet, with sweat this time, and bright red. He was panting, but smiling.

Xi replaced his own stick in the rack and lifted his own mask from his face.

"Master Zhao, I have to leave. As soon as I can get my new passport from Mr Fang," Gabriel said between heaving breaths.

Xi nodded, barely sweating, his breathing normal. "Then before you go, tell me how you intend to draw out the snake far enough to kill it."

Over tea, Gabriel explained the plan he'd been formulating ever since his first meeting with Wūshī.

56

Day Trip

TWO days later, Gabriel was back in England. He called Britta the same evening.

"*Hej*! What's up? Where are you?"

"Home, for now. After I called you last time, I went to Hong Kong. I stayed with Zhao Xi. He showed me where Michael was killed. And where he's buried. Then he introduced me to a triad boss who suggested a way to get to Sutherland. Then an assassin called Sasha Beck tried to kill me but I drugged her and took her phone. This computer geek called the Wizard hacked Gordian's email servers, so now I have concrete proof that Sutherland isn't just corrupt but evil, too."

"Shit! No boring days with you, are there? What do you mean, she's 'evil'? Isn't that a bit melodramatic?"

"You know how our patrol was ambushed in Mozambique the day we lost Smudge?"

"Sure. You were overrun. The place was supposed to be clean."

"Sutherland passed classified military intel about our mission to Robert Hamilton, Gordian's CEO. He gave it to N'Tolo's gang of terrorists. Sutherland and Hamilton were trying to protect a scheme to take over a diamond field. That's what N'Tolo's plans were all about."

There was a pause, during which Gabriel could Britta breathing.

"I'm sorry."

He frowned. "What for?"

"For not believing you before. When you suspected her the first time. For pushing you into danger just for hard proof."

"You didn't push me anywhere, darling. I had to go to Hong Kong. Everything else happened because I made it happen."

"You're going to kill Hamilton." It wasn't a question.

"Yes. I am."

"What about Sutherland?"

"I saw the original documents in Hong Kong. But I only have scans and digital copies. It could be argued they were faked by terrorists trying to blacken her name. I'm going to draw her out into the open and find a way to get her to incriminate herself."

"Be careful, then. *Den spik som sticker ut blir slagen.*"

"What does that mean?"

"It's a Swedish proverb. The nail that sticks out gets struck."

"True. But *Lyckan står den djärve bi.*"

"What? You learned Swedish in Hong Kong, too?"

"No. Just that one phrase. For you. *If I am bold, maybe Fortune will favour me.*"

"I hope so, Wolfe. You need all the luck you can get."

Gabriel hung up then called Don on his mobile number, unsure whether it would even ring. Would he just get a "this number has been suspended" message? He did not.

"Hello, Old Sport. Thought you'd never call. What's going on with you?"

Gabriel sketched in the details he'd just given Britta.

"And how are you after your little adventure in Africa?"

"Better now I know you're still in the frame. I thought you'd been canned, or thrown into the Tower. Or worse."

Don chuckled. "I was beginning to wonder myself. I heard you went looking for me in Essex."

"I did. The guys on the gate said they'd never heard of you."

"I know. Sorry. Just a bit of the general subterfuge. I've temporarily suspended The Department's operations. At least in terms of formal facilities and missions. I suppose you could say I'm working from home. I believe that's the current parlance. I still have my guys on standby, but we're all keeping our heads down."

"Can I ask something, Don? You seemed really out of sorts last time we spoke. What was the matter?"

"I have been under a certain amount of pressure from a nasty individual going by the name of David Brown. He behaves like a spook, but I have a feeling he's part of something," he paused, "cross-departmental, shall we call it? I think we all know who's pulling Brown's strings. Which brings us to the main problem. Our mutual friend in SW1."

"I have a plan for dealing with that particular individual. But I need some help getting to the States. Fast."

"What can I do to help Old Sport?"

Gabriel explained.

At nine the following morning, Gabriel was zipping himself into the olive-green folds of a flight overall. It was noon, and he was standing on the apron at the Empire Test Pilots' School at MOD Boscombe Down, Wiltshire, just a few miles from his cottage.

"I need to get to the US as fast as possible," he'd said to Don. "Any chance of a ride in a fast jet?"

"Only two-seaters I know of in this country are the SAAB Gripens at the ETPS. You won't even have to find a hotel . . ."

"Ready to go then?" the pilot asked, a smile playing over his fair-skinned face, dotted here and there with pale freckles. He'd introduced himself as Flight Lieutenant Craig Hendricks.

Gabriel nodded. "How long will it take?"

"We'll be flying between Mach One and Mach Two. I've got a midflight refuel booked with a Vickers VC10 from 101 Squadron RAF. We'll be there in three hours."

"There" was York Airport in Pennsylvania, ten miles from Tactical

Campus in Shiloh. Allowing for the time difference, Gabriel had calculated he'd be touching down in Pennsylvania at eight a.m. local time. Plenty of time to equip himself for what he had planned.

Gabriel strapped himself into the co-pilot's seat behind Craig, who was conducting his pre-flight cabin checks. The cockpit was narrow. Gabriel's fears were restricted to spiders, but had he suffered from claustrophobia, he would have been popping tranquilisers by the handful. His shoulders were separated from the cold wind slicing across the airfield by nothing more than a few inches of pressurised air, and then the inner and outer skins of the airframe and whatever avionics were sandwiched between them. He pulled the strap adjuster tight until he felt he couldn't move in his seat then leaned back, flipped the polarising visor down on his flight helmet, and waited.

He heard Craig's voice, and the air traffic controller's, through his in-helmet comms.

"Roger, Tower. Golf Alpha Hotel One Niner Three taxiing to takeoff."

"OK, Golf Alpha Hotel One Niner Three. Proceed at your own discretion. You're cleared for takeoff. Over and out."

"Roger, Tower. Thank you. Over and out."

Gabriel felt, rather than heard the Volvo RM12 turbofan engines spin up, the vibrations thrumming inside his chest. Then he did hear it, as Craig pushed the throttle lever forward and set the Gripen moving along the apron towards the end of the runway. The roar was still muted by the sound insulation inside his helmet, but there was an insistence and urgency to the rumble in his ears that promised something spectacular.

As they reached the end of the runway, Craig's voice crackled in his headset.

"OK, Gabriel. I don't how fast that car of yours accelerates, but I promise you, this is going to be fun. Hold on!"

Gabriel could hear the smile in the young man's voice and readied himself, clenching his stomach muscles and pushing his helmet back against the headrest. He glanced to his left, then right, at the rolling Wiltshire countryside, bleak and grey at this time of year. Ghostly green reflections of the flight instruments curved over his head on the Plexiglas canopy. Then, while his eyes were upturned, Craig pushed the throttle all the way forward.

The muted roar Gabriel had almost grown used to increased in volume and violence, to a screaming bellow. He felt his internal organs compress as the Gripen accelerated past six hundred miles per hour. Craig maintained a running commentary as the jet surged into the air at an angle so sharp Gabriel's perceptions of gravity, direction and his own bodily position in the plane simply vanished.

"Tower, this is Golf Alpha Hotel One Niner Three. On a bearing two-seven-seven, airspeed nine hundred miles per hour, climbing to twenty thousand feet. See you tomorrow. Over and out."

"Golf Alpha Hotel One Niner Three from Tower. Roger that. Bring doughnuts. Over and out."

"Gabriel? I didn't ask. Ever been in a fast-jet before?"

"No. I did a bit of work with a couple of Typhoon pilots a while back, but this is my first flight. Only choppers and C130-Js before this, and the odd light plane."

"Typhoons? Lovely planes. I've flown a couple. Like ice skating in your bare feet till you get used to it."

"So I've heard. You said we'd be flying between Mach One and Mach Two. How fast are we going now?"

"Now? Just subsonic. We have to reach thirty thousand feet before we go supersonic or we'll run through too much fuel. Look down, that's the Bristol Channel. Once we're over the Atlantic I'll light the afterburners. That'll be fun." Moments later, it seemed, Gabriel was looking down at a dull, petrol-blue sea. "OK, Gabriel. Hold onto your breakfast."

What happened next made the takeoff feel like pushing a family saloon car through the gears. As the afterburners sucked in the exhaust gases and re-combusted them to provide extra thrust, the Gripen didn't so much accelerate as snap into the future. Gabriel could feel his eyeballs being squashed into their sockets and his lungs trying to leave his back through the gaps between his ribs. Breathing the faintly plasticky air through the oxygen mask became a struggle and points of light danced at the edge of his vision.

Suddenly, the pressure eased off, as if an elephant had tired of sitting on his chest and jumped up. He inhaled in a gasp.

"Fuck!" was all he could say.

"Indeed. Did you like it?"

"It was . . . brilliant, actually. But," he added hurriedly, "that will do me for a while."

Craig laughed, an oddly robotic sound as the comms clipped the higher frequencies and smoothed out the volume. "Don't worry, that's it for a while now. I'll give you a prod when we're about to refuel. It's fun to watch. But I'm afraid it's just a glorified taxi-ride for an hour and a bit now."

Craig knew what he was talking about. The clouds closed in and he took the plane higher until they broke through into glorious sunlit air. The sun glinted off the silver of the wings and made Gabriel squint, but once he'd admired the mountainous landscape of cumulus clouds for a few minutes the flight became as monotonous as any commercial trip on a Boeing 777 or Airbus 380.

Eighty-nine minutes later, as Gabriel was running through the next steps in his campaign, Craig's voice in the intercom made him jump.

"Gabriel? If you look over to starboard, you'll see our tanker."

Gabriel holstered the pistol in his mind and turned his head to the right. Flying ahead and above them was a dark-grey Vickers VC10. Trailing from the rear of the converted airliner's fuselage was a refuelling hose, tipped with a conical drogue basket. The hose snaked out to seventy feet, and Gabriel wondered how anyone could possibly engage the cone to receive the aviation fuel they needed to stay in the air. He wanted to ask, but felt he should keep quiet. He needn't have bothered.

"We're going to ease up behind mother and stick our refuelling probe into the drogue. Then I flick a switch and she dumps three tonnes of pressurised aviation fuel right into our tank. OK, here we go. Tanker from Golf Alpha Hotel One Niner Three. Ready to engage, over."

"Golf Alpha Hotel One Niner Three, clear to engage. Over."

"Roger that, over."

Craig flew in close behind the VC10. Craning round the pilot's helmet,

Gabriel could see the drogue basket growing bigger in the windscreen as Craig closed the gap.

Twenty feet.

Fifteen.

Twelve.

Ten.

Seven.

Five.

There was a muffled *clunk* as the refuelling probe and the drogue interlocked and formed an airtight seal. For the next three minutes, Craig held the Gripen steady behind the VC10. There was another *clunk*, and the refuelling hose dropped away and began retracting into the VC10's fuselage.

"All done," Craig said. "Tanker from Golf Alpha Hotel One Niner Three. Thanks, mum. Going to pat my back like usual? Over."

"Very droll, Golf Alpha Hotel One Niner Three. Have a good trip. Over and out."

"Thanks. You too. Over and out. Right," Craig said, to Gabriel this time. "Next stop, York, Pennsylvania."

*

Standing on the tarmac at York Airport, at eight a.m. local time, Gabriel shook hands with Craig.

"Thanks for the ride. I'll see you later, all being well."

Craig smiled. "Hope it goes well. Whatever it is."

Gabriel nodded. "Me too. Better get rid of this first, I suppose."

He unzipped the flight suit and shrugged his way out of it, then handed it, folded in half, to Craig, who slung it over his arm.

He walked away from the plane towards the terminal building. Don had arranged a security detail to escort Gabriel through the airport. He could see them now, waiting for him at the small, one-storey, glass and brick building: two fit-looking guys in identical navy overcoats over black two-piece suits, white shirts and dark ties. One navy, one burgundy, he saw, when he was close enough.

His own outfit was less severe: black trousers, dark grey running shoes with violet stripes, dark green sweatshirt and a dark brown leather biker jacket. Just the sort of thing a runner for an international hitwoman – assassin, he corrected himself – would wear. A runner with no idea of what sort of temperatures Pennsylvania could plummet to in February he reflected, determining to buy a coat before anything else.

His escorts introduced themselves with perfunctory greetings and the minimum amount of information consistent with explaining procedure.

"Johnson," Navy Tie said. He was tall and blond, with a mountainous build, his craggy features bearing a watchful expression.

"Baylesford," Burgundy Tie said. Also tall, also blond, but slim and gangling. Left eye, a startlingly bright blue, not perfectly coordinated with the right, so his gaze seemed unfixed. "This way, please. Passport?" He held out his hand, palm uppermost.

Gabriel handed over his passport.

The two men turned in unison and marched him off to the double doors of the terminal building. It was hard not to feel like a prisoner as they strode up to the single immigration officer, sitting in a small glass cubicle and looking bored.

Baylesford leaned over and muttered a few words into the guard's ear. Showed the passport. Got it stamped. Straightened and returned it to Gabriel. All three men walked through into the open area of the building where executives, military personnel and a few families milled about, buying coffees and newspapers, checking phones and looking for the people they were meeting, either frowning or smiling, depending on whether they'd found them or not.

Baylesford stopped and placed a hand on Gabriel's forearm to slow him.

"Call me when you're ready to go. We'll send a car." He handed Gabriel a card, which he slid into his wallet alongside those belonging to Don, Fariyah Crace, Mr Fang, Darryl Burroughs and Tatyana Garin.

Johnson spoke, handing Gabriel a sheet of paper, folded in half. "Take this. It's a four-eighty-four, ten-fifty: temporary Federal law enforcement accreditation. It'll get you what you need."

Baylesford and Johnson left without another word, and Gabriel headed outside to find a taxi.

57

Tactical Campus

DOWNTOWN York, Pennsylvania, like many American towns, offered the visitor as many retail diversions as she – or he – could think of. The food choices alone would choke a whale: burgers, tacos, burritos, pizzas, lobster rolls, hot dogs, gyros, frozen yoghurt and ice cream, even in February, plus buckets of fizzy drinks and pints of hot, sweet, milky coffee.

Gabriel bought a hot dog from a cart outside a department store and washed it down with a can of Coke before entering the shop. Ten minutes later, he emerged clad in a thick woollen overcoat belted round his waist, and a fur-lined trapper hat, the flaps, mercifully, covering his ears just in time to stop them breaking off. Black leather gloves, stitched with three radiating lines on the backs, brought warmth back into his fingers.

For his next purchase, he headed for East Market Street. The store, Falcon Sporting Goods, was double-fronted. The display window to the left of the door was filled with brightly-coloured balls for basketball, soccer, America football, softball and baseball. Someone with an eye for merchandising had arranged them so they appeared to be spilling from a giant, golden conch shell – a sporting horn of plenty.

The window to the right held Gabriel's attention. Behind a steel grille were arrayed enough small arms to equip an SAS platoon. Semi-automatic pistols rubbed shoulders with assault rifles, hunting rifles and shotguns. There were crossbows, slingshots and longbows, too, should the customer be in more of an old-school state of mind. A hand-lettered sign behind the weapons stated:

HOME DEFENSE – HUNTING – COLLECTORS – COMPETITION
In-store Range – Shoot Before You Buy

Inside the shop, which was doing a slow but steady trade, to judge from the beeping of several tills, a sign pointed the way to the gun counter. The owners were maintaining the interior of their establishment at a temperature that made Gabriel sweat inside the heavy coat, so he loosened the belt and undid the buttons. He threaded his way between a couple of toned and tanned soccer moms buying boots for their daughters.

Behind the counter, a slab of thick glass scratched and pitted from the merchandise, Gabriel guessed, stood a muscular man wearing a forest-green polo shirt with the shop's logo – a falcon perched on a pistol – stitched onto the left side. He wore his grey hair in a military buzz cut, and his rolled-up sleeves revealed thick forearms, covered in dense, black hair through which tattoos that could have been regimental badges showed, in faded shades of navy and crimson.

He looked up from a shooting magazine as Gabriel approached and flashed a smile, though Gabriel noticed his muscle tone tighten by a fraction and the way he let his his hands drop out of sight behind the stainless steel back wall of the counter display.

In the seconds it took Gabriel to reach the counter, he noticed the professional summing-up the man performed, gaze alighting first on Gabriel's eyes before dropping to his coat, his hands and back to his eyes.

As if receiving the message Gabriel was beaming him through his open expression and smile – *That's right, I'm a regular citizen, not a crazy* – the man relaxed visibly, replaced his hands on the counter and allowed his smile to reflect genuine good humour.

"Yes, sir. What are you looking for?"

Gabriel looked beyond the man's left shoulder at the display of rifles mounted behind another steel grille. *What I'd really like is one of those.* Then down at the handguns displayed in angled ranks beneath the glass.

"A semi-automatic pistol. With a suppressor. Nine-millimetre. SIG Sauer P226 for choice. But anything reliable."

"You're British, right?"

"Yes. Would you like to see my passport?"

"No, sir. But you do need an LTCF issued by the State of Pennsylvania."

"And that would be?"

"That would be a License to Carry a Firearm. I'll also need to conduct background checks and run them through the Federal NICS . . ." He stopped himself, smiled, and explained the second acronym. "The National Instant Criminal Background Check System. That's a couple of bucks. And then, if you pass all that, I need you to fill out a purchase application. After all that, you can walk out of here with anything you see."

Gabriel reached into his inside breast pocket, noting the man stiffen again, then relax as he brought out the folded sheet of paper Johnson had provided.

"I'm afraid I don't have an LTCF. And I won't show up at all in your NICS, being a British citizen" – *subject, technically, but I don't want to confuse you* – "but I do have this."

He handed the folded sheet of paper across the counter. The gun dealer unfolded it, read for a minute or so, held it under an ultra-violet scanner behind the counter, then refolded it and handed it back.

"Only the second time I've ever seen one of those. Some guy built like a terminator produced it and walked out with an AR15, a couple of Glocks and enough ammunition to start a small war. Didn't ask what he wanted it for. So, a nine-mil, huh? Well, you got your Glock 17, Glock 19, Beretta FS92, that's a nice weapon, SIG Sauer P226 like you said, 1911s, American Tactical, GSG, basically pretty much everything."

"And a suppressor?"

"Yeah, we got the full range. Name your brand. One thing, we just sold our last SIG with a threaded barrel. If you're in a hurry it'll have to be a Glock 19."

Gabriel shrugged. "The Glock's fine. Do you stock Gem-Tech suppressors?"

"Yes, sir, we do. A lot of our customers who shoot suppressed like the GM-9."

"Good. I'll have a Glock, the GM-9, and a box of ammunition."

"OK. We stock all the major brands. I'm not going to ask what you're planning on shooting, but I'm guessing it ain't targets. You have any strong feelings there?"

"Hollow-points."

The gun dealer screwed his eyes up as he looked at Gabriel. "Well now, for personal defense," he laid heavy, ironic emphasis on these two words, "I'd go for the Remington Golden Saber in nine-millimetre Parabellum, jacketed hollow-points. Folks'll argue forever about which round is best, but this is a man-stopper, right enough. You got decent expansion, penetration and velocity. Do you want to try it out, get the feel of the gun?"

Gabriel shook his head. "I'm sure it's all fine."

"You want a holster?"

"No thanks. This has nice deep pockets," Gabriel said, flapping the overcoat.

∗

With the pistol bought and paid for, along with a couple of extra bits and pieces, Gabriel left the shop, overcoat pockets now weighed down by roughly four pounds of steel, plastic, brass, lead, copper and smokeless powder.

He hailed a cab on the street and gave the Gordian Group address. The taxi dropped him on a smooth curve of tarmac directly outside the main entrance.

Tactical Campus was a one-storey building. Why build up when you can sprawl? The exterior gave nothing away as to the kind of business transacted beyond the mirrored doors. It could have been a technology company, an engineering firm, a pharmaceuticals manufacturer or a business school.

To the left of the doors stood a bright silver sculpture – the knot Gabriel had seen on the unlock page before Wūshī had slashed through it with the cursor of his mouse. As he passed the six-foot tall metal tangle, he saw himself reflected back dozens of times in the distorting mirrors of its inch-thick strands. He checked the date on his phone. *Yes. This is the day 'Sasha' told you her runner was coming for the bearer bonds.*

Inside the building, the air was pleasantly warm, unlike the sub-tropical atmosphere in the gun store. Gabriel unbuttoned the coat and stuffed the hat and gloves into the capacious pockets. In the centre of the ground-floor space, the architects had positioned the reception desk. It was an aggressive, angular structure that appeared to be built of carbon-fibre, the intricate grey-and-black weave sending a message to visitors: strength, high-tech, functionality and fuck the aesthetics. A bit like the two burly security officers who stood each side of the reception desk, glaring at Gabriel from under lowered brows and military buzz-cuts, hands resting on pistol-butts at their waists.

The receptionist, on the other hand, appeared to have been chosen specifically on aesthetic grounds. Whether she had a PhD in weapons engineering or not, it was impossible to say. But he had no doubt her looks would cause even the most hardened defence procurement executive to lower his guard before a sensitive negotiation. Her lips, coloured a pale, frosted pink were wide, and curved into a genuine-looking smile, that popped dimples into both cheeks. Her glossy auburn hair was tied in a bun at the back of her head, exposing a slender throat.

"Yes, sir. How may I help you?" she said.

"I have an appointment with Robert Hamilton."

"Your name?"

"Lang, but it's not important. My employer's is. Just tell him I work for Sasha Beck."

"Let me just check to see if he's expecting you, Mister Lang."

She stared at the screen in front of her. Her smile slipped, and the dimples disappeared, to be replaced with a frown. "I'm afraid I can't see your appointment in his diary."

He leant across the reception desk, placing both hands flat on the pale wood each side of the visitors' book, and looked deep into her eyes, which were, he noticed pale blue, with darker rings of pigment around the edges of the irises. He glanced at her name badge.

"That doesn't surprise me, Tatum. But, as I said, it's not my name that matters. Why don't you try calling Mr Hamilton? Or his PA. He's expecting me."

She picked up her desk phone, shooting Gabriel a tight-lipped smile that lacked the warmth of its predecessor.

"Hi Patricia, it's Tatum," she said, half-turning away from Gabriel. "I have a gentleman here, a Mister Lang, who says he has an appointment with Mr Hamilton . . . Well, that just it. He seems awfully sure of himself. He says Mr Hamilton is expecting him and that his employer's name is the one that matters . . . It's Sasha Beck," she said, looking at Gabriel to check she'd got the name right. He nodded. "OK. Thanks, Trish." She replaced the handset in its cradle and looked at Gabriel, who had stepped back from her territory and now stood, hands in coat pockets, waiting for good news. "Mr Hamilton's PA is just checking his appointments diary. Would you take a seat, Mr Lang?"

Gabriel wasn't enjoying pushing the receptionist's buttons, would much rather be doing something similar, but with more force, to her boss. But he needed to create the right psychological impression on everyone with whom he came into contact. So he refused her request and maintained his position, directly in front of the reception desk and an obvious obstacle to anyone who might enter the building after him.

He looked around while they waited for Trish to call back. Although the exterior of the building was devoid of clues to the company's line of business, the interior was another story. Behind Tatum's head, fixed to the wall by oversized black bolts, was a piece of stainless steel, two feet deep by eight across. In acid-etched type that suggested the text on the sides of military vehicles, it repeated the company's slogan in capitals:

FIGHTING THE GOOD FIGHT.
ALWAYS. EVERYWHERE.

The material and the message seemed to be at odds with each other, suggesting a fascist worldview rather than something from the Bible.

Gabriel became aware that Tatum was speaking to him.

"Sir? Mr Lang? Mr Hamilton will see you right away." Her expression, eyes wide, lips parted, suggested that this was not the answer she'd been expecting when Trish called back. "You follow the corridor down to the end. Mr Hamilton's office is the door on the right."

Without another word, Gabriel spun on his heel and marched off towards his appointment with the man who had very nearly caused his death, not once, not twice, but, as he now knew, three times.

The dark wood door bore a label: Robert Hamilton, CEO. It was done in the same acid-etched steel as the overbearing slogan in reception. Gabriel didn't knock. He just pushed it open and strode through. As he'd expected, he was standing in an outer office, dominated by a large desk, around which an efficient-looking woman of forty or forty-five was already stepping. She wore high heels and a forbidding frown, and she looked as though she would like nothing better than to ram one of her stilettos though his eye socket. Instead, she contented herself with a clipped utterance. "You must be the *gentleman*," how she loaded that much disdain into three syllables, Gabriel had no idea, "that Mr Hamilton is expecting. Follow me, please."

She walked ahead of him, knocked twice on another dark door – mahogany was Gabriel's guess – and stepped through.

Sitting in a thickly padded, leather swivel chair was the man Gabriel had come to kill.

58
The Debt Collector

WITHOUT turning, Gabriel sensed the PA leave the room, feeling the minute change in air pressure as she closed the door behind her, listening to the brush of its lower edge over the thick pile of the carpet. Good tight fit, he mused. Probably deadens the sound when Hamilton's negotiating.

Hamilton was on the phone. A power play, Gabriel assumed. He tried to catch Hamilton's eye but the man was staring intently out of the window as he spoke. Gabriel stuffed his hands into his trouser pockets, curling his right hand around the steel cylinder he'd not used in Mozambique, or Zimbabwe, but had held onto and brought all the way from the UK.

Not without a few plays of his own, Gabriel wandered around the room as if he was considering moving in. He pulled a dead leaf off a potted olive tree. Then, one by one, he began picking up framed photographs of Hamilton with smug-looking men in expensive suits, giving them a cursory glance, then lying them flat on the shelves they'd come from. On one wall hung an antique map of the world. There was no glass, so its rippled parchment surface was open to the air.

Reaching into his coat pocket, Gabriel pulled out one of his additional purchases from Falcon Sporting Goods, a hunting knife with a six-inch blade.

He poked it into the northwest corner of the map, just on the eastern coast of Alaska, and drew it diagonally down, southeast, until it bisected Australia

---

before hitting the moulded wooden frame. The sound of the parchment pulling apart was a harsh creak, and, looking round, Gabriel found he'd managed to attract Hamilton's attention.

The man's long face, clean-shaven and tanned to an even, pale caramel, was contorted with fury, lips curled up, nose wrinkled like a predator's.

"I'll call you back, Frank," he said, then slammed the phone down. "What the fuck do you think you're doing?" he snarled, the patrician mask slipping for a moment. "That came from the USS Constitution."

"Miss Beck sends her regards," Gabriel said, strolling over to Hamilton's desk and sliding into the chair facing the enraged CEO. "I'm here to collect three million in US bearer bonds. And if you press that button under your desk, your new young wife's car will explode exactly five minutes after she collects your stepkids from Morgan's Vale Preparatory School." He inspected his reflection in the blade of the knife. "Esme and Henry. Cool names."

Hamilton's face lost its high colour in a flash, as if someone had changed the filter on a digital photo.

"If you harm . . ."

"Yeah, yeah, I've heard that speech before. 'A hair on their heads, I'll blah blah blah.' Listen, do you have the bearer bonds or not?"

Without another word, Hamilton reached into a drawer on his left and pulled out a large, rectangular, brown envelope. He pushed it across the desk towards Gabriel.

Enjoying Hamilton's discomfiture, Gabriel laid his knife on the polished surface of the desk, then took his time with the envelope. He turned it over in his hands and untwisted the wire tag that closed the flap.

The documents that emerged, gripped between his right thumb and forefinger, were elaborately engraved on sheets of thick, stiff, off-white paper. Stamps, signatures, presidential portraits and insignia competed for space with copper-plate text declaring that each sheet could be exchanged on presentation by the bearer for the sum of one hundred thousand US dollars.

"Thirty, right?" Gabriel said, looking at Hamilton while flicking the edges of the bonds with his thumb.

"They're all there, if that's what you mean."

"Better count them. I don't want Miss Beck to be disappointed. Who knows what she might do."

Licking the pad of his thumb, Gabriel separated each bond from its neighbour in the stack and counted out loud, placing them face down on Hamilton's desk to the right of the knife. Reaching seventeen, Gabriel paused.

"Oh, shit. Was that seventeen or eighteen?"

Hamilton's lips tightened. "Seventeen."

"Nope. Can't risk it. I'm starting again."

"Oh, for Christ's sake, is this really necessary?"

"Hey, you want to wake up with your own head on your nightstand, that's up to you. Me, I like that connected feeling. Now, one, two, three . . ."

By the time Gabriel reached thirty, Hamilton was fidgeting with a fountain pen on the blotter in front of him, clamping his jaws and chewing the inside of his cheek. *Good, you bastard. Imagine feeling ten times this stressed, fighting your way past a gang of terrorists who knew you were coming.*

He folded the bonds and slid them into an inside pocket.

"Happy now?" Hamilton asked, glaring at Gabriel.

"No, Mr Hamilton. I am anything but happy. I am so unhappy I feel like shooting you right now."

He pulled out the Glock and pointed it at Hamilton's head.

The effect was instantaneous. Hamilton reared back in his chair, eyes popping, hands scrabbling for grip on the armrests. For added emphasis, Gabriel racked the slide and let it snap back with a crack against the receiver.

"You've got your money. Sasha's money, I mean. What are you doing? Is that even loaded?" Hamilton gabbled, his voice several tones higher pitched.

"Why don't we find out?" Gabriel replied, extending his right arm towards Hamilton, until the end of the suppressor was less than three feet from Hamilton's sweat-slicked forehead.

"No! Please. Don't."

"Relax, Hamilton. I'm not going to. Not yet," Gabriel said, keeping the Glock held straight out in front of him.

Hamilton appeared to have made a deduction. His eyes widened.

"Wait. Do you even work for Sasha?"

"No. I don't."

Hamilton's eyes, which had resumed their normal shape, popped open again like twin flashbulbs.

"Fuck. I know who you are. You're the British operative. You're Wolfe."

"Yes, I am. Although if you use that name again, I'll put a hollow-point in your ear. And I know who you are. You're the man who took military intelligence from Barbara Sutherland in 2012 and used it to set up an ambush for me and my men in Mozambique."

Hamilton clamped a hand around the back of his neck, as if holding his head steady.

"If you know that, then you know exactly who you're dealing with. Kill me and you'll bring some very powerful people into play. People who, believe me, you don't want to tangle with."

"What did you say just then? 'Kill me'? I suppose I could. It would save a lot of time."

Gabriel tightened his finger around the trigger.

Hamilton put his hands out in front of him, palms towards Gabriel. "No! Jesus! Look, just tell me what you want. I'm sure we can work something out. You've got three million there in untraceable bearer bonds. I'll double it. In gold."

Gabriel got to his feet.

"I've got a better idea. You can buy me a coffee."

Hamilton's brow creased with the effort of decoding this offer.

"What?"

"A coffee. Come on. Take me out for a coffee. We'll go and tell Trish we're concluding our chat at the nearest Starbucks, find your car and shoot the shit about people whose deaths we've caused. Oh, and one last thing. Anyone spots anything off in your act and calls the police or your in-house security team and, boom! 'Soccer mom tragedy, three killed'. If I don't make a call to a certain number at a certain time and leave a certain code, blam! 'A town mourns as kids, mom, stepdad, die on same day.' Understood?" Hamilton grimaced, then nodded. "Oh, and what's your phone unlock code?"

"Nine-zero-zero-five."

"Unlock it and hand it over."

In the outer office, Trish looked up from her computer as Hamilton emerged, with Gabriel following a few seconds later. He'd used the gap to twist the top on the electromagnetic pulse generator, setting a five-minute delay, before pushing it below the soil surface of the potted olive tree.

"I'm taking Mr Lang out for coffee, Trish. Cancel my meetings for the rest of the morning, would you? He's an old friend. We have a lot to catch up on."

Hamilton even managed a smile as he led Gabriel passed his PA's desk.

The temperature had dropped, even though the morning was wearing on and there were a few slashes cut in the blanket of high, white clouds. Gabriel was glad of the coat and pleased to see Hamilton shivering in his elegantly cut, but lightweight, suit.

"Where's your car?" he asked Hamilton.

"It's round the back. The parking lot."

"Fine. Let's go then. Keep the happy face on and think of Esme and Henry."

At the back of the building, the company's parking lot sprawled over a couple of acres. In the spot closest to the rear door sat a gunmetal Aston Martin DB9. Hamilton blipped the fob and seconds later both men were sitting in the mulberry-coloured cabin, which smelled of expensive leather and the man's own equally expensive aftershave.

"The nearest coffee shop is back in York," Hamilton said.

"We're not going for coffee. Do you have a proving ground out here? A place you show off the toys to the boys who come to do deals?"

Hamilton nodded.

"Two miles down the road. There's some land we own. Forest, tracks, a mocked up Afghan village, a lake."

"That's where we're going. Same rules apply. You flash your lights at a cop car or hit a panic button and hairs on heads get harmed. OK?"

Hamilton nodded, lips set in a grim line.

59
Reckoning

THE road leading from Gordian's headquarters to their proving ground was empty, and the sleek British sports car purred along the blacktop without meeting so much as a single oncoming car of any kind, let alone a York PD cruiser or a Pennsylvania state cop doing the rounds.

Checking his rearview mirror, Hamilton flicked on the right indicator and pulled off the highway onto a slip road. The blacktop ran out after half a mile and for the last five hundred yards the Aston's suspension had to soak up a constant juddering from the rough and ready road surface that led to the proving ground.

Ahead, a pair of steel gates came into view. They were eight feet tall, and topped with razor wire, with more of the lethal fencing stretching away left and right into the scrubby vegetation on both sides. As the car came within thirty yards of the gates, Hamilton slowed. The gates clanked once and swung back silently on their oiled hinges as pneumatic rams pulled them apart.

"Transponder in the engine compartment," Hamilton said. Clearly he was a perpetual salesman and unable to resist demonstrating a bit of the company's attention to technological detail.

He accelerated through the gap between the gates and a minute later hit the brakes and brought the car to a stop in the centre of a group of low, white houses through which a wide road snaked. The engine silenced. Hamilton turned in his seat to look at Gabriel.

"Out," Gabriel said. "Let's go for a walk."

As Hamilton exited his side of the car, Gabriel took the Glock from his coat pocket and eased off the safety. Then he followed, pushing the door closed behind him with a damped *clunk*.

Hamilton was already walking away from the car as Gabriel rounded the bonnet, and he strode with long paces to catch up, Glock pointing at the small of the man's back.

"Everything we supply is legal," Hamilton said, a pleading note in his voice. "The weapons systems, the comms, the men. Gordian is involved in peace-keeping, regime-change and legitimate conflicts only."

"Shut up. I read the copy on your website. I don't need the pitch a second time. And since when was ambushing British troops based on classified military intelligence legal?"

"She didn't tell me!" Hamilton said, turning to face Gabriel. "She said there was a rogue team of Special Forces guys down there in Mozambique that had to be taken out. How was I to know you were legit?"

Gabriel ground his teeth together in his efforts not to either speak or drill the man where he stood. When they reached the centre of the mocked-up village, he spoke again.

"Ever been in a place like this for real, Mr Hamilton?"

Hamilton shook his head. "Our operations director is a former Marine, though. He has."

"Yeah, well I have. And others like it. And it was always OK, fighting the enemy. That's what we signed up for, that's what we did. Go in, do your job, get out and go home. And if you lost people, you brought them home with you, buried them, mourned and moved on. But there was this one man, Michael Smith. We called him Smudge. He was killed by Abel N'Tolo's men when they overran us. You know about N'Tolo, don't you?" Hamilton's lips were a thin line. "Don't you?"

"Yes, I know about him."

"Of course you do. Because you and Sutherland were helping him seize control of a diamond field, weren't you?"

"Look, it wasn't like that," Hamilton said, lines creasing his forehead. "He wanted the diamond field, of course. But he was the best chance for peace in that part of Mozambique. He –"

"Shut up!" Gabriel barked. "Finish that sentence and I'll call my associate then gut-shoot you. I assume you know what happens when you get a hollow-point in the stomach?" Hamilton nodded. Said nothing. "Because of the men you tipped off – and supplied – we had to leave Smudge behind. They crucified him. Stood his body against a baobab tree and stuck machetes through his hands and into the trunk. As the chopper took us away from the scene of the firefight I looked down out of the open loading door. Do you know what my last sight of Smudge was?"

"No."

"A buzzard was sitting on his shoulder, eating his brain through the bullet hole in the back of his head. I went back to find him, as you know, since you tried to have me killed. Twice. But you failed."

"Look, Gabriel isn't it? I said I'd double the three million. That was insulting. To you and to Smudge's memory. I am truly sorry for what happened. It was Barbara, I mean Sutherland who pushed me into it. She's the prime minister of the UK, for God's sake. She's an immensely powerful woman. What can I do to make things right between us?"

"I'll . . . tell you what . . . you can . . . do to make . . . it right between . . . us," Gabriel said, altering his breathing patterns and performing a precise and disorientating series of eye movements as he broke his speech patterns into nonsensical fragments. "You can . . . take . . . this Glock 19 . . . and you . . . can . . . stick it . . . in your mouth and . . . pull the . . . trigger . . . you will pull . . . the trigger."

As Gabriel spoke, he watched Hamilton closely, alive to the minute changes in blood flow through his skin, and the coordination between left and right eyes. Hamilton's breathing had started to match Gabriel's own and the lids of his blue eyes were drooping spasmodically as he fought the effects of the ancient hypnotic routine.

"I . . . will . . . pull the . . . trigger," Hamilton said.

Gabriel smiled and extended his arm towards Hamilton, releasing his own finger from the Glock's trigger and letting the gun drop slightly so it was pointing at Hamilton's feet.

As if animated by a puppeteer, Hamilton's right arm stretched out and his hand closed around the suppressor. He took the pistol from Gabriel, reversed his grip and opened his mouth wide. His eyes were closed all the way now.

Hamilton encircled the end of the suppressor with his lips and hooked his index finger around the trigger.

Then his eyes popped open.

He withdrew the suppressor from his mouth and turned the muzzle to point at Gabriel's chest.

"No," he said. "I don't think we'll do that after all." He smiled. "I never was in one of these shitholes with the grunts. That was true. I was CIA. We operated out of a nice air-conditioned office in Guantanamo Bay. I was an interrogator. And guess what? As part of our training, which was very, very good by the way, we were taught how to resist torture. Not just that fairground hypnosis act you just pulled on me, either. I'm talking about the hardcore stuff. Up to and including waterboarding. So fuck you, Mr Wolfe. And fuck Smudge Smith."

Hamilton straightened his arm and pulled the trigger.

60

With Interest

SUPPRESSED by the GM-9, Hamilton's shot was still loud enough to startle a flock of roosting birds from a nearby tree.

Gabriel flinched at the muzzle flash.

The particles of burnt propellant that shot towards him stung his nose.

And the projectile hit him dead-centre in his chest.

It bounced off his coat and fell harmlessly to the ground.

Hamilton gasped, looking down at the crumpled and burnt wad of paper lying at his feet.

Then his mouth closed and his lower jaw began to quiver.

Gabriel stepped towards Hamilton, swiped the gun from his hand, and thumbed the magazine release switch. He pulled a second magazine from his coat pocket and inserted it into the grip. Racked the slide to chamber a round, and aimed at Hamilton.

"I researched your background. I know all about your CIA training. So guess what? I gave you a blank round. But you know what GSR is, don't you? Gunshot residue. It's one of the first things the police look for in an apparent suicide. And now it's all over your hands."

"Wait," Hamilton said, putting his hands out in front of him, palms towards Gabriel. "My children. You're going to create two orphans."

"They'll have their mother. And anyway, I've created orphans before. As you have."

Hamilton opened his mouth to scream.

Gabriel took another step closer to his target, pushed the gun between his teeth and pulled the trigger.

Hamilton's mouth contained the blast from the pistol, meaning little or no GSR escaped to coat Gabriel's gloved right hand. The back portion of Hamilton's skull flew away in a spray of blood, brain and bone fragments that spattered the off-white wall of the nearest house. The body collapsed backwards into the dirt, one knee bent, arms flung out to the sides.

Gabriel knelt and wrapped Hamilton's right hand around the Glock's butt, taking care to press the pads of his thumb and fingers against the trigger and the plastic grip. Then he dropped it a few feet in front of the body. Next he typed a short note on Hamilton's phone and left the app open.

On the short walk back to the Aston Martin, Gabriel called his welcoming committee from York Airport.

"Baylesford."

"It's Gabriel Wolfe. I'm done. Can you meet me at the airport?"

"Sure. We'll be out front."

"I'll be two hours."

Gabriel walked past the Aston. Resisting the urge to gouge the paintwork with a stone, which would undermine somewhat the suicide scenario he'd left for the York Police Department to find, he marched on towards the open gates. He covered the seven miles from the Gordian proving ground to the airport in just under the two hours.

He was met outside by Baylesford and Johnson.

"We'll need your firearm, sir," Baylesford said. "And the four-eighty-four, ten-fifty. Can't very well have you in possession of such a useful document, can we?"

Was that the hint of a smile on the agent's face? Gabriel thought it might have been. Or maybe the guy was suffering from trapped wind. He handed over the document, the spare magazine, and the remaining rounds of ammunition in their boxes, blanks and hollow-points alike.

"I can't give you the weapon. I don't have it any more. If you monitor the York PD radio frequency for a couple of days or just buy the paper, I'm sure you'll hear of its location."

The men nodded. A grim expression that said, "we're not going to ask you any questions, and you won't tell us any lies". They walked Gabriel into the terminal building, escorted him through the various uniformed functionaries of the Federal and State Governments standing, literally, between Gabriel and his ride home, then shook hands and left.

Thirty minutes after that, Craig, the Gripen pilot, opened the throttles on the jet and they were airborne.

*

Back in England at half-past-eight that same evening, Gabriel thanked Craig and walked to the car park. The whole exercise had taken less than twelve hours, from takeoff to touchdown.

In the Maserati, Gabriel unlocked Hamilton's phone and scrolled through the contacts until he came to "S". There she was. With a photo, too. He composed a text.

```
Wolfe came to kill me. He's dead.
```

Then he pulled out from the access road and into the surrounding network of everyday residential streets that surrounded the school and muttered under his breath.

"One down, one to go."

61

Speak Truth to Power

MIDNIGHT. Gabriel made a phone call.

"Hello?"

"Britta, it's me."

"How come my phone says unknown caller?"

"I'm not using my own phone. It's more secure that way."

"Where are you?"

"In a hotel in the Peak District, the Bull, in Hartington."

"What? Why the fuck are you there?"

"I'm laying a trap and I need your help."

"OK. What do you need me to do?"

Lying on his back on the flowered bedspread, Gabriel explained what he needed from Britta. They agreed on the meeting time then ended the call.

Gabriel had already transferred Barbara Sutherland's number from Hamilton's phone into the one he'd lifted from Sasha Beck's prostrate form in The Golden Dragon. He used it now, with a voice-changer he'd bought in an electronics shop. When she answered, the Prime Minister sounded guarded to say the least. Gabriel tapped the record button on the call recorder app he'd installed.

"This is an unlisted number. Who are you?"

"I am a friend of Robert Hamilton's, Prime Minister. I carried out a hit for him on your behalf. I believe he texted you about it."

"What do you want?"

"I want to meet you."

"Why? Robert paid you I assume."

"He did. But I think you can afford to pay a little more."

"What?"

"You heard me. Robert was a little indiscreet. So now I know about your little arrangement. And I have the dossier Philip Agambe compiled on your dealings in blood diamonds."

There was a long pause. Gabriel counted it. Ten seconds.

"What do you want?"

"I want to meet you."

"Impossible. It's the middle of a session in Parliament. And my diary is solid."

"I said, I want to meet you. Or shall I send the dossier to the media?"

"No! Don't do that. Where and when?"

"I thought the Peak District. The day after tomorrow. Seven a.m. I'll send you a GPS reference."

"Impossible." Sutherland's flat Yorkshire tones still carried authority even know he knew she was on the defensive. "I'm leaving for a trip. India."

"Cancel it."

"I can't just cancel a trip like this. Look, I don't know who you are, but you clearly don't know anything about –"

"Cancel it!" Gabriel shouted. Then, quieter. "Have a health scare. A death in the family. Tom fell out of a tree. Children do get hurt, you know."

At the mention of her son's name, Sutherland's own voice became strident. "Don't you *dare* threaten my son. I'll come after you."

"Yes, you will. To the GPS reference I'm going to send you. And no reinforcements."

*

Early on in her days as Prime Minister, Sutherland had discovered just how hard it was to meet people privately. Anything official and she could expect to be accompanied by a squad of ministers or civil servants. Anything unofficial and there would be a couple of burly Special Branch officers tailing her, more or less discreetly. Nevertheless, she had found ways to place enough distance between herself and her minders to conduct the occasional meeting on her own.

Such a meeting was in progress now. In a soundproofed room in the Cabinet Office, its walls packed with foil-wrapped insulation to prevent electronic eavesdropping, she sat at a round table opposite David Brown.

"Someone has leaked," she said. "No, not leaked. Someone has opened the bloody floodgates. I got a call from some bloke in the middle of the night who claims he knows all about us and Robert Hamilton. Said he wants to meet me in the bloody Peak District, for God's sake."

"And you're telling me this, why?"

Her eyes flashed wide. "What do you mean? Why the bloody hell do you *think* I'm telling you? Because you have to do something about it."

Brown leaned back in his chair and clasped his hands behind his head.

"I'm not sure there's an awful lot I *can* do about it, Barbara." He pushed off from the floor until his chair was canted backwards, and stuck out his feet so the toe-caps of his shoes caught under the table.

"Now, listen to me," she said, pointing at him. "I still hold the reins of power. And I say you'll have to think of something."

He looked at her, without speaking. Then jerked his bodyweight forward and let it pull the chair back onto all four legs with a thump on the thick carpet.

"Shall I tell you about power, Prime Minister?" he said in a quiet voice. "You have a certain brand of power, bestowed upon you by your party and, shall we say, activated by the electorate. You're only in Parliament because you're an MP. Those same voters who put you there could choose someone else to represent them and you'd be out of a job. Just. Like. That." He snapped his fingers, a dry, percussive pop in the acoustically dead room. "Now, take me. In contrast to the precariousness of your own position, I am an appointee. So no worries about *my* job every five years. The voters might choose, in their infinite wisdom, to elect a pig-ignorant bigot to run this country, or an exdinner lady for all I care. But they can't get rid of me. In fact," he smiled, a predatory expression that showed his canine teeth, "nobody can get rid of me. You see, I don't really exist. Not in any way that would make sense to the bureaucrats. You knew that when we first began working together. How else do you think I was able to act on your behalf with some of the people you chose to do business with?"

"But I thought you worked for MI6. That still places you under official power of some kind."

"I work *in* MI6. The difference in preposition is small, but significant. Most importantly, it confers on me real power. I have a budget beyond scrutiny. I have highly skilled people at my disposal. And, I have the kind of freedom of action you might wish for but will never acquire."

"Are you telling me you're a double agent? Are you working for the Russians?"

He laughed. A genuine sound, warm and amused.

"Oh, dear. How quaint," he said, when the paroxysm had passed. "The Russians. No. I'm not working for them. Though a few of them work for me. The group of which I'm a member has what one might call transnational interests. We set the wheels in motion for globalisation decades ago. Trade deals, treaties, financial deregulation, loosened labour laws, free movement of people and capital. They were all our ideas." The smile left his face. "Here's the thing, Barbara. You don't have any power. Not really. And you've become a liability. I'm tired of your whining. So I'm not going to do anything to help you." He paused. "Actually, there is one thing I can suggest."

"What?" she asked, leaning forward.

"Get yourself a decent pair of boots. The Peak District's murder on high heels."

*

Two days after calling Sutherland from the hotel in Hartington, Gabriel woke at four. He showered, shaved and dressed. Merino base layer, top and bottom, then black moleskin trousers, long-sleeved T-shirt and fleece, finally Gore-tex over-trousers and a Berghaus shell jacket. Lined gloves, a black fleece watch-cap, a tactical facemask and Italian walking boots completed the outfit. Into a black rucksack went a pair of night-vision goggles, a bottle of water and some energy bars . . . and something couriered to him by Britta the previous day. Something heavy.

He left the Maserati in the hotel's car park and set off towards his rendezvous with Sutherland. The town was silent. A few flakes of snow drifted here and there but Hartington's streets were clear, bathed in the pinkish-orange glow of streetlights.

There was an alley between two shopfronts – an optician's and a pizza place. He turned down it, walked fast for a quarter of a mile, crossed a residential street at the far end and was climbing a stile into the beginnings of the National Park a few minutes later. The only part of him exposed to the air was a narrow strip of his face. The skin round his eyes puckered against the biting cold, he began the two-mile journey to the place where he would confront Sutherland. The moon provided enough light to see by, though he was careful picking his way through the bracken, gorse and heather as he navigated the terrain to the GPS reference. Twisting an ankle wasn't part of the plan.

Arriving, he scanned the area. *Perfect. Thank you Google Images.* Flat. Featureless. The nearest peak was well over a mile away, out of range for even the best sniper. Even though kills at well over two-and-a-half-thousand yards had been recorded, Gabriel was counting on the conditions, and the lack of light, to make that an impossibility.

He raked up a nest of dry bracken and moss and dug himself in to wait.

It was the faint crack that alerted him. He had been huddled down, munching one of the energy bars and thinking about Britta, when the snap of a bracken stem brought him back to the present. *They're here!*

He reached into the rucksack and withdrew Britta's present. Black, dull surface, moulded plastic handgrip. The Glock 19 was loaded with fifteen 9 x 19 mm Parabellum rounds. Hollow-points like the ones he'd used to kill Robert Hamilton. Stuffing it down into the squashed bracken between his thighs to muffle the sound, he racked the slide to chamber one of the rounds, then pushed the safety off.

Next, he slid the power switch over on the night-vision goggles and, as the electronics came to life with a mosquito's whine, pulled them down over his eyes.

The landscape in front of him swam into view: green and black but as clear as if it had been seven in the morning in June, not February. Three figures were stalking across the ground towards him, in a tight group. The figure in the centre of the group was shorter by a head than the other two. All were dressed in padded gear that bulked them out.

All three stopped, while one consulted a handheld device, a GPS presumably. The figure pointed in Gabriel's direction, then made a hand signal: *spread out.*

Flattening himself into his squashed nest of vegetation, Gabriel observed as the figures drew pistols, increased the distance between them to fifteen yards, and began a crouching approach to his position.

He'd anticipated that Sutherland wouldn't come alone. *He* wouldn't, whatever he'd been instructed to do.

The question was what to do about the protection team. They didn't look like they'd tagged along merely to stand guard. Their intent was clear.

But given the precariousness of Sutherland's position, he doubted they'd be soldiers, or even armed police. Not MI5 or MI6, either. She couldn't just order up a hit team and whisk them off to the middle of the Peak District on two days' notice. There'd be too many questions. No. These would be private contractors. Probably working for some British equivalent of Gordian.

He scraped bracken back over the flattened basin where'd he'd been lying in wait and belly-crawled parallel to the advancing team. There was a shallow trench running through the bracken and the soil beneath it, some sort of natural formation where the rock under the moorland had shifted downwards, thousands, or hundreds of thousands, of years ago.

Gabriel slid down into the trench and continued his knee-and-elbow progress away from the armed bodyguards. The road lay ahead. It was the only road leading to this remote spot. It ended in a wide scrape of tarmac surrounded by wooden post-and-rail fence: a viewpoint, and a starting point for circular walks through this "area of outstanding natural beauty" as the tourist guides put it. Though what was about to happen was not, to Gabriel's mind, in the slightest bit beautiful.

He reached the parking area while his opponents were still heading away towards the GPS reference. A solitary vehicle, a dark Land Rover Discovery, sat there, with the interior light on. And inside the solitary vehicle sat a solitary figure. A woman, wrapped up warm in a dark-coloured parka with a fur-lined hood pushed back from her face. A woman with a slash of red lipstick, despite the horrifically early hour she must have risen to be here at this time. She stared out through the passenger window, eyes wide, biting a fingernail. *Hello, Prime Minister.*

Gabriel crawled over the lip of the trench and crept up to the rear of the Discovery. Apt name, he thought as he kept low and made his way forward, along its near side. The engine was idling and the smell of unburnt diesel from the exhaust was pungent in the otherwise crisp, clean Derbyshire air.

As he reached the B-pillar, behind the window of the front passenger door, he straightened and tapped once on the glass with the muzzle of his pistol.

The effect was all he'd hoped for.

62

Nemesis

BARBARA Sutherland's head snapped round and she jerked back in her seat, eyes wide, mouth frozen open.

He pulled the door open and said a single word.

"Out."

She complied. What choice did she have?

"Where are you taking me?" she said in a shaking voice. "Who are you?"

"We have an appointment," he said through the tactical mask, which muffled his voice, though he didn't think it disguised it enough for her not to recognise it. "Move. Scream and I'll shoot you."

She stumbled ahead of him, zipping up the parka against the cold.

As they moved back towards the GPS reference, a shot rang out. Several bursts followed, four or five rounds at a time, two shooters overlapping their fire.

Sutherland stopped but Gabriel prodded her in the back with the pistol.

"No! They're shooting," she said.

"I know. Keep moving," he said.

Now they could hear shouting. Two male voices. One deep, rough, East End of London. The other higher pitched. A Geordie.

"Luke?" the Geordie called.

"He's down," East End replied.

"Shit! Sniper?"

"Think so."

"What do we do?"

"She said kill him."

Gabriel tightened his jaw at this and had to will himself not to drop Sutherland on the spot.

"There's nobody here." Geordie again.

"Fuck!" This was East End.

There was a rustle: squashed bracken springing back as a man lying on it stood up.

A split second later, another single gunshot rang out across the moorland.

Completing a triplet of sounds was the scrunch of dry vegetation as the man fell back to the ground.

"Johnno? Johnno?" East End called out. "Shit!"

By this time, Gabriel had manoeuvred Sutherland into position, just ten yards from the man's back.

He pushed her to the ground, gripping the back of her neck and crouched beside her.

At the noise, East End whirled round, his ghostly, green form sharp in Gabriel's night vision, his eyes pinpricks of white.

He brought his pistol up, a Beretta, Gabriel noted, and fired wildly, running through the remaining rounds in his magazine in a few seconds. He'd kept his arm straight out in front of him, firing at head-height.

Now Gabriel stood, and held his pistol out in front of him in a classic shooter's stance, feet parallel, slight lean forward, barrel level with his eyes.

He shot the man where he stood. Five rounds centre-mass. A white spray behind him filled the viewfinder of the goggles. Then the man sank to his knees and fell forward onto his face. Gabriel closed the gap between them and put another two rounds into the back of the man's head.

Turning, he was surprised to see Sutherland running off back towards the Discovery. He ran after her, taking high steps to avoid tripping, and caught her within thirty feet.

"No, Barbara. Not this time. Come with me."

At his use of her first name she whirled round and peered into the goggles.

"Who the bloody hell are you?"

"Who am I? I'm your nemesis. I'm somebody you've tried to have killed over and over again. And yet here I am. Alive and well."

Her eyes popped open as she processed this information.

"You can't be. You're dead."

Gabriel removed his watch cap and tugged the goggles over his head. Then he lifted the front edge of the tactical mask away from his chin and pulled it up and over his forehead before stuffing it in his pocket.

"I'm afraid not."

The dawn was late to arrive in this part of England's green and pleasant land, but there was enough pale light seeping over the terrain from the east to light Gabriel's features.

"Robert texted me. How did he not know?"

"Robert Hamilton killed himself three days ago. Apparently he couldn't cope with the crushing sense of guilt he felt for fomenting civil war, for the creation of child soldiers, and for torture, just to line his own – and others' – pockets." Her eyes fell. "Or, at least, that's what the note on his phone says."

Three or four minutes elapsed during which they picked their way past the three bodies on the ground and found the precise spot indicated by the GPS reference he'd texted her. Gabriel said nothing. Nor did Sutherland.

They stood facing each other, she panting, he breathing steadily, slowly, dark eyes narrowed. Then she did speak.

"What do you want, Gabriel, love? I promise I can get it for you. Money? Name your price. You know I have the conflict diamonds. They're untraceable. Take them to Amsterdam or New York or anywhere in Africa. You'll get a good price. I can even introduce you to the right people." He looked hard at her, but couldn't trust himself to speak. Not yet. "Or a job? In Government. You could be a security czar. Or honours? How about that? A knighthood. It's easy. The old bag will sign whatever I tell her to."

Finally, Gabriel spoke. In a low voice he began.

"You bent and twisted the law, handed out defence contracts to evil men, all to line your pockets."

She scowled. "Do you know what the world I move in is like?" she asked. "I'm a woman. They used to take the piss out of me. At every level. I had to be twice as tough as the men, had to jump just that extra bit higher. When Robert Hamilton approached me, he presented it as just a small favour. Building British defence industry competitiveness. The fee was hardly the stuff of Fleet Street exposés. But it got bigger. I came from nothing, Gabriel. Nothing! My dad was a farmer. We barely scraped by when I was growing up. Then Robert showed me what was possible. He said all my predecessors were at it, one way or another. The amounts weren't even that big. Barely bigger than the wastage from the MoD in a single month. Surely you can see that?"

Gabriel's right hand jerked out in front of him, finger tightening on the trigger. She gasped and drew back, flinching.

"If it was just the money, I'd walk away. You're all bent, one way or another. Hamilton was right. But you traded military intelligence for money. You put your own soldiers' lives in danger."

"What are you talking about? I helped Robert with defence contracts and I brokered a few arms deals in Africa for him, that's all."

"Have you really forgotten, Barbara? When you were Defence Secretary? You diverted operational intelligence within 22 SAS to Hamilton to protect Abel N'Tolo. My men and I were caught up in that. I lost a good man that day. And another of my men lost his left arm. A little girl had to grow up without her dad, and his wife became a widow."

"Gabriel, love, please. Kids are orphaned all the time. Women are widowed. That's war. They all know that when they enlist."

"Yes, they do know that. They know they could be maimed, or mutilated, or killed. By the enemy. But what they don't know is that they'll be ambushed because their own Government minister has betrayed them for a handful of blood diamonds and cheap African land."

Something in Sutherland seemed to snap. Maybe she realised she wasn't going to reason her way out of it.

"Fine. I traded military intel for blood diamonds and land. So what! Those idiots don't know what to do with it, do they? We've been pouring aid into Africa since the seventies. And for what? Civil wars. Terrorism. Torture.

Genocide. Corrupt leaders who use their national treasuries like other people use credit cards. It doesn't matter, does it? So if you're going to shoot me, let's get it over with. But frankly, you've done so much talking, I don't think you've got the balls. Otherwise, tell me how much you want to keep quiet and we can get out of this fucking cold."

Gabriel extended his right arm and leaned forward, breath misting in the air between them, and pressed the muzzle of the pistol against her forehead until the skin dented. He enjoyed watching her stiffen and shrink from what was coming. Then he took it away and stuffed it into his jacket pocket.

"I want you to disappear. Completely. I want you to resign. From the Government. From Parliament. From your party. From politics. From public life altogether. Your last act as Prime Minister is to reinstate Don Webster, and me, and put The Department under direct control of the Privy Council."

"I thought so. You realised what I already know. You can't murder me. It would destabilise the country you love. It would push the economy into freefall. You need me alive. Well I've got news for you, love. The answer's no."

Gabriel smiled. Then he called out.

"Did you get all that?"

There was a rustling and a quiet *clink* about twenty yards to the west of the place they were standing. Sutherland turned to her left, Gabriel to his right.

Walking towards them was a shambling, shaggy form. Fronds of bracken, thorny branches of gorse and sprigs of purple heather hung from it in a swishing mass. The form was humanoid. Visible over its right shoulder was the long barrel of a rifle. It was a Finnish model: a Sako TRG-42. Gabriel knew this even though the barrel itself didn't give enough away for him to make a visual ID. He knew because it was the shooter's weapon of choice for sniping.

When the shooter arrived, looking more like a human-plant hybrid than a person, it stood still, reached up with a leafy, twiggy limb and removed its head.

Inside the monstrous mass of canvas, netting and vegetation was a smaller head: red hair tied back in a plait coiled and pinned to the nape of the neck, freckles decorating the face.

"Every word," Britta said, holding up a small remote control and clicking the STOP button.

"You shit!" Sutherland spat. "This is blackmail. Not really the moral high ground you've been making such a fuss about, is it?"

Britta spun to her right and shoved Sutherland hard in the chest. Then she hit her. An open-handed blow to the left cheek.

"You bitch! You tried to have us killed. You're a disgrace to democracy. One more word and I'll shoot you myself."

"She will, Barbara. I promise. We have a high quality recording of your confession. So here's the deal. You keep quiet and so will we. You make any noise about this at all, or make trouble for us and this goes straight to the world's media."

Silenced by this outburst, Sutherland suddenly seemed to realise what had happened to her. Her shoulders sagged, her head dropped forward and she sighed deeply.

"Let's go," she said. "I'm tired."

63

One Last Roll of the Dice

REACHING the Land Rover, Gabriel pulled open the rear door. Barbara Sutherland climbed back in. She hadn't said a word on the walk back. The interior was still warm, and smelled of her perfume. Britta was just climbing in next to her, one boot inside the footwell, when the sound of a helicopter approaching made her stop.

"Who else did you tell?" she asked Sutherland.

"Nobody. I swear," she said, her eyes wide, her brow deeply furrowed.

"Stay here with her," Gabriel said, handing Britta his pistol. "If anybody approaches, give them one warning, then shoot. Let me have the Sako."

Britta nodded, handing over the rifle. She turned to Sutherland. "Don't think of shouting, or fighting me. I'll shoot you, too."

Gabriel turned and ran back towards the cover of the thick bracken. He slid to his knees and pulled more of the ragged brown stems over himself, then worked the smooth bolt of the Sako to chamber a round.

Fifty yards to the east of his position, a helicopter materialised out of the cloud, descended, and hovered a couple of feet above the ground. A single, black-clad figure jumped out, carrying a machinegun, a Heckler & Koch MG5. The belt-fed gun was a full-fat infantry weapon and could take out light aircraft. Somebody was playing for keeps.

As the helicopter ascended and wheeled away to the north, Gabriel decided it was time to change the odds. He sighted through the precision optics of the scope mounted on the Sako and squeezed the trigger.

His shot was dead on target. The bullet penetrated the MG5's receiver, smashing the sophisticated mechanical parts inside and rendering the powerful weapon impotent. As it swung right from the force of the impact the stranger had to let go or have his wrist broken. He dropped into a crouch, but not before Gabriel had taken a good look at his enemy.

The man was old to be a fighter, in his early sixties at least, Gabriel estimated. His silver hair was cut short and his eyes were heavily lined at the corners.

As Gabriel crept closer, hugging his body to the ground, the man pulled out a phone and spoke briefly. Then he drew a pistol, a Glock, aimed in Gabriel's direction and fired, twice, into the bracken. The shots were nowhere near him. If the man's aim had been even close, Gabriel would have dropped him with another round from the rifle.

Then the man stood upright and shouted.

"Gabriel Wolfe, I know that's you with the rifle. Nice shooting, by the way." His upper-class accent jarred with the black tactical outfit he wore. "You think you've won, because you've managed to fool that woman into betraying herself. But I'm afraid I can't let that stand. You see, there are powerful people whose interests I protect who want you out of the way." Gabriel manoeuvred clear of a frond of bracken and laid the cross-hairs of the sight over the man's right eye. "Before you pull the trigger, let me ask you something. Are you really going to kill me without knowing the first thing about me? Like you killed Philip Agambe?"

Gabriel watched the man through the scope. Nodded. And smiled.

A clump of moorland vegetation had just risen to its feet behind the man. It pushed the muzzle of a Glock 19 hard against the back of the man's head then immediately stepped back.

"Drop your weapon," the clump said. "Or I'll drop you."

The man complied, and raised his hands above his head.

Gabriel broke cover and raced over to join Britta.

"Sutherland?" he asked.

"Cable ties."

He turned to face the man. "Who are you?"

"Why don't you call me David?" the man said.

"Who are these people you're working for?"

He smiled. "I'm afraid that would be telling. Something I am not prepared to do."

His next move caught Gabriel and Britta by surprise.

He spun, fast, dropping to a crouch and kicking out at Britta's right knee. She buckled with a scream of pain, and as she brought her gun arm up again he smashed his knuckles down onto her wrist and broke her grip on the pistol, before clawing her across the eyes.

Then his hand was closing round the butt, ripping it out of her hand and swinging it round to aim at Gabriel.

Gabriel closed in, pushing himself to get inside the man's reach, and slammed the heel of his right hand under the man's chin. The *clack* as his jaws snapped closed was clearly audible.

Now Gabriel grabbed the Glock's barrel and pushed it out wide to the left.

Britta was still down, hands over her eyes, moaning with pain, helpless.

The noise of rotor blades made Gabriel look up, a big mistake. The next moment he felt an explosion of pain as the man hammered his other fist into Gabriel's throat. Choking, he staggered back, regrouping.

The chopper was landing now, rotor blades *whop-whopping* at deafening volume.

His gun arm free again, the man was levelling the Glock, aiming straight at Gabriel's face.

There was a look of cold triumph on his face. The crinkled blue eyes and the smile stealing over his face said it all. I win. You lose.

Then the eyes opened wide and the mouth dropped open, allowing a thin stream of dark red blood to emerge, sliding over his lower lip and down his chin.

The Glock fell from his outstretched hand and landed with a soft rustle in the bracken.

He collapsed to his knees and fell forwards onto his face.

Britta was standing behind him, squinting through half-closed eyes. Her right hand dangled at her side.

Protruding from the back of the man's neck was the hilt of a knife. Not a single millimetre of the blade was visible.

Gabriel turned round, bent and retrieved the Sako. Working the bolt and bringing it up to his shoulder in one, fluid movement, he aimed at the chopper, whose pilot, seeing the action on the ground, had clearly just decided to leave and had throttled forward, producing a whine of increased thrust from the engine.

The skids were only just kissing the bracken as the .338 Lapua Magnum round tore into the fuselage just below the main rotor mast. With a shrieking explosion, the gears, turbine rotors and the engine itself disintegrated. The rotor blades canted crazily to one side before the tip of one blade dug into the soft ground and snapped with a bang.

Gabriel pushed Britta to the ground, drawing a scream as her injured wrist hit the earth. The air above them was filled with shrapnel as the other three rotor blades fractured. The helicopter settled back down with a crashing thump, black smoke coiling up from the engine, rear rotor spinning down to a standstill.

With the chopper disabled, its rotors crumpled like the wings of a squashed insect, Gabriel bent to retrieve the Glock and ran towards the cabin, where he could see the pilot frantically trying to free himself from his flight harness. He wrenched the door open and stuck the pistol into the man's face.

"Enough!" He shouted. "It's over."

64

Return to Mozambique

SIX floors above the swarming pedestrians, in a small apartment on Ko Shing Street, Hong Kong, a young computer genius by the name of Wūshī clicked on an email in his inbox. He nodded as he reviewed the names of the encrypted files attached.

"Sweet!" he whispered.

He uploaded the files to a secure server he maintained, set up a distribution list, and encrypted the release software. No timer, but an instant SEND if he received a code word by text, email or instant message.

*

Five thousand miles to the west, in the basement of a Stockholm house owned by twenty-five-year-old IT teacher Matteo Falskog, a similar procedure was taking place.

*

In the office of a small terraced family home in Peckham, southeast London, the widow of an SAS trooper was sitting at her computer. She was making her own careful preparations should she ever need to release the recording sent to her by Gabriel, as well as the digital scans of the dossier she held on Barbara Sutherland, the former Prime Minister of the United Kingdom of Great Britain and Northern Ireland.

*

Two days after the recording had been distributed, Gabriel arrived in Maputo, traveling on the fake passport provided by Mr Fang, who'd refused several attempts by Gabriel to pay for the work that had clearly gone into producing the document. After checking in at a hotel – The Excelsior – he called Darryl and arranged to meet at a downtown bar.

From the street, Montebello had appeared to be just another of hundreds of urban bars he'd seen in his lifetime. A double-width frontage between offices and shops. But it hid a secret. A garden, visible from the interior of the bar. Gabriel carried a gin and tonic into the miniature urban Eden.

It wasn't huge, maybe forty or fifty feet square, and mostly paved, but it was lush with vegetation. Fruit trees, flowering vines, huge glazed pots overflowing with trailing geraniums in saturated shades of crimson and coral, and a blowsy bougainvillea, smothered in cerise-pink flowers. The perfume was a heady blend of sweet and spicy that made Gabriel smile for no reason he could fathom. In the centre of the paved area was a small, raised pool with a cascade of more glazed pots above it mounted in a copper framework, delivering a never-ending stream of bubbling, splashing water onto the heads of the goldfish that swam close to the surface.

The space was crowded with tables set with mosaic tiles; all were occupied. Gabriel scanned the area, looking for Darryl.

"Hey! Gabriel. Over here. I got us a nice corner table."

Darryl was standing at the far end of the garden. He wore another lurid Hawaiian shirt, this one featuring World War II warplanes, their camouflaged noses painted with snarling shark-mouths. His Southern tones cut through the chatter, causing a few other drinkers to turn their heads. Moments later, the two men were shaking hands before sitting down and clinking glasses.

"You said you had to abort your mission," Darryl said.

"We did. We were attacked. Twice. First, by some private contractor types in a Humvee. Then by a warlord, or his gang at any rate. The Zambian air force pulled us out, with a little help from your countrymen, for which many thanks, by the way."

"Nothing to do with me, but I'll take the thanks on behalf of Uncle Sam."

He tilted his glass at Gabriel before taking on pull on the golden brown liquid. "Then what?"

Well, then the shit really hit the fan.

"Well, we decided discretion was the better part of valour. We left."

"But you're back now."

"I am. Look, I'll be honest with you. I could really use some help. You said you'd been involved with the US Defense POW/MIA Accounting Agency?"

"Yes, I did." Darryl drained his drink, letting the ice cubes click against his front teeth.

"I made a promise to my friend's widow and her daughter to bring their man back to them and I intend to carry it out."

Darryl scratched the stubble on his cheek. "On the record? There's nothing I can do for you. I haven't heard from Don in a while, so to me you're just Joe Schmo from Kokomo. Off the record, I got a lot of respect for what y'all are doing. Let me go and get us some more drinks and you can tell me what's on your shopping list."

Gabriel finished his gin and tonic and handed the empty tumbler to Darryl, who squeezed his way between the other tables. With surprising grace for a man carrying as much surplus weight as he did, Gabriel thought.

When Darryl returned – "G and T for you, old boy, eh what? Rum and Coke for me," – Gabriel laid out his requirements for his second trip up-country.

"I need a vehicle. Four-wheel drive, obviously. GPS. Spare gas. Rations and bottled water. Medical kit. Some kind of sealable plastic bags. A decent knife. Water purification tablets. Sleeping bag. And, although I'm not expecting any trouble this time, a sidearm and rifle."

"That's it? You don't want a couple Hellfires? What I heard, one shook up those dudes who sprung it on you last time you were here, with that pretty little redhead."

"Yeah, and maybe throw in a handful of Claymores while we're at it."

"Why stop at anti-personnel mines? How 'bout I throw in a drone or two?"

"Or get me a Bradley and I'll just go in a straight line all the way. Just hop out at the other end."

Darryl laughed, then took a long pull on his rum and Coke. He leaned back, expansive now.

"Tell you what. I'll make a call, get you a fucking Apache. Why drive when you can fly?"

Gabriel laughed too, enjoying the slobby American's company and easy humour. Then he noticed Darryl wasn't smiling any more.

"Darryl? What's the matter?"

The man's brow was furrowed with deep lines. Then he grinned.

65

Here Comes a Chopper . . .

FLYING in helicopters had been a regular part of Gabriel's life during his Army service days. It was two days after his conversation with Darryl at Montebello and now the two men sat, strapped in side by side, as the pilot and crew of a fully loaded Apache Gunship made their final flight preparations.

"I have to ask," he said, leaning close to Darryl. "How on earth did you swing this? Doesn't it cost a shitload of money to put one of these birds into the air?"

"Damn straight. You're looking at lots of zeroes. Thing is, I play poker once a month with a group of guys working down here and one them is a Colonel in AFRICOM. That's the United States Africa Command. He owes me a lot of money and I traded it for a favour."

"Thank you. Which doesn't sound like enough, but, really, that means a lot."

Further conversation became impossible as the big helicopter's rotor blades started turning, chopping the air into turbulent currents that howled and swirled around its fuselage.

Darryl gave Gabriel the thumbs up and then bent his head to his chest. Gabriel couldn't think of anything better to do so he, too, closed his eyes. He felt the Apache bank left as it climbed away from the ground to begin the flight to the GPS reference Gabriel had sent to the pilot from his phone. He found the vibrations thrumming through his chest oddly soothing, and his eyes grew heavy.

The bump when the chopper landed jolted Gabriel awake. But something was wrong. Terribly wrong. Beside him, head dangling to the right, Darryl was dead, his throat gaping, blood soaking the front of his camouflage jacket. Both hands were pinned to his thighs with machetes. Up front, he could see red splashes on the Plexiglas windscreen, which was starred and cracked, pocked with bullet holes. The pilot and co-pilot had been shot. Their bodies lolled sideways, flight helmets touching, and smashed open like eggs where large-calibre rounds had penetrated the thin plastic shells.

He punched the release button at his waist, but it was jammed. The four-point harness held him in place like a baby in a pushchair. He wrenched his body round in an attempt to reach the knife he'd strapped to his calf but his fingers fell agonisingly short. Then he heard men laughing beyond the open door in front of him.

A muscular brown hand grabbed hold of the side of the doorway and hauled its owner on board. The man wore a bright yellow Adidas T-shirt with the distinctive three stripes running down each sleeve to the point where they ended at massive biceps. He carried a chrome-plated, Desert Eagle semi-automatic pistol.

"Oho, what have we got here? Captain Wolfe. Did you come back for more punishment? That can be arranged you know. But first we have to release you from your harness, yes?"

He pulled the slide back, racking a .50 calibre hollow-point round as thick as a man's finger into the chamber.

Gabriel was struggling, writhing in the nylon webbing, but it seemed to be tightening, constricting around his ribs like a python.

"Goodbye, Captain Wolfe," the man said with a grin displaying a double row of gold teeth.

Then he pulled the trigger.

Gabriel screamed as the hollow-point hit the release button on his harness and ploughed into his guts.

A hand was shaking him violently. He jerked his head up. The Apache was just setting down in a treeless area of forest.

"Gabriel, man? Wake up. You were having the mother of all nightmares. They heard you from up front, through their cans."

Gabriel was hyperventilating. His pulse was thumping painfully in his neck. He wiped away the greasy slick of sweat that had covered his face and exposed neck.

"Oh, Jesus! Sorry. That was a bad one."

Darryl's forehead crinkled and he pursed his lips.

"You seeing someone for that?" he said.

"What, nightmares?"

"No, not nightmares. You know damn well what I'm talking about. I've seen it in plenty of our guys. I ain't going to say it if you don't want me to."

Gabriel shook his head.

"No, it's OK. And, yes, I am seeing someone about it. But I'm so close to finding Smudge this time, I guess it all just came flooding out."

"That's what you called him, huh?"

"Yeah. We all had nicknames. Before I was the boss they called me Wolfie. Not very original, I know."

"Never mind original, it's what bonds us. Man's got a nickname from his comrades, he feels part of something bigger, you know. I've never seen combat, just gone along afterwards to recover our MIAs, but my old man did. Vietnam. Two tours. Got three Purple Hearts, and a Silver Star for taking out a Viet Cong machine gun nest. His name was Dwight but they called him 'Yogi'. Know why?"

Gabriel shrugged. "Tell me."

"You ever hear of a baseball player called Yogi Berra?"

"No, sorry."

"Fucking Limeys. Bet you would have if he'd played cricket, don't you know." Darryl whipped out his cod upper-class British accent for this last sally before continuing. "Man was, like, the greatest. Amazing hitter. But what he did better'n anyone was catch. My Dad was on patrol down in the jungle one day, and this kid, maybe eleven or twelve, runs out onto the path about twenty feet away and lobs a grenade at him and his men. My Dad drops his M16 and damn if he doesn't catch the grenade. No time to think, he just throws it back at the spot where the kid vanished into the bushes. Grenade goes off and a foot comes flying over their heads and gets stuck in a tree. After that, they always called him Yogi." He shook his head and sighed. "It's the bonds that matter between fighting men. What do you say we get out and get it on, start looking for Smudge?"

Gabriel nodded. Five minutes later, having agreed with the pilot they'd check in every ten minutes by radio, he and Darryl walked away from the Apache. They headed for the village where that last, disastrous skirmish with the People's Army for the Liberation of Mozambique had taken place. Both men wore general purpose camouflage fatigues and brown army boots. Both carried Beretta M9 semi-automatic pistols in holsters on their right hips, and both had freshly oiled M4 carbines slung across their backs.

The village, when they reached it, had the dilapidated look of abandoned human settlements everywhere, whether in an African forest or a Florida subdivision after the debt-burdened residents have upped sticks and left. Tin-roofed shacks sagged drunkenly, their corrugated roofs rusty and spattered with greyish-white bird droppings. The paths between the buildings, once swept clean every morning, were now barely discernible tracks of grass. No feet had pounded the red earth into a flat, dusty surface for years. Lying against a collapsing mud wall was a cracked terracotta pot that might once have been used for cooking. Its black glaze had weathered to a matt finish and then scabbed off in flakes, revealing the red-brown clay beneath.

"This where it happened?" Darryl said.

"The chief's place was that one over there," Gabriel said, pointing to a larger, but still ruined house on the edge of the central clearing. "That's where we took out N'Tolo. He'd brought a few guys with him for protection and we dealt with them, but when we came out, the place was swarming with his men." *And our own Defence Secretary betrayed us for a handful of fucking diamonds.*

"So which way did you guys go?"

Gabriel paused. Looked around. Closed his eyes. Willing the memories of that day to come back and yet terrified that they would . . .

Small arms fire.

Five-round bursts from the M16s.

Full-auto fire from the AKs.

Hot brass and cordite.

Sweat.

Fear.

"They hit Smudge!"

"We need those plans, Smudge. Get them back."

"On it, Boss."

Smudge stumbles. He's taken a round in the back. He flings the case containing N'Tolo's plans to Gabriel.

Then another hits him. Back of the head.

Blood. Brain. Bone.

"Put down area fire! Drive them back!"

Exfil, still firing, to the extract point.

Gabriel opened his eyes. "The extract point was northwest from here. I remember looking down from the chopper. The tree where they . . . where they took him, it was behind the chief's house somewhere."

"Come on, then. Let's go find your boy."

They strode through the abandoned settlement, reached the chief's house and skirted it on the right. The forest beyond was dense and green, and alive with birds, whose calls and songs would have entranced Gabriel in any other circumstances. Now they were a distraction. Swatting away biting flies, the two men picked their way between the trees, lifting their boots high to avoid tripping in the tangled undergrowth that swarmed and coiled around their feet.

Gabriel staggered, catching his right boot on a vine as thick as a python. He freed his boot and stood again. Then his eyes widened and he extended his right arm, the index finger pointing.

66

Finding Calvary

BROKEN by tree branches into alternating bands of gold and dark green, sunshine lit up a clearing.

Standing in its centre was a single, fat-trunked baobab.

Two low branches extended out from the trunk about six feet above the forest floor.

Gabriel pushed through the few trees remaining between him and the baobab. This was the place. This was the tree those murderous bastards had pinned Smudge to through his hands. He clenched his fists and ground his teeth as he looked at those branches spread like arms, as if to say, "Don't blame me. I wanted no part of it. They crucified him on me. I had no choice".

And there, stuck into the wood, all the way through the bark and the cambium beneath, were two rusted steel machetes. Wasps and termites must have eaten away the wooden handles years ago, leaving the narrow tangs and those deep-bellied blades in the flesh of the tree. But of Smudge, there was no sign. No finger bones dangling from the blades, no bones at all. Gabriel fell to his knees in front of the tree and scraped at the bare ground with his hands, scrabbling through the hard surface to the softer earth, splitting nails, cutting his fingertips. He was swearing under his breath – a constant stream of the vilest curses he could conjure – and sweating profusely.

Then Darryl bent and laid a hand on his back, between the shoulder blades.

"Gabriel. You need to step back. We need to think."

Gabriel jumped to his feet, about-turned, marched away from the tree for eight or ten feet, Darryl following, and drew his Beretta.

He spun round, thumbed off the safety and started shooting.

The noise as the 9 mm bullets left the barrel was deafening. Darryl stood back and watched as Gabriel unloaded all sixteen rounds into the tree. Wood chips and needle-pointed splinters flew in all directions, one catching Gabriel on the left cheek and opening a cut.

"Fuck you!" he yelled. "Fuck you all!" Then he hurled the empty M9 at the smoking tree.

"Feel better now?" Darryl asked in a dry tone, brushing bits of bark from the front of his jacket.

Gabriel nodded, then went to retrieve his pistol, slammed home a fresh magazine and holstered it, safety on again. "Sorry. I think I was expecting find a skeleton pinned up there, or even just his hands. But there's nothing."

Darryl shook his head. "There's never nothing. If you can find the site of a soldier's death, you can find something. Probably what happened was, scavengers took him. The bigger elements get taken by hyenas, maybe even leopards or lions. Then you got your jackals and wild dogs. Vultures, too. Finally you got smaller birds, and the damn flies and beetles will get in on the act. But they don't eat metal, OK? So his dog tags should be around here somewhere. Maybe a couple of bones the hyenas and vultures missed. We need to search the immediate environment."

Gabriel swiped a palm across his forehead. "I understand. Good. What are we looking for?"

"Somewhere a scavenger might have hidden a trophy. Maybe a watercourse where stuff could have gotten washed away. What were your tags like?"

"Two metal discs in rubber silencers. Green nylon cord, although we used plug chains too."

"None of that's edible and it's not going to corrode either. So let's grid this. You go to the left of the tree, I'll go to the right. We'll start with a ten-yard square each. You walk over it in one-foot wide paths, north-south first, then east-west. Something we learned from crime-scene investigators."

Head down, Gabriel began to pace the virtual grid he'd overlaid on the ground. It took forty-five minutes and by the end he had discovered nothing. He called across to Darryl.

"Anything?"

"No. You?"

"No." Gabriel looked back at the tree as he said this and changed his mind. "Did you say watercourse?"

Darryl came over to join him. "Yeah, I did. Why? You see one?"

"I'm not sure. Look over there." He was shading his eyes and pointing at a sweeping curve of smooth, cracked mud beyond the tree. "Could that be a stream-bed do you think?"

"Let's go and find out."

Boots crunching on dry leaves and twigs, the two men made their way to the curve of mud, which had a concave surface like a shallow gutter. The sun had dried it to a hard, crisp finish, patterned with ripples and cracked like dry skin under a magnifying glass. Flecks of translucent mica glittered on the surface like diamonds.

"Yes indeed, my friend. That is a dry stream-bed. Look at the direction of the ripples. It was flowing that way," Darryl said, looking towards the tree line. "Come on, we'll follow it along. Grab a stick and start breaking open the surface. Maybe we'll get lucky. Like a couple of old-time prospectors, y'know?"

Armed with branches cut from nearby trees, they began smashing the top layer of the mud as it meandered downstream from the baobab tree. The first ten or fifteen times Gabriel struck the hard-baked surface, it cracked open to reveal nothing more than a slightly darker, crumblier version of the same soil. No metal, no bone, no fabric.

Swearing, he brought the branch back over his head then crashed it down into a mosaic of rippled crust in a circular wash, where a rock had diverted the now dried-up stream. Gasping with the effort and wiping dust from his eyes, he peered down. And gasped. Something glinted at him from the red earth. A crescent of dull silver-grey metal.

Gabriel let out a yelp of delight. "Found them! I've found them. His discs."

As Darryl knelt by him and watched silently, Gabriel picked away the polygonal fragments of crust and uncovered the discs, still seated in their black rubber silencers and attached to their nylon cord and half-buried in the softer soil. The stainless steel was dull and pitted but otherwise intact. Gabriel picked them free with his index finger and held them up, blowing the dust away. He read out the sparse text, ignoring the eight-digit service number:

O POS
SMITH
MA
CE

"That your boy?" Darryl asked.

Gabriel brushed at his eyes, where tears had spilled over onto his cheeks, running through the dust like this stream must once have done.

"That's him. Michael Anthony Smith. We found him." Gabriel looped the cord around his own neck and tucked the discs inside his shirt. "Oh, Jesus, we found him, Darryl." Gabriel was smiling. He leant over and clapped Darryl on his meaty shoulder.

Darryl was smiling too. "That's fantastic. Well done. Now, there may be some bones 'round here too. It's possible something carried him this far. Keep looking downstream and maybe back up a ways, too."

Still on their knees, they began a fingertip search in the stream bed. This time it was Darryl's turn to shout.

"Got something!"

Gabriel ran back and squatted beside Darryl, who was raking back some of the mud, exposing a small white knob of bone. "What is it?"

"Hold on and I'll tell you." Darryl flicked away a few more fragments of dried mud and prised the bone free with the tip of his knife. He held it up.

"Vertebra. Cervical. C3 or C4 I'd guess."

"You can tell by looking?"

Darryl nodded, still scrutinising the vertebra. "They trained us pretty well in skeletal anatomy. Had archaeologists, pathologists, anthropologists, every kind of 'ologist' you can imagine."

Over the next two hours, the two men scraped away the entire surface of the stream-bed, but found no further bones.

Straightening and leaning back to ease the muscles in his back, Gabriel spotted a vulture wheeling in lazy circles against a bank of low, white clouds. *Did you take him? Did you leave me anything else?*

He looked back to where Darryl was dragging the point of his knife through the mud, and then beyond. A second baobab tree stood sentry about seventy yards from the first. At the base of its swollen trunk was a black oval. At first Gabriel thought it must be a shadow, but then, realising there were no objects close by that could create such an inky, sharp-edged shape, he walked closer to get a better look.

What he had at first taken to be a shadow was actually a hole. Maybe it had been hollowed out by some burrowing rodent or insect colony. As he got closer, he broke into a run. He heard Darryl shouting to him but ignored him and kept going, skidding to stop and dropping to his knees in front of the tree. He was reaching towards the hole when Darryl's shout stopped him.

"Gabriel, wait!" The American came lumbering over, too out of shape to sprint. He was sweating heavily in the camouflage fatigues, dark stains under his arms and in the centre of his chest. "Could be any damn thing in there waiting to bite you. Some pretty bad critters in Mozambique. Snakes, spiders, scorpions, every-fucking-thing."

Looking around, Gabriel grabbed a stick and poked it into the hole, stirring it around in the leaf mould within for good measure.

Both men waited, ready to jump back if something venomous and pissed-off appeared. Nothing. No giant spiders or angry cobras. No gang of killer bees or monster centipedes.

Gabriel drew a breath then stretched his arm out and pushed his hand into the hole.

He felt around in the rotted leaves and powdery wood fragments chewed up by whatever had made the hole. Then his fingers touched something hard, smooth and curved, right at the back of the hole. He explored the surface, placing his palm over it and feeling all around it with his fingers.

"Oh, my God. I think I've found him, Darryl."

He pushed his fingers underneath the object, found a grip in its ridged underside, and pulled, gently. With a soft *shushing*, the object came free of the leaf mould. Gabriel sat back on his heels and brought it out into the sunlight.

Held in Gabriel's cupped hands was a skull. The lower jaw was missing. The rear surface was cracked and splintered, with a circular hole distorted by sharp-edged triangular gaps high on the crown. There was no other damage. The top teeth were all there, some of the molars filled with blackened amalgam, and the eye sockets and nasal cavity were intact.

Gabriel looked around, half-expecting to see a brown-skinned man in SAS camo waving from the treeline, but there was nothing. Just birds singing, and the sun hot on his face. He brushed the flakes of leaf and dried wood fragments from the bone and sat, staring into the empty eye sockets.

He bent his head until his forehead touched the skull and closed his eyes.

67

A Cold Land

THIRTY hours later, Gabriel stepped out into the arrivals lounge at Heathrow. Darryl had promised to get Smudge's skull and identity discs back in a diplomatic bag to the US Embassy in London. Bored-looking drivers held placards in front of their chests, scanning the emerging passengers for the people they'd been hired to take to hotels, offices and meeting rooms. Nobody waited for Gabriel. He stopped at an ATM, then walked out of the warm terminal building into the February air.

A freezing wind bit into his cheeks, blowing sharp flecks of sleet into his eyes. Someone a few places ahead of him in the taxi queue was smoking, and the acrid smell of the cigarette smoke caught in his nose and made him sneeze.

A middle-aged woman next to him, bundled up in a purple padded coat and wearing a white, fake-fur hat, turned and looked at him. Then frowned.

"You don't want to walk about without a coat, love. You'll catch your death."

Then she turned back. Eventually a taxi drew level with Gabriel and the driver lugged his bags around to the back and loaded them into the boot.

"Where to, guv?"

"Salisbury, please."

The man frowned. "That's going to cost, I'm afraid. Two hundred."

"It's fine."

Gabriel closed his eyes as soon as the taxi pulled away and slept for the entire journey. He woke when the driver asked him for his address. It was nine in the evening. He gave it and, twenty minutes later, walked in through the front door of his cottage. Post had piled up on the mat and he stepped over it, heading for the kitchen.

His answer phone told him he had fifteen messages. He ignored it. He retrieved a bottle of Tanqueray and a handful of ice from the freezer, clinked the cubes into a cut-glass tumbler and poured a couple of inches of gin over them. He emptied a tin of Schweppes tonic on top, then took a long pull on the drink before sitting at the kitchen table.

There were people he needed to speak to, but right now he needed to sleep. He sent a single text, to Britta.

Found him. Back at home. Going to bed. Speak tomorrow. X

He took the gin and tonic upstairs and drank it in bed, reading an old copy of *The Pickwick Papers* until Dickens's characters began blurring into one another.

The next morning, Gabriel shopped for food and returned to the cottage carrying a bag full of bacon, sausages, eggs, mushrooms, tomatoes, tea, coffee, milk, bread and marmalade. He made what his old Regimental Sergeant Major would have called "a proper breakfast" and spent the next thirty minutes eating, drinking tea and listening to jazz on the radio. Breakfast finished, he called the US Embassy in London's Grosvenor Square. After bouncing around the automated call-response system, he found himself talking to a pleasant-sounding female voice that he hoped belonged to a flesh-and-blood human.

"Thank you for calling the American Embassy. This is Melissa. How may I help you today?" She delivered this mini-speech in a singsong voice, the accent somewhere on the East Coast.

"Yes. My name is Gabriel Wolfe. I believe one of your overseas . . ." *What? Spooks? Facilitators? Operatives?* "staff members couriered something to you for me to collect. I have a reference if you'd like it?"

"Yes, of course, sir. Please go ahead."

"It's Darryl Burroughs and reference DB/MIA/GB/717."

"Please hold."

Gabriel stared at the rain streaking the kitchen window and the bedraggled garden beyond. Seconds ticked by and he started taking bets against himself on which of a pair of raindrops would reach the bottom of the pane first. The tinny Muzak playing on a twenty-second loop was beginning to grate when Melissa came back on the line.

"Sir? Yes. I have a package in our mailroom marked for your attention. You can come at any time during our operating hours, which are eight-thirty a.m. until five-thirty p.m. Please bring two forms of ID including at least one with a photograph. Is there anything else I can do for you today?"

"No, thank you. You've been very helpful."

"Have a nice day."

Gabriel doubted he would, although the next call at least would be a pleasant one.

"Oh, thank, God," Britta said when she answered her phone. "You could have called last night, you know. I didn't sleep a blink."

"I'm sorry. Just done in, I'm afraid."

"So where have you been? What's going on?"

Gabriel laughed. "Slow down. The good news is, yes, we found Smudge. I have his ID discs here, and a neck bone. We found his skull, too and I have to collect it from the US Embassy." As he spoke, he fingered the discs, the stamped information about Smudge's name, number, blood type and religion still ingrained here and there with particles of red soil.

"Wait, we? You had a partner?"

"Darryl Burroughs. Remember him?"

"With his Neanderthal attitude to women and that horrible shirt, how could I forget?"

"He came through for me. We flew up there in an Apache. Remember he used to work recovering MIAs for the US Government? He knew all kinds of practical techniques. He's one of the good guys."

"Maybe. But he could still lose a few pounds and get a decent wardrobe.

What are you going to do now?"

"I'm going to come up to town and get Smudge and take him to Melody and Nathalie. I made them a promise and now I can keep it."

"Will there be a military funeral?"

"I don't know. I hadn't thought. I'll ask Melody."

68

Family and Friends Only

A man's skull doesn't weigh much. Without the brain, most of the mass is gone. Strip away the muscle and skin and remove the lower jaw, and you're left with a surprisingly light object. The young girl who brought the box to Gabriel, as he waited in the reception area of the American Embassy, clearly had no trouble carrying it. It was almost completely wrapped in dull, silver-grey duct tape. On its upper surface was a printed label with his name on it, and Darryl's, along with the reference code.

"Mr Wolfe, sir?" she said as she reached the small group of sofas where Gabriel stood.

"Yes, that's me."

"I just need to see your ID, please."

Somehow he'd imagined all the staff would be Americans themselves, so her east London accent surprised him.

He fished out his passport – his real passport – along with his driving licence and handed them over. She checked them, face impassive, taking her time and glancing from the two digitised photos to Gabriel face several times. Satisfied that he was who he claimed to be, she handed over the carton.

"Thank you," he said. Then he turned and left, holding the carton reverently as if it contained treasure.

An hour later he pulled into Denman Road. As he rang the bell, he monitored his heart rate with interest. It was ticking along at a steady fifty-five, but then, as the door began its inward swing, it shot up to ninety.

Standing in the doorway, wearing a pair of faded jeans, a crumpled pale blue shirt and soft suede moccasins on her feet, was the widow of the man whose remains he carried in the carton held in both hands between them.

Melody looked down at the top of the box. Neither moved for several seconds.

Gabriel waited, watching as tears emerged from the inner corners of her eyes and tracked down her cheeks, before dropping from her chin onto the fabric of her shirt, creating dark-blue splotches.

Finally, she looked up. "Is that him?" He nodded, suddenly unable to talk, swallowing against the lump that had formed in his throat. "Sorry, Gabriel. Come in."

In the kitchen, they sat facing each other across the table, the carton between them. Realising the experience was going to be a shock for Melody, civilians tending not to come across many skulls at all in their lives, let alone the bullet-ridden skulls of their own husbands, Gabriel brought out an envelope from his suit jacket.

"We found these, too. They're his."

Melody took the bumpy envelope from him and slit the seal with a pencil that was lying on the table, left, perhaps, by Nathalie. She cupped her hand and slid the contents out into her palm. She gasped as the vertebra bobbled across her skin before the two stainless steel discs fell on top of it, arresting its progress.

"Oh, God," she said in a whisper, looking from the discs to the carton

"Here," he said, opening a small penknife. "Let me open it for you."

He slit the tape around the top and opened the flaps. Then he smiled, a small tight-lipped smile. Someone, and he suspected he knew who, had placed Smudge's skull inside a soft, unbleached cotton shopping bag, such as a Mozambican woman might take to market with her. He reached in and lifted the package out and placed it softly on the table.

Her eyes widened. It was obvious what the bag contained. Her lower lip trembling, she opened the neck of the bag and reached in, then inhaled sharply as her hand touched bone. Holding the bottom of the bag with her left hand, she withdrew her right. It was fixed like a claw around the cranium.

"No!" she cried, a choking, broken sound. "Oh, no, Mike!" Sobbing, she turned the skull around on the table, pausing as the bullet hole came into view. She looked at Gabriel. "Is that?"

He nodded. "Yes. That's where the bullet hit him. The one that killed him."

Melody poked her index finger into the hole then pulled it out again and stared at the tip of her finger, end-on.

"It doesn't look big enough, does it?"

Then she laughed. A cracked, mirthless eruption of emotion. "Oh, Mike. I'm sorry, my love. We'll bury you properly, now. Me and Nat."

This was the moment Gabriel had been waiting for. He reached across the table and took Melody's hand.

"Melody, have you thought about the burial? He's entitled to a full military funeral, if you want."

She shook her head violently. "No!" she said in a harsh voice, roughened by her reignited grief. "They took him from me. He loved the SAS, but I never did. I'm not one of those army wives who feels gratitude to the Regiment. I hate them, Gabriel, I hate them!" She shouted the last three words and Gabriel realised he'd misjudged the situation. Not for the first time, he reflected.

"I'm sorry. It was the wrong thing to say. But the guys would want to pay their respects."

"That's up to them. It's going to be quiet. Just family and friends. And you, of course. What were their names? Daisy and who?"

"Dusty. Ben Rhodes, really. And Daisy's Damon Cheaney."

"You three, then. But that's it. No flags, and definitely no guns."

"No flags. No guns. I'll let them know. Will you call me with the date?" She nodded. "Thank you. I have to go."

Another nod. She was staring at her husband's ID discs, turning them over and over in her fingers. Gabriel got up, kissed the top of her head and left.

*

The funeral took place at Camberwell New Cemetery. The day was cold, and a bitter wind blew across from the north, so that even dry eyes began leaking tears from their corners within seconds of leaving the long, black cars that brought them.

Gabriel had attended many military funerals in dress uniform. Today, he wore a dark grey suit. He stood to one side in the foyer of the chapel, with Damon Cheaney and Ben Rhodes, as the other guests arrived.

Smudge's side of the family was numerous: he'd had five brothers and two sisters, who all arrived with spouses and kids in tow. His mother, a large lady, carried herself with the dignity of a queen, the centre of attention for her family. She enveloped Melody in a hug, crushing her against her bosom and smothering her with kisses, leaving deep red lip prints all over her cheeks.

Melody's family was smaller, both physically and in number. Her parents were both slight, timid-looking creatures, pale-skinned and fair-haired, but they clearly loved and were loved by the louder, more colourful black family whom their children had joined together.

After the service, and the hymns, during which the soaring harmonies of the black women mourning their lost soldier made Gabriel smile despite his tears, the congregation moved outside.

Melody had asked Gabriel to be one of the pall-bearers along with her brothers-in-law. As he walked in step with the others, he pressed his cheek to the varnished coffin and whispered four words:

"I've got you, Smudge".

THE END

Andy Maslen

Andy Maslen was born in Nottingham, in the UK, home of legendary bowman Robin Hood. Andy once won a medal for archery, although he has never been locked up by the sheriff.

He has worked in a record shop, as a barman, as a door-to-door DIY products salesman and a cook in an Italian restaurant. He eventually landed a job in marketing, writing mailshots to sell business management reports. He spent ten years in the corporate world before launching a business writing agency, Sunfish, where he writes for clients including The Economist, Christie's and World Vision.

As well as the Gabriel Wolfe series of thrillers, Andy has published five works of non-fiction, on copywriting and freelancing, with Marshall Cavendish and Kogan Page. They are all available online and in bookshops.

He lives in Wiltshire with his wife, two sons and a whippet named Merlin.

*

News of the fifth Gabriel Wolfe thriller coming up . . .

Want to know more?

To get regular updates on new Gabriel Wolfe books, and exclusive news and offers for members, join Andy Maslen's Readers' Group at www.andymaslen.com/first_casualty.

Email Andy at andy@andymaslen.com

Follow and tweet him at @Andy_Maslen

Like his page "Andy Maslen Author" on Facebook

Gabriel Wolfe returns in a new novel, *Fury*. Turn the page to read the first chapter.

FURY

1
Words in the Wind

GUY, the chauffeur, held the rear door open, but the woman who called herself Erin didn't feel like riding in the back this evening. She motioned him to close the door and went round to the other side of the car and climbed into the passenger seat.

"How was the dinner, ma'am?" Guy asked as he settled himself beside her and buckled in.

"For a start, you can knock off the 'ma'am' bit. I'm not the fucking Queen. You can call me Erin, or boss, I don't care which. And since you ask, it was a fucking train wreck. That smug bitch Simone Berrington told me moneymaking was one thing but that 'politics is best left to those who know what we're doing'." Erin's mimicry of the Foreign Secretary's home counties accent was wickedly accurate, even down to the trace of a lisp her party-appointed speech therapists had all but erased.

"I'm sorry to hear that, m . . . boss."

"She even gave me her card in case I ever wanted to talk about donating to the party."

"There are always others you could approach."

"Oh, don't you worry. Berrington will rue the day she turned me down."

They cruised through the streets of Mayfair, quiet now evening had fallen. Erin looked idly out of the window to her left at the artworks and designer dresses displayed in the windows. Suddenly, the Bentley jerked to a stop and Guy swore under his breath as a Lycra-clad cyclist swerved in front of them. The lights ahead changed to red and they drew alongside the cyclist, who turned out to be a middle-aged man bearing a hostile scowl. Rather than taking a foot out of his pedal clips, he stretched out his right hand and rested it on the Bentley's roof.

Erin buzzed her window down and spoke.

"Get your fucking hand off my car, you moron. And while you're about it, learn some manners."

The cyclist whipped his head round and down and spat into the open window.

"How's that for manners, you Tory cunt?" he shouted. Then he gave her the finger and jumped the light across to the next quiet stretch of road leading towards Park Lane.

Guy looked sideways at Erin, eyebrows lifted fractionally.

She nodded back. He returned his eyes to the road and once the lights turned to green accelerated smoothly across the junction, using the full might of the Bentley's sixteen-cylinder engine to catch the cyclist. He drew level and slowed to match the man's speed. Then with a sudden wrench left of the steering wheel, he slammed the two and a half tonnes of car into the cyclist's right side, crunching man and bike into the side of a stationary removals van, parked for the night.

He pulled in to the next available space. Erin got out of the car and walked back towards the fallen cyclist, her high heels clicking on the tarmac. He was unconscious, his legs twisted beneath him at unnatural angles. Two bright shards of bone protruded through the flesh of his right calf muscle and there was a spreading pool of blood beneath his head giving off a coppery smell.

She stooped and placed a small rectangle of card with a Foreign and Commonwealth Office crest on his fluttering chest, then sauntered back to the Bentley.

"Home, James," she purred. "And don't spare the horses. We have to be in Manhattan tomorrow and I haven't packed."

*

The sheet of pale-blue, lined notebook paper swirled high above Central Park, snatched by the wind from a home office desk in Erin Ayer's twenty-first floor, 5th Avenue penthouse. Written on it, in elegant, sloping calligraphy, was a list of eight items:

House
Car
Money
Teacher
Comrades
Friends
Boss
Girlfriend

A gust of gritty, fume-laden air rose up from the canyon that was 5th Avenue between East 84th and East 85th Streets and carried the list south. It whirled away, over the spire of St Paddy's, then shifted eastwards onto Park Avenue. Caught in a vortex of air moving around the stainless steel cladding of the Chrysler Building's terraced crown, it fluttered over and over, traveling southwest towards Mott Street in Chinatown. A downdraft like a cold, wet hand pushed it out of the thermals, so that it dropped out of the grey sky into a cobbled alley running between a vacant lot and the backs of a row of Chinese restaurants. It landed in a puddle of week-old cooking oil. Moments later, a rat darted out from a pile of rotting cabbage stalks, sniffed at the paper and, perhaps deciding it would make good nesting material, fastened its long, yellow incisors into it and pulled it free from the oil before trotting off to a grating and disappearing. The list had vanished. Its consequences would begin two weeks later.

*

In the kitchen of a flat in Chiswick, west London, Gabriel Wolfe and Britta Falskog were drinking Pol Roger champagne. She held the flute in her left hand; her right was heavily bandaged.

"So, what's the special occasion?" Britta asked.

Gabriel raised his glass to his lips, sniffed the stewed-apple aroma of the wine and took a brief sip.

"There's something I want to ask you."

"What is it? If it's a trip anywhere except to bed, the answer's no."

He smiled and shook his head.

"I want to ask you if you'll marry me."

Her blue eyes popped wide with surprise. She put her glass down. Then she turned to face him. His breathing was steady but his heart was beating fast as she opened her mouth to speak.

"It would be tough on our kids, you know," she said.

It wasn't either of the answers Gabriel Wolfe had been playing in his mind. "What?' the ex-SAS Captain asked. "What kids? You're not . . .?"

"No, idiot! But can you really see us as a cosy married couple with a couple of, what is it, ankle-biters? Daddy off to kill bad men in Africa for the British government's black ops hit squad, Mummy going undercover to defeat a terrorist plot? I mean, it's not exactly home sweet home, is it?"

Gabriel scratched the back of his head and ruffled his short black hair into spikes. He had just proposed and somehow hadn't been expecting a logical analysis of the pros and cons. More fool him for not knowing how the redheaded Swede standing opposite him, glass of champagne in hand, would react.

"No, I guess not. But we don't have to have kids." He noted her eyes flashbulb in surprise, the whites showing all the way round the irises. "Not straight away, anyway. Do we? We could just be . . . unconventional."

"Well, for one thing," Britta drained her champagne and started counting off points on her fingers. She'd picked up the habit from Gabriel who in turn had adopted the mannerism from his boss at The Department and former CO in the SAS, Don Webster. "Yes, we do have to have kids. Otherwise what's the point of getting married? Two, 'unconventional' doesn't really begin to cover it, does it? Children need stability. You of all people should know that." Gabriel's eyes fell and his mouth compressed into a thin line.

"Oh, Jesus, sorry my darling. I didn't mean about Michael."

Michael Wolfe was Gabriel's younger brother. Until very recently, Gabriel would have sworn he was an only child. Then a series of events had led him to realise that not only was that untrue, but he had been responsible for his brother's death, while Michael had been just five years old.

"It's OK," Gabriel said, then smiled a small, sad smile. "You are right. Kids need a stable home. Somewhere safe. But couldn't we provide that? Surely there's a way? And why can't you give an answer to the main question? It's not the most romantic way to respond to a proposal of marriage."

She closed the two-foot gap between them and wrapped her arms around his waist. "Okay. Answer time. I can't think of anything I'd like more. So, yes, please. But," she added hurriedly as his face broke into a wide grin and his dark brown eyes crinkled at the corners, "it's a yes, please with conditions."

"Fine! Tell me. SAS and Swedish Special Forces guard of honour with fixed bayonets? Knife-throwing at the reception? Tell me."

"Give me till the end of the job they're sending me on next. Just to work out some of the practicalities."

*

The gondola seemed like a tourist cliché, but the assassin was happy enough to trail her long, maroon-tipped fingers in the green water as her muscular gondolier poled the narrow craft along the canal. She looked up at him. *You look good enough to eat*, she thought, a smile curving her black-cherry lips upwards. He caught her expression and smiled back, puffing his chest out a little further and sucking in his stomach. *That's my boy. Maybe I'll invite you back to my hotel after we're through.* A buzz on her left hip switched her frame of mind back to business. She had few friends, and those she did have never contacted her on this phone.

She pulled the customised, steel-grey iPhone from her pocket and glanced at the display. Unknown caller. Well, this should be interesting. Not one of her regulars.

"Sasha Beck," she said. Then waited.

"Ms Beck, my name is Erin Ayer. I have a job for you, but I don't know whether I should come to you or have you flown out to meet me here. I'm in Manhattan."

Sasha looked up at the gondolier, who had adopted a comically macho pose – all bulging biceps and jutting jaw that almost made her laugh – then turned away from his so that she was facing in the opposite direction. "Well, 'Mizz' Erin Ayer, you're going a little too fast. If you don't mind we'll slow things down. One, I'm a Miss. Two, nobody flies me anywhere. Three, I don't know you from Adam, or Eve, and I want to know how you got this number."

"I'm so sorry, *Miss* Beck." The caller's clipped English accent laid heavy emphasis on the title with unmissable sarcasm, piquing Sasha's curiosity further. "Let me begin again. I was given your number by a Kazakh gentleman named Timur Kamenko. I believe you have worked for him in the past. And, of course, I should be quite happy to come to you. Wherever that might be. Is that splashing I hear in the background? Are you on the water? Ooh, church bells. And those acoustics – all that stone and water. You must be in a gondola. I do love Venice."

"Bravo. So you're a distant relative of Sherlock Holmes and you know Timur. Meet me at Caffè Florian at eleven o'clock the day after tomorrow. If you're late, you won't find me waiting."

There was humour in the other woman's voice. "Very well. I'll pack extra euros – my treat."

Assuming that anyone with the connections necessary to gain access to her business number would also have no problems making the rendezvous or recognising her, Sasha ended the call and smiled hungrily up at her gondolier.

Printed in Great Britain
by Amazon